PERFECT
VENGEANCE

FBI STRIKE FORCE SERIES

TEE O'FALLON

Edited by Karen Grove
Cover art and design by LJ Anderson, Mayhem Cover Creations. Stock art by GettyImages, Shutterstock, and DepositPhotos

ISBN 979-8-9925967-0-0 (ebook)
ISBN 979-8-9925967-1-7 (print)

Manufactured in the United States of America
First Edition June 2025

ALSO BY TEE O'FALLON

For my Family. Matt - you have the patience of a saint for listening to me pitch my plot ideas all these years!

Chapter One

A soft click shattered the silence.

Gina punched off the tiny penlight, plunging the room into darkness. She froze, crouching before the floor safe inside the closet and praying her ears were playing tricks on her. Instinct told her those prayers were about to go unanswered.

The crush of shoes on carpet. Breathing, not just hers. Then, a *click*.

"Don't move a muscle." The deep, masculine voice sliced through the early morning stillness, eliminating any doubts Gina may have had about what she'd heard—a gun's hammer being drawn back. It was like no other sound in the world. One she'd never forgotten...

And never would.

"Do exactly as I say," the voice growled, "or this will be the last safe you ever lay hands on."

Her heart raced, the beat pounding in her ears. Somehow, the intel on Rocco Lambrusco's whereabouts was wrong. Dead wrong, and now the mobster had caught her inside his apartment, breaking into his safe.

I am dead meat.

"Get off the floor." The way he spat out the words told her he was pissed. *Really* pissed. "Now!"

And she was in deep, deep shit.

The metal ridges of the old safe's combination dial bit into her fingertips as she gripped it tighter.

"Are you deaf or just stupid?" Unbridled fury didn't begin to describe the undertone of Rocco's question. "If you don't get moving, I'll ram my boot straight up your ass."

"Okay, okay." Her throat was so tight she could barely choke out the words. Her voice had sounded raspy, more like a man's than a woman's.

In a heartbeat, she ran down the list of possible weapons on her utility belt.

Lockpick set.

Screwdriver.

Pepper spray.

Better yet, the stiletto strapped around her ankle. With luck, she could slide the knife out, bury it in Rocco's gut, and be out the door with the cash before he knew what hit him.

Quietly, she clipped the penlight to her belt. Her arm brushed the strap of the empty black duffel bag slung across her chest. She slid her hand down the inside of her thigh to her calf until her fingers grazed the stiletto's ebony handle. One more second and she'd have it. Then drive it into Rocco's beefy belly.

"Quit stalling and get off the floor."

Her gut clenched tighter than she thought possible. Any wrong move and he'd kill her. Two bullets to the back of the head—the same way Franco Falzone murdered her father.

"Keep your back to me, and don't even think of going for that blade on your ankle."

She dropped her hand from the knife. How could he see anything? The bastard must have the eyesight of a panther.

So much for Plan A.

A bead of sweat trickled down her temple. Her breaths quickened, along with the crazy pounding in her chest. As she got to her feet, she eased her hand toward her utility belt until her fingers contacted the hard plastic handle of the screwdriver. Another inch and she'd jam *that* into Rocco's belly.

"Stop," he bit out. "Make another play for one of the toys on your belt and your life ends here."

With a sinking feeling, she let her hand fall from the screwdriver.

There goes Plan B.

She hadn't heard Rocco move, not even a rustle of clothing, but his voice had come from a different direction this time. He was circling her as if she were prey about to be mauled to death. Why didn't he clip her and be done with it? Maybe he didn't want to bloody his plush pile carpeting.

No way was she giving up. Not only was she *so* not ready to die, but there were too many desperate women counting on the money in that safe. Still facing the open closet, she fisted her hands, then froze as the muzzle of a gun pressed against the back of her head. The tip of the metal barrel bit straight through the thin fabric of her hood.

Taking a deep breath, she lashed out, knocking the barrel of the gun away from her head. Rocco cursed. Gina jabbed first, one fist, then the other, hitting nothing but air. She struck out with a right cross. One of her knuckles grazed his jaw.

Left jab. A miss but close. Her right hook finally connected with something solid—his wrist. She peppered him with blow after blow. Jab, cross, hook, uppercut. Each time, he parried, blocking her shots with expert precision. The man had skills. If she didn't take him down soon, she'd tire and he'd overpower her.

Backing off, she whipped her leg up and around, executing a flawless roundhouse kick. The duffel hindered her movement, but her foot still made contact.

He grunted. "Sonofa—" A large hand spun her, shoving her against the wall.

She flung her hands in front of her. Too late. Her forehead smacked into the drywall, sending pain splintering through her head.

"Next time, do what I tell you *when* I tell you." He loomed over her, keeping his hand rammed between her shoulder blades, pinning her to the wall.

She squirmed beneath his hand, but he only mashed her face tighter against the wall. If he'd wanted to pump her full of lead, or at least activate her dental plan, he would have done it by now. Teeth-bashing had always been a mob favorite.

Through the haze of pain jabbing her forehead, it occurred to her that Rocco really was looming over her. But he shouldn't be.

At five foot four, the plump little mobster was an inch shorter than she was. Gina knew that from surveilling him steadily off and on for the last four weeks. She'd never heard the man speak, but it had to be him. This was his apartment, after all. Who else would it be?

Yet the man towering over her had to be a good foot taller than she was. Come to think of it, his voice didn't have that unmistakable accent all New Jersey mobsters were known for. This voice was deep and rich, reminding her of a country music singer. A very pissed-off country music singer.

Of all the things to take notice of with a gun jammed against your thick, stupid skull.

"I'm not in a good mood tonight, and your bullshit isn't helping." His hand dropped from her back. "Turn around. Slowly."

Gina obeyed his order and turned. *Click.* A bright light blinded her, and she squinted. Figures he had one of those fancy cop flashlights. Tiny white stars danced in her vision. She couldn't see a thing other than the guy was huge with broad shoulders and a chest as wide as a gorilla.

Something touched the back of her head. The hood of her skintight catsuit was yanked off and fell onto her back.

"Ouch." She flinched and massaged her stinging scalp where he'd pulled out several strands of her hair.

"You've gotta be kidding." He let loose with a string of colorful words, some of which she'd never heard before. "A woman."

"Last time I checked." The words had flown from her mouth before she could stop them.

"Listen, wiseass." His hand clamped around her arm, and he hauled her upward, forcing her to stand on her toes. The flashlight was so near her face, the light so harsh, she had to squeeze her eyes shut before her retinas fried. "You weren't invited to this party, so you're damn sure gonna tell me who you are."

"Dream on, caveman." His viselike grip on her upper arm tightened. Strong fingers bit into her flesh. She gasped, and he eased his hold, as if he hadn't realized he'd been hurting her.

"Once more," he said, pulling her closer but surprisingly more gently this time, "tell me who you're working for."

"You first," she snapped with more volume than intended, considering *he* was the one holding the gun.

She gulped hard, and the microphone Velcroed around her neck bobbed up and down. That microphone was a dead giveaway she had communication with someone else. Revealing her name wasn't an option, and she'd die before giving up her accomplices. If anyone discovered she and her friends were stealing from the Falzone Crime Family, they'd either be whacked or get tossed in jail, where the long arm of Franco Falzone would eventually reach out and knife them in the back. Literally. And the helpless women Gina and her friends had been donating money to for the last two years would also be imprisoned. A different sort of prison, one filled with savage beatings and emotional hell for the rest of their lives.

"Lady, you have no idea what you've walked into or how much you've royally screwed things."

"*I* screwed things?" She tried opening her eyes to glimpse his face, but the light from the flashlight was too intense. "Forgive me if I don't apologize, but your presence here doesn't exactly help me out either."

He snorted. "Helping you isn't at the top of my list. Now for the last time, who—"

The sound of the apartment's front door opening filtered into the bedroom.

"Shit," he whispered, then released her arm so abruptly she nearly collapsed on the floor.

It had to be Rocco. The *real* Rocco.

The flashlight clicked off. She still couldn't see anything but flashes and pops of white and yellow. She was as helpless as a bat in daylight.

A long, powerful arm shot around her chest and shoulders, dragging her backward into the closet. She closed her fingers around her captor's forearm and began struggling. "Let. Me. Go."

6

"Knock it off, or we're both dead." He leaned forward and pulled the closet door closed, barely making a sound. "And keep that big mouth of yours shut."

Whoever this guy was, he didn't want to get caught any more than she did. Again, begging the question... Who was he? Was he also trying to rob Rocco and was ticked she'd gotten there first?

She blinked several times. The fireworks dancing before her eyes had finally disappeared. A shaft of light shot through the crack between the bottom of the closet door and the carpet.

Rocco was in the bedroom.

She tried putting more distance between the tips of her boots and the door. As she moved, the duffel bag's strap caught on the corner of a box, throwing her off balance until she nearly stumbled over the same safe she'd been attempting to break into.

Her captor adjusted his arm around her upper body to steady her before she could fall, catching her with his hand over her breast.

She fought the urge to yank his hand away, but the tiny closet was packed to the gills with swag—stolen merchandise she'd noticed earlier. Stacks of boxes on either side of them jabbed into her arms. The way they were crammed between all the boxes, the slightest movement could have Rocco firing a round through the closet door.

Warmth from his hand permeated the suit to her breast. From head to toe, she was pressed against a towering body that seemed to be comprised of only two things: muscle and steel. Not one inch of him was soft or flabby. To make matters worse, every breath she took shoved her breast more firmly into his hand.

The guy's jaw flexed against the side of her head. He

exhaled through his nose, cutting off the soft growl she heard, as much as felt, emanating from deep within his chest. Without meaning to, she gripped his muscled forearm. Even through the thick material it was obvious he was in amazing shape.

Warm breath blew across the top of her head, riffling her hair and sending goose bumps prickling along her neck and shoulders. She inhaled a wisp of mint along with leather from his jacket and something else she hadn't noticed before. His clean, fresh scent, as if he'd just stepped out of the shower five minutes ago. Well, if she had to hide for her life in a closet, practically skin to skin with a mysterious stranger, at least the guy smelled great and practiced good oral hygiene.

Water from the shower pounded against the adjacent bathroom wall. The shaft of light inches from her feet flickered, casting shadows on the floor as Rocco walked in front of the closet again. She tensed and leaned back, pressing into the man's chest.

He stiffened, and his hand tightened even more over her breast. As if realizing what he'd done, he eased his hold on her. That wasn't the only involuntary action going on inside the closet, as her nipple hardened beneath his touch. This could *not* be happening.

I'm getting turned on by a really buff guy while hiding in a closet from a mobster who won't hesitate to shoot us both. Sadly, it was the hottest sexual encounter she'd had in a very long time.

She heard the shower curtain being drawn open, then closed. Followed by singing. Bad singing, totally off key. Puccini? Some kind of Italian opera. *Figures.* She hated Italian opera.

Warm lips pressed against her ear. "Get ready to haul ass. Front door when I give the command."

"Ya think?" she whispered in a sarcastic tone. "For the record, I don't take orders from a low-life mobster, and I don't need you to state the obvious."

"What *you* need is irrelevant. You're nothing but a thief." Gone was the deep country music bass. In its place was a deadly warning.

"And you're what?"

"Your worst nightmare." His breath fanned her cheek. "Wait for my signal or I'll strangle you and hang your body on a hook in Rocco's closet."

For an instant, she believed he might actually do it, then he reached in front of her and cracked the door. His stubbled jaw grazed her cheek, and she got another whiff of his minty fresh breath. Gradually, he pushed the door open and propelled her from the closet with a solid shove. "Go. Now."

Not needing any more direction from Mr. Tall, Dark, and Bastard, she took off. Steamy, shampoo-scented air swirled from the half-open bathroom door along with Rocco's horrible singing.

Gina raced into the hallway, running lightly on the balls of her rubber-soled boots. If she didn't get away from her closet buddy pronto, who knew what he might do. She was a witness, maybe someone he couldn't allow to live.

She glanced at the security system box on the wall by the front door. Two steady green lights. She silently thanked Rocco's carelessness in not resetting the alarm. It would have taken her precious time to disarm it the way she had when she'd picked the lock and broken in.

Soft footsteps indicated her hard-nosed companion was

close behind. She eased open the door and sprinted for the stairwell exit at the end of the long hallway. The empty black duffel smacked against her hip, an irritating reminder of her failure. She and her friends had stolen thousands of life-saving dollars over the last two years, but tonight... Zilch.

At the end of the hallway, she threw her weight against the gray metal door to the stairwell and shoved it open. Dank, musty air surrounded her as she raced down the two flights to the first floor.

Every one of her footfalls echoed like thunder in the narrow stairwell. It was nothing compared to the reverberations of the much heavier footsteps following in her wake or the thumping of her heart hammering against her ribs.

This guy meant trouble. Whoever he was, evading him was just as vital to her mission as escaping from Rocco. It meant the difference between life and death. *Hers.*

The footsteps behind her grew louder, closer. A brief glance over her shoulder was all it took to see the large shadow half a flight above and bearing down fast.

Her feet hit the concrete landing of the ground floor, and she threw her weight against the heavy exit door. A blast of cold, late-November air slammed into her face and bit through her suit.

She leaped onto the front lawn and raced across the grass. The door she'd just flown out of hadn't slammed shut behind her. That could mean only one thing.

He was gaining on her.

Gina pumped her legs until her calf and thigh muscles burned. At the corner of the complex, she hooked another left and bolted along the side of the building, heading down a dirt path.

She raced for the back alley that paralleled the complex. Mullet Street. Gina knew the preplanned escape route by heart. She'd run surveillance the week before and practiced an emergency extraction in her head a hundred times. This was the first time a job had gone bad and she'd actually had to put one of those plans into action.

At 3:00 a.m., the street was deserted. With no street-lights, she could barely see what was in front of her. It didn't matter. She knew what was behind her.

He was.

With every stride and every breath, freezing air burned her lungs. She touched the microphone on her throat. "Kinsey," she gasped. "I'm heading south on Mullet." She veered right, practically plowing headfirst into a dumpster. "Trouble. Someone was inside. He's on my six. I need emex."

The tiny receiver crackled in her ear. "On my way."

Heavy footsteps pounded behind her. For such a big man, he was faster than expected.

Headlights illuminated the empty road ahead. Behind her, the rented Dodge Charger roared. She couldn't resist the urge to look over her shoulder. A dark figure loomed not ten feet away. She cut sharply across the alley to be closer to the passenger door when Kinsey picked her up. Her momentum was so great she crashed into the chain-link fence on the other side of the street.

The Charger tore down the alley, tires screeching as Kinsey braked next to where Gina clung to the fence. The back end of the car careened, and the acrid smell of burning rubber drifted to her nose.

She heard a muffled *thump*, then a resounding *whack*—the horrible sounds a car makes when it hits something. A body slid off the hood of the Charger and slumped to the ground.

Oh, crap.

Gina hunched over and planted her hands on her thighs. Sweat dripped down her forehead, and white puffy breaths billowed in front of her face.

The Charger's doors flew open. Kinsey and Annabelle jumped out and bolted to the front of the car.

Margo rushed over to where Gina stood. Her teardrop-shaped eyes widened. "Are you all right?" Wisps of cropped hair stuck out from her hood, outlining her face in a blond halo.

"Fine," she huffed, still hunched over and gasping. Every inhalation of chilly air made her throat feel as if it had a bad case of freezer burn.

Annabelle's curly red locks bobbed in the light breeze. "I think you killed him," she said in a quiet, worried voice. "I told you to slow down."

Kinsey knelt beside the man who lay on his side, one arm outstretched on the pavement, the other tucked beneath him. She pulled off her glove and touched her fingers to either side of his neck, checking for a pulse and seemingly not finding one. In the glow of the headlights, Kinsey's fuchsia pink nail polish contrasted against his pale flesh.

Gina's stomach muscles clenched again and again as she fought the urge to throw up. *Please don't be dead.* Manslaughter hadn't been in the ops plan.

Her hands trembled as she dragged herself to the front of the car. As much as she wanted to scream, the last thing they needed was more noise and chaos to muddy things worse than they were already. Who was she kidding? They'd far surpassed chaos and were well on their way to FUBAR. *Fucked up beyond all repair.*

"Well?" Annabelle prompted, a mixture of anger and outright fear on her cherubic face.

"Don't yell at me." Kinsey swept her long box braids over her shoulder. "We don't want to wake the neighborhood."

"Wake the neighborhood?" Annabelle's voice rose, a sure sign she was about to go ballistic. "You're our getaway driver. You're supposed to be as good as Dale Earnhardt, Jr., and you just ran over a guy."

"It was an accident." Gina clenched her hands to stop them from shaking. "Besides, it was either that or he'd have caught me." She swiped the icy sweat from her brow with the palm of her hand. "Did you find a pulse?"

"He's dead." Annabelle waved her hand toward the slumped body. "We're all dead."

"Knock it off." Kinsey stood to her full five foot ten and glared down at the petite woman. "You always were a terrible backseat driver. And for the record, it's not my fault he didn't stop. He had to have seen my headlights, and this car doesn't exactly purr like a kitten. It roars."

"This isn't the time or the place to argue over what happened." Margo, ever the voice of reason, inserted herself between the two women. She nodded to Annabelle. "Go over there and keep an eye out."

With an audible huff, Annabelle stalked to the end of the alley where it intersected one of the secondary roads.

Margo crouched near the body. "There's blood on his forehead."

"My first hit-and-run." Kinsey finally sounded appropriately worried. "At least he's a no-good, thieving mobster."

Gina knelt next to Margo and swallowed the lump in her throat. No matter what he'd wanted, she never meant for anyone to get hurt. Then again, he might have been planning to beat her to a pulp.

Daring to hope Kinsey didn't know where to find a

carotid artery, Gina rested two fingers on the man's neck. Nothing. A renewed shiver of fear crept up her spine, lifting the hair at her nape.

The skin beneath her fingertips was warm and stubbled. She shifted to the other side of his neck and pressed her fingers into the hollow beneath his jawbone. Still nothing. She adjusted her fingers a fraction and was rewarded with the faint thumping of a pulse. "Thank God." She let out the biggest sigh of relief she'd felt in her entire life. "He's alive." But a thin, steady rivulet of blood trickled from his hairline.

"That bump on his head might not be his only injury," Margo said.

"I know, but we can't risk moving him. We have to call for help." Gina ran her hand down his arm, hip, and leg. "If he does have broken bones or internal injuries, jostling him might cause more damage."

"Wow, he's huge." Kinsey crouched beside them. "No wonder it felt like I creamed a water buffalo." She pointed to his outstretched arm. "I think his wrist is broken. See where it's turning colors and all puffy?"

Gina's heart squeezed. *This is all my fault.*

"Uh, guys?" Margo interrupted. "It's great that he's alive, and I'm sorry his wrist may be broken, but Annabelle's right. We can't stay here any longer. We have to clear out before someone sees us."

"We can't abandon him." Gina's voice cracked, and she felt more and more guilty about what they'd done. She was the team leader. Whatever happened was ultimately her responsibility. "What if he really does have a serious injury, like a broken back or a skull fracture or a ruptured spleen?"

"You've been watching too many medical shows," Kinsey said.

"No, she's right." Margo massaged her chin. "We can't

leave him like this, but we can't hang around here either. We'll hit the road and immediately call 911." She tucked her hand around Gina's upper arm. "Let's go."

"Wait a minute." She swatted her friend's hand away. "It's freezing out here. He could go into shock. Check for a blanket or a spare jacket in the car, anything we can cover him up with."

"All right," Margo relented. "But we need to be fast."

While Margo and Kinsey searched the Charger, a twinge of suspicion niggled away in her brain. Could be the guy was just another mobster, maybe from a rival family. Something still bugged her about who he was and why he'd been chasing her instead of making his own getaway.

"This was the closest thing to a blanket I could find." A scraggly cloth tarp dangled from Margo's hands.

"It'll do." She grabbed the cloth but stopped before draping it over him. "I want to search his pockets, try to find some ID."

"Who cares who he is?" Kinsey asked. Patience had never been her strong suit. "Let's get out of here before someone catches us."

Gina pulled open the man's jacket, looking for an inside pocket. A wicked-looking gun stuck out from a black leather holster on his belt. Odd that he carried his gun in a holster and not stuffed in his pocket or waistband the way criminals did.

She shook it off and continued her search. "Don't just stand there, help me. But be careful. I don't want to hurt him."

"Little late to worry about that, dontcha think?" Kinsey began patting down his chest. "He's got great pecs." Her roving hands had hiked up his knit shirt, and she let out a low whistle. "Whoa, nice abs."

15

"This is no time for groping." Gina lifted the back of his jacket. "Check his pants."

Kinsey ran her hands over his rear jeans pockets and let out another whistle. "And what a great ass."

"Kinsey!" Margo threw her an impatient look. "We're not at a strip club. Hurry up!"

"Okay, okay." Kinsey tugged a black wallet from one of his pockets. She flipped it open and held it in front of the Charger's headlights, illuminating the laminated ID.

Gina's heart skipped a beat. Then another.

Margo gasped.

"Holy shit," Kinsey whispered.

For several seconds longer, none of them said another word.

Gina continued gaping at the man's wallet as everything fell into place.

His words: *You have no idea what you've walked into.*

Why he didn't want to get caught in Rocco's apartment.

Why he didn't shoot her on the spot, and why he was chasing her down as if she were a common thief. To him, she was.

Annabelle ran over. "What is it? What's wrong?"

Kinsey angled the wallet for Annabelle to see.

Annabelle's eyes went as wide as serving platters. "Oh. My. God." She clapped a hand over her mouth.

"He ain't God," Kinsey muttered.

"He's worse." Margo shook her head. "Much worse."

"FBI." Gina swallowed. Hard. "We are so screwed."

Chapter Two

Frustration and panic sat like balls of lead in the pit of Gina's stomach. If it weren't five in the morning, she would have slammed her front door shut to ease the tension stretching her muscles tighter than a bowstring, but that would have woken half the tenants in her East River high-rise.

The voice of reason won out, and she flicked on the crystal chandelier, holding the door open for Margo, Kinsey, and Annabelle to follow her inside. She locked the door behind them, then leaned back against it. The breath she exhaled sounded more like a rumble of thunder. Any second now and Zeus himself would blast her with a bolt of lightning for all the heinous crimes she'd committed in the last three hours.

J. Edgar Hoover, or whoever was in charge of the FBI these days, would have her head on a platter for running down one of his G-men in the middle of the street like he was roadkill. *Special Agent Roadkill.*

The idea she could joke at a time like this made her sick to her stomach. The man was their victim, and he had a name. They'd all seen it on his government credentials. Now it was permanently etched into her brain.

Jack Gates. *Special Agent* Jack Gates.

A lump as big as a grapefruit clogged her throat.

After draping the cloth tarp over the hunky fed, they'd hauled ass from the alley and dialed 911 on a disposable, untraceable cell phone to anonymously report an unconscious man lying on the side of Mullet Street in Union, New Jersey. Then they'd returned the rental car back to the lot, picked up Gina's personal vehicle, and raced through the Holland Tunnel back to Manhattan.

God, she hoped he was all right. They'd made sure he hadn't been lying in the middle of the road where someone else might run over him, but his face had been so pale, and they'd left him there. Alone. Bleeding.

She could practically hear the judge's gavel slamming onto the bench as he pronounced them guilty. Where did people who crushed FBI agents with rented Dodges go? She could already see her and her friends toiling on their knees, doomed to scrubbing stinky prison latrines in the federal lockup for the next twenty years. Even the normally soothing *tick tock* from the grandfather clock wedged in the corner of the foyer gave no sense of peace. Tonight, it reminded her of a death knell. *Theirs.*

The black duffel bag slid off her shoulder, smacking the floor as it landed. Empty except for the utility belt she'd stuffed inside.

She took a steadying breath and inhaled the scent of lemon polish her housekeeper had used. With the adrenaline overload beginning to ebb, every muscle in her body—even her bones—felt as if they were about to melt into a giant puddle on the floor. Rational thought was impossible. Not with the long list of emotions stacking up fast.

Worry. Fear. Anger. Not to mention total disbelief. They'd just stepped into a mile-high pile of poop.

Annabelle plopped onto the long white sofa and turned on the Tiffany lamp perched on the end table. She crossed her arms over her chest and glared at Kinsey. "I can't believe you ran over an FBI agent."

Gina noted Annabelle's thick "New Yawk" accent intensified whenever she got emotional, which had been pretty much nonstop for the last hour.

"How many times do I have to tell you it was an accident?" Kinsey plunked down on the opposite side of the sofa. "And I didn't run him over. *He* ran into *me*." She stabbed a finger at her chest.

Likewise, while Kinsey's Kenyan lilt was normally a lyrical blend of British English and Swahili, now it also took on a slight New York punch, courtesy of living in the Big Apple for the last ten years. And from Annabelle getting under her skin.

Annabelle rolled her eyes to the ceiling. "What's the difference?"

"Stop it, you two." Margo took up her usual mediating position between the two women. "This isn't helping matters."

Annabelle huffed. "Fine, but we still need to talk about what happened."

Gina clenched her hands, fighting the urge to smash something expensive to pieces. If she hadn't already sold every luxury knickknack in her apartment to help the woman's shelter, she would have.

The sounds of her best friends bickering made the stabbing pain in her forehead and temples worsen. There was only one remedy.

She pushed from the door, kicking the black duffel

aside, then stormed through the living room. Her friends' voices followed her as she beelined for the kitchen.

"Where's she going?" Annabelle asked as Gina blew past.

"Duh," Kinsey said. "Where she always goes when she's pissed off and needs to calm her nerves."

"Let her go," Margo interjected. "She's on a mission."

They'd all used the murder weapon—the Dodge—to quick-change into sneakers and warm-up suits to cover their black stealth garb. Now, Gina's sneakers squeaked as she stepped onto the kitchen tile and flipped on the lights.

She charged to the pantry and snapped open the folding doors with a loud *whack*. She grabbed one of several slim, red foil-covered boxes from a lower shelf and tore off the wrapper. The box's cover came next, and she flung it onto the kitchen's island. A tall copper pepper mill toppled and clattered as it smacked onto the black granite counter.

The heavenly scent of deep, rich chocolate flooded her nose. With shaking fingers, she plucked out a chocolate-covered lychee nut from the plastic tray and shoved it into her mouth, barely chewing it before swallowing, then stuffing in three more. She squeezed her eyes shut, savoring the smooth, creamy chocolate slithering down her throat and contrasting with the juicy, sweet tartness of the lychee. After a few more seconds, the ability to think clearly returned. Marginally, that was.

During their post-op briefings, they normally discussed how the op went and ways they could improve their tactics, and all while counting the money they'd stolen. Tonight there would be no money counting and no post-op briefing. *Postmortem, maybe.* On top of which, now there was that other teensy, weensy little problem crawling up their asses.

Assaulting an FBI agent and abandoning him in a freezing cold alleyway.

He'd probably be okay. He was breathing fine, and she could clearly feel his pulse—after she'd stopped freaking out. Still, they never should have left him there. Guilt and more worry gnawed at her insides. She'd be going straight to hell when she died. Maybe sooner.

She snapped open her eyes and glanced longingly into the pantry, three shelves of which were fully stocked with every grade and variety of chocolate known to womankind. Within twenty-four hours, she'd have to restock at least one entire shelf. It was her cross to bear. When her life turned into a chaotic mess, she gorged on chocolate.

Gina grabbed another box of chocolate-covered lychees, anticipating with dire certainty the need for a second fix long before the sun peeked over the horizon.

With the two boxes of chocolates balanced in her hand, she turned to face her friends for what would surely be their most depressing post-rip-off briefing yet. At the doorway between the kitchen and shabby chic–inspired living room, she paused and looked at each of her friends' worried faces, feeling even more like crap because this whole crazy scheme had been her idea from the beginning.

One minute they'd been laughing and drinking martinis while watching the old *Robin Hood* movie with Errol Flynn, and the next they were plotting how to steal from the mob and give the money to their favorite charity. One thing had led to another, and here they were two years later with their first notch in the failure column. Add to that a vehicular hit-and-run—on a federal agent, no less—and they were batting oh-for-three tonight.

Tears burned her eyes, and she blinked them back. She'd learned the hard way that relationships didn't last and were a waste of time. People she loved always left. But these women had become the closest thing to family she had, and she'd really screwed things up.

Could things possibly get any worse?

She mentally chastised herself for even thinking such a stupid question. Things could *always* get worse. *The FBI can make it worse.* She knew that from firsthand experience. If the FBI hadn't arrested her father, Franco wouldn't have murdered him.

The blinking red light on Gina's answering machine caught her eye, and she frowned. She'd recently broken it off with Paul, a stockbroker at the Wall Street investment firm where she worked, so the message wouldn't be from him. The only other person she'd ever given her home number to besides Margo, Kinsey, and Annabelle was Linda Hernandez of the Manhattan Women's Crisis Center.

She gripped the boxes of chocolate tighter. This couldn't be good. With a sinking feeling, she pushed the button and listened as Linda's urgent message echoed off the kitchen walls.

Gina, this is Linda. Marilyn's husband found the safe house and beat her up pretty badly. Her nose is broken along with two ribs. He was about to start in on the children when the police showed up and arrested him. He won't stop until he gets Marilyn back or kills her and the kids. Please, if you were successful in getting that large donation you mentioned, call me right away. It doesn't matter how late it is.

She didn't need to copy down the number Linda recited. She knew it by heart. Linda had been her contact with the Center and the grateful recipient of the anonymous cash Gina and her friends provided to abused women and their children to help them escape and make a better life. A life that cost money.

Setting up an entire family in another city was an expensive endeavor. New ID, a place to live, a car, cash for food and other necessary supplies. Freedom from abuse wasn't free, and it didn't come cheap.

The corner of one of the boxes dug into her palm where she'd crushed it with her fingers. She glanced into the living room where the other women sat in a row on the sofa. From the gloomy looks on their faces, they'd heard every word of Linda's message.

"That settles it." One by one, she locked eyes with each of her friends. "I'm going back."

"Back?" Kinsey leaned forward. "Where? You can't mean Rocco's." Her striking amber-brown eyes widened.

"Yes. To Rocco's. Not tonight, but soon." She strode into the living room and perched on the rolled arm of the love seat. "You heard the message. Marilyn needs that money more than ever, and she needs it yesterday."

"You're crazy." Annabelle shook her head, making her shoulder-length, curly red hair shimmer. "Rocco might be waiting. He might even set a trap."

"I doubt it." Gina popped another lychee into her mouth, then held out the box to her friends. "Want any?" She knew they didn't. They'd never understood the choco-late-lychee fetish she took to addictive levels. Not even Kinsey, whom she'd first met at a chocolate tasting event put on by her family's international cacao company.

"Yuck." Kinsey's perfect, twenty-six-year-old's complexion crinkled as she grimaced. "Chocolate-covered raspberries maybe, but not that weird-ass nut-fruit."

"Me neither." Annabelle held up her hand. "I don't know how you can eat at a time like this."

Margo likewise declined, shaking her head. "What makes you think you can successfully get into Rocco's apartment again? He has to know you were there. Don't you think he'll move the cash to another location?"

"I don't think so." She finished chewing and swallowed, feeling more and more certain their original plan could still work. "Even though Rocco showed up, I don't think he has a clue anyone was inside the apartment with him. Me *or* that FBI agent. We hid in the closet while he was in the shower. He never got the chance to eyeball us. Plus," she added, tossing the boxes onto the coffee table, "I never cracked the safe, so there's no money missing. There'd be no sign we were ever there."

"That's another thing." Annabelle crossed her arms, tightening her jacket across her plump bosom. "It's way too risky now that the FBI is on to us."

"What do you mean, they're *on* to us?" Gina held her arms from her sides. "They have no idea who we are. That agent might have seen my face, but he doesn't know my name, and there's no way he could have gotten the tag off our rental car, what with it being pitch-black outside and that little matter of him being unconscious." She prayed he wasn't lying in a full body cast in some hospital.

"You don't think getting run over would be motive enough for a federal agent to track us down?" Annabelle's accent was thickening to new levels. "He's the FBI. They know *everything*."

"Stop whining." Kinsey faced off against Annabelle again. "*I* was the one behind the wheel. If anyone's going to get hunted down like a waterbuck it will be me."

"All right, calm down, both of you." Margo angled on the sofa to focus on Gina. "I agree that under the circumstances it would be difficult for the FBI to identify us. We should consider having another crack at Rocco's place, but first we need to analyze what went wrong and whether it could happen again."

Annabelle opened her mouth to object, but Gina cut her off. "I know what you're going to say, but tonight was a fluke. Everything else went like clockwork. Rocco's alarm system was decrepit and simple to bypass." She reached into the pocket of her black warm-up jacket and plucked out the jumble of wires and alligator clips Margo had concocted, courtesy of having been a top-notch electrical engineer. She tossed it on the table where it landed with a *thump*. "And with everything Sergio taught me about lock picking, I was inside Rocco's door within thirty seconds. I can do it again."

"What about the safe?" Annabelle shot her a dubious look.

"Your lack of faith wounds me." She pressed a hand over her heart. "That safe is so ancient I could hear the tumblers falling into place from across the room. Besides, there hasn't been a safe I couldn't get into in the two years we've been doing this." Thanks to one of many unsavory people she'd known in her life.

Early on, Gina had explained to her friends that she once worked for a colleague of her father's—a professional locksmith who repaired everything from simple residential locks to complex electronic security systems and specialized in troubleshooting and repairing safes. Only after he was arrested for multiple burglaries did Gina realize Sergio Mattuci had a lucrative side hustle. Sergio always said she had a natural talent—*a gift*—and he'd taught her everything he knew.

Gina grinned, her juices beginning to flow as they did

whenever she talked about picking locks or safecracking. "You really are a pessimist."

"I'm a realist." Annabelle huffed again and settled back against the cushions.

"I'm getting inside Rocco's safe if I have to give it open-heart surgery." She laced her fingers and cracked her joints.

"What's to keep Rocco from showing up again unexpectedly?" Margo asked. "Your source told you he was supposed to leave yesterday afternoon for Atlantic City and be there for the entire weekend."

"I know." She frowned. "I should have been updated with any changes in his itinerary." That particular mob informant had always fed her accurate intel in the past. He was a childhood friend, and she paid him well enough for his information. "Maybe he changed his plans at the last minute or postponed until next weekend. I'll check with my source and find out if he rebooked at the hotel. Either way, we can't put this off. This location is our best opportunity to grab a large amount of money quickly."

Margo stroked her jaw again, and the sleeve of her brown jacket slid down, revealing a forearm toned from regular sessions with her personal trainer. "It's still a risk going back there."

Gina balled her hands on her knees. "We don't have a choice."

"Maybe there's another way," Kinsey piped in. "Why don't we pool our own resources again and donate more money to the Center? I've got nothing better to do with my trust fund. My parents keep adding to it, hoping the bigger it gets, the less guilty they'll feel for not having anything to do with me."

"I can't let you do that." Gina shook her head, but overwhelming affection and pride for Kinsey nearly sent her to her knees. At eight years her junior, Kinsey was the kid sister Gina never had. Kinsey's sad family state reminded her of her own life right after she turned eighteen, completely devoid of family. "You've tapped into your trust fund for these women enough as it is. But thank you."

Next, she glanced to Margo, her dearest friend and confidant of five years now. "You have two children in Ivy League colleges, and the way your husband is pushing them, they'll be going to grad school for their MBAs, MDs, PhDs, or something else that costs oodles of money." To Annabelle she said, "And if your husband catches you withdrawing more cash from your accounts, you know he'll threaten you with divorce again."

The three women sitting before her were amazingly big-hearted and generous to a fault, and despite their differing and unique backgrounds they'd forged a friendship she treasured above all others.

She swept her gaze through the living room and adjacent dining area, searching for something pricy she might have missed that she could auction off or sell at a local pawn shop.

"Don't even think about it," Margo interrupted. "You may be a hotshot investment banker, but you've already sold off far more of your stocks and personal property than you should have for the Center. No one would ever accuse you of being stingy."

Margo was right. She might be living in a fancy, well-furnished apartment, but she'd sold off most of her gold and diamonds and couldn't recall the last time she'd taken a vacation to somewhere with a beach, palm trees, and pina coladas. Still, she would do whatever it took to effect the kind of change the women at the Center needed. The kind of assistance her mother hadn't gotten in time.

"Then that settles it." She slapped her hands on her thighs. "I can't let us all go bankrupt, and there's no need. Not when there's unreportable cash lying around that's totally available. Rocco and his buddies probably made that money running numbers, selling stolen goods, or loan-sharking. He'll never report it missing. And you heard Linda Hernandez. Marilyn is running out of time. So is a long list of other women."

Judging from their furrowed foreheads, she still wasn't sure whether she'd convinced her friends to go along with her plan. She hoped so. Otherwise, the things that could happen to Marilyn were unthinkable. Like getting beaten to death. Exactly what had happened to Gina's mother after her father had been killed.

"Based on our surveillance of Rocco's activities, there should be thousands of dollars in his safe." Her blood pumped faster at the idea of hitting Rocco again. He was one of Franco Falzone's biggest money earners. For her, the closer they got to stealing from Franco himself, the sweeter the payback. For her father, mother, and the life she'd been forced to live without them. "I have to go back."

"What do you mean, *I*?" Kinsey shot Gina a look of disbelief.

"What I mean is that I understand if you don't want to come with me, and maybe that's for the best after what happened tonight."

"No way." Kinsey came around the coffee table to tower over Gina. "You go," she said, pointing a long, pink fingernail at her, then sweeping her arm toward the other women and adding, "we go."

"She's right." Annabelle had also come around the table and rested her hand on Kinsey's slim shoulder. "We're a team. Remember?"

Annabelle's words tugged at Gina's heart. They *were* a team, a team of friends who loved each other unconditionally. She couldn't suppress the grin forming on her lips at the vision the two women standing before her made. Annabelle would chew her ass out if she said so, but tucked in next to Kinsey, the two of them reminded her of Friar Tuck and Will Scarlett. They were as different in physical appearance and personality as night and day and fought outwardly like cats and dogs. Secretly, they adored each other.

"We knew what we were getting into when we formed our little band of merry women." Margo joined them and drew Gina up from the love seat into their tight circle until they stood with their arms linked. "We're family. Whatever happens, we do it together."

Family.

Guilt stabbed her deeply enough that she had to avert her eyes. Each of her friends was in this with her because someone close to them had been a victim of domestic violence. What would they think if they knew *her* real story? Or that twelve years ago she'd legally changed her name to keep that story permanently buried? She wasn't about to risk them learning her original motives behind their scheme weren't necessarily as pure as she'd led them to believe.

People you love will always leave. That had been her ironclad mantra since she turned eighteen. Since then, she hadn't gotten close to anyone. Except these women. If she lost them, she'd have nothing. She'd *be* nothing. Having their love and support, helping others who were powerless to help themselves, was all that mattered, all she needed in life to be happy. Without it...her life would be empty, meaningless.

For a moment, none of them said a word. Kinsey began to sniffle, then Annabelle, followed a second later by Margo, and Gina couldn't help but join in. Suddenly, they were all crying and laughing, hugging each other tightly.

A few minutes later, Gina walked her friends to the door. "As soon as I confirm, we'll reschedule."

"It's a date." Annabelle stood on the tips of her toes to drop a light kiss on Gina's cheek. "Let's just pray there's no story in the papers tomorrow about an FBI agent killed in a hit-and-run."

"Don't start that again." Kinsey dragged Annabelle out the door and into the hallway.

Margo was the last to leave. Her eyes held no small amount of understanding. "He'll probably just wake up tomorrow with nothing more than a major headache, a cast on his wrist, and a foul disposition."

"I hope so." Yet the pressure in her chest only worsened. "I really, really hope so."

An hour later, she sat cross-legged on her sofa, staring at the empty chocolate boxes on the coffee table. With a grand total of five hours sleep in the last two days, her eyelids were closing but sleep eluded her. The mother of all worries glared in her mind like a neon sign.

That they hadn't seen the last of FBI Special Agent Jack Gates.

Chapter Three

Monday morning, three days after getting run down, Jack's skull still pounded. Beneath the fiberglass cast, his busted wrist throbbed even worse than after the doctor had set the bone. Sixteen years as an FBI agent and no injuries. Until now.

He fumbled with his good hand to flip the cap off a bottle of aspirin. The cap sailed end over end before splashing into the saltwater tropical fish tank on his credenza. His two clownfish—John Wayne and Annie Oakley—darted away as the cap sank to the bottom of the tank.

"Sorry, guys." The brightly colored orange-and-white fish were the highlight of his mornings, something beautiful to look at when his days went to shit. Like today.

John Wayne rose slowly to nibble on a blade of algae-tipped seaweed. Over the last week, JW had become listless, swimming around the tank with sluggish swishes of his fins. A pang of remorse hit Jack in the gut. He recognized the signs. The old fish had reached the end of his lifespan.

He let out a long exhale. Just like people, fish came and went.

Jack flipped the lid back over the tank and shook his head in disgust. He'd be a one-armed man for the next five weeks and one sorry excuse for an FBI agent. If Smitty and the paramedics hadn't found him knocked out cold behind Rocco's building, he'd have frozen to death.

As Jack's backup, Smitty had been parked a block away. Being in hot foot pursuit, Jack hadn't had the opportunity to reach out to him. Only the arrival of a patrol car and an ambulance had alerted Smitty something had gone down.

Jack pinched the bridge of his nose. He had nothing to go on.

There were no cameras in the alley where he'd been hit. Somehow, his assailant had avoided getting picked up by any other city cameras during that timeframe. He'd even checked with the emergency communications center, hoping to ID a witness from the 911 call. Turned out the anonymous call that had come in reporting a man lying on the side of the road was made from an untraceable burner phone, and no one had stuck around. Leaving him wondering if the caller had been the same person who'd run him down.

Or the woman he'd been chasing.

A spasm of pain shot through his injured wrist. He jerked his arm, whacking it against his coffee mug. Mud-brown droplets spattered on his white dress shirt and gray slacks.

He gritted his teeth, though what he really wanted to do was heave the mug and its remaining contents against the wall. This wasn't his day. Or his week.

Truth was, the last six months had been the worst of his life. That interfering little cat burglar had only added to his frustration. Whoever she was, she'd made a serious mistake wrecking his op. If it weren't for her, he'd have had that bug planted and been long gone before Rocco had shown up. As it was, there was no bug, and he was totally screwed.

Stopping the Falzones before they become a major player in the modern-day world of organized crime meant everything to him, and that's where his listening devices came in. The Mafia was more insidious than ever and spreading like a cancer. Just because they didn't make headlines anymore didn't mean they were gone. They were reorganizing.

In the fifteen years he'd worked on the FBI's Organized Crime Strike Force Team, he'd witnessed the mob growing smarter and more sophisticated. Technology was transforming every day and becoming increasingly complex. So was organized crime. Where once the Mafia's bread and butter came from extortion, heroin trafficking, and waste management, now the almighty internet provided a virtually covert way for them to make millions off scam cyber-crime businesses. Although, when it came to modern innovation, the Falzones were running behind.

The phone on his desk rang, interrupting his thoughts and hammering into his skull. He grabbed the receiver. "Gates," he snapped.

"Is this Special Agent Jack Gates?" a female voice with a heavy Italian accent asked.

"Yes." He narrowed his eyes. Something about the voice was familiar, but he couldn't place it. "Who's this?"

Click.

He replaced the receiver, then wolfed three aspirin and washed them down with a swig of rotgut coffee that only added to his sucky mood. With a groan, he rose to retrieve the bottle cap from the fish tank. He plunged his good hand into the water to scoop out the cap. Again, his clownfish bolted in opposite directions.

Jack's partner sauntered into the office and headed for a chair opposite Jack's desk. The chair creaked as he sat. The buzz cut Smitty had gotten last week made him look like a blond, blue-eyed—albeit very out of shape—marine. His lime-green dress shirt stretched across his broadening gut to the point where two buttons defied the laws of physics by not popping off. Smitty's customary Monday morning after-shave—eau-de-doughnut—wafted across the desk.

Smitty swiped at the powdered sugar on his orange-and-purple tie, flinging some onto Jack's files. "Still pissed, I see."

"Getting run over will do that to a guy." He glanced at the cast covering half his right hand and extending up his forearm.

"Getting outrun by a woman must sting too."

When Smitty snickered, Jack drew his brows together and instantly regretted it. The movement was enough to tug on the strips of tape an ER doctor had used to close the cut on his scalp. "Did you get the memo?" he bit out. "I'm on the disabled list."

"I got it." Smitty leaned forward, wearing a more serious expression. "You know Morrison had no choice."

He gave a slight nod. "Yeah, although I didn't think he'd assign you to another squad. I can easily get back into Rocco's to finish the job there, but I don't have a key to the deadbolt on Psycho Fiori's front door." Between Rocco's apartment and Psycho Fiori's house, he'd have two of Franco Falzone's top soldiers covered. "Even if I could climb a twenty-foot rope to get onto the balcony, which I can't with a busted wrist, I'm no locksmith, and all our tech teams are still tied up on the west coast. How does Morrison expect me to get that second bug planted before the court order expires?"

"I don't," Special Agent in Charge Michael Morrison boomed from the doorway. He strode into Jack's office and planted his beefy hands on the desk. "You're on light duty until the doc clears you. You'll have to get an extension on your Title III orders for those bugs."

"I can't." He reached for the manila folder in his in-box and smacked it on the desk. "This was the last extension Judge Ortiz would sign. Said our probable cause was getting stale." Jim Spencer had given his life to get that PC and Jack would be damned before letting an agent's ultimate sacrifice be meaningless. "If I don't get these devices planted within the next four days, this case is dead."

"Better the case dead, than you." Morrison straightened to his full six feet and crossed his arms over his massive chest. Glare from the overhead lights glinted off his balding head. "I won't risk losing another agent just to nail Franco and Tino Falzone."

The mention of that trigger-happy piece of garbage had Jack grinding his teeth.

"What happened to Jim Spencer wasn't your fault."

"The hell it wasn't." Renewed guilt ripped through him as it had every day for the last six months. Since he identified Jim's bullet-riddled body in a Pennsylvania cornfield. His gut told him Tino had personally done the hit, with or without Franco's blessing. "He was too young, too inexperienced, and I put him in anyway."

"He was good," Smitty said. "That's why you picked him."

Jack stared at the file on his desk, not really seeing it. No matter how many times he heard that he hadn't been responsible, and that he'd done everything by the book, he'd never forgive himself for Jim's death. Worse, it reminded him of someone else he'd once been responsible for. A cooperator he'd wired up to gather evidence against the Falzones. That was nearly fifteen years ago, but he'd never forgotten the way that bookie's face had looked when the body was discovered behind the old Meadowlands Arena. Gunshots to the man's head had all but obliterated any identifying features.

Morrison held up his hand to stop Jack from objecting further. "Agent Spencer had the requisite five years' experience as a field agent. He aced every practical problem and scenario Quantico's undercover school could throw at him. The board reviewed his qualifications and blessed him as a UC operative."

Jack dragged his hand down his face. That might be enough to mollify some agents. Not him. He'd failed Spencer and could never make it up to him. "I should have waited for Mark Simmons to get freed up on that other case. He had more experience." But Jack had been impatient, too eager to get an undercover inside the Falzone organization before the secret Mafia Commission meeting took place.

Jim Spencer's murder had to be avenged, and it was his responsibility to do it. It was a matter of honor among agents, and the only thing that mattered in his life right now.

He looked at the manila folder containing the soon-to-expire court orders, then at the calendar blotter on the desk. Midnight Thursday. The deadline was approaching fast.

"Don't even think it." Morrison's baritone cut through Jack's haze of revenge. "You're a senior agent in this office. You and your brothers are the best I've got on the Strike Force teams. No offense, Smitty."

Smitty shrugged. "None taken."

Jack's brothers, Kyle and Deke, were also top agents in the FBI. If his youngest brother, Lance, wasn't doing some kind of black ops assignment for an agency he suspected didn't really exist—officially, that was—there was no doubt in Jack's mind that he'd have made a top-notch FBI agent too.

"If I so much as get wind of you doing any field work before the doc clears you," Morrison continued, "I'll take your badge, your gun, and give you thirty days on the beach for insubordination."

Jack clenched his jaw. His boss was a good man and a fair supervisor, but right now it was all he could do not to smash his good fist through the wall. With his luck he'd hit a stud and end up wearing casts on *both* hands.

For the first time in his career, he felt useless, and it was driving him out of his mind. "I can't sit on my ass for the next five weeks." He flipped open the manila folder to double-check the expiration dates on the court orders, hoping he was wrong and knowing he wasn't. "The information we'll get from these bugs is critical. Word on the street is that the Commission is set to give the Falzones a fully recognized seat. If Franco Falzone becomes head of a sanctioned Mafia family, there'll be no stopping him. Worse, when Franco gets taken out—and someday he will —Tino will take his place."

"That's all we need," Smitty muttered. "A sick psychopath running a mob family."

"Smitty's right." Jack tossed the folder back onto his desk. "Franco's a killer, but Tino likes to mutilate his victims." Rumors of Tino's "treasure jars" containing body parts he'd hacked off his victims were infamous.

Due to the nature of his death, Jim Spencer's funeral had been closed-casket. When his wife asked for the return of her husband's wedding ring—a unique gold band with an emerald—to one day give to their son, it about killed him to tell her that her husband's ring was missing. Along with his finger. More evidence that Tino Falzone had rightly earned his nickname "the Beast" because of his extreme cruelty and sadistic methods of torturing his victims.

"You've got a broken wrist and a concussion," Morrison said. "You shouldn't even be here. You should be home with your girlfriend."

The last thing he needed was a reminder of yet another relationship he'd let disintegrate to dust. Susan's parting shot had been to accuse him of constantly ignoring her in favor of sitting surveillance with Smitty at all hours of the night. She'd been right. Since Jim had died, he'd been obsessed with nailing the Falzones. He felt like crap about hurting her, but he had no time for personal attachments. He had a job to do.

"Give me someone else for four days." Or, somehow, he'd find another way.

"You know the policy." Morrison shook his head. "Only an FBI-certified tech agent can install Title III court-ordered devices."

"I *am* certified."

"I know that." Morrison recrossed his arms. "You're the only field agent in this office outside the tech teams who is, but you're not medically fit. What's more, from what you've told me about Fiori's house, you'd need the best locksmith agent we've got to break in there, and he's on the west coast. And before you ask, your request to mobilize a team from Philly or Boston was denied. Too short notice, and they're tied up on other cases. I know it sucks, but you're outta luck."

"Mike, there's too much at stake." He stood, intending

to stare down his supervisor. Another bolt of pain shot from his wrist straight up his arm, and he hissed in a sharp breath. "If I can get enough evidence to indict Franco and Tino for murdering a federal agent, the Commission will never consider giving the Falzones an official seat. It would mean too much heat and unwanted publicity for *all* mob families."

"I'm well aware of the timetable, but I won't let you back in the field until you're cleared." Morrison's voice held a note of anger and frustration, and for the first time Jack realized just how much of Spencer's death the man had also shouldered. "I know Spencer isn't the first one you've lost to the Falzones. Yeah, I read those reports too. It was a long time ago. That wasn't your fault either. This is a dangerous business and people do die in it."

"Mike—"

"Give it up, Jack, and stop kicking yourself for things you can't change. You're desk-bound until I say otherwise." He turned and strode out the door.

Jack lowered himself back onto his chair. "Christ." He closed his eyes, trying to shut out the images of old crime scene photos he could still recall with bloody clarity. Seemed like all his best did was get people killed. Part of him had started questioning his own judgment.

Smitty pointed at the bottle of aspirin on Jack's desk. "You didn't take any of those painkillers, did you?"

"Can't. The minute I take one of them, I can't even report to the office for desk duty, let alone drive a G-ride." He'd go insane stuck at his condo without his government vehicle. More importantly, he needed a clear head to figure out how to get around Morrison's orders.

"You mean you *won't* take anything."

"Same thing." In the last ten minutes, his headache had

worsened considerably, and he wondered how much aspirin he could take without overdosing.

"I know what you're planning." Smitty narrowed his eyes. "I'm going with you."

"No, you're not." Smitty had a wife and four kids to support. Going against orders could land Jack in seriously hot water, but he wouldn't take his friend down with him. "For the record, I'm not going anywhere."

"Don't lie to me." Smitty glanced over his shoulder as the sounds of the office coming to life filtered in. "We've been friends and partners for way too long. You're going back to Rocco's, so don't feed me a line of bull."

Jack looked at the framed photo on his desk of him with his three younger brothers. As the eldest, he'd spent his entire childhood protecting them. They still looked up to him, but they shouldn't. He didn't deserve it, and he didn't deserve their respect. Not after what had happened. With Jim Spencer and that bookie, he'd failed. Like his brothers, Smitty was family. Jack would protect his partner's job *and* the man's life if they were the last things he did. "You're not coming."

"Sonofabitch." Smitty pounded the chair's arm, then stormed out the door.

Jack pressed the heel of his good hand to his forehead, rotating it over the tight muscles. He didn't need this. Not when he had more important things to do, like getting Kenny "Meat" Canzona to verify Rocco's and Fiori's locations for the next seventy-two hours. Meat was one of his best informants over the years, and the guy owed him.

Six years ago, Meat's four-year-old daughter was kidnapped by a pedophile. Jack was instrumental in the girl's safe return to her family. While they kept it on the down low, Meat was indebted for life and fed Jack whatever information he could. Recently, Meat gave him a tip regarding a witness to Jim's murder. One who might be willing to talk. So far, it was only a rumor. Like the one he heard about an unknown faction that had been ripping off the Falzones for the last two years. He'd assumed it was a rival family, or maybe the Sicilians. After his encounter with that wiseass little witch and her NASCAR driving buddies, he wasn't so sure.

He ignored the ringing of his phone and stared out the door, watching his fellow agents settle into their cubicles as he considered what had happened the other night.

That woman was a professional. The belt around her slim waist had been loaded with the tools of an experienced safecracker. And how could he forget the ebony-handled stiletto strapped to her ankle? Pretty, but deadly. Even with the muzzle of his gun shoved against her head, she'd still planned to ram a screwdriver into one of his body parts.

During his career, he'd busted every kind of lowlife the streets could puke up, but something about her didn't fit. Except the way her lush curves had fit into his hand.

His lips twitched. In addition to having a set of brass ovaries, which he grudgingly admired, she certainly had curves. While they'd been jammed in the closet like sardines, he hadn't been able to stop himself from running down a less than professional inventory of her assets.

From what he'd seen—and felt—he'd guess she was in her early thirties, five-five, a hundred and twenty pounds. At first, he'd thought she was skinny. Until he'd gotten a good feel of her long, firm muscles beneath that sexy suit. She had to work out regularly to achieve a body like that, although the full breast he'd cupped in his hand was definitely au naturel. He knew because his ex-girlfriend's weren't.

When all that thick brown hair had sprung from beneath her hood he'd nearly choked. And the way she smelled...no perfume, just a sweet, womanly scent. Like vanilla and sugar. But her voice...nothing sweet about that. Hard, biting, snapping at him with all the pent-up venom of a pit viper. Yet at the same time, it was soft and husky.

While he didn't give a rat's ass that she was stealing from the Falzones, she was nothing more than a thief. On top of which, she and her cohorts had not only obstructed a major investigation but assaulted a federal agent. After he threw the Falzones in jail, he'd put enough money on the streets to turn something up on her, then he'd charge her for violating every federal statute in the book.

The cell phone on his belt vibrated. "Meat, what've you got?" His informant rattled off the itineraries Jack had been waiting on. "Outstanding."

He might not have the resources to get into Psycho's, but Rocco's place he could manage. And Rocco would be out of town in Atlantic City. Tonight.

Chapter Four

"Aw, shit." Tino jumped back. The bookie's severed ear smacked onto the concrete floor, spattering blood on his brand new Ferragamos. "Shit, shit, shit."

The bookie howled in pain. Not even the industrial fans the size of small Chevys rumbling overhead were enough to keep the man's annoying screams from echoing off the bloodstained walls.

Tino clenched the roughened wood handle of the butcher knife tighter and raised his arm to take another swipe. "Fuck it." He flung the knife to the floor. The ten-inch blade clattered before skidding to a stop near a metal grating. "Will you look at this mess?" He pointed to his shoes. "I should hack the rest of the guy's head off for that alone."

"Serves you right for wearing designer shoes." Rocco crossed his arms, stretching the black sweater covering his beach ball–sized belly. "It's Monday, so what's with the Sunday best?"

Rather than flipping the older man the bird, Tino flicked the tips of his fingers beneath his chin, a silent FU. "I gotta take Ma out for dinner tonight. She likes it when I show up dressed nice, like I'm going to church."

"*You* go to church?" Rocco planted his hands on his belly and roared with laughter. "Hate to break it to you," he said between laughs and the bookie's moans, "you're going straight to hell no matter what you're wearin'."

"As long as I look good when I go"—he indicated with both hands to his Armani suit— "I don't give a damn where I end up."

"You and your freakin' wardrobe." Rocco snorted. "You spend more money on clothes than my four sisters put together."

"You should talk." He sneered as he made a show of checking the other man out. "You look like you buy your clothes at Dollar Tree."

A loud moan came from the man tied to the chair. The bookie's sobbing was beginning to grate on Tino's nerves almost as bad as Rocco's constant nagging. He glared at the bookie and held his arms wide. "Would you shut the fuck up? We're trying to have a conversation here." He began checking the sleeves of his suit for blood.

"What did you expect?" Rocco laughed. "You just chopped the guy's ear off."

As Rocco picked up the knife Tino had thrown away, Tino looked around the abandoned meat-packing ware-house, double-checking to make sure they didn't have any unexpected guests.

Aside from the rusty metal chair the bookie was tied to, the only other things in the fifty-square-yard room were a few stainless steel carts on wheels and dried blood-encrusted hooks attached to conveyer belts hanging from the ceiling.

He glanced at the ear lying in the puddle of blood at his

feet, then at the skinny man writhing and twisting in the chair. Tears poured down the man's face. Blood dripped from the ragged flesh still attached to his head where his ear used to be. The man's black T-shirt darkened steadily as it absorbed more blood.

"Cut him loose," Tino said, then yanked a silk handkerchief from his breast pocket and leaned down to wipe his shoes.

Rocco set the butcher knife on one of the carts and dug into the front pocket of his slacks to pull out a small folding knife. As soon as the bookie's hands were free, the man held both of them to his head. Blood oozed between his fingers as he whimpered, rocking back and forth on the chair.

"You ruined my shoes, asshole." Tino finished wiping his Ferragamos, then threw the bloody handkerchief in the man's face. "Now beat it."

The bookie stared at him, his eyes going wide. "I-I can leave?"

"What's the matter?" Tino got in his face. "Didn't you *hear* me?"

Rocco chuckled.

"I'll get the money to you next week." More candy-assed tears. "I swear it."

"I know you will." He pointed to the door. "Now get outta here before I change my mind and cut your dick off."

With one hand jammed against the gaping wound on the side of his head, the bookie bolted from the chair and stumbled across the warehouse floor, his footfalls echoing with every step. The door slammed shut behind him.

"This place still stinks like rotten cow." Tino lifted the lapel of his suit and held it to his nose, grimacing. "Do I have any more blood on me? I don't want Ma asking questions."

Rocco stepped closer and looked him over, sniffing the air. "Nah, you're good. You do stink a little like dead meat, though." He used the same cloth he'd wiped down the knife with to grab the bookie's ear off the floor. "For your collection?" A long strand of gooey blood dangled from the ear as Rocco held it at arm's length.

"Wrap it up and hang on to it for me." He rechecked his suit for spatters, running his hands along the smooth silk jacket. "I can't go to dinner carrying a bloody ear in my pocket."

"That's one sick habit you got." Rocco folded the cloth around the bookie's ear and stuffed it into his pocket.

"What can I say? I like mementos. John Gotti's hit man collected jewelry and watches from all the guys he whacked."

"A bloody ear ain't exactly a gold watch." Rocco found another cloth to wipe his hands on. "And remind me again why we didn't just whack this guy. I mean, rules are rules, right? If you skim money, you get taken out. Franco has a zero-tolerance policy where bookies are concerned. It ain't even this guy's first indiscretion."

"Franco's orders." He couldn't contain the disgust in his voice. "No more bodies before the big meeting. Besides, the more body parts I hacked off, the more of this dickhead's blood would have ended up on my suit."

"Since when do you care about orders?" Rocco dragged the metal chair across the floor to the center of the warehouse, allowing the blood on the armrest to drip through the metal grating. "You didn't wait for Franco's blessing before clipping that fed."

Out of habit, Tino scanned the warehouse again. "The fed had to go. Franco didn't have the balls to order the hit."

He headed for the switch on the wall to shut off the fans. "Franco's gone soft."

"You don't get to be head of a Family by being soft." Rocco plodded to where Tino stood. "Maybe he's just smart. Maybe there was a better way to deal with the fed than drilling him fulla lead and dumping the body in that cornfield."

He glared at the other man. "How many times do I gotta explain myself?" The top of the older man's head didn't even come to his chin. "I wanted to send a message to the FBI."

"Yeah, you sent a message all right." Rocco nodded. "It's been six months and that agent—Gates—is still all over us."

"No kidding." Tino spat on the floor. "The guy's a fucking pit bull."

"You should be careful around Franco." Rocco planted a beefy hand on Tino's shoulder. "He still blames you for bringing heat down on the Family. With all the feds tailing us after the hit, revenue tanked, and it's still not where it used to be."

"Don't push it." Tino's fingers twitched as he seriously considered slamming his fist into Rocco's jaw. "I don't need you to remind me of all the shit my old man blames me for." Like the fed. Like his own wife, Maria. And especially the thieves who'd been ripping them off.

"Look, all I'm sayin' is you gotta be more careful what you say about your old man and who you say it to. People, and I'm not saying who, are starting to think you don't respect him."

"Maybe I don't." He gestured for Rocco to follow. "The old man's time is over. We're trailing the other families because Franco's still living in the past. The 'old ways,' he calls it. We need to move into the twenty-first century before we fall behind."

He picked up his pace, being careful not to step in the trail of blood the bookie had left behind. He didn't give a damn that Rocco practically had to run to keep up. If Tino didn't get his ass in gear, he'd be late for dinner. One more thing for Franco to bust his balls over.

"Bookies, numbers games, shylocking, extortion, heroin," Tino continued. "Pennies compared to what we could be making. New drugs like vaping products are where it's at. We should be getting more into cyber-crimes and sending our people to computer school, not onto the streets. That way of life for us is gone. Dead and buried. Franco doesn't understand new drugs or the online potential for making money and deals."

To his credit, Rocco played it smart and kept his trap shut. Rocco was only a soldier in this Family, while he, Tino Falzone, was the Boss's son and a capo.

He turned as Rocco lumbered up behind him. "As soon as the Commission meets and Franco gets a seat, it might be time for a change."

"I didn't hear nothin'." Rocco threw his hands in the air.

"Good." Tino switched off the lights and shoved open the rusty, squeaky door. "Let's get outta here." He grabbed his Christian Dior shades from his pocket and shoved them on. "How do I look?"

Rocco scratched his double chin. "Like a movie star."

"Maria says I look like George Clooney." Too bad his wife was such a pain in the ass lately.

"Yeah, yeah, yeah." Rocco brushed past him, heading for the black Escalade parked behind the warehouse. "Whatever."

"Hey!" Tino started after Rocco. "What's your problem?"

"I don't have a problem. I'm heading down to Atlantic City tonight with some of the guys." He paused before hauling himself into the driver's seat of the SUV. "We were supposed to go a couple nights ago."

"You've got a night of gambling, drinking, and whores ahead of you. So why are you acting like you're on the rag?" Tino got in and pulled the door shut.

"Cuz maybe I am." Rocco shot him a pissed-off look before starting the engine.

"Buy a tampon and get over it." He eyed Rocco from beneath his dark shades as they pulled out of the warehouse lot and headed back to Staten Island. Rocco had been a real prick lately, and it wasn't like him. When the guy wasn't busting someone's kneecaps or breaking all their teeth, he was freaking jolly. Kids loved him.

Scenery flew by as Tino stared out the window in silence. Something was biting at Rocco's hairy ass, but he had more important things to worry about. Like staying in Franco's good graces.

Nailing the sonsofbitches who were ripping them off was the best way to keep Franco off his back. For now.

After his old man got that Commission seat and, with it, the official title of "Don Franco," Tino would make his move.

He couldn't stop the smile twisting his lips.

Don Tino sounded fine. Damn fine.

Chapter Five

The Porsche Cayenne's turbo-charged engine rumbled in protest when Gina eased her foot off the gas. Flakes of snow drifted through the beams of the Cayenne's headlights, twinkling like glass.

New York City truly was the city that never slept. Though it was well after midnight, cars still meandered along the side streets of the Upper East Side. Antique streetlamps bathed the deserted sidewalks in dim, almost ethereal light as she guided the SUV through the narrow streets.

Still not satisfied she hadn't picked up a tail after returning the rental car and dropping off her friends, she circled her block, rechecking the rearview mirror for what seemed like the hundredth time in the last twenty minutes. No one was behind or in front of her.

Her thoughts glided back to the gently falling snow and the last time she and her father had a snowball fight on their front lawn. That had been right before his body had been discovered half-submerged in thick swamp mud off the New Jersey Turnpike.

Gina swallowed the aching lump in her throat. Stealing from Franco's capos and soldiers was sweet revenge, but she and her friends couldn't keep it up forever. What would happen when they called it quits? Their capers had created a seemingly unbreakable bond between them. Would that bond remain intact when they retired from their Robin Hood days?

Tears burned the backs of her eyes as she gunned the Cayenne down the block.

About a year after her father was murdered, her mother had been lured into marriage by a smooth-talking bastard who'd moved into their family home. By the time Gina discovered the extent of the man's physical abuse, it was too late.

She'd found her mother on the living room floor, her face bloody. Her stepfather was sitting on the sofa, a beer bottle at his lips as he watched a football game on TV. A dozen more empty bottles lay at his feet. She'd rushed over to her mother, trying to wake her up. She'd even tried mouth-to-mouth resuscitation, knowing it was no use. The body wasn't cold, but it wasn't warm either.

"You killed her!" she'd screamed, barely able to see through the tears.

"If you don't get your ass out of here," he'd said, pointing a gun at her and pulling back the hammer, "I'll kill you too."

She'd fled the house and called the police. Her stepfather had pleaded guilty and gone to prison where he'd later died of an aneurism.

With her parents gone and the stain of the Mafia on her family, everyone Gina had thought was her friend abandoned her, practically disavowing her existence. She had faith that her current friends would never leave her. These women were her present, and her past was just that. Now she had other things to worry about. Things that could get her and her friends killed if she dropped her guard for even a second.

Another quick scan of the street, then she used her magnetic entry card and headed into the private parking garage beneath her building. After swinging the car into her assigned spot near the elevator, she shut off the engine and uncurled her fingers from the shiny olivewood steering wheel. She closed her eyes and leaned her head back against the headrest, breathing in the comforting smell of the Cayenne's buttery-soft leather interior.

Thank God tonight was finally over, although there were still more rips to plan. She patted the duffel bag resting on the passenger seat. Bulges of cash jutted against the rough nylon fabric beneath her fingers, but even so, she couldn't contain her sigh of disappointment.

Breaking into Rocco's place again had been as easy as slicing into her favorite seven-layer chocolate cake—as was getting into his safe. Problem was, there hadn't been nearly as much money as they'd expected. Mostly small bills stacked beneath larger ones. Nowhere near enough to set up Marilyn and her kids on the west coast, far away from the woman's scumbag husband.

If the fundraiser this Saturday night didn't raise enough cash, she'd sell the Cayenne. *Anything to help Marilyn and those sweet children.*

She opened her eyes and stared through the windshield at the gray concrete wall. Despite not getting as much cash as they needed, everything had gone as planned tonight. *So why can't I shake the feeling something's wrong?*

After slipping out of Rocco's apartment, she'd had the bizarre sense someone was watching her. During the drive from New Jersey back to Margo's Sutton Place brownstone for their post-rip briefing, she could have sworn they were being followed.

Paranoia. That's what it was. *Everything's going to be fine.* So why didn't she feel fine?

Duh. Because she and her friends had nearly killed a man.

To say she had no love for the FBI was an understatement, but she was still human. Fearing the worst about Special Agent Gates's condition, she'd checked the newspapers all weekend until she was bleary-eyed, searching for articles about an FBI agent injured in a hit-and-run.

Still worried out of her mind, the first thing she'd done this morning was call every FBI office in New Jersey and New York until she'd found Agent Gates at 26 Federal Plaza in New York City, not ten blocks from her Wall Street office. Even if he hadn't used his name when answering the phone, she would have known that sexy country-music voice anywhere. Relief at knowing he wasn't in some hospital, deep in a coma with tubes and IVs sticking out of him, practically made her giddy with relief.

After several shrugs to ease the growing knot between her shoulders, she got out of the SUV. The air inside the parking garage smelled musty and of exhaust. When she shut the car door, the sound echoed off the concrete walls like a gunshot, making her flinch and her heart pound a little faster.

Calm, Gina. Think calm. This was her home. Her haven. She was totally safe here. One benefit of the hefty price she paid for her apartment was guaranteed privacy. No one could access the garage without a magnetic swipe card, and the ex-cop security guard stationed at the front door had strict orders not to allow visitors inside unless they'd been vetted first by a tenant. If she didn't stop donating her own money to the women's shelter, she'd have to give up this nifty little pad and downgrade to something more affordable. Right at this moment, however, the added security gave her a sense of peace.

She went around to the passenger door and dragged the black duffel from the seat, slinging it over her shoulder. Tonight, the strap dug only slightly through her jacket. She sighed. Small bills actually seemed to weigh less.

Two minutes later, she stepped into her apartment and flicked on the lights. Relief rushed through her veins. *Home sweet home.* The bag dropped to the wood floor where it landed with a soft thud. She nudged the door closed behind her, not waiting for it to click shut before heading to the kitchen. Spicy smells of the mu shu pork she'd picked at hours earlier for dinner still hung in the air. Her empty stomach grumbled, but there was only one sure way to ease the tension cramping her muscles.

"Chocolate," she said on another sigh. "Lots of choc—"

Something crashed behind her—the door whacking against the wall.

Gina spun. Then froze.

A man towered in the doorway. No, make that a *huge* man.

The scream rising in her throat died. Nothing came out. Not even a gurgle.

He's a burglar. Worse, a rapist.

Gina's chest rose and fell faster as she struggled to breathe.

Move. Do *something.*

Like, run. Throw things. Too bad her body wouldn't respond. She might as well have been tacked to the wall behind her for all the good her legs did her.

It wasn't the intruder's size or the obvious strength in his powerful physique that chilled every cell in her body. It was the look of venomous fury shooting from his silvery gray eyes. If anger could be harnessed into optical lightning bolts, she'd have been fried by now.

He slammed the door shut behind him. Glass panes on her grandfather clock in the corner of the foyer rattled but stayed put.

Gina flinched, then balanced her weight on the leg planted behind her. She raised her fists. This guy looked like a linebacker for the New York Giants and could tackle her like she was nothing bigger than a football.

Bring it, you sonofabitch.

Oddly, he just stood there on long legs encased in faded blue jeans. He crossed his arms, tightening the black sweater and leather bomber jacket over his broad chest. Something white flashed at one of his jacket cuffs, but her eyes were drawn to the frown twisting his lips.

To her amazement, she found her voice. "I'm assuming you didn't come here for late-night tea, so if you're going to rape me or rob me, what the hell are you waiting for?"

The man's frown deepened and a look of what she could only describe as disgust came over him. He clamped his square, lightly stubbled jaw, emphasizing high cheek-bones and a hard, angular bone structure. Brows as dark as his close-cropped hair drew together, furrowing the skin on his broad forehead. A definite Cary Grant-possessed-by-Satan look but without the cleft chin.

Flinty eyes blazed into her, but the guy didn't move. More perplexing was that he actually looked as if he was...*thinking?*

Fine, pal. While you're thinking, I'm gonna gut you from the top of your movie-star head down to your size twelve boots.

She lunged for the stiletto strapped to her ankle.

A dark blur bore down on her. Before she could bolt and roll, powerful arms hauled her to her feet. He spun her, pinning her arms to her sides and lifting her off the floor.

She kicked backward, aiming for his legs, but missed. She twisted in every direction, but his thickly muscled arms were tighter than steel vise grips. Extricating herself from a locked bank vault would have been easier. She tried to scream when a hand clamped over her mouth.

"Stop fighting me, you little witch," he growled in her ear. "I don't want to hurt you, but if you don't quit struggling you *will* get hurt."

Dead is what I'll get. No thanks, asshole.

Even with only one of his arms around her now, she was still completely immobilized. She could only flap her hands at her sides like a trained seal. Under the circumstances, all her martial arts training was completely useless.

Something hard and rough dug into her arm as he held her tightly against his body. Her heart continued to race as she racked her brain for a way out.

What other weapons do I have? None, and even if she had any, she wouldn't be able to reach them.

Rough calluses dug into her lips. *Time to get in touch with my inner vampire.*

Gina maneuvered her mouth until she could get her teeth around two of his fingers. She bit down and the metallic taste of blood trickled into her mouth.

The guy grunted, but his hand didn't budge. With her luck, he probably had some communicable disease. It was either that or die a worse death in far less time.

She clamped her teeth down harder, putting everything she had into it, and was rewarded with a half growl, half grunt of pain, followed by a string of muttered curses.

More blood streamed into her mouth and she nearly gagged.

Yuck.

"Jesus, lady." Uttering more colorful curses, he wrenched his hand from her teeth and wrapped that arm around her chest too. "You already broke my wrist, the least you can do is leave my other arm intact."

She continued squirming, flapping her hands uselessly at her sides. Then his words filtered through to her brain. She stopped struggling and hung there, legs dangling a foot above the floor.

Annabelle's favorite phrase came to mind.

Oh. My. God.

She widened her eyes. Now her heart galloped faster than when she'd thought he was a rapist. *It can't be.* Then again, there *had* been something familiar about his face right before she'd lunged for her knife.

The same leather bomber jacket. And that voice—pissed off but still smooth and rich like melted chocolate. How could she have been so stupid?

The white on his jacket cuff and that rock-hard feeling against her arm made sense now. *His cast, you dope.* The one on the wrist that she and her friends were responsible for breaking. She closed her eyes and groaned.

It was *him.* FBI Special Agent Jack Gates.

Her muscles went limp. If Gates hadn't been holding her, she would have slipped to the floor like warm jelly.

I'm so screwed.

Of all the sticky situations she'd gotten herself into over the years, this was one she couldn't run from or pick her way out of. Looked like her future really would be filled with stinky prison latrines. Meals that looked and tasted like puke. Chain gangs and collecting garbage on highway shoulders.

Orange jumpsuit, here I come.

Gates's breath might have been warm against her ear, but his granite-hard tone held a clear warning. "I'll let you go, but if you try to bite me, kick me, knife me, or break any more of my bones, I'll cuff you and hang you by your ankles from the chandelier."

Gina didn't answer. She couldn't. *Crap.* She'd lost her voice. Again. Twice in one night.

"Do you understand me?"

"Y-yes," she finally whispered, nodding.

Her feet met the floor and his arms dropped away as he let her go. Something brushed her ankle, and before she knew what was happening, he'd whipped up her pants leg and slid her stiletto from its leather sheath.

Adrenaline that had been storming through her veins drained away as if someone had pulled the plug in a bathtub.

It was over. Everything they'd worked so hard for. What would happen to all those other women who needed cash to help them escape? For that matter, what would happen to *her?* To Margo, Kinsey, and Annabelle?

Nothing. She'd take the blame for all of them. Stealing from the Falzones had been her hair-brained idea from the beginning. Charity and revenge all rolled into one. *She* was responsible for masterminding every rip.

She held back a laugh of disgust at how similar her mantra was to the Mafia code of silence. *Omerta.* Never dime out your friends.

No matter how much she tried to deny it, she really did have Mafia blood flowing through her veins. It was ensconced in her DNA. Much as she wished it, even leeches couldn't suck that out of her.

She turned to see Gates standing a good three feet from her, palming the stiletto.

"This is what you were planning to gut me with the other night?" He shot an annoyed look at the knife. "Looks more like it's made for scaling fish."

"Or a snake." She sucked in her lower lip. The last thing she should be doing was taking potshots at Gates. He'd only add "mouthing off to an FBI agent" to the lengthy list of charges she was about to be arrested for.

What was it about this guy that punched all her buttons? She didn't have to think hard to drum up the answer to that question. Being an FBI agent was reason enough.

One corner of Gates's mouth lifted, not quite reaching what she would ever call a smile. Adding to her annoyance was the undeniable fact that he looked as cool and in total control as one of those arrogant feds on TV. *Figures.*

"For someone about to go to jail, you're pretty cocky." Carefully, he stowed her stiletto in the rear pocket of his jeans. Those hard eyes locked onto hers, reminding her of smoky quartz crystals she'd seen in a mineral exhibit. "Hiding anything else under that sweat suit?"

"No." She willed herself not to look at the black duffel bag near Gates's feet.

Please, please *don't look at the duffel.* As long as he didn't look in the bag, there was still a chance Margo could get the cash to Marilyn. Margo would have to be Gina's "one call" when she got to jail.

"Take it off," Gates ordered.

She narrowed her eyes. "Take what off?"

"The sweat suit. Forgive me if I don't take your word for it that you're not hiding a machete under there."

"Oh, no." She began shaking her head. "I'm not taking anything off."

"Either *you* take it off, or *I* will."

This cannot *be happening*. It was and she had no choice. Besides, they'd search her in jail anyway.

Exhaling a quick breath, she tipped her head to the ceiling and rolled her eyes. She pulled down the zipper on her sweat suit jacket and slipped it off her shoulders. As she flung it against the wall behind her, Gates's eyes dipped to her breasts.

"Now the pants."

Gina gritted her teeth, then stepped out of her sweat-pants and dropped them to the floor. Aside from her face, hands, and neck, the skintight black suit covered nearly every inch of her body, but beneath Gates's head-to-toe perusal she felt completely naked.

The muscles in his square jaw flexed. His next movement was so quick she didn't have time to react.

He grabbed her arm, spinning her and shoving her against the wall between the foyer and the living room. Jeez, the man had this move down to an art form, and his strength was off the charts.

In no time, he had her feet spread apart and her hands splayed on the plaster above her head. With one hand pressed securely against her back, he reached around and with quick, efficient movements patted her down. Starting with her breasts.

"Hey!" She tried pushing from the wall, but he pushed back, gently but firmly, immobilizing her again.

"Stand still or you'll only drag this out longer." The hard ridge of his cast dug into her back where he held her in place. His other hand was everywhere, roaming her breasts and belly, then her waist, crotch, and legs. "You might look like a cover model for Burglars R Us," Gates said, "but I won't underestimate you a second time."

The material of her suit was so thin she felt every touch, every squeeze, and every skim of his hand over her body clear to her bones. To the cellular level, even.

Humiliation at being groped again by this muscle-bound Neanderthal turned to anger, and she balled her hands against the wall. It was all she could do not to kick backward and permanently sterilize one of the FBI's finest.

He must have sensed her thoughts, because the next thing he said was, "Don't even think it. Your attorney's going to have his or her hands full as it is." The last part of her body he patted down was her ass. He cupped first one cheek then the other, squeezing lightly. "My professional recommendation is not to add more assault charges to the list."

She growled under her breath.

"Don't take this personally," he said as he completed his pat down. "I search all my prisoners before cuffing them."

She whipped around and slammed into a wall of muscle. More specifically, Gates's hard, pectorally perfect chest. He gripped her upper arms until she regained her balance. She pushed at him, spreading her fingers wide, but he held fast. God, but the man really did have the most incredible body. All those rippling, flexing muscles.

He gave her that half-assed smile again. "Now who's copping a feel?"

"Oooh," she gritted out and shoved again at his chest.

"Knock yourself out, honey."

"Let me go," she snapped.

He did. Abruptly.

The back of her head whacked against the wall as she stumbled. A jolt of pain exploded in her skull. For a second, she saw stars, but no way would she go down, not in front of the most overbearing, pig-headed—

Regaining her balance, she planted her hands on her hips and faced him head-on, though she had to crane her neck to accomplish that.

The corners of his mouth lifted again. "When I said 'knock yourself out' I didn't mean literally."

She rubbed the back of her head and prayed he'd just arrest her and get it over with before humiliating her further. The memory of her body's involuntary reaction to his hand on her breast while they'd been stuck in the closet washed over her like a heat wave, and her face flushed. "Bastard."

"You have no idea." He crossed his arms, hiking up his sleeve to reveal more of his cast. Then he smiled—broader, this time—and darned if it didn't transform his face, softening all those hard planes and angles, making him appear younger than she'd originally thought. Maybe in his mid to late-thirties. Under any other circumstances, she'd have to admit the man was not only handsome, he was downright gorgeous.

Don't judge this book by its cover. Gates was no cover model. He was a gun-toting, badge-carrying, handcuff-wielding FBI agent who was about to throw her smartass mouth in jail. Before the night was over, she'd be cuffed to a chair and put under interrogation lights until she gave up her friends. He probably already knew who her friends were. Like Annabelle said... *The FBI knows everything.*

"Let's get one thing straight here, G-man." She pointed a trembling finger. "I won't tell you anything."

The smile on his face disappeared. He rubbed his forehead with his thumb and forefingers, as if he had a headache.

Serves you right. Big, pompous jerk.

When he lowered his hand, narrow strips of white medical tape she hadn't noticed earlier were visible at the fringe of his hairline. An unexpected twinge of guilt jabbed her gut. Who could blame the guy for arresting her? After all, she *had* run him down. Kinsey might have been behind the wheel, but Gina took full responsibility for her friend's actions.

"We'll start out easy." He hooked his thumbs on his belt. The movement spread his jacket wide, revealing the holstered gun on his hip. "What's your name?"

Her eyes widened in disbelief. "You don't already know? I thought the FBI knew everything."

"Knock it off." There was a discernible growl in his tone. "You're in enough hot water to boil your butt as it is."

"Okay, okay." She held up her hands. "My name's Gina. Gina Perot." *Gulp.* Yet another lie. Technically, anyway. "Sorry about the smart-mouth remarks. I can't help it, it's in my blood."

At the mention of blood, she noticed the red droplets dripping to the floor from Gates's hand where she'd bitten him. What was one more assault charge tacked onto the list?

"You might want to wipe your mouth," Gates said.

"Why?" She narrowed her eyes.

He held up his chomped, bloody fingers and scowled.

"Oh. Yeah." She swiped her hand across her lips, then glanced at her fingers and giggled. Not because she'd made him bleed again. She actually did feel kind of badly about that.

"Keep it up and you'll make tossing you in jail that much easier on me."

Given the trouble she was in, she really needed to stop laughing. "I was just thinking how red your blood is."

"What did you expect, alien green?"

"Guess I thought a federal agent would bleed all patriotic-like." She couldn't keep from giggling again, and realized it was more because she was on the verge of hysteria rather than actual amusement. "You know, red, white, and blue."

Aside from arching a dark brow, Gates ignored her barb. "Who are you working for?"

"No one."

"Who are you working *with*?"

"N-no one."

"You just pegged a perfect ten on my bullshit meter." As if his tone hadn't been hard before, now it was icy. "If I haven't mentioned it, lying to a federal agent is a felony. Up to five years in jail for that charge alone."

"It's the truth." She swallowed so hard she heard herself gulp. She might be an ace cat burglar, but lying was something she'd never acquired a talent for. "I work alone."

He snorted. "I don't need to be a human polygraph to know you're handing me a line of crap. Someone else was driving the car that ran me down, probably the same person driving like a crazed lunatic through midtown two hours ago."

Gina couldn't stop her eyes from widening. They *had* been followed. Good to know her instincts were still dead-on accurate.

"That's right," Gates said, nodding. "I followed you after you left. I lost you somewhere in midtown, but this time, since I wasn't lying in the street unconscious, I *did* get the tag off your rental car and tracked it back to you. But *you* weren't the one driving the car last week. Give me a name."

She chewed her lower lip. *Not gonna happen.* There was only one thing to do here. The right thing.

"Go ahead." She took a deep inhale and held her arms out in front of her. "Cuff me."

Gates didn't move. He stood there, watching her. Correction, make that *examining* her. His eyes were like twin lasers, splaying her soul wide open, and God how it made the hair on the back of her neck prickle.

She'd never thought of herself as a coward, but she was beginning to understand that when Gates had no decipherable expression on his face—which, frankly, was most of the time—he was at his most dangerous. She could almost hear the gears in his head spinning and churning.

After a full minute, she lowered her arms. Clearly, he had no intention of cuffing her. Yet, anyway. He wanted information and probably figured he'd get more out of her in the comfort of her own home, rather than handcuffed in the back of a police car, or paddy wagon, or whatever feds transported prisoners in these days.

She shifted her weight from one foot to the other. The silence was getting to her, and he knew it. This was worse than getting hammered with questions. The man must be an ace interrogator. She wanted to tell the truth, felt obligated to spill her guts. He was the law, after all. But no way would she tell him about Margo, Kinsey, and Annabelle.

"The names of your friends," he bit out. "Now."

Slowly, she shook her head.

"Loyalty is for movies." Only the slight narrowing of his eyes told her he was getting impatient. "Prison is for liars."

Silence stretched between them. The only sound was the ticking of her grandfather clock in the foyer, one of the few things she couldn't possibly have pawned. The clock was a family heirloom and meant too much to her.

Agent Gates knew how to work the moment. All he did was stare and, dammit, she looked away first. When she glanced back, alarm bells clanged in her head. He'd abandoned his interrogation of her and was kneeling next to the black duffel.

She gasped, then covered her mouth with her hand. *No, no, no!* Her heart somersaulted over and over. If the FBI seized the cash—and they would—the money would probably end up in some generic government bank account used to buy new furniture for all the FBI offices. Or buried in a warehouse full of crates, like in the *Lost Ark of the Covenant*.

Gates yanked the zipper and several bundles of cash spilled onto the floor. He glanced up. "You look as if you're about to cry." She was. "This cash is from tonight." He nodded at the bag. "What did you do with the rest of the money you've stolen?"

"There is no other money." Though she willed them not to, her lips trembled. She really wished they'd offered Lying 101 in college. "This was the only time."

"Yeah, right," he snapped. "You and your friends have been ripping off the Falzones for at least two years."

Her jaw dropped. "How did you—"

"Know about your operation?" He gave her a *duh* look. "I've been investigating the Falzones for fifteen years. It's my job to know *everything* about them."

Fifteen years? She stood by her original assessment that Gates had to be in his mid- to late-thirties, so he must have become an agent in what, his early twenties? Fresh out of college, she'd bet.

"Until now, I didn't know who it was." He turned in a

slow circle, taking in the rest of her apartment. "Costly crib."

"I can afford it." She held her head high. "I work on Wall Street." She'd worked her butt off to get there, putting herself through college and business school while working for a chocolatier at night and on weekends.

"What about jewelry, furs?" His tone had become demeaning. He obviously assumed someone with her Upper East Side address would be drowning in diamonds. "What else does a cat burglar crave?"

"I only own jewelry with sentimental value, and fur coats disgust me."

"I'll have the Humane Society send you a Christmas card."

She bit her tongue, and this time, it was her own blood she tasted.

Sarcasm like that from anyone would normally have been more than sufficient cause for her to verbally ream them out with a caustic quip no man could recover from. Coming from a know-it-all FBI agent made clamping down on her colorful vocabulary that much harder.

Luckily, her father's words of wisdom sprouted forth from the depths of her memory. *Choose your battles wisely. Or you might get clipped.*

Well, he'd never said the second part to her, at least not in so many words. She'd been smart enough to get the gist of what he meant.

"I'm telling the truth." She tried keeping her voice steady, which was difficult when her hands were shaking like tree limbs in a hurricane. "Check my bedroom. My jewelry box is practically empty." She'd pawned all the good stuff and given the cash to the Center. "I assure you, there are no furs in any of my closets."

Gates rose, reminding her of a huge jungle cat. He strode toward her and gripped her chin between the thumb and forefinger of his good hand. His grip was firm but not painful. In fact, it was ridiculously gentle. She couldn't help but breathe in his minty breath, or take notice of how unexpectedly thick his eyelashes were. A supermodel would kill for those lashes.

She gave a mental snicker. He probably hated hearing that.

"Cooperation goes a long way in this business." The taut set of his mouth created tiny fan lines at the corners of his lips. "Tell me what you did with all the money you've stolen. It might lessen the amount of time you'll spend wearing an orange jumpsuit."

Oh, no. I guess inmates really wear those.

She swallowed and tried wresting her chin away. When he didn't let go, she grabbed his wrist above his jacket sleeve. His skin was warm, with a light coating of springy hairs. "I —I can't tell you that," she whispered.

"You can." He moved in closer, his warm breath washing over her face. "And you will."

"No, I—" She began shaking her head. "Please."

"Please what?"

"Don't ask me that."

"Why, did you spend it all on manicures? Wire it to a Swiss bank account?"

"No," she snapped.

"What then, jetting to the French Riviera? Caviar and champagne?" He narrowed his eyes. "Answer me."

Fear clawed at her insides. At this rate, she might as well surrender. Gates had her dead to rights, and he knew it. Case closed. No jury. No trial. Do not pass go, go directly to jail.

"This may be a game for you," he said, releasing her chin, "but believe me. It's no game, and people's lives are at stake."

"I know." Marilyn's and three small children.

"You don't know *anything.* You and your friends are obstructing a federal investigation. Your little scheme just set my op back for months."

"What do you mean?" How could their stealing have done anything negative except piss off the Falzones, which was exactly what she intended?

"Every time you steal from them to go buy yourself something pretty, it takes me three months to clean up the damage you leave behind."

"What are you talking about?" She took a step back. "And I told you before, we *don't* steal for personal gain."

"No? Then why?" He clasped her upper arms. As before, there was no pain in his grip, quite the opposite. Every one of his fingers branded her skin straight through her suit with a warmth that made her shiver. "You have no idea what can happen to a pretty little thing like you in prison. Now for the last time—"

"I gave the money away," she blurted out.

He angled his head. "To whom?"

She glanced at the ceiling. He was giving her no choice.

"You've got three seconds."

Forgive me.

Unable to look him in the eye, she stared at the corded muscles in his neck. "I gave the money to a women's shelter."

His hands dropped away, and his eyes went wide as he took a step back. For a full five seconds, which for this guy was probably a record, she detected emotion. Real, live, raw emotion.

Steely gray eyes pinned her again, but for the first time since he'd busted into her place, she detected no anger. Dark brows furrowed, and renewed fear tingled along her backbone.

He doesn't believe me.

"I'm telling you the truth." She held out her hand in a pleading gesture. "These women have no one to turn to. Their husbands will kill them *and* their children. They need cash to escape, to get new identities, to—"

"I *know* how women's shelters work." He tilted back his head and took a deep breath.

"That money"—she nodded to the duffel—"is for a woman and her three children to get set up on the west coast. As soon as she's released from the hospital, that is. Her husband beat the crap out of her and almost got to the children."

The shock had long since faded from Gates's face, replaced by a blank look.

"I know you're going to arrest me no matter what I say," she continued, "but believe me when I say we never stole anything for personal gain. We gave it all to the shelter." Still no reaction. "And if that's not a good reason to steal from a bunch of murdering, thieving mobsters, I don't know what is." The blank look on Gates's face seemed frozen in place. Another moment of frustrating silence passed. "Aren't you going to say something?"

"Why are you doing this?" he asked. "What do you get out of it? There has to be some kind of reward for you."

"There *is* no reward." She gritted her teeth. "Except the satisfaction of doing something good for someone, of helping people who can't help themselves." And, at the same time, hurting the dickheads who deserve it.

Gates stared intently, as if gauging her truthfulness.

Gina knew she must look and sound credible, because most of her tirade was true. Except for the little part she'd withheld about her own personal revenge against Franco Falzone being the icing on the cake.

"Maybe you've been a federal agent for so long you aren't capable of believing anyone. Maybe it's left you so jaded you can't possibly understand there are people in this world who take their reward by giving to others."

He began stroking his stubbled, square jaw with his good hand, then he started to pace the length of her foyer.

"Listen to me," she cried, stepping in his path and nearly getting run down as he strode into the living room to the large window overlooking the East River. "You've obviously never suffered any personal loss in your life or you wouldn't be such an emotional iceberg. Can't you have compassion for other people's pain and suffering?"

Slowly, he turned to face her, and for a second she could swear there was genuine hurt in his eyes. In the time it took to blink once, the look was gone, the chiseled lines of his profile tightening as he turned to stare out the window.

This is so *not good.* She could see his reflection. He was thinking again. Glowering, even.

Taking a chance, she grabbed his arm. "What about *your* job? You help others, don't you? What you do gets bad people off the streets, criminals who hurt others, shoot them, whack them, whatever. Can't you understand?"

When he looked down at her, one thing was clear. The man hadn't heard a word she'd said. It was over. Her impassioned speech had fallen on deaf ears. His heart had to be made of one hundred percent, grade-A ice.

She released his arm and stared out the window right alongside him. This might very well be the last time she enjoyed the twinkling red, green, and white lights of the many bridges spanning the river. As a free woman, that was. There was a similar view from the opposite bank of the river. Where the women's prison stood.

"I'll never tell you who my friends are," she whispered. "You might as well arrest me and be done with it."

"I have no intention of arresting you."

She snapped her head up to see a strange gleam in his eyes. "You don't?"

"No." The corners of his mouth lifted. "I have a better idea."

Her muscles tightened. Whatever was stewing inside his head was trouble, and the look he was giving her made her feel like prey again—like an animal that knows it's trapped and at the mercy of a predator. An *FBI* predator.

"Only one thing will keep you and your friends out of jail."

Gina swallowed. "What?"

This time he made no attempt to hide his sly grin. "Work for me."

Chapter Six

"You want me to *what?*" Gina's incredible big brown eyes grew impossibly bigger.

"You heard me. I want you to work for me. As an FBI cooperator."

Jack's proposal was met with near dead silence. The only sound in the room besides the annoying grandfather clock ticking away, was the low whir from the apartment's heating system as it cranked warm air from the vents.

Her voice cracked as she backed away. "I can't think of a single reason I'd want to cooperate with the FBI."

He cocked a brow. "If that's what you think, you need a major reality check. Before you kiss off my proposal you need to hear me out."

"That whack to your skull must have knocked your brains loose." She began shaking her head. "There's nothing you have to say I'm interested in, and there's nothing I could possibly offer the FBI."

"That's where you're wrong." He frowned, distracted as blinking beacons on the RFK-Triborough Bridge glinted off Gina's hair. It wasn't plain brown as he'd originally thought.

Red highlights shimmered in the thick waves that swirled around her face and brushed the tops of her shoulders. "And you don't really have a choice."

"No, that's where *you're* wrong." She parked her fists on her hips, stretching that already tight-as-sin black suit even more across her full breasts. "I *always* have a choice." The pissed-off glare she shot him was hot enough to laser his cast in half.

"News flash, babe." He intentionally invaded her personal space again, near enough to breathe in the same vanilla-sugar scent he'd noticed when they'd been jammed in the closet tighter than a box of ammunition. "No matter how well-intentioned your motives are for stealing from the Falzones, you just landed your butt in the middle of a major criminal investigation and screwed it up royally. There's no way you won't get indicted." He couldn't contain the hint of anger in his tone at how much rectal irritation she'd caused him. "Unless you agree to work off the charges—*all* the charges—by cooperating."

"*All* the charges?" She took a deep breath, again stretching her suit until he was sure the fabric would split at the seams. The way it molded to every shapely curve of her lithe body it could have been tattooed on. "How many are there exactly?"

"Let's see." He walked to the end of the sofa. This time, *he* was the one who needed space. As much distance as he could get between himself and this woman whose assets he couldn't seem to stop cataloging.

He held up his hand, counting off on his fingers. "Assault on a federal agent, leaving the scene of an accident, obstructing a federal investigation, breaking and entering, burglary, and conspiracy. That's the short list."

"Burglary?" Her voice rose and her chocolate-brown

eyes widened even more. "Why do you care if I steal from a bunch of thieving mobsters who probably stole that money from someone else, or got it by some other illegal means?"

"I don't." In fact, he applauded her for it. Officially, he could never tell her that.

"Then what's the problem?" She held open her arms in question.

"The problem is, every time you and your friends rip off the Falzones, they quit talking."

"I don't understand. Italians never stop talking." As if to emphasize her point, she began motioning with her hands. "It's a genetically foregone conclusion. Even when their mouths are shut, Italians keep talking with their hands."

He crossed his arms. "Like you're doing now?"

"Yes, like—" She bit her lower lip.

A blood-red warning flag waved in the back of Jack's mind. What slip had she been about to make? And there was something vaguely familiar about her. Not that they'd ever met before. He'd have to have been run over by a tank and gotten total amnesia to forget a woman like her. No, it was more that she reminded him of someone else. He couldn't put his finger on who that was.

"Now, maybe you'll let me finish." He ground his teeth, fighting to take a breath that didn't have Gina's distracting scent stamped all over it. "In the last six months—"

"And what do you mean I obstructed a federal investigation?" Challenge burned in her eyes. "How could my stealing have obstructed anything?"

"Let. Me. Finish." If he had some duct tape for that pretty mouth of hers, he could get this done and be out of her apartment before she drove him nuts.

"Okay, okay." She held up her hands in surrender.

More hand gestures. He'd have to run a thorough background on one Gina Perot, cat burglar-at-large. Her name might sound French, but there could be some thick Italian blood running through her veins, and with it, hidden ties to the Falzones or some other mob family.

"If you repeat anything I'm about to tell you—to *anyone*," he continued, "the offer I'm about to make you goes down the toilet, and you'll spend at least the next decade in jail. Capiche?" He waited for her to nod. "In the last six months, I've planted listening devices in key mob locations. You and your friends have hit four of them. Do you know what happens when a mobster's crib is broken into and he gets ripped off?"

Gina opened her mouth, but he held up his hand to silence her, which, miraculously, worked. "He abandons that location and I get nothing. I was about to break into Rocco's again tonight when I saw you sneaking out. Any bug I planted would have been worthless. Even when you rip off mob hangouts where I *don't* have a bug, they still get real cautious about what they say to anyone, anywhere."

Begging another question that had been bothering him. "You sure know a lot about who the key players are and where they keep their money. Just where are you getting your intel?"

She looked away and, before turning back, cleared her throat. "You were at Rocco's trying to plant a *bug*?"

"Yeah. Trying to." Now enough red flags to decorate a used-car dealership whipped back and forth in Jack's brain. The woman was exhibiting classic physical and verbal evasive maneuvers to avoid his question. "Until you got in the way. Like tonight."

"Until *I* got in the way. Let's be clear on this. *You*," she said, pointing a slim finger at him before pointing it at her chest, and adding, "got in *my* way."

"No kidding." He held up his broken wrist. "Is this what you do to anyone who gets in your way? Run them down and leave them unconscious in the street?"

"I'm sorry. It was an accident. We would never deliberately hurt anyone. We called 911. I don't know what else I can say or do to apologize."

"I do." He sat on the rolled arm of the sofa. "I need a bug installed in a location that, thanks to you"—he glanced at his cast—"I can't access. I'm officially on the disabled list and can't do it alone."

"Can't you get some of your FBI friends to help you?"

He shook his head. "Unavailable."

"Why are they unavailable?" She reached out to the table behind the sofa where he sat and plucked something silver from a crystal bowl. Her fingers made quick work of unwrapping silver foil from whatever she'd grabbed.

"They're on other assignments. Unlike what you see on TV, the FBI doesn't have unlimited resources." And if SAC Morrison ever found out he was in the field against orders, without medical clearance, and all while recruiting an unsanctioned FBI cooperator, Jack would be toast.

He grimaced as he identified the shiny brown ball in Gina's fingers just before she popped it into her mouth.

Chocolate.

His stomach lurched. Chocolate was like hemlock to his body.

"Then why not wait until they *are* available?" she asked between chews.

He hesitated. He'd already disclosed enough about the bugs. Discussing the existence of sealed court documents violated so many federal policies, he could get suspended without pay for a month. Then again, if he didn't convince Gina to help him, he could kiss his investigation goodbye, and with it his only chance of nailing the Falzones for what they did to Jim Spencer.

And to so many others he'd lost count.

A nauseating whiff of chocolate blew into his face, nearly making him heave. "The court order authorizing the bugs expires this Thursday at midnight."

"Can't you get an extension?" Even with her mouth half filled with chocolate, it was obvious from the tone in her voice she thought he was the most brainless agent on the planet. "Or why not just get another court order for another bug? You are the great and powerful FBI, are you not? Able to leap tall buildings, stop speeding locomotives, and all that other superhero stuff?"

"Great." He rolled his eyes. "A thief with a sense of humor."

"You have no idea." Her mouth curved into an impish smile that left him struggling to ignore how beautiful she was.

"There are no more extensions and no more court orders," he growled. "Either I get this bug planted fast, or my investigation is over."

"Okay, I get the picture." She swallowed and headed for the love seat opposite where he sat. Her catsuit made soft swishing noises as she walked. She sat on the arm of the chair, swinging her leg back and forth. "But I still don't understa—" Her mouth fell open. "You want *me* to plant the bug for you?"

"Not exactly. I'll plant the bug, but I need your cat burglar skills to get me inside."

"Oh, no." She quit swinging her leg and began waving her finger at him. "I'm not about to start playing spy games for Uncle Sam." The expression of disbelief on her face echoed her words. "I'd rather be sucked out of an airplane window at thirty thousand feet."

Using his good hand, he reached to the small of his back and whipped out a set of handcuffs, letting them dangle on the tips of his fingers. "There's always the alternative."

"I'll hire a good lawyer." She held her head high, but her voice wavered. "Any judge who hears why I did this would only give me probation."

"Doubtful." He looped the cuffs over the front of his belt where she could still see them. "Charges are way too stiff, and you'd have to ID your accomplices and name the women's shelter. As soon as you walk out the door of the courthouse, the mob will come after you and the shelter for their money. Trust me, *they* won't be sympathetic to your cause." And within a week, Gina Perot would be as dead as Jim Spencer.

His gut roiled at the image of her body floating in New York Harbor. He felt like garbage for what he had to do next. Play on her Achilles' heel.

"Think about your friends," he said in a low voice. "Prison doesn't exactly cater to rich women accustomed to having their hair coiffed and their nails manicured on a weekly basis."

Her perfect brows furrowed. The anger shooting at him only seconds ago was gone, replaced by fear. Not for herself, he was sure. For her friends. He had to admire her loyalty, but the job came first. It had to.

She slid fully onto the love seat and grabbed a throw pillow, hugging it to her chest. After another minute, she lifted her eyes to meet his. "I take full responsibility for everything." Her voice trembled. "I still won't tell you who my friends are."

"You don't really have to." He watched her fingers dig

deeper into the pillow. "The visitors log downstairs in the lobby is a road map to whoever you've been palling around with. I can also subpoena your phone records. With or without your cooperation, in a few days I'll have your friends' names, addresses, where they play tennis, polo, and wherever else rich, pampered women go to spend money."

"Please, don't do that." Her voice was soft, pleading. With her face still mostly in shadow, he couldn't be certain but was she about to—

He reached for the stained-glass lamp on the sofa end table and yanked on the metal beaded pull cord. *Ah, hell.* Her eyes shimmered with unshed tears. He swallowed the big lump of guilt choking his windpipe. She was a thief, but unlike most, she was also a real do-gooder. Not like the usual lowlifes he busted.

To her credit, she sniffed back the tears before a single drop spilled.

There is a god.

Anger he could take. Cursing he would understand. Even projectiles—bullets *and* knives—aimed at his head he could tolerate.

Her waterworks affected him like no other woman's ever had.

Shit.

She licked her lips. "You're not giving me a choice."

Now that he thought about it, her light olive complexion revealed what very well could be Mediterranean lineage. "I know." He didn't have a choice either. Not if he wanted to get that bug planted in time. "You've got a decision to make," he added before her expressive face did more of a number on his conscience.

Gina sifted her fingers through her hair, making him wonder if it was really as soft and silky as it looked. The throw pillow fell to her lap, and he decided then and there, skintight catsuits should be outlawed in all fifty states. And in all US territories.

The grandfather clock seemed louder, sounding more and more like a machine gun with every swing of its pendulum. Heaving it out the window onto the East Side Drive and watching it smash into a million pieces seemed like a stellar idea.

Jack's muscles ratcheted tighter, but now for an entirely different reason. It was the look of vulnerability on Gina's face, the one tugging on every vein leading to his heart.

Man, he was going soft. He clenched his hands and a shaft of pain shot through his busted wrist.

Gina's slim fingers sifted back and forth through the throw pillow's fringe. Her eyes filled with a mixture of worry and suspicion as she stared at him across the coffee table.

Come on. Take the deal.

If she didn't, they were both screwed.

She bit her lower lip again, a habit he'd learned in the last hour she did when there was a major battle going on inside her head. "You said all your FBI buddies were on other assignments. We'll need help running countersurveillance, but I won't involve my friends unless you promise that, no matter what happens, they go free when this is over. No charges filed on *any* of them. If something goes wrong and you need to blame it on someone, it will be me. *Not* them. Capiche?"

Wiseass. "Capiche."

A few more seconds passed before she finally said with a degree of determination, "Assuming my friends aren't inclined to wear orange jumpsuits any more than I am, when do you want us to do this?"

Relief flooded his body, and he dragged a hand down his face. "Wednesday night. Thursday will be our backup."

"That's not much time." She stood, then tossed the pillow on the sofa and began pacing in front of the window. "With prep and surveillance, it might be doable. My friends and I need to check out the location and start putting a plan together."

"Negative." Laying down ground rules with her was a no-brainer. *He* was calling the shots. Not her.

"Negative?" She laughed, and a rosy hue tinted her cheeks. "Is that cop talk for 'no'?"

"This deal comes with conditions. *My* conditions. The first one is that you and your friends don't go anywhere near the location until I say so and never without me present."

"Fine." She also crossed her arms. "When do *you* want to go with us?"

"You really do have the biggest set of—" He blew out a loud breath. The woman loved to irritate him, something she was way too good at. "You can't stand relinquishing control, can you?"

She pressed her hand to her chest. "Not when it's my ass on the line."

"Too bad." He strode to the window and planted his hand on the glass pane above her head. "Welcome to the wonderful world of the FBI."

Her lips compressed tightly. It was probably taking every ounce of her self-control not to whack him over the head with that glass lamp. He wanted to laugh at the speed with which she shifted gears. Totally vulnerable to completely kick-ass in a heartbeat. He liked her better this way. *This* side of her personality he could deal with.

"I can see you're going to be a handful." *She already is.*

She stiffened. "A handful of what?"

82

"Trouble." Needing space, he backed away.

Her lips twisted into a sexy pout. Her eyes might not be shooting fiery bullets at him anymore, but the steady glow told him he had to keep his distance or risk having every hair on his head singed off.

"Fine. You win." She headed back to the crystal bowl of chocolates. Seconds later, she had another chocolate ball unwrapped and stuffed into her mouth.

Despite the sickening effect chocolate had on his stomach, he couldn't tear his eyes from her mouth as she savored the candy. Or the way her tongue worked the inside of her cheeks.

She made a soft sighing sound as she swallowed. "May I ask a question now, Mr. President?"

"Could I stop you?" *Not likely.*

"Does your case have anything to do with the FBI agent who was murdered earlier this year?" Her voice held a sympathetic tone. "I read about it in the newspapers. There was speculation the Falzones were behind it."

"Speculation my ass." He fisted his good hand.

"Was he a friend of yours?" The tender look she gave him twisted his guts.

I don't deserve anyone's tenderness. "Yes." He stared out the window, focusing on the bridges spanning the river. She was doing a good job of dredging up feelings he'd stashed so deeply, ones he prayed would never resurface.

"I'm sorry." He flinched at the light touch of her hand on his arm. "About everything. Interfering in your investigation and about your colleague too."

"Forget it." He risked a glance at her and instantly regretted it. She'd dropped her hand, but the softness in her eyes tugged at his conscience. He was already beginning to rethink the wisdom of recruiting her and her friends for such a dangerous job. Like he had with Jim, he'd be putting them in danger. Then again, these women had been parking themselves front and center of more danger than they realized.

The clock in the foyer chimed twice. Christ, it was two in the morning. While he'd been making a sappy ass of himself, time had seriously flown.

"Here's the deal." He retucked his handcuffs into their usual place at the small of his back. "Get me into this location, and you and your friends don't go to jail. I forget I ever saw you. I forget your name and what you did to me." As if on cue, his wrist began to throb. "But there's one more thing."

"More ground rules?" A slight smile tugged at Gina's lips.

"Yes, and they're nonnegotiable."

"What?"

"As long as my investigation remains active, there'll be no more rips. Your little caper is shut down until I say otherwise."

"*What?*" Anger flashed in her eyes. "You can't do that. After I help you, you can't tell me what to do."

"You're wrong. I can." He lasered her a sharp look of his own. "And you should be thinking more about your own safety and the lives of your friends. You're tangling with people so vicious and cruel they'll torture you just for the fun of it. Then they'll kill you to send a message to others not to mess with them."

"Don't you think I know that?"

"You don't know anything about the people you're dealing with."

"Yes, I do. I—" She clamped her mouth shut.

"You what?" He narrowed his eyes. "What else do you know about the Falzones?"

"Nothing." She lowered her gaze to his chest. "Except they're mobsters, so of course they're dangerous."

Yeah, right. Gina Perot might be a world-class thief, but her lying skills sucked. The only question was what she was hiding. As long as she did the break-in for him, he didn't really care. At least, he *shouldn't* care. Oddly, he did.

"No more rips." He ignored her I-hate-you glare. "That's the deal. Take it or leave it."

She tilted her head and narrowed her eyes. "How do I know that after this is over, you won't arrest us anyway?"

"You don't. Except that I gave you my word. In return, I want yours that you won't plan any more heists."

He counted off ten more seconds.

Finally, Gina held out her hand. "Deal."

When he clasped her hand, a soothing warmth passed from her smooth, shapely fingers to his large, callused ones. For several seconds their gazes met and held. Finally, he released her hand. "Where do you work?" he asked.

After she gave him the address, he headed for the door. "Today at noon," he said over his shoulder. "I'll pick you up and we'll go over details at the location. Be ready." He pulled the door open but stopped before stepping into the hallway. "Stealing from the mob to give to a women's shelter is about the most courageous and admirable thing I've ever heard of." The ridged knob bit into his hand as he yanked the door shut behind him. He really was turning into a sappy pile of mush.

At the elevator, he pushed the down button. The brass arrow above the elevator doors moved until it pointed to Gina's floor and pinged. The doors creaked open and, as he stepped inside, he cast one last look toward her apartment.

How much of what was driving him was to stop the Falzones, and how much was to put an end to his own burning need to avenge Jim's death? He wasn't sure.

The elevator doors slid shut, and the car lurched as it descended. He leaned back against the metal wall and closed his eyes. *Thank God she took the deal.* Locking her up sat about as well with him as a dislocated shoulder.

He scrubbed his hand along his jaw, the day-old growth of beard pricking his fingers. Like Gina, Jim Spencer's wife, Tasha, was young and beautiful. Jack had personally delivered the news of Jim's death. During the funeral, he'd held her hand. It had reminded him of the bookie's funeral fifteen years earlier. Although he hadn't held that widow's hand.

He'd attended the funeral to pay his respects and out of a sense of obligation. Knowing the family wouldn't appreciate his presence, he'd kept his distance. As he'd driven from the cemetery, he'd glimpsed the widow silently weeping and the tears streaming down his daughter's face. The girl couldn't have been more than seventeen or eighteen.

He'd practically been fresh out of Quantico at the time himself. He'd been privileged and flattered beyond belief to be assisting on such an important organized crime case at such a young age. His gut told him he'd done it right, but his conscience would never let him forget the consequences of his actions.

If it was the last thing he accomplished in his career, he'd get that bug planted and make an airtight case against Tino and Franco Falzone. And as long as Gina and her friends were involved in his crazy-ass plan, he'd protect them. At all cost. He'd die before letting anyone else get hurt on his watch.

Chapter Seven

Gina jumped when the intercom on her desk buzzed. The black marker she'd been holding slipped from her fingers, leaving a zigzagging trail on the cuff of her green silk blouse. *Wonderful.* With only a few hours of sleep under her belt, her mind was so preoccupied she couldn't even hold a pen.

Noon. Be ready, Jack had ordered. She was so *not* ready it wasn't remotely funny. Her stomach had more butterflies than a rainforest.

"I'm going to lunch," Charlotte, Gina's fiftysomething secretary announced over the intercom. "You should too."

"Thank you, Charlotte." She smiled at her admin's attentive nature, but her smile quickly faded. The gold-edged clock perched on her ebony desk read 11:55, five minutes to the witching hour.

She was about to start working for the FBI against her will. Just like her father had. Only unlike her father, she was determined neither she nor her friends wound up dead. She picked up the framed photo of herself with Kinsey, Annabelle, and Margo at the last fundraiser they'd attended for the Center. Sighing, she carefully set the picture down, then stood and began pacing the length of her spacious office on the twentieth floor.

As soon as Jack had left her apartment, she'd grabbed the phone and conferenced in her friends to give all of them his ultimatum at the same time. They took it far better than she could have expected.

Kinsey had replied that it would be *cool* working for the FBI. Margo took the news the way she took everything—calmly and rationally. It was Annabelle who surprised her the most by stating they were bound to get caught sooner or later, and better to be caught by the good guys than by the mobsters they were stealing from. Then again, *The Untouchables*, that Kevin Costner flick about Elliot Ness and Al Capone, was Annabelle's favorite movie.

The click of her black pumps echoed on the floor as she made two complete circuits of her office before coming to a stop beside the solid brass coatrack by the door. "Good guys, huh?" The FBI hadn't taken care of her father. Why should she expect Jack Gates to take care of her—of *all* of them? She and her friends were merely the means for him to get what he needed. At least he'd been magnanimous enough to leave her the cash in the duffel bag. *Gee, what a swell guy.*

She curled her fingers around the coatrack. She hated the FBI with every fiber of her being. Despite their role in how her father had died, they'd done nothing to help her and her mother afterward. Without her father's income, money became tight overnight. They were on the verge of losing their house. Sadly, that was a big reason her mother wound up marrying that evil man a year later.

The system had let them down, and she worried it would again. Could she really trust Jack to keep his word and let them all go with no charges after they'd fulfilled their part of the bargain? *A bargain with the devil himself.* Was this what her father had felt like when the FBI had given him no choice?

She grabbed her cashmere coat from the rack and took a steadying breath that wasn't so steadying at all.

Back then, she'd vowed never to be that vulnerable again, never be so completely taken advantage of, but here she was. Essentially blackmailed and working for the big, bad G. Placing her fate in another's hands, let alone the *FBI's* hands, made her sick to her stomach.

Before heading out the door, she reached for her black Gucci tote with its stash of nerve-calming chocolate-covered lychees.

Three minutes later, she pushed through the revolving door of her building, squinting when a shaft of sunlight peeking through the towering skyscrapers nearly blinded her. A wintry blast of air whipped her hair in front of her face and blew her coat open. She fumbled with the closures, all while trying to keep the tote from slipping off her shoulder.

"You're late," a familiar voice said from behind her.

Jack gently took her by the elbow and guided her down a short flight of concrete steps to a blue Ford Expedition with darkly tinted windows parked at the curb. A curb, she thought wryly, that no one else in the busy city was permitted to park at.

She slanted him a frosty look, fully intending to remind him she might be going along with his forced labor scheme, but that didn't mean she had to make it easy on him. The snide remark died on her tongue. She had to swallow at just how good the man looked.

Unlike the last time she'd seen him, this time his chiseled face was clean shaven, and the beautifully tailored navy-blue suit he wore made his shoulders appear even broader, his arms more powerful, and his legs even longer. The man was eye-catchingly drool-worthy. Minus the little downside that he carried an FBI badge in his pocket.

He opened the passenger door and waited for her to slide onto the seat. Even stepping onto the running board, she had to grab the handle above the door to haul herself inside. "I suppose you have special parking privileges the rest of us little people don't," she quipped as she unceremoniously fell onto the passenger seat.

"Uh, yeah." He cleared his throat, his eyes focusing not on her face but lower. "Perks of the job."

Despite the freezing cold outside, her face heated to the temperature of a safe-cutting blowtorch. During her less-than-graceful entry into the Expedition, the sides of her unbuttoned coat had parted and her skirt had ridden up her legs practically to her hips, giving him an eyeful of her flesh-colored, lace-trimmed, thigh-high stockings.

Wriggling on the seat, she jerked the hem of her skirt down, covering her upper legs with her coat. "You can close the door now," she snapped. Embarrassment washed over her in waves. Regular workouts kept her in shape for the constant demands of breaking and entering, but exposing herself to Special Agent Jack Gates hadn't been part of the plan.

A slight smile tugged at his lips right before he shut the door.

With a groan, she let her head fall back against the headrest. She couldn't help but notice when Jack smiled for real—even a little—his usual I'll-crush-you-if-you-defy-me look vanished and... *Oh, girl.* When he wanted to use it, Jack Gates had a killer smile.

Keep your sex-starved body in check.

She needed to remember who he was. More to the point, *what* he was and the power he wielded over her and her friends.

As he shut his door, he reached to the dashboard for the laminated placard sporting a huge gold badge and the word POLICE emblazoned on it. He tucked the placard behind the visor.

With his left hand, he grabbed his seat belt and pulled it across his chest. He fumbled with his other hand—the one with the cast—to buckle himself in. "Dammit." A flash of pain crossed his features.

Only then did she realize how much his broken wrist actually hurt him. Again, guilt swamped her that she was the cause of his pain. After a few more seconds of watching him struggle with the receiving end of the buckle, which had now sunk deeper into the crack between the seat and the console, she couldn't take it anymore. "Here," she said softly, placing her hand on his cast. "Let me help you."

As the pain on his face receded, a little bit of her anger melted away and a disturbing thought insinuated itself. Jack was a lot of things, but he was still just a man and could feel pain like anyone else.

She slid her hand to his fingers where they protruded from the white fiberglass cast. With a gentle tug, she eased his hand from the seat belt and finished buckling him in.

"Thank you," he said in a gruff voice.

It could have been her imagination, but the disarming intensity of his eyes seemed softer, not quite so hard and unapproachable. His forehead furrowed, calling attention to the red gash peeking out from the edge of his dark hair. *I did that too.*

"You're welcome." Something about this guy got to her. She jerked away and sat ramrod stiff. "I'd have thought the

FBI would force you to take medical leave until you're fully healed."

"They tried." He started the engine. "I didn't listen."

With his good hand on the wheel, he steered the SUV toward the West Side Highway and the Holland Tunnel. Even one-handed, he maneuvered the large vehicle through the busy side streets with admirable finesse.

He slowed to merge into the long line of vehicles waiting to enter the tunnel. Another ten minutes and they hadn't made it more than twenty feet. To alleviate the tension, she tried focusing on the op for today.

Surveillance. Access points. Entry. Egress. Complete the job and get out from under the FBI's way too big thumbnail. She began strumming her fingers on the strap of her tote, then chewed on her lower lip.

"Nervous?" He chuckled.

"No." She refused to look at him. "Did I say something funny?"

"Not yet, but you usually do when you're uptight."

"What makes you think I'm uptight?"

"You're biting your lower lip."

When he smirked, she gritted her teeth. *Crap.* He'd known her for a total of what, four hours? Already he knew too much about her emotions. Must be something they taught federal agents. Mind Reading 101.

As they continued crawling through traffic at a slug's pace, Jack was silent, but his presence was as big as a Mack truck. Powerful and commanding, which only irked her more. She suspected he already had a plan and would get to it in his own time. The silence made her edgier by the minute.

When his cell phone rang, he grasped the steering wheel with the tips of his fingers sticking out from the cast and grimaced from the pain even that small movement caused him. With his good hand he tugged the phone from his belt and held it to his ear. "Kyle. What's up, bro?"

Jack had a family? Then again, *bro* could just be one of those macho terms men used when referring to each other.

"No, I didn't forget." His mouth tightened. "I was working. You know I'm right in the middle of—"

He blew out a heavy breath. The voice on the other end of the phone got louder to the point where Gina heard every word.

"You're breaking Mom's heart. It's been six months since you showed your ass at Sunday dinner."

"I'll try to make it one of these weekends," Jack grumbled. "I promise."

More cursing. "Your promises are about as reliable as a drug lord swearing he's going straight."

Jack glanced at her. Embarrassed at having been caught staring and eavesdropping, she glued her eyes to the brake lights ahead.

"Gotta go. Wait! Do me a favor and feed my clownfish for the next couple of days. John Wayne is old. Make sure he eats."

"Mind telling me how I make sure a clownfish eats?"

"There's a can of freeze-dried shrimp and flaked seaweed by the tank. Just lift the lid and tap some in. John Wayne and Annie Oakley will do the rest."

"Fine," came Kyle's terse response.

Jack clipped the phone back onto his belt. When he repositioned his left hand on the wheel, he gripped it so hard his knuckles cracked.

No wedding ring. Then again, maybe he was married and didn't wear one. A lot of men did that these days.

While it was none of her business, she couldn't help but

analyze the conversation she'd overheard, and another chink of her inherent animosity tumbled to the ground.

Even stern, hard-assed federal agents had families. Jack had a mother and brother who obviously cared for him very much. Whatever family issues existed, he was apparently upset over them.

"It's probably none of my business," she began, "but—"

"Probably not." His chiseled jaw tightened as he stared out the windshield at the stopped lanes of traffic looming ahead.

"But," she continued, ignoring his none too subtle message, "family is something you should never take for granted."

"Eavesdropping, huh?"

"Hard not to. Your brother was yelling loudly enough for the car next to us to hear. It was like listening to someone use a megaphone." She frowned when Jack didn't respond to her attempt at lightening the conversation. His anger she was used to, but this silent brooding thing was beginning to bug her, and *that* really did make her nervous. "So you actually have a mother?"

"Did you think I hatched from an egg?" The annoyance on his face was priceless.

"Certainly not." She snickered. "Humans aren't birthed that way. I think you were one of those clandestine genetic government experiments. You know, grown in a test tube and born in an underground laboratory. Like on the *X-Files*."

"To hell with this." He cut the steering wheel hard left and darted the Expedition into the thru-traffic lane, causing several drivers to pound on their horns.

Gina grabbed the armrest as he stomped on the accelerator, swerving as he drove. He hung a sharp right down a short street that dropped them directly in front of the tunnel entrance. A uniformed Port Authority cop blocked the way. Jack rolled down his window, flashed his badge, and was immediately waived through. In no time, they were speeding through the Holland Tunnel toward New Jersey.

"Another perk of the job?"

"For official business, yes."

"And while we're at it, you must know that talking on a cell phone without a hands-free device is illegal in New York."

His brows drew together. "What are you, a cop?"

"Speaking of which, your brother sounds like one. Is he? And how many brothers do you have?"

"You ask too many questions." He scowled, and she couldn't hold back a giddy grin.

The drive was becoming far more entertaining than she could have imagined. She held no power over this man whatsoever, except the instinctive ability to annoy him. Anger at the FBI aside, something about cracking through Jack's emotional armor and goading him was downright fun and something he couldn't arrest her for. *Too bad, so sad.*

Lights lining the tiled tunnel walls blurred into a pale gold streak. The faint smell of exhaust came through the air vents.

"Three," Jack muttered.

"Three what?"

"Brothers."

Ah. Progress. "Are they also in the FBI?"

"Two are, both in other OCUs—organized crime units. The other works for... Well, we're not quite sure *what* agency he works for."

"Must make for scintillating conversation at family dinners." She lowered her voice, trying to impersonate a man's much lower octave. "Hey, bro, kung fu anyone into confessing lately? How many hoods did ya throw in the slammer this week? Why, today I busted three little old ladies peddling whacky weed out the back of a flower shop. One of them tried hitting me over the head with her cane." She laughed and turned to see Jack scowling again, which, naturally, only made her laugh harder.

As they exited the tunnel into New Jersey, he glanced at her, but this time amusement glimmered in his eyes. "You're lucky I don't have any duct tape for your smart mouth."

"Sorry." Nah, she wasn't sorry at all. "It's hard for me to imagine you doing the family thing."

"Why?"

"Well, because...because..." She twisted her lips, struggling to find the answer to his question. When it finally hit her, she held out her hands. "Because you're *you*."

"How's *that*, exactly?" He swerved to avoid another vehicle.

"Mysterious, moody, tight-lipped, and tight-a—" She clamped down a giggle. "All that testosterone in one room must be overwhelming for your poor mother."

The SUV's engine roared as Jack gunned it onto the ramp for the Pulaski Skyway.

"I have no doubt you're the life of the party at *your* family gatherings," he said in a tone laced with sarcasm. "Your mother and father must be very proud."

"I wouldn't know." The smile on her face faded. "They're dead." And she was *so* not going deeper into any conversation about her parents. Especially not with an FBI agent.

"Sorry." He sounded sincere.

As they headed west, commercial jetliners heading into

Newark Liberty International Airport soared overhead. When she turned to follow one plane's descent, she couldn't stop from admiring Jack's sternly handsome profile. "Do you ever smile?" she asked. "Other than when you crack a suspect during an interrogation under those bright lights, of course."

"No."

"Do you ever laugh just for enjoyment?"

"No." He swerved through traffic and merged onto Route 280. "Do you ever stop asking inane questions?"

"Never." She smiled. Lord, but she hadn't had this much fun since the second grade when she teased the school bully, Jimmy Corelli, until he cried. "Bet *I* could make you laugh."

"FBI agents aren't allowed to laugh. It's in the manual."

"Is that a challenge?"

"No." His lips twitched.

"So, clownfish? Really?"

He snorted. "Yeah. Really."

She snorted back. "I didn't figure you for a tropical fish kind of guy. I see you more with a giant German shepherd, one with snapping jaws and huge fangs."

He surprised her by uttering a genuine laugh. "My father got me started on tropical fish when I was a kid, and I got hooked on them."

"And your fish is named John Wayne?"

"One is. The other—his girlfriend—I named Annie Oakley. My brothers and I used to watch all the old John Wayne westerns with my dad on Saturday afternoons. I actually did want a German shepherd, but since I'm never home..."

Well, dunk my head in a vat of chocolate. Maybe the

man is human after all. "That's a beautiful way to spend time with your father. You must love him very much."

"I did. He passed away three years ago." He exited onto the Garden State Parkway, heading north.

"I'm sorry." His words had been laced with a hint of grief, reminding her of her own loss.

He shrugged, clearly not comfortable talking about his family. "Our ETA's in fifteen. When we get there, I'll make a couple passes so you can get a feel for the area. House schematics are in the back of the truck. You can study them tonight."

Finally, they were getting down to the business that brought her one blessed step closer to concluding their pact and never seeing him again. Odd how she'd actually been enjoying their conversation.

"Whose house is it?" she asked.

"Psycho Fiori's. He's a high-ranking Falzone soldier."

"Psycho?" Gina grimaced. She'd heard of him, but she and her friends hadn't ripped him off yet. "I have a bad feeling there's a reason for that nickname."

"There is." The dark edge to his voice told her she wasn't going to like what he said next. "Not only does he enjoy killing, Psycho goes to a shrink on a regular basis."

"Aside from the killing thing, dare I ask why?"

"Anger management. He's got the temper of a wild boar and the fighting skills of a lion. A bad combination."

"Great." She began tapping on her Gucci bag again. "Can't we plant this bug at some other mobster's house, someone who doesn't have insane, homicidal tendencies?"

"No." He gave her a quick but meaningful look. "Court orders are location specific."

Gina clasped her hands. She'd honestly had no idea of the damage they'd done by ripping off the mob.

Ten minutes later, they drove into Montclair. When Jack braked at a traffic light, she noted with irony that such a charming town was home to a number of high-ranking mobsters. She'd known that since childhood, having accompanied her father on "payouts" to the numerous capos and soldiers who lived here. She'd stayed put in her father's car while he'd gone inside, but she always knew why they'd gone to Montclair.

As they passed through the town's main intersection, not even the two- and three-story brick-fronted shops with their gold-gilded signs and colorful canopies or the beautifully landscaped parks could ever make her think fondly of this place. Her heart ached as if her parents had died only yesterday.

Before she realized it, they'd driven out of the town's center and onto a residential road.

"We're here," Jack announced, breaking into her trek down Sad Sack Memory Lane.

"Number 42." He pointed to the right. "The corner house. Stucco with green trim."

"Posh for a crazed lunatic." She switched to op mode and began assessing the structure and its surroundings. From a B and E—breaking and entering—perspective, that was. "Mind if I take notes?"

"Do whatever you need to." He slowed the Expedition without making it obvious they were surveilling the place. Traffic was light but constant, helping them blend in.

"Two-story, around twenty-two hundred square feet. About a third of an acre. Grass front and back lawns. Concrete driveway." While continuing to itemize more relevant aspects of the location, she dug into her bag for a small spiral notebook and pen. "Two motion sensors on either side of the driveway. Metal grating on all first-floor windows." She paused to jot down her observations.

"Check out the rear of the house," he said as they cruised past the front yard.

She looked over her shoulder. "Second-story balcony. Wrought iron railing, sliding glass door. I take it there's a problem breaking in through the front door?"

"Several." He braked at the stop sign and turned right at the corner. "A sophisticated deadbolt lock with anti-pick pins."

"You think I can't pick that?" She pressed a hand to her heart. "My ego is shattered."

"Even if you can, it would take too long." He made another right turn, heading back around to the front of the house. "The front door is lit up at night like Madison Square Garden. Risk of exposure's too great."

"So you need me to pick the lock on the second-story balcony?" She tapped the end of her pen on her chin. "Easy enough to access with a rope."

"Unless you've got a busted wrist," he grumbled so low Gina barely caught his words.

"I heard that. Point made. For the hundredth time, I really am sorry."

The tautness in his jaw eased. "Forget it."

As he recircled the block, she made a quick sketch below the notes she'd taken.

"Hmph."

She looked up to catch him eyeing her pad. "What's wrong?"

"Nothing." He refocused on the road, but not before she detected something different in his expression.

Admiration? Respect?

Can't be. The only thing the FBI respects is the FBI.

He made one last turn and Psycho Fiori's house came into view again. He parallel parked midway down the adjacent block and across the street between two other SUVs. "We'll sit here for about fifteen minutes," he said. From their position, they had partial views of both the front door and rear balcony. "In addition to the metal grating on the lower windows, Psycho has a standard security alarm package."

"Do you know what make it is?" she asked.

"A residential Protector system."

"Ahhh." Gina made another notation.

"You're familiar with it?"

She rolled her eyes. "Once again, you wound me. Protector makes a very common, very simple residential security package. I assume he has a monitoring contract."

"He doesn't."

"You're kidding. What kind of psychotic idiot installs an unmonitored alarm system?"

"The kind that doesn't want the police responding to a burglary at a house that's loaded with illegal cash."

"Right." This time, she did feel stupid. At least it made the job easier. There'd be no need to cut outdoor phone wires or internet cables before the alarm was triggered and a signal sent to the monitoring company. "Okay, then we're dealing with a self-contained system with audio and visual alarms. Bells and whistles positioned inside the house to notify the owner of a break-in." She jotted down a few more notes before continuing. "The basic Protector system uses a six- to eight-zone setup, including one motion sensor that's usually installed on the ground floor to detect anyone breaking in through the front door."

Jack tapped the steering wheel. "I assume there'll be

some kind of detection unit set up on the second-story balcony door."

"Maybe, maybe not." She eyed the rear balcony. "Most break-ins occur at ground level because it's easier on petty crooks than hauling around a ladder to access upper floors. There could be glass-break sensors upstairs, but I don't plan on breaking any glass. Most systems also use closed circuit, surface-mounted magnetic contact window and door sensors. Each window and door has a two-part, side-by-side sensor. One side of the sensor is a magnet and the other houses an electrical circuit that's either wired to an alarm box or set to send a wireless signal. As long as the two parts are within an eighth of an inch of each other, the circuit remains closed. Any increase in distance opens the circuit and triggers the alarm."

"How do you plan to get around that?"

"I can easily bypass the sensors."

"How?"

"By simulating the magnetic contact."

"How do you squeeze a magnet between two locked sliding glass doors?" The look of skepticism on Jack's face was amusing.

"I don't. I jimmy a slim strip of supermagnetized metal into the tiny space between the door and the jamb, close enough to simulate the magnetic contact required to keep the circuit closed. As long as that magnet remains in place, the alarm stays silent."

"You didn't learn *that* working on Wall Street." Jack's laser-sharp gaze could have burned a hole right through her.

"A girl's gotta have her secrets." She winked and was rewarded with a sexy half smile that sent a shaft of not unpleasant heat arrowing up her spine.

"Okay." He nodded. "I'm assuming picking the lock on

the balcony door should be a slam dunk for a burglar with supermagnetizing skills, but how do you plan to access the second floor?"

She held her hand out, palm facing up. "Like I said, with a rope."

"You can't leave anything behind, so how will you detach the rope after you climb back down?"

"Another of my inventions." Again she couldn't stop herself from winking.

"I won't bother asking." He shook his head. "Anyone who can supermagnetize metal can devise a way to remotely unhook a rope from a railing."

She grinned. "So true."

He turned back to the house. "There are no motion sensors in the backyard. Psycho ripped them out because his dog kept setting them off, but he might have installed extra motion sensors in the upper floor."

"There's a dog inside?" She loved dogs but didn't want to tangle with one.

"Not anymore," he said, shaking his head. "Apparently, the dog annoyed him."

"He killed his own dog?"

"Dunno." Jack shrugged. "Could be he gave the dog away. Can't say for sure."

Bastard. Now she hated Psycho Fiori even more. She shook her head to clear it of the awful image and concentrate on the task at hand. "Interior sensors are easy to check on before I step into the room and easy to get around if they're there. Most motion sensors are placed in such a way to detect people, not animals, and since Psycho had a dog, he would have placed the sensors up high or the alarm would be going off every five minutes. All I have to do is hug the floor."

"Anything else?"

"I'll have to watch for pressure mats."

"What are those?" Jack's brows rose.

"Pressure mats look like ordinary floor mats, the same kind you'd put just inside an exterior door to wipe your feet on. Only in this case, when you step on the mat, two metal strips are pushed together, completing a circuit and triggering an alarm."

Jack's lips quirked and amusement glimmered in his eyes. Gina suddenly felt as if she'd been whacked upside the head. "You already know all of this, don't you?" She slumped back into her seat. "I'm such an idiot. You were testing me."

"Don't worry." He grinned. "You passed."

The man probably knew as much about breaking into a house as she did. Maybe more. When she'd broken into Rocco's apartment, Jack was already inside and she hadn't even known it. The rest of her team never even saw him go in. He was only using her because he was injured, on a deadline, and there were no other agents available for the job.

"Once you're in," he continued, "go downstairs and deactivate the front door alarm. Hit me on the radio, and I'll come to the door and knock as if I'm a visitor so the neighbors or anyone driving by won't be suspicious. You let me in, I plant the bug, then you let me back out the same way. Got it?"

"Yes, Dad."

Other than arching a dark brow he ignored her sarcasm. "Then you'll relock the front door, reset the alarm, exit out the balcony, and leave everything the way it was." He gave her a pointed look. "I mean it. You have one mission and one mission only. No searching for cash and no safecracking. Is that clear?"

"Perfectly." *For now.* Once Jack's investigation was over, she could drum up a plan to return and grab more cash. "Except, I'm starting to think we don't need to involve my friends in this." More like didn't *want* to involve them. The more she thought about it, she and Jack could tackle this one alone, giving her friends that much more of a buffer from all this.

"Countersurveillance. They'll keep watch while we're inside." With his good hand, Jack gripped the wheel.

"Why aren't you using other FBI agents for countersurveillance? You don't need a special tech team for that."

His knuckles cracked. "The fewer people who know about your involvement in this, the better off you are."

"Does anyone besides you know about us?"

A long moment of silence filled the SUV. "No."

"Why not?" She couldn't keep the suspicion from her voice. "Don't you have to do everything by the book? Reports? Government red tape?"

"Not this one." His square jaw clenched. "It's better this way. Trust me."

She almost choked on his last words. *Trust me.* There wasn't a single chance of that happening. "How do you know Psycho won't be home tomorrow when I break in?"

"Good intel." He scanned both sides of the street, then checked his mirrors.

Gina drew her brows together, realizing she had no first-hand intel on the target, something she normally made a point of researching herself. "What about Psycho's wife? Any kids?"

"Psycho's estranged wife grabbed the kids and moved to Florida, making him even more psychotic."

"Ah." She nodded. "I should have known you'd know all this. FBI informants and all."

"Speaking of which, you never answered my question the other night. How do *you* know so much about the Falzones?"

The interior of the huge SUV suddenly shrank to the size of a mailbox.

"How do you know what targets to hit and when?" he pressed. "You've either got a crystal ball or some kick-ass informants yourself. And how did you pick up enough breaking and entering skills to get into this business in the first place?"

Gina sucked in her lower lip. She had no intention of answering his questions. Time to derail this interrogation train. "That wasn't part of our deal."

"What wasn't?"

"You peppering me with questions."

"Let's compromise. I already ran your criminal history, so I know you've never been arrested." He paused, making her dread what was coming next. "Is there anything else in your background I should know about?"

"Like what?" Sweat began trickling down her back.

"I don't know." His voice softened, making her wonder if this approach was some kind of sneaky FBI technique. "You tell *me*."

"There's nothing to tell." If she gave him any reason to suspect there was something ugly in her past he'd only dig deeper. "What you see is what you get." *Plus a scooch more.* Like the little factoid that she was the daughter of Franco Falzone's former bookie, Tony Perotti. If Jack discovered that, he'd almost certainly throw her, Margo, Kinsey, and Annabelle in jail on the spot. Guilt by association. *Mob* association. Never a good thing to be with the FBI dogging your every move.

More sweat trickled down her back, making her silk shirt stick to her skin. There was only one antidote. She dug into her tote for her stash. When her trembling fingers contacted the small baggie, she nearly groaned with relief. A moment later, she had a chocolate-covered lychee in her mouth. This time, she did groan, like a drug addict injecting herself with a quick fix.

With slightly steadier fingers, she unwrapped a second lychee and was about to pop it into her mouth when she caught sight of Jack with his back pressed against the driver side door. His face was pale, his mouth pinched. He looked ready to puke.

"What's wrong?" She shoved the second piece of chocolate into her mouth.

He cracked his window and every other window in the SUV. A gust of frigid air blew inside, ruffling his hair.

"Hey, it's freezing in here." More cold air poured into the Expedition, and she pulled her coat closed around her body. "Raise the windows. I'm cold. The least you can do is keep your employee happy."

He ignored her request and sucked in long lungfuls of air. "You're not my employee."

"What am I then?"

"A cooperator." His Adam's apple bobbed as he swallowed.

"Hmm, let's see." She intentionally laced her voice with sarcasm. "A cooperator, by definition, is someone who joins with another for a common purpose, but who acquiesces *willingly*." She practically spit out the last word.

"I didn't force you." His throat continued to work. "I gave you a choice and you made it. *Willingly*."

"Whatever." Man, she'd lost that debate a solid ten to zip. "At least raise the windows so your *cooperator* doesn't freeze to death." She unwrapped another piece of chocolate.

"No."

"Why not?" She twisted to face him, pulling her coat tighter. She was freezing her butt off, but his terse responses were getting her steamed. He eyed the bag of chocolates in her lap as if it were a bomb with a lit fuse. "This?" She raised her brows. "You don't like the smell of chocolate?" He shook his head. "Who doesn't like the smell of chocolate?"

"I don't."

"You're kidding."

"Do I look like I'm kidding?" He definitely didn't. In fact, he looked green around the gills.

She popped the chocolate into her mouth, chewed quicker than she would have liked and swallowed. Jack exhaled, as if he'd been holding his breath. He turned to take another gulp of air at the open window.

"What's with you and chocolate?" Come to think of it, he did have a less than thrilled look on his face last night at her apartment when she'd thrown back a couple dark chocolate balls to take the edge off.

He sucked in more air before turning back to her. "I'm allergic to it."

She blinked. *Huh?* Her stomach muscles began to quiver, and she pressed her lips together until she couldn't contain it and burst out laughing. She laughed until tears pricked at the corners of her eyes. "You're kidding?"

"Once again"—he curled his lip at the bag of chocolates—"do I look like I'm kidding?"

"Oh my God." She pressed a hand to her belly. "I'm sorry. I never met anyone with a chocolate allergy."

"It's rare." Sweat beaded on his forehead. "I've had it since I was a kid. It's gotten worse with age."

"Rare? It's unheard of." She wiped the tears now streaming down her temples, loving the irony of the situation. Here she was crying with laughter and he was sweating bullets. "What happens if you accidentally eat chocolate? I mean," she added with a hint of mischief, "what if one of your enemies gets wind of your rare allergy and slips some into your drink or your food?"

He pointed a long finger at her. "Don't get any ideas."

"I know, I know, or you'll throw me in jail for assaulting a federal agent. No, really, what would happen if you ingested chocolate?"

He gave her another threatening look. "My throat would close up."

"I'll keep that in mind, Agent Gates." She smirked and batted her eyelashes.

"See that you do." He dipped his chin to the baggie. "And put that shi—stuff away."

After one more snort of laughter, she obediently returned the stash to her bag. Jack waited until she complied, then another full minute more before raising the windows.

"Street's pretty quiet today." With a click, he eased his seat back. "Not much to see. We'll head out in a few minutes, so take notes on anything else you need to."

She watched the house, but she'd already seen everything she needed to. An American flag attached to the front of the house whipped helplessly in the wind. Guess even the mob could be patriotic.

Jack reached out and pushed a button on the dashboard.

Italian opera filled the SUV, and she wrinkled her nose. She was thrown back to the horrible day of her father's funeral. Someone had played Verdi the entire time.

She crossed her arms and glared at him. "How can you like Italian opera when you spend your whole life throwing Italian citizens in jail."

"I don't throw Italian *citizens* in jail. I throw *criminals* in jail, many of whom happen to be of Italian descent." He cranked up the volume, making her wince. "My mother practically raised me and my brothers on opera. There's a certain irony in that, but I find it soothing." He started to grin. "From the look on your face, you obviously don't care for opera."

"Understatement," she mumbled. That and she hated when men grinned at her.

"In fact," he added, "you look like you're about to be sick. Why do you hate Italian opera so much?"

Oh, no. Not gonna go there. "I just do." She uncrossed her arms and had to restrain from diving back into her stash.

"Why?" He made a sound that was close to an outright laugh but not quite there.

For the second time since they'd met, she caught him smiling at her. A real smile, with straight white teeth and everything. The shock of seeing it again in all its masculine beauty almost made her forget her irritation. Almost.

"Don't tell me you're allergic to opera?" His smile broadened.

"Now who's asking too many questions?" *Dammit.* Just when she thought she'd found the great and almighty Special Agent Gates's Achilles' heel, he'd spun things around and found *hers.*

Oh, he's good, all right. She recrossed her arms and turned away from his way too handsome, way too disconcerting smile. But it was infectious, and she soon found herself smiling too. "Touché," she admitted.

To her surprise, Jack burst out laughing—a rich, resonating sound. "I have an idea," he said.

"Oh yeah?"

"A truce." He shut off the music, dousing the SUV in blessed silence. "No opera in exchange for no chocolate."

"Hmm." She knitted her brows, feigning deep thought. "I don't know. My opera allergy isn't nearly as dangerous to my health as your chocolate allergy is to yours."

Another one of those killer smiles curved his lips, and for a nanosecond she wondered what it would be like to have his mouth on hers, kissing her. *Get. Real.* "Deal." She extended her hand.

The instant their fingers touched, a jolt of awareness sparked up her arm to her neck, shooting straight out the top of her head, and leaving tingly goose bumps parading across her skin. She jerked her hand away.

Jack's eyes widened. His nostrils flared and the muscles in his square jaw flexed. When he refused to stop staring at her, the hair at her nape began to prickle.

Once again, she could practically hear the gears turning in his head, and again she longed to dive into her bag for a chocolate-covered lychee. But she'd given her word.

"What, do I have chocolate on my face?" she asked in a light tone, hoping to diffuse whatever thoughts were occupying his far too suspicious brain.

At first, he didn't answer. "Sometimes you look familiar. I don't know where we could have met before."

"Maybe you saw my picture in the society pages. My friends and I are occasionally photographed at fundraisers we attend for the women's shelter." Like the one this Saturday night.

"That's not it." He gave a quick shake of his head. "We've been here long enough, but there are a few things we need to discuss." He tilted his seat fully upright and maneuvered the SUV back onto the road. "The most important thing is that you have to trust me."

"Fat chance."

"You may not like me, but I never lied to you."

"I seriously doubt that."

"No." The tone of his voice hardened. "I *never* lied to you. Good, bad, or ugly, I'll always give it to you straight."

"How can I believe that?"

"Because it's the only way I do business."

"You work for the federal government. That makes you and anything you say suspect."

At a traffic light, he rested his broken wrist on the back of her headrest. "What we're doing is too dangerous for me to hide anything from you and for you to hide anything from me. We have to trust each other or someone could get hurt, and that's not acceptable. No one else gets hurt on my watch."

No one else?

After the playful banter they'd established, the seriousness of his expression was a bit frightening. "Okay." She nodded and assumed he was referring to his dead colleague, that agent the Falzones had supposedly killed. No, not supposedly. She, too, had firsthand knowledge of what they were capable of. If Jack was certain the Falzones murdered his colleague, that was good enough for her.

"Sorry. Didn't mean to go ballistic." He shut his eyes and massaged the bridge of his nose with his thumb and forefinger. "I just don't want anything to happen to you or your friends."

When he opened his eyes there was no doubting the

truth of his words. It was written on his face as clearly as a commandment. Was she wrong? Did he actually care about what happened to them? The possibility upended every preconceived notion she had about the FBI.

A horn sounded behind them, and he stomped on the accelerator. Moments later, he turned onto the Garden State Parkway and broke every posted speed limit. The only times he spoke to her again during the drive were to firm up details of their plan.

There was nothing special about this break-in. At least not on the surface. But she'd learned enough from Sergio to expect the unexpected.

Barely twenty minutes after they'd passed the Leaving Montclair sign, Jack maneuvered the SUV through the narrow streets crisscrossing the Wall Street section of Manhattan. After parking in front of her building, he got out and retrieved the rolled schematics for Psycho's house from the back of the SUV. Before she could finish buttoning her coat, he came around to her side and opened the door.

Wind blasting across the concrete courtyard in front of the building blew her hair from her face. Behind her, the enormous American flag atop a thirty-foot pole whipped back and forth.

"I'll be at your place tomorrow night. Eight sharp." He handed her the schematics, barely making eye contact. "We'll do a briefing before heading out. Make sure your friends are ready to go."

Yup. Hard-assed fed back in place. All is right with the world again.

Or was it?

Without another word, he left her standing at the curb. While she watched the SUV disappear around a corner, a chill ran through her, and it wasn't from the strong winds or the sub-zero temperature.

This deal with the FBI... Things were about to change. Their days of ripping off the Falzones might be coming to an end.

As she clenched her fingers around the rolled documents, a plan took root, one that could grab them an absurd amount of cash in one night. Then they could call it quits.

Her conscience prickled with anxiety. Breaking her promise to Jack wasn't an option. The ramifications were too great. There had to be a solution, and she'd find it. She had to. Because lives were at stake.

Chapter Eight

"Oh, Mister Franco!" Chita gasped as Franco's hips slapped against the woman's ass cheeks.

The petite maid grunted as he continued rocking into her, making the cans and tools on the wooden workbench rattle.

Franco squeezed Chita's full breasts beneath her maid's uniform, breathing against her neck and inhaling whatever that thick scent was that she wore. The smell reminded him of air freshener. If she wasn't such a good fuck, he'd have ordered her to quit wearing that cheap stuff long ago.

Uttering a low growl, he slammed into her one last time. His chest heaved as he sucked in more of Chita's cheap perfume mingled with garage grease and oil. "Honey," he managed between breaths, "you've got the sweetest pussy in all of New York."

"Thank you." She wriggled free and reached down to hike up her panties and pantyhose. "I'm gonna be sore tomorrow."

He slapped her buttocks before she could cover herself,

loving the feel of her smooth flesh beneath his hand. He chuckled when she jumped.

"That's what you get for extending your vacation." He tucked his custom-made silk shirt back into his slacks and yanked up the zipper. "I'm a horny old man and three weeks is too long. Now get back inside before the missus sees you're gone."

Chita tugged down her skirt. "Yes, Mister Franco."

He watched her sashay between his blue Cadillac Escalade and silver Lincoln Town Car as she headed to the door connecting the garage and the house.

Sixty years old, and I still got it. Whoever said it was all over after fifty was full of shit. Some Friday nights he'd fucked Chita so hard, pumping between her thighs from every position, it was a wonder she could walk the next day. That was what a *gumada*—a girlfriend—was for.

As Chita opened the connecting door to the house, she threw him a flirtatious look over her shoulder and nearly slammed into Tino. She lowered her eyes as Tino brushed past her, practically shoving her out of the way. Chita disappeared into the house, closing the door behind her.

Tino leaned his hip against the hood of the Lincoln, then crossed his arms, tightening his suit jacket over his broad, steroid-bulked shoulders.

At six feet tall and with dark, handsome Italian looks to match, Tino should have been what every father wanted in a son. Too bad it was only skin deep. Beneath that polished exterior was a calculating little rat Franco had begun to trust less and less.

He buttoned his slacks and fastened his belt. "You didn't have to be so rude."

"*I* was rude?" He jabbed a finger in Franco's direction. "What about *you* being rude to Ma?" He glanced at the

116

connecting door to the house and spoke with less volume. "You once told me Friday nights you take out your gumada, and Saturday night you take out your wife. All the other nights are for family. Not getting your rocks off."

Franco narrowed his eyes. "Don't you *ever* speak to me with such disrespect again. You're my only son, but I'm head of this family, and lately you seem to have forgotten that."

"You wanna talk about disrespect?" He shoved off the car and stopped short a foot from where Franco stood. Challenge gleamed in his son's eyes, another thing Franco had noticed with increasing frequency. "You don't respect my mother," Tino gritted out, "or you wouldn't be banging the maid right under her nose and in her own house."

"*Her* house?" He glared at his son. "Who do you think paid for this place? I did, and you know it." Heat rose to his face as he considered the balls it took for one of his own capos—his son, no less—to confront him in this insubordinate manner.

"Don't ever forget your place. You're my capo, and you take orders from *me*." They locked stares long enough for Franco to count the gold flecks in Tino's dark eyes. "I don't owe you any explanation about who I fuck and where I do it. As my son, I tell you it's *because* I respect your mother that I screw the maid. I would never disrespect your mother by asking her to do half the things I do with Chita."

"Fine." Tino unclenched his jaw and blew out a breath. "But get off my ass about Maria."

"Stop beating the crap out of her, and I will." Franco backed off. "Women are fragile and need to be treated like queens."

"You want me to stay out of your personal life. Stay out

of mine." He fisted his hands. "What I do with *my* wife is *my* business."

"Bullshit." Franco smacked the garage door opener on the wall with the heel of his hand.

The motor whirred as the massive garage door creaked, then opened. A gust of cold air blew into the garage, but Franco barely felt it. Anger at Tino's increasingly shitty attitude was pissing him off and making him hotter under the collar than he could ever remember being.

He hooked his thumb, indicating Tino should follow him. The house was swept regularly for bugs, but there was no sense taking a chance discussing business inside. The FBI had ears everywhere.

Their shoes crunched on the white stone driveway as they walked to the wall overlooking Lower and Gravesend Bays. Cawing seagulls hovered overhead. Wind whipped up the cliff, ruffling Franco's thinning hair.

Briefly, he considered throwing Tino over the ledge and ridding himself of a major pain in the ass, but Tino's mother would be heartbroken, something Franco couldn't live with. Instead, he turned on his son and slapped him in the face.

Tino flinched from the blow. A tick worked overtime in his jaw, and his cheek reddened where Franco had slapped him.

"You listen to me and listen good." Franco's heart hammered. This was the first time he'd ever laid a hand on his son.

The shocked look on Tino's face quickly disappeared, his eyes blazing with a different emotion now. If murdering looks could kill, Franco had no doubt he'd be fish bait.

"When you pound on Maria to the point where she has to go to the hospital, you bring unwanted attention and heat down on the whole Family, and that affects business." He waved his finger in front of Tino's nose. "I will not tolerate that, especially with the Commission meeting set to happen any day now. The last thing I need are more feds tailing us everywhere we go. You fucked things up enough when you took out that fed without my sanction."

Tino's nostrils flared so wide he thought his son was about to snap and come at him.

"Yeah, I know about that," he continued. "There's nothing I *don't* know. There's too much at stake for you to run around half-cocked all the time. If I can't control my own people, let alone my own son, the Commission will never grant me a seat."

He paused to gauge Tino's reaction. Aside from clenching and unclenching his hands, the little prick kept his mouth shut. Good thing too. Franco detested using his hands for violence. That's what God invented guns, knives, and ice picks for, for shit's sake.

"Now that we've got that straightened out, we can talk business." He paused, making sure Tino wasn't about to whip out a gun and plug him. "What are you doing to catch the assholes who've been ripping us off?"

Tino's lips compressed as he took a deep breath through his nose. "I ordered my guys to beef up their security systems. My shore house is tighter than Fort Knox. Psycho's latest security enhancement is something *extra* special. When he told me about it, I nearly pissed my pants. Whoever tries ripping Psycho off is going to end up really rattled." He snickered. "And dead."

Franco held up his hand. "I don't want to know. If that guy wasn't such a motivated enforcer, I'd have him committed for being one sick motherfucker."

"The man does love to kill." Tino chuckled. "Good

thing he's on our side. Whoever these guys are, I'll get them."

"It's taking too long." He shoved his hands in his pockets. "Make this your priority. Work with Rocco. The Commission won't respect a boss who can't safeguard his own assets."

"I can handle it."

"I'm not gonna say it again." He stared into his son's dark, emotionless eyes. "Bring Rocco more into the loop. The man gets things done."

"Fine," he gritted out.

Franco breathed in the briny smell of the bay, thoroughly disgusted. Slapping his own son went against the most important thing he believed in. Family. Family values and protecting the people he loved most meant everything.

"Your mother and I will be attending a society event this Saturday night, and as a member of this family, you and your lovely wife will join us. Maria needs to get out more. You keep her so locked up, she's as pale as these rocks." He kicked at the white stones, sending several flying against the wall.

Tino's lip curled. "I hate those stupid charity things."

"I don't care." His patience was tanking fast. "You *will* go, and you'll exercise decorum while you're there, particularly toward your wife. Are we clear on this?"

Tino's jaw muscles flexed. "Yes."

Another gust of wind bit through Franco's shirt, and he indicated for Tino to follow him inside. "Dinner should be ready. About that business yesterday, everything go okay?"

They headed to the front of the mansion Franco had specially built to mimic deceased Gambino crime boss Paul Castellano's Todt Hill estate on Staten Island not a quarter mile away. Fluted white columns flanked the entryway to the enormous stucco structure.

"It's done." He took the few steps to the massive, carved oak door and reached for the knob.

Franco placed his hand on Tino's arm, stopping him. "So he got my message?"

"Yeah." Tino smirked. "Loud and clear."

"Excellent." Knowing precisely how Tino had delivered the message, he smiled at the obvious quip and clapped his son on the shoulder. "There's been far too much trouble with bookies lately, and we can't afford to have any more bodies show up right now."

That thought brought to mind a bookie he'd taken out a long, long time ago. One he never would have suspected of crossing him. *Trust no one.* That was how he'd survived three attempted hits on his life and avoided going to jail for more than a few days.

Tino opened the door, and they stepped inside onto the pink marble floor separating the hallway from the dining room.

"Dinner is ready, Mister Franco," Chita called out.

"Wonderful." He rubbed his hands together to warm them. "What are we having?"

"Roast pork and orriechiette," Chita answered, giving the name of the pasta that, in Italian, meant *little ears.*

Franco laughed. "How appropriate."

Despite his warning not to, Tino threw Chita a derisive look behind her back. With each passing day, he was behaving less like his son and more like a rival. In this line of business, an all-out power struggle was something one of them would not walk away from. It was clear Tino no longer had his father's back.

Son or no son, it was time to activate Franco's watchdog.

Chapter Nine

Jack strode through the elegant hallway to Gina's apartment. He still couldn't believe he was going through with this. For every reason that tonight should go off without a hitch there were twice as many reasons why it could bite him in the ass. Gina Perot being one of them.

The database queries on her social security number only covered the last twelve years. Thanks to the flu sweeping through his office, the analyst he'd assigned to conduct a more in-depth query was out on sick leave. Other than piquing his curiosity, that one oddity in her lookup raised no real red flags. Besides, by the time he got the full lookup, his association with her would be history.

He glanced at his watch. Eight sharp. Gina had better be ready. The risk of what he was doing was astronomical. If something went wrong tonight, he'd lose his job. If it didn't, and he got that bug planted in time, it would all be worth it. Especially with the latest intel he'd received this morning from Meat about the Commission convening as early as next week.

That still didn't stop the guilt from spreading through

his system like venom. When he'd told Gina no one else gets hurt on his watch, he'd meant it. If anyone else died because of his actions, he honestly didn't know if he could handle it.

Taking a deep inhale, he pressed the buzzer on her door. It opened a few seconds later, and he was met by a tall, willowy African princess lookalike wearing a pink warm-up suit and who made short order of checking him out like he was a piece of meat. Her amber eyes dipped down, then up. She smiled, revealing a perfect set of white teeth. *Model* teeth. Like the rest of her.

"You must be Jack. Come on in." She hooked her hand around his elbow and guided him inside as if they were life-long pals. The door shut behind them, giving him the distinct feeling he'd just sealed his fate. "I'm Kinsey Prescott. Gina's busy in the kitchen, but don't worry. We'll take care of you until she's ready."

Take care of me?

The woman sure smelled good, like some fancy flower. Though he preferred Gina's more subtle vanilla-sugar scent.

Two other women, also sporting sweat suits, rose from the sofa. Beneath the gym garb they probably wore the same skintight black getup he'd seen Gina wear the other night. It was like working with Emma Peel and Charlie's Angels all rolled into one. If any of these women called him Bosley— even once—he'd cuff them just to make a point.

"Margo Kim, Annabelle Rudolph, this is Gina's FBI agent." Kinsey threw him another seductive smile. "Jack Gates."

The woman with short, curly red hair pursed her lips and crossed her arms, plumping her bosom beneath her blue warm-up jacket. She looked ready to claw his face off.

123

Margo, the trim blond in the brown suit, nodded, watching him silently.

They stared at him as if he were the devil incarnate. And that annoying grandfather clock in the foyer kept ticking away, grating his nerves raw. More, now than ever, he wanted to toss the thing out the window.

Kinsey tapped one finger lightly on his cast. "I should probably apologize for that." She gently tugged on his arm, drawing him deeper into the living room. "I'm the one who ran you over." She batted her long, dark eyelashes, wearing a contrite but still flirtatious expression. "I swear I didn't see you, and as I'm sure Gina explained, we had no idea who you were. We assumed you were a mobster trying to kill her. Surely you can see our side of the story."

"Surely." He cocked a brow. Tell that to his busted wrist and his cracked skull.

"Now that we've got that settled..." Kinsey's face lit with a smile. "Have a seat and we can get down to business." She urged him to sit on the love seat and plunked herself down on the sofa next to the pouting redhead.

"Speaking of business." Jack searched the living room. "What's Gina doing in the kitchen that's so important?"

"She's"—Kinsey glanced over her shoulder—"prepping. Yes, she's prepping."

"Prepping?" he asked.

"She's a little nervous." Margo's voice was even, cultured. "Given the circumstances, surely you can understand that."

"Surely," Jack repeated. That seemed to be the word of the day. "What's she *really* doing?"

The redhead pursed her lips tighter. Margo glanced toward the kitchen.

While pressing her thumb and forefinger together,

Kinsey explained, "Gina has a teensy, weensy little fetish. It's a chocolate thing. When she gets uptight she—"

"Oh, that." Jack relaxed. For a second, he half expected Gina to ditch and run. But that didn't really jibe with her spitfire personality. A little high-strung maybe, but he'd never peg her for a coward. Just the opposite. The woman had more guts than was safe for one person to have.

"You know about Gina's chocolate thing?" Annabelle's large green eyes reminded Jack of pale limes.

"Yeah." He crossed his arms, mimicking Annabelle's surly demeanor. "I know about it."

"Hah!" Kinsey slapped her knee. "You were right, Anna. The FBI really *does* know everything."

He could only *wish* the FBI knew everything. Like when the Commission was set to vote on conferring Franco Falzone with Godfather status. That meeting would be a target-rich environment for every federal law enforcement agency on the east coast.

The redhead rolled her eyes. "How can you find humor at a time like this?"

"Oh, I don't know." Kinsey draped an arm over Annabelle's shoulders. "Maybe because life's too short to always look at the downside of things."

Annabelle slanted Kinsey an annoyed look. The brunette giggled, but he detected an undertone of sadness. Guess money really couldn't buy everything. Like happiness.

"So, Jack," Margo interjected. "Gina briefed us on the plan, and we studied the schematics. We agree, the second-story balcony is the optimal access point, and Gina can easily pick the balcony sliding door lock and handle the rudimentary security system. Is there anything else we should know about?"

He pegged Margo as the rational, levelheaded one of the team. Kinsey, the sassy, good-natured rich girl who liked to party. And Annabelle, the pessimistic worry wart.

"Yeah," Annabelle piped in on cue. "Like whether you'll stick to your word and let us go after you plant that insect."

"Bug," Kinsey corrected. "It's called a bug, not an insect. With your love of cop movies, you should know that."

"Bug, insect, worm, whatever." Annabelle flicked her hand in a dismissive gesture. "I still want an answer to my question, *Jack*."

"Be nice to the hunky federal agent." Kinsey winked at him.

Quantico didn't train agents for this level of abuse. Facing off against Gina's sharp wit was like standing in front of a firing squad and waiting for them to shoot. Now Annabelle wanted to slice him up for shark bait, while Kinsey looked ready to eat him for dessert. God only knew what Margo had in mind. Winning an argument against one woman was statistically a losing proposition, let alone four of them simultaneously.

"We don't have a choice about this," Margo cut in. "We broke the law and Jack is only doing his job. Isn't that right, Agent Gates?"

He looked at each of the women. "I gave Gina my word that after tonight, your obligations to the FBI are over. That promise extends to all of you."

"How do we know you won't—"

"That's enough, Anna!" Gina's eyes flashed, and something silver glittered in her hand. Chocolate.

Despite his body's involuntary shudder, he stood, a tribute to the etiquette his mother had pounded into his and his brothers' heads to stand when a woman entered the room.

"As Margo said," Gina continued, "we've already discussed this as a group, and *as a group*," she emphasized, "we agreed to go through with this to pay our debt. There's no need to keep rehashing things. And don't forget," she said, pointing a finger at Annabelle, "you were the one who said we were bound to get caught sooner or later, and better to be caught by the good guys than by the mob."

"I'm starting to rethink that." Annabelle fell back against the sofa.

"Well, don't." Gina's voice softened as she took a seat next to Kinsey.

Jack sat, noticing the other women looking expectantly at Gina, as if waiting for her next command. It was clear she wasn't only their leader but the very heart and soul of the group.

"We'll do this job as professionally as all the others we've undertaken." She unwrapped the silver foil-covered chocolate in her hand and tossed it into her mouth.

His stomach took a nosedive. Apparently, she'd forgotten about their truce.

"As much as it pains me to say this," she said, sliding her hand into her pocket and coming out with another piece of the offensive stuff, "for tonight, we take orders from Jack." Her mouth worked as she sucked on the candy.

Jack couldn't tear his gaze from her lips. The things he imagined her tongue must be doing to that warm, melting—

Hell. Her words finally sank in to that mushy gray stuff between his ears. Or what was left of it. She'd actually relinquished control of this op to him. It was a good thing he was already sitting or he'd have fallen on his ass.

Kinsey cleared her throat and grinned at him, dragging

his brain back on line. Sweat broke out on his forehead. Was it a tropical rainforest in here, or was it just him? He stripped off his bomber jacket and draped it on the armrest.

"Oooh, nice toys." Kinsey eyed the gear strapped to his belt—Glock, extra mags, expandable baton, tactical Master knife. "Do we get to play with those?"

"Sorry, no." He chuckled. Kinsey was exactly the kind of woman his crazy youngest brother, Deke, would go for. Even the FBI hadn't mellowed that kid out yet.

"Too bad." Kinsey bobbed her dark brows like Groucho Marx. In a deep, sultry voice, she added, "Your gun looks so big and powerful. Is it true that size doesn't matter?"

"Puh-lease," Annabelle elbowed Kinsey in the ribs.

Margo stifled a laugh.

Gina clapped a hand to her forehead.

"Will there be any other agents out there with us?" Margo hiked up the sleeves of her jacket.

"No."

"Why not?" Annabelle pinned him with suspicious eyes.

Time for more half-truths. "As I already told Gina, the fewer agents who know you're involved, the better off you are." Truth being, as an unsanctioned FBI op, he couldn't request backup. Not even Smitty.

"What if something goes wrong?" Annabelle asked.

Gina tossed a balled-up piece of foil onto the table. "We'll make sure it doesn't."

"What if it does? No, wait. Let me guess." The redhead held up her hand. "As always, Jack, if you or any of your special team are caught, the United States government will disavow any knowledge of your existence. This tape will self-destruct in five seconds."

He snorted at the *Mission Impossible* reference. "Tom Cruise, I'm not."

Annabelle's surly expression lightened until the edges of her mouth quirked. Finally, a thaw in her prickly disposition.

He pulled a combination earpiece-microphone from his jacket pocket. "We should go over a few more things before we head out, communication being the first." He tossed the combo kit with its mini power box and wire attachment onto the glass-topped coffee table. "I know you have your own rigs, but mine have a secure channel allocated solely to the FBI and used only for undercover ops. No one else can break into this channel or hear us."

Gina picked up the kit and unwound the wire coiled around the battery box.

"I'll help you hook it up before we head out."

She nodded, and he turned to address the other women, who seemed to have put their antipathy toward him aside and were now listening intently. They might hate his guts, but beneath that veneer of pampered richness, they had a professional side that took over when there was work to be done. Yesterday, he'd admired that same quality in Gina. Her lightning-fast assessment of Psycho's house and security system was balls-on accurate, and her detailed drawings had impressed the heck out of him.

"Both vehicles," he continued, "will have a hand radio set to the same frequency as the transmitter Gina will wear. She and I will be in my truck with Kinsey. Margo and Annabelle in the rental. Margo and Annabelle will run countersurveillance along the street behind the house. Kinsey will take the street in front of the house and pick us up when we come out."

He dug into his other jacket pocket, fumbling with his

injured hand until he pulled out a small gray plastic box. Using his thumb, he flipped open the hinged lid, exposing the slim, black pea-sized device nestled in a piece of foam padding. He gave it a quick inspection and was about to close the lid.

Gina edged forward on the sofa. "Is that the bug you're going to plant?"

"Yes." He handed her the box. "You can take it out, just be careful with it."

She plucked the bug from the padding and held it under the lamp on the end table.

"How does it work?" Annabelle eyed the gadget with curiosity. "It's so small."

"True, but in this case"—he flashed Kinsey a quick smile —"size *doesn't* matter. This little beauty can pick up a whisper thirty feet away."

"Wow." Annabelle nudged Gina's shoulder and held out her hand. "Let me see." Gina stuck the device back into the padding and handed her the tiny box. "How long does the battery last?"

"There is no battery. I'll wire it into the internet cable to power up."

Annabelle passed the bug to Kinsey. "Is there a tape recorder inside here too?"

"No, that would require too large a device, something that could easily be seen and too difficult to retrieve." He was surprised at the redhead's sudden shift from nagging to interested.

Margo examined the bug next. "Then how do you record conversations?"

"This bug detects sound and transmits conversation off-site via microwave signals to a nearby tower. From there, the signal is sent to another location where it's recorded."

"Amazing." Annabelle eyed him with fascination, no longer intent on cutting him up for shark bait. "Just like in the movies."

"Annabelle is our resident Hollywood expert," Kinsey explained, tucking her long dark braids behind her ears. "She's seen *The Untouchables* at least ten times. Elliot Ness is her idol, and she's in love with Kevin Costner."

Jack grimaced. Kevin Costner was only an actor. Hardly the real thing.

"Please." She waved her hand at him. "Call me Anna."

Gina groaned. "Oh, brother."

Anna inched forward. "I realize you can't reveal too much information, but what kinds of things do you hope to record with this bug?"

"General intel, evidence of crimes committed by any mobster, particularly Franco and Tino Falzone."

"Ahhh." Anna nodded. "But why don't you just plant a bug in Franco's or Tino's house?"

"I would if I could. I don't have PC—probable cause—to plant devices in *their* homes."

"Do you have PC to plant one in the house tonight?" Margo asked.

"Yes. And with the info from that bug, hopefully I can get PC to install devices at Franco's and Tino's and record evidence good enough for an indictment. That's how the FBI nailed Gambino crime boss Paul Castellano back in the eighties."

Anna scrunched her eyebrows. "How so?"

"FBI agents planted a device in Castellano's kitchen. Using those recorded conversations, Castellano was indicted for extortion, theft, prostitution, drug trafficking, and multiple murders."

"How much jail time did he get?" Kinsey asked.

"None. Before we had a chance to convict him, he and his underboss were gunned down outside a Manhattan steak house."

"Who did it?" Margo asked.

"The way the story goes, it was set up by Castellano's own capo, John Gotti, aka the Dapper Don, and Sammy "The Bull" Gravano, a Gambino Crime Family hit man."

Anna's eyes widened. "So all that work for nothing?"

"Not really. As a result of that case, we learned more about the Mafia than we knew before." Including those rare, secret meetings held by the Commission.

Margo pinned him with shrewd eyes. "You hope to get the big fish by first reeling in the little fish."

"Exactly." The grandfather clock chimed once, and Jack glanced at his watch. Eight thirty. "You need to get ready while I outfit Gina with the com microphone and transmitter."

As he set up the earpiece, Margo and Anna went down the hallway and disappeared into another room. Kinsey padded into the foyer and opened a closet filled with coats.

Gina unzipped her jacket, revealing the skintight suit that made every article of clothing in the Victoria's Secret catalog seem grandmotherly in comparison.

Focus, brain cells.

When he looked up, her eyes were twinkling. She wasn't making this easy on him. Knowing her, she was playing with him.

"You're going to have to help me out here," he said.

"Ya think?" Grinning, she shrugged out of her warm-up jacket and tossed it onto the sofa. Next, she unzipped her catsuit down to her waist and spread the fabric by placing her hands on her hips.

She did not *just do that.* He actually had to squeeze his eyes shut for a second. When he reopened them, the view was the same. Creamy swells of the most perfect breasts peeked out of the laciest, sexiest black bra he'd ever laid eyes on.

His heart beat a little faster, and he prayed he didn't get a colossal boner. Adding to his discomfort, that intoxicating scent of hers mingling with her natural body heat was like a warm vanilla-sugar bath. One he was on the brink of drowning in.

"What?" At her question, he snapped his eyes from her chest to her face. "I don't have any pockets on this thing."

"Yeah," he muttered. "I see that."

From the hallway, Kinsey snickered. Way too much amusement at his expense.

With the unsteady fingers of his good hand, he gently pressed the com kit's power supply box against Gina's taut abdomen. Heat from her bare skin seared his fingertips as he adjusted the box to fit into the hollow beneath her rib cage. "Hold that." His voice sounded like someone had rubbed his vocal cords with sandpaper.

She held the box in place while he tugged her zipper up. With each tug, he had to reach inside her suit with his injured hand to keep threading the ear wire out the top of the material so it would reach to her ear. With every touch of his fingers on her soft skin, his body temp went up a degree. The same way it had yesterday when he'd gotten a good view of her shapely legs...those same legs that made him dream about dragging those incredible stockings off them with his teeth.

With a final tug, he yanked the zipper up to her neck and began hooking the earpiece around her ear. More sweat beaded on his forehead. If things got any hotter, his Glock would go off on its own. The woman didn't seem to notice the torture she was inflicting on him. Or maybe she did, and that was part of her diabolical plan to exact revenge.

When he finished draping the ear wire beneath her thick hair, her eyes were bright, her cheeks flushed, and her pink lips parted. With every breath, her chest rose and fell a little too fast. The same way his was doing.

"You two really should get a room." Kinsey's voice sliced into his consciousness. He and Gina practically jumped apart. "Merely an observation." She giggled and winked over her shoulder as she returned to the hallway.

As Gina shrugged back into her warm-up jacket, her lips pressed together tightly.

"You okay?" When she didn't answer, he rested his hands on her shoulders. "You can do this. The mission might have changed, but the tactics are no different from the rips you've been doing."

"I know." She took a deep inhale. "Thanks for the pep talk."

"Anytime." For what must have been the tenth time tonight, their gazes locked and held. He wished that would quit happening. Every time it did, one—if not *both* of his heads—stopped thinking clearly.

Stay. On. Target.

Gina might be a beautiful, intelligent, sexy woman, but she was a cooperator. An essential element of his job and the mission he'd focused on nearly every waking minute of his life for the last six months.

"Remember," he said as he jammed his arms into his jacket. "There's only one mission tonight. We get in, do the job, and get out."

His words were as much to himself as to her. After tonight, he'd do the same and get the hell out of her life.

Chapter Ten

"Girl, he is smokin' *hot*." Kinsey whistled for emphasis as Margo maneuvered the rented black Charger out of Gina's parking garage. "The man makes sweaty look g-o-o-d *good*."

Anna giggled from the front passenger seat. "Did you see how that black sweater stuck to his super buff bod?" She made a suggestive, gurgling sound in her throat. "Yowza."

Resisting the urge to elbow Kinsey in the ribs and smack Anna in the back of the head, Gina leaned forward between the headrests and pointed to Jack's SUV double-parked ahead. "Pull up behind that Expedition and try to keep your libidos in check. We've got a job to do, and if we botch it, we could all wind up wearing orange jumpsuits for the next decade. You should be focusing on *that* visual." While she knew her friends were only teasing, it was irritating to hear them discussing Jack like he was a piece of grade A sirloin they were about to gobble up. Not that she disagreed with their observations.

Kinsey snickered. "Oooh, someone's a little possessive."

"What do you mean *possessive*?" She frowned as she caught the smirk on Kinsey's face.

"Oh, come on, Gina," Margo said as she pulled up behind Jack's Expedition. "Even I can see the chemistry between you two. It was so hot in your apartment I thought the fire alarm would go off."

"You should have seen his face when you yanked open your suit and your boobs practically popped out," Kinsey said. "He clenched his manly jaw so hard I heard his teeth crack."

This time, she *did* elbow Kinsey in the ribs, and her friend let out a little grunt mingled with more laughter.

"You could do a lot worse," Anna added. "Take Paul, for instance. The guy might have been loaded, but he was *sooo* boring. I wonder what Jack's like in bed."

Kinsey's dark brows bobbed. "The things you can do with a set of handcuffs."

Gina rolled her eyes. "Do I have to remind you *what* Jack is?" Somehow, despite the do-what-I-tell-you-or-else choke hold he had on all of them, his hidden charms seemed to have wormed their way past her friends' normally bone-deep sense of caution. "He's an FBI agent, and we're a fly's hiccup away from getting arrested. The only thing between us and a jail cell is getting this freaking bug planted. After tonight, we should all be praying we never see Jack Gates again."

"Point taken." Margo put the car in park. "Beneath all that twisted steel and federal agent sex appeal is a man we should never cross."

Headlights illuminated Jack's tall form as he got out of the SUV. Even the street's semidarkness couldn't hide the man's aura of tightly reined-in power. Power he could unleash if they got on his bad side. Again, that was. She'd lost count of how many times that had already happened.

Margo lowered her window. Jack's cast made a *thunk* as

he rested his forearms on the window frame. He handed Margo a slim, black radio. "It's turned on and tuned to a discrete FBI frequency. All you have to do is key the button on the side to talk."

"Ten-four," Anna declared as she took the radio from Margo. She was loving this Elliot Ness thing far too much, in Gina's opinion.

"Ready, ladies?" Jack asked, but it was Gina's eye he caught.

"As ever." Though she didn't think she'd ever be ready for this job. Not in a hundred years. Not in a thousand. "Let's get it done."

After getting out of the Charger, she hefted her utility belt and a coil of knotted rope over her shoulder. Kinsey joined her and headed for the driver's side of the SUV. Cold, wintry air bit through her polar fleece jacket and the microfiber of her suit.

Jack waited for Kinsey to slip in behind the wheel of his Expedition. As he shut the door, Gina realized he must have deactivated the SUV's interior lights so they wouldn't light up when the doors opened. She could just barely make out Kinsey stripping off her sweat suit.

She and Jack both reached for the rear passenger door's handle at the same time. Their hands brushed, but when she tried letting go of the handle, he held his hand firmly on top of hers. The handle was cold. Jack's fingers were warm.

"You okay?" His eyes were hooded by shadow, but there was unexpected concern in his voice.

"You asked me that back in my apartment. And yeah, I'm always okay before a B and E. Turns me on, actually." She could have been imagining the spark in his eyes, but she definitely felt it from his touch.

He released her hand as she opened the door, then

waited for her to get in before shutting the door behind her. Who'd have suspected a gentleman lurked behind the badge?

Ironically, in the last few days, Jack had touched her —*literally*—more than Paul ever had in their entire two-month relationship. No, that wasn't exactly true. But Jack's professional searches of her body for weapons and wiring her up for that earpiece had gotten her oodles hotter than Paul ever had.

She let the utility belt and rope drop to the seat so she could shrug out of her sweat suit.

"Head to the Holland Tunnel," Jack ordered Kinsey after he'd gotten into the front passenger seat and shut the door.

"Nice ride." Kinsey gunned the SUV down the block. "Whatcha got under the hood?"

"Six speed, V8, 5.4-liter engine, 310 horsepower, 365 pound-feet of torque."

While he outlined more of the Expedition's vital statistics as if it were a hot chick, Gina couldn't tear her eyes from his mouth. Those lips. Not for the first time, she wondered what his kisses would be like.

She rolled her eyes. *FBI. Remember that.* Besides, he might be gorgeous and hunky and everything Kinsey and Anna said he was, but he was such a tight-assed control freak. He probably kissed like a robot—stiff, with no passion. One of the reasons she'd broken it off with Paul was because he *was* boring, and his kisses were an extension of that personality trait. Locking lips with him had been like kissing a limp noodle. *Major ick.* So why did her skin ignite every time Mr. Uber-Robocop touched her?

"Niiiice." Kinsey stroked the dashboard. "I love having all that power beneath me."

Kinsey looked about five seconds away from having an orgasm. Gina couldn't be sure whether it was from flirting with Jack or from driving his SUV. The woman did love a souped-up vehicle.

As they whizzed past a streetlight, Jack smiled at Kinsey, and a brief stab of jealousy kicked in. Why, for the life of her, she couldn't imagine. Kinsey *was* gorgeous. If he wanted to flirt back at her friend like a lovesick teenager, why should she care?

With Kinsey's lead foot, they crossed into New Jersey and were now heading west toward Montclair. Gina cinched her utility belt around her waist, tightening it over her suit before slipping on her black gloves.

A short time later, Jack directed Kinsey onto Psycho's block. "Pull over here while we do a radio check." He pointed to the sidewalk about fifty feet before Psycho's driveway. As Kinsey pulled over, he keyed the radio. "Annabelle, radio check."

Jack's deep voice came through Gina's earpiece.

"Loud and clear," Anna answered. "We're in position one street over. Negative countersurveillance."

Jack twisted in the seat to face her. "Did you get that?"

"Ten-four, good buddy." Ignoring the annoyed look he shot her in the dark, Gina pulled on her hood and stuffed her hair beneath the snug-fitting garment, being careful not to dislodge the earpiece. Next, she adjusted the attached microphone until it was a quarter inch from her lips.

"Your mic will automatically transmit anything you say over the radio," Jack said. "Ready?"

"Ready."

He nodded once. "Let me know when you're in."

She slung the rope over her shoulder and opened the door.

"Wait." He caught her arm. "I already verified the house is empty, but if anything goes wrong, don't stop to think. Just get out. I mean it."

"You don't need to pretend to care about me. About us." She tipped her chin to Kinsey, who watched them with a curious expression. "Don't worry. I'll get you inside so you can get your precious bug planted." She yanked her arm away and stepped onto the sidewalk.

Quietly, she nudged the door closed. Adrenaline surged through her body as she sprinted to Psycho's driveway. The padded hook at the end of the rope slapped against her shoulder as she ran.

Though it was a moonless night, between the street-lights and the lamp over the house's front door, the place was lit up like Times Square. The rest of the house and the property were dark. No light shined from any of the windows. She stayed in the shadows as much as possible, being careful to step over the invisible line running between the two motion sensors on either side of the driveway. If she tripped it, a signal would probably go directly to Psycho's cell phone. The same thing would happen if she messed up picking the balcony door's lock.

Her heart rate kicked up as she ran into the backyard, hugging the side of the house. Frost-covered grass crunched beneath her boots. She paused with her back against the stucco and quickly scanned the yard. Wisps of condensed breath swirled before her face.

She slowed her breathing to listen. Aside from the pulsing of her own heartbeat in her ears, the neighborhood was as quiet as could be expected. It was only ten o'clock. Gina and her friends didn't normally do rips this early. People weren't solidly in their REM sleep stage until around two or three in the morning, making that the preferred time for a break-in. If it were up to her, she would have waited until at least after midnight, but Jack was calling the shots, and Psycho wasn't supposed to be at home. Just because the driveway was empty didn't automatically mean the house was.

Gina let another few seconds pass before slipping deeper into the shadow cast by the balcony twenty feet above her head. She slid the knotted rope from her shoulder and grasped the hook in one hand while setting the remainder of the coiled hemp carefully on the grass at her feet. Gripping the rope a few feet from the hook, she began swinging the hook back and forth, building momentum.

One more swing and she flung the hook upward, letting the rope slide through her gloved hand. The hook made a soft thud as it landed on the balcony. She tugged steadily on the dangling rope, waiting for the hook to catch on the metal railing. It didn't and fell back to the grass.

Again, she recoiled the rope and swung the hook back and forth. With a final heave, she hurled it in the air. This time, when she tugged on the rope, it caught.

Using the knots as gripping points, she began climbing. Even with the knots, her muscles strained as she hauled herself higher and higher until her fingers met the balcony rail. She swung her leg up to the edge of the deck and grabbed onto the vertical posts, heaving herself upright until she stood on the outside lip of the deck. The top metal rail was slippery with frost. Any mistake and she'd fall twenty feet. With her luck, she'd land on her head instead of her cushy butt cheeks.

Gripping the top rail, she vaulted over and landed on the wood deck. She crouched and spun, taking another quick scan of the yard below. Empty. A slight smile tugged at her lips as adrenaline lit a fire in her veins. This was the rush Sergio told her would hit during times of danger. When the stakes were high and the risk beyond calculable.

With a flick of her hand, she tugged the penlight from her belt and clicked it on. She'd retrofit the light with a red lens, so as not to affect her night vision. Still crouching, she went to the balcony's sliding glass door and easily found the magnetic sensor on the inside, right at the seam where the door met the frame. She pulled the strip of supermagnetized metal from a pouch on her utility belt and jimmied it around until it found its way between the sensors.

Piece of cake. Chocolate, of course.

Now to rake the lock. She eyed the keyhole on the brass handle. Even a first-day B and E student could get in. She clicked off the penlight and slid it back onto her belt. This little job could be done by touch alone.

Without looking down, she plucked out her tools. A slim metal lock pick with a wide tip, a lock rake, and a tension wrench. She inserted the pick all the way to the back of the lock, then inserted the rake. She pulled the rake out quickly, feeling the lock's pins bounce. With her other hand, she turned the lock plug with the tension wrench and *voilà.*

Before opening the door fully, she applied several strips of tape to the magnetized piece of metal to hold it in place, then held her breath, tensing as she crouched low and opened the door wider. Nothing. No lights, no sirens. She stashed her tools back in their case and again clicked on the penlight and scanned the room, particularly the walls, searching for motion sensors. This was the master bedroom, with its giant, king-size bed taking center stage, and—

You've got *to be kidding.* Was that a Velvet Elvis hanging above the headboard? Talk about truly tacky artwork. Then she saw it. A tiny red dot.

Sure enough, in the corner of the room next to the bed and about five feet up the wall, a sensor box faced the balcony door. No problemo. All she had to do was keep hugging the floor.

On a hunch, before stepping inside she aimed the flashlight beam down. A floor mat sat just inside the door. Grinning, she lifted one corner of the mat, knowing full well what she'd find. A pressure sensor.

As expected, a thin white wire ran from under the mat to a tiny hole in the floor. Two metal strips glinted in the flashlight's beam. If she'd been sloppy and had stepped on the mat, the two metal strips would have made heavier contact, initiating the alarm sequence. She would have had about fifteen seconds to punch in the correct code at the main box downstairs before the system started screaming out a signal that someone had broken in.

Carefully, she lowered the mat back to the floor and stepped over it. She eased the door closed behind her and paused. "I'm in," she said.

"Copy that." Jack's silky smooth, chocolaty voice rumbled in her ear.

She stifled a snort. The man had a bizarre chocolate allergy, and she'd just equated his voice to chocolate.

Keeping low, she crossed the room, scanning the path ahead as she went. She swept the flashlight beam into the hallway, searching for hidden surprises, but there were none. None she could see, anyway.

Between the wrought iron grating on the first-floor windows, the motion sensor guarding the second-floor balcony door, and the security box wired to the front door, Psycho probably figured he had the entire house protected.

Sergio's warning clanged in her head. *Expect the unexpected.*

143

After a quick check of the other bedrooms, all located exactly as shown on the schematics she'd studied, Gina padded down the carpeted staircase and onto the tiled entryway, sweeping the flashlight beam in all directions. More heinous artwork hung on the walls. As far as interior decorating went, Mrs. Psycho was clueless. Or it was all swag, stolen from seriously low-end motels. The kind that charged by the hour and had vibrating beds. Fifty cents for ten minutes of shake, rattle, and roll.

The control box on the wall by the door glowed a steady red, indicating the alarm system was fully engaged. She continued past the living room and into Psycho's study where Jack would install his bug. No more wall-mounted motion sensors or pressure mats.

Last, she checked the kitchen, aiming the beam around the room. As with the other rooms on the first floor, nothing unexpected.

Tap. Gina dropped to the floor, crouching. Every muscle in her body went to DEFCON 3. She was definitely alone inside, so...

Tap. Tap. Tap.

There it was again, only this time she determined its source. The refrigerator, or freezer, more likely. Probably chunks of ice from the automated icemaker.

Whew. She let out a breath and returned to the hallway to address the control box. First, she plucked a tiny screwdriver from her belt and unscrewed the plastic facing. Then she pulled out her code-breaker kit, the same one she'd used to deactivate Rocco's decrepit alarm system. She attached the kit's alligator clips to the box's metal contacts and watched as the kit did its thing.

A steady stream of changing numbers glowed green on the digital readout as the kit searched for Psycho's security code. This unit required seven numbers, three more than Rocco's. As she waited for the telltale *click* announcing the kit had found the code, she tapped her hand against the side of her leg. Four numbers. Five numbers. Six. Seven.

Click. The tiny light on the code box turned green.

Taking a steadying breath, she turned the deadbolt, then the knob, cracking the door a mere quarter inch. A beam of streetlight spilled inside, and she quickly shut the door.

The alarm system had been successfully deactivated, but something about this job still bugged her, pardon the pun. Maybe it was her Spidey-sense talking. For her, the hard part was over. That didn't stop the worry niggling at the back of her mind that something was wrong here.

"Jack," she said into the microphone. "Front door is open."

"Copy that. ETA one minute."

Less than a minute later, there was a knock at the door, prearranged so that anyone passing by would assume he was a legitimate visitor. She opened the door to let him in, then closed it behind them.

In one hand he carried a black, metal briefcase. He rested his other hand on her shoulder. Even with the cast on his wrist, he managed to give her a gentle squeeze. "Good job. Any other motion sensors on this floor?"

"No, I checked."

"Anything else I should know about?"

"No." Other than her Spidey-sense being wigged-out.

He flicked on a flashlight, also red-beamed, and headed directly for Psycho's study. Not surprisingly, he already knew the interior layout of the place. He set his briefcase on the desk and flipped open the catches. Inside the case was a high-tech tool kit, including wire cutters and splicers, screw-

145

drivers and wrenches of all sizes, an ammeter, fuses, penknives, and several different colors of electrical tape.

Even with a cast on one wrist, he wielded the tools with expert precision, first splicing into Psycho's internet line. Deep concentration etched into his handsome features. He'd pushed up the sleeves of his bomber jacket, and as he carefully concealed the tiny listening device to the underside of the cable, thick muscles in his forearm rippled and bunched in a sensual dance. When he touched a voltage meter to the bug, a bulb lit on the meter.

"I need to wait for confirmation the bug is actively transmitting," Jack said as he tapped a text into his cell phone. "It'll be a few minutes."

"Great." *Not.* Those niggly-wigglies were getting worse by the second, and she was eager for them to get as far away from Casa Psycho as possible. Unable to stand still, she shifted repeatedly from one foot to the other.

Jack gave a soft laugh. "Why don't you keep an eye out the front door?"

"Good idea." She nodded, happy to be given a task to keep her mind occupied.

Back in the hallway, she peered through one of the glass panels next to the door. The street was quiet. With no other useful assignment, she began checking out the artwork more closely, grimacing at a particularly wretched piece on the wall just outside the kitchen. If Bozo the Clown took up painting and decided to do a self-portrait, this was what—

Tap, tap, tap, tap.

She froze. This time, the noise didn't sound like ice dropping. It was too fast, more like a rattle. So what was it? The ghost of that poor dog Psycho murdered?

Gina padded into the kitchen, darting her eyes in every direction. She clicked on her penlight, bathing the room in an eerie red glow. Nothing had changed. The kitchen was still empty, and she was positive the sound was coming from the freezer. Running her fingers along the rubber gaskets of the stainless-steel side-by-side doors, she searched for trip wires. Next, she checked the back of the unit. The *unplugged* unit. So much for the ice theory.

If she were sensible and smart, she'd beat feet. Something deep inside, something only an experienced burglar would understand, drove her onward. This was a puzzle to be solved, and her gut told her something interesting lay behind the freezer door. Like on that game show, *Let's Make A Deal*. She had to know what was behind Door #1. She no sooner could have stopped now than she could have stopped breathing.

She placed a gloved hand on the left side door and closed her eyes. Nothing. No vibrations. Slowly, she tugged on the handle and cracked the door. Shivers of anticipation crept up her spine.

Don't be stupid. Leave. Now.

"Can't help it," she whispered.

After opening the door all the way, she shined her light inside and her jaw dropped. If she were standing in front of a mirror, her eyes would be bigger than chocolate chip cookies.

Staring back at her were five shelves jammed with cash, each piled high from front to back, mostly with hundred-dollar bills.

She chewed on her lower lip. This was more than enough to get Marilyn and her kids to the west coast. All this cash was hers for the taking. It would be so easy. Minus the little part about the FBI agent in the other room. If she stole cash, Psycho would know someone had broken in, and

Jack's bug would be rendered worthless, and... *Federal obstruction charges here we come.*

What if she just grabbed a few stacks from the back, say, one from each shelf? If those really were all hundreds, five stacks would be around five thousand dollars. Psycho would never know.

Neither would Jack.

She reached into the freezer and took a stack from the front of one shelf. Then she reached to the rear of the shelf and pulled another stack forward to make it look as if nothing was missing. She stared at the cash, biting harder on her lower lip.

Leaving this money behind sat about as well as turning away a box of Godiva chocolates, but she'd made a deal. No more rips until Jack completed his investigation. The idea of breaking her word to him bothered her more than she expected. More importantly, she could never risk getting her friends in more trouble than they were already in. They'd just have to pray the Center raised enough cash for Marilyn at the fundraiser.

Sighing, she started to put the stack of cash back on the shelf. That's when she heard it. A rattle followed by a hiss. Something darted from behind the stacks of cash, knocking the light from her hand. She gasped, letting go of the money and jumping back. Her hip slammed against the kitchen table. She might be a city girl, but she'd watched enough episodes of *Animal Planet* to have a complete—albeit *late*—understanding of what that rattling sound was.

Rattlesnakes.

Behind her, a chair toppled to the floor, clattering loudly. She lost her balance and fell. Her head whacked against the edge of the table as she went down. Despite the pain shooting through her skull, she crab-walked backward on the floor.

The penlight had rolled beneath the table, yet still illuminated the inside of the freezer where three coiled rattlesnakes each protected their own shelf of cash.

Holy—! That psychotic lunatic had booby-trapped his cash with pit vipers. What if the one that had lunged for her was slithering on the tile floor? *Getting closer.*

She scrambled off the floor and vaulted onto the counter. Her heart raced, and she sucked in deep breaths. Somehow, she had to retrieve her penlight and return the room to its original state, but how could she be sure the floor wasn't covered in writhing, spitting, biting snakes?

"Gina!" Jack rushed into the kitchen. She could just make out his silvery gray eyes glaring at her. "What happened?"

"Stop!" She held up her hand. "Don't come in here!"

"Why not?" A distinct note of anger laced his question.

"Rattlesnakes," she whispered, as if saying the word in normal speaking volume mattered at this point. "There are rattlesnakes in the freezer. One of them tried to bite me, and I don't know if it got out."

"Are you *kidding*?"

Adamantly, she shook her head and pointed to the freezer. "Do I *look* like I'm kidding?"

A light clicked on—Jack's flashlight.

"Stay there." Leading with the flashlight, he edged into the room, swinging the beam back and forth across the floor and giving the open freezer door a wide berth.

"Copy that." She prayed she didn't sound half as panicked as she really was.

"Are you guys okay?" Margo's voice came through

149

Gina's earpiece. "Did I hear you correctly? Did you say 'rattlesnakes?'"

"Everything's fine," Gina whispered, rolling her eyes at the ridiculous lie she'd just told.

After clearing the floor, Jack shined his penlight into the freezer. A split second before he slammed it shut, he tensed.

When he faced her, she gulped. Every sculpted ridge and muscle in his face had gone as hard as a diamond. Except for the flames shooting from his eyes. Those were hot enough to *melt* a diamond. "Did you take any?"

"No!" Her voice *and* her body trembled. "It's not what you think. I heard a noise in the freezer, and I was curious. I opened the door and—"

"Curious, my ass. We're getting out of here," he bit out through his clenched jaw. "*Now*." After righting and repositioning the chair that had fallen over, he strode from the kitchen, leaving a trail of pissed-off vibe in his wake so potent she could feel it on her skin and taste it on her tongue.

Her next breath left her lungs in a *whoosh*. When they got back to her apartment, she was in for a tongue lashing of cosmic proportions.

Still not convinced there wasn't a pit viper patrolling the floor, she scanned the tile thoroughly before easing off the counter.

Jack waited for her by the front door. Virtual smoke shot from his ears. "Margo, I'm on my way out." Throwing her one last venomous glare, he opened the door and closed it behind him.

She locked the deadbolt, then reached for her penlight, which wasn't on her belt where it should have been. *Crap.* In all the chaos she'd left it on the kitchen floor.

At the entrance to the kitchen, she hesitated before inching her way inside. With every step, she scoured the floor for snakes. She reached under the table for her penlight, snatching it up, then spinning to sweep the light back and forth across the floor. The beam hit on something and she sucked in a breath. Wedged beneath the freezer, was a bundle of cash—the one that had slipped from her hand when the snake attacked. In her state of panic, she must have nudged the bundle partially under the unit with her foot. In the near darkness, Jack hadn't seen it.

"Oh shit." Double shit, actually. No, make that triple shit.

She'd made the decision to honor her agreement and not take any of the cash. Now what was she supposed to do? If she took the bundle on the floor, Jack would kill her first, *then* throw her body in jail for breaking their deal. Opening that freezer door again...*not happening*. Jail would be preferable.

Taking a deep breath, she scooped up the stack of bills and unzipped the top of her suit just enough to stuff it inside. She yanked the zipper back up, then took one final look around, verifying all was in its place before heading to the front door.

With shaking fingers, she unhooked the alligator clips from the control box, reset the alarm, and reinstalled the cover. After stowing the kit back in the pouch on her belt she went up the stairs. At the door to the master bedroom, she hunkered low to the floor so as not to activate the motion sensor.

Her belly knotted with enough anxiety to keep a psychiatrist busy for at least a year. She opened the sliding glass door, stepped out, and pulled it shut behind her. After resetting the lock, she retrieved her magnetic strip from the door sensors and shoved it into the pouch on her belt.

"On my way down."

"Copy that." Jack still sounded angry. "We're in place ready to pick you up."

She climbed over the metal railing and grasped the knotted rope, lowering herself down. When her feet hit the grass, she wanted to weep for joy. That was, without a doubt, the freakiest job she'd ever pulled.

With a strong tug on the rope, her hook release worked like a charm and the rope fell to the ground. She coiled it around her shoulder and hauled ass to the driveway, carefully avoiding the motion sensor beam.

True to his word, Jack and Kinsey waited for her in the Expedition not ten feet away. She sprinted for the passenger door, opened it, and practically flung herself inside. "Let's go!" Damn, she sounded freaked out. She grabbed her warm-up jacket from the seat and shoved her arms quickly inside, zipping it straight to her throat. Anything to hide the telltale bulge beneath her suit.

Jack turned in his seat. "What took you so long?"

Kinsey hit the gas, and the SUV shot forward.

"Nothing. I just needed to make sure I left everything the way it was when I came in."

In the dim light, Jack sent her the same penetrating look he'd given her that first night in his apartment. Like he could see right through her.

He knows I'm lying. Probably scored another perfect ten on his poop-o-meter.

Just before he turned away, he gave her one last meaningful look. The kind that unequivocally shouted: *We* will *talk later.*

Her head began pounding with the mother of all headaches. *God, I need chocolate.*

Jack keyed his radio. "We're done," he notified Margo and Annabelle. "Head back to the city."

"Ten-four," Anna responded.

Forty minutes later, they parked outside Gina's apartment building, where Jack thanked the women for their assistance. When it was obvious to her friends that he planned on debriefing Gina—*alone*—Kinsey winked at her, Anna smirked, and Margo gave her a hug.

"We're outta here." Kinsey latched onto Anna and Margo's arms, pulling them away. "Gotta return the rental car."

Seconds later, she stared at the Charger's red taillights as Kinsey took the corner at about twenty miles above the speed limit. She turned to leave, hoping in her fantasy world that Jack would just let her go.

No such freaking luck.

"Not so fast." He fell in step beside her, holding open the heavy glass door to the lobby of her building. "I'm going up with you."

"Why? I thought we were done. Mission accomplished. Ten-four, good buddy, over and out."

Undeterred, he stepped into the elevator with her. By the time they reached her apartment door, she was biting her lower lip so hard she drew blood. The stack of cash beneath her suit was burning a hole in her chest. The only thing covering it from Jack's scrutiny was her warm-up jacket.

As expected, he followed her inside her apartment. She didn't bother trying to keep him out. He'd only force his way in.

The door clicked shut behind them, and she kept going through the living room, heading for the kitchen. The only thing that could possibly ease her nerves was chocolate, something with a lot of cocoa solids. Tonight was an 80% night if ever there was one.

"Gina." Jack grasped her arm gently but forcefully enough to turn her to face him. The movement caused the zipper of her jacket to slip down a few notches. *Please don't look.* If he found out she'd taken any cash—no matter the circumstances—she'd be toast. "What were you really doing snooping around in the freezer?"

"I told you already. I was curious, and I was bored. I heard a sound, so I opened it." His eyes narrowed to gray slits, a clear sign that meter of his was pinging into the red zone. Not that she could blame him. Her story sounded lame and ludicrous, even to her. She shoved a hand through her hair and flinched.

He touched his fingers to her head. "You're hurt. How did you get this?"

She reached up to feel the beginning of a good-sized goose egg. No wonder her head pounded so badly. "When that snake lunged for me, I fell."

The look in his eyes softened. "And how did you get this?" He grasped her hand, the one she'd held to her forehead.

She blinked. On the top of her hand, midway between her knuckles and her wrist, was a long red mark. "Oh, no." That snake's fang must have grazed her skin, and she'd been too juiced on adrenaline to feel it.

"Did a *snake* do that?" His brows furrowed deeper. When she nodded, he examined the mark more closely and inspected both sides of her hands. "It doesn't look like it punctured the skin. If it had injected you with any venom you'd have felt it by now."

Realization of just how near she'd actually been to dropping dead on Psycho's kitchen floor had her sucking in ragged breaths. Her chest rose and fell rapidly.

"What the—" Jack focused on her chest where her jacket zipper had descended farther.

She swallowed. The bulge beneath her sweat suit was clearly visible.

He yanked the zipper to her waist, then did the same with the zipper of her catsuit. The bundle of cash fell out, making a smacking sound as it landed on the floor.

She thought she'd been freaked out by those snakes, but the furious look on Jack's face was far more frightening.

"What did you do?" She opened her mouth to explain, but he cut her off. "You couldn't let it go, could you? Was the money calling your name? Last I checked, cash can't talk."

"It wasn't like that," she cried. "I *didn't* break my word to you, I swear it. I only went back into the kitchen to get my penlight, and I found the cash on the floor. I couldn't very well open that freezer door again, could I?" Tension from everything that had transpired over the last week slammed into her like a two-ton safe. "Fine. Don't believe me. Throw me in jail, but keep my friends out of this."

Leaving him standing in the living room, Gina spun and dashed into the kitchen. She whipped open the pantry doors and grabbed a bar of 80% Brazilian chocolate. She tore off the wrapper and broke off a chunk, about to shove it into her mouth when Jack ripped it from her hand.

"Did you eat any of that stuff yet?" He threw the chocolate bar to the floor. The look on his face was ten shades past furious. It was...dangerous. "Did you?"

"No, not that it's any of your bus—"

He pulled her into his arms and covered her mouth with his. For a microsecond, she resisted, shoving her hands against his iron-hard chest. When she opened her mouth to tell him precisely what she thought of his manhandling her, he took full advantage and slipped his tongue between her lips.

Any resistance on her part died then and there. She melted into his warm body, absorbing his heat, his very breath, as he kissed her deeper. His big hands threaded through her hair, and he groaned into her mouth. The kiss became feral, all-consuming. Her mind went totally blank, but every square inch of her skin shimmered with sparks igniting simultaneously. In one split second, Jack had accomplished what no man ever had.

Gina felt alive in the arms of a man. *Really* alive.

She slid her hands beneath his sweater, awed by the flex and play of thick muscles beneath her fingertips. Moaning, she dug her nails into his firm flesh, wishing she could get closer, tighter against this man who inflamed her body with desire she'd never experienced.

His hands roved her back, massaging, caressing, burning straight through the fabric of her jacket and catsuit, and all the while his incredibly talented mouth and tongue continued their assault on her mouth.

He cupped her buttocks and hauled her against his arousal. *More.* She craved more. All she wanted was to wrap her entire body around him.

Suddenly, he broke the kiss and eased away. She nearly cried out from the loss of his body heat, his fiery touch, and the promise of something incredible. Her chest heaved, and she stood there, gasping for air.

He stared at her, his back pressed against the kitchen

counter as he sucked in ragged breaths. Even with his eyes hooded as they were, the burning need in those gray depths mirrored her own. They might be standing four feet apart, but she still felt his touch straight to her core.

"That shouldn't have happened." His voice was hoarse, and she could have imagined it, but he seemed as confused as she felt right at that moment. That theory went out the window after he cleared his throat. "You've fulfilled your part of our bargain. Consider your debt to the FBI and to me paid in full." The look of regret on his face intensified, and the tone he'd used was about as passionless as a roll of duct tape.

He'd just given her the most incredible, soul-rocking kiss of her life, and just like that it was over, back to business. Guess that's all she'd ever be to him. Business.

He grabbed the towel hanging on the oven door, then went to her freezer and dispensed ice onto the terrycloth. Wordlessly, he gently pressed the makeshift ice pack to the bump on her head.

"I believe you," he said, clenching his jaw. "About what happened tonight. You can keep that stack of cash, but remember...no more rips until my investigation is over. After that, what you do is at your own risk."

Anger, mixed with a healthy dose of rejection, fueled the bite in her next words. "And how will I know when your investigation is complete? Will you send me a memo?"

"You can read about it in the papers. In the meantime, it's too dangerous for you to continue ripping off mobsters. If you're smart, you'll call it quits. For good."

She took control of the icepack. "What do you care?"

For a moment, he didn't say a word. "I just do."

"That's a laugh. From the look on your face, you're thrilled to be rid of me."

He gave her another look, this one different—and one she couldn't decipher. On anyone else, she might have thought it was...longing.

Then he was gone. A moment later, her front door slammed shut.

Shock hit first, followed by so much numbness she nearly slid to the floor. The sensible thing would be to shrug it off. It was just a kiss, after all, one that clearly meant nothing to Jack. It was merely a sudden urge, an adrenaline rush between two people who were physically attracted to each other.

Her belly quivered. The urge to cry was overwhelming. Rather than give in to tears, she wrapped her arms around herself and sank to the floor. She shivered, but it wasn't from the cold tile beneath her. It was from the unforgettable desire Jack's touch had awakened within her.

Worse, she'd gone and done the stupidest thing possible. She'd actually begun to like the muscle-bound fed. He might be a stern, hard-assed pain in the butt, but she'd glimpsed the other side of his personality, the one buried deep beneath his exterior wall of iron. *That* man was caring, passionate, and—

Had rejected her. Completely and totally. She was a fool for considering there could be more to that kiss than there so clearly wasn't. *Just as well.* Like all the good men in her life—the few that there'd been—he eventually would have done what they all did. Leave. Not that she'd really been thinking about Jack in those terms.

She pressed the ice pack harder against the goose egg and flinched. It was time to face facts. Time to move past this little glitch in her life and focus on what was really important. Helping Marilyn and the other women at the shelter. That was all that really mattered. She could continue getting by in life and being happy just by helping others who couldn't help themselves. Who needed love, anyway? From what little she'd seen of it, love was not only seriously overrated, but it never lasted.

With more rips out of the question, she'd have to be at her smooth-talking best at the fundraiser and sweet-talk all those rich people into writing big fat checks.

Chapter Eleven

Franco propped his feet on the coffee table, being careful not to scratch the gold inlaid figurines with the heel of his shoe. He grabbed a remote and punched one of the buttons. Vertical blinds *whooshed* open, revealing the best view of the bay money could buy.

As long as he could look at the bay any time he chose, he couldn't care less what the inside of his mansion looked like. He'd given carte blanche to his wife, Carmen, to decorate the place. His only stipulation was that it had to look expensive. After all, a man's house should reflect his title. Carmen had done her characteristically impeccable job.

Italian marble floors gleamed everywhere on the main level. Rich silk drapes hung from the picture windows. The overstuffed down pillow furniture was covered in imported European fabric and had gleaming wooden feet that reminded him of eagle talons. Velvet pillows with gold frilly things dangling from the edges were part of what Carmen lovingly referred to as "accessories." Ridiculously *expensive* accessories, but as long as they'd been married, he'd never been able to deny his wife a thing. Nor did he want to.

A strong wind had kicked up and whitecaps covered the bay. The water was alive, a living breathing entity that answered to no one. Just as he, Franco Falzone, answered to no man.

"Franco." Carmen stood with her hands on her trim hips, partially blocking his view. "How many times have I asked you not to put your feet on the coffee table? It's an antique and the beautiful gilding is original."

"I'm sorry, sweet." He rose to take his wife's fragile hand and hold it to his lips. "*You* are more beautiful than any gilding and as lovely as the day I married you." That had been over forty years ago, and she was still the love of his life.

Carmen's graying chestnut hair piled high on her head reminded him of an upside down seashell. She smiled, a shrewd, knowing look shining in her lovely green eyes. "And you still know exactly what to say to get yourself out of hot water."

He laughed. "You know me too well." It was one of the things he cherished about her.

"I do," she called over her shoulder as she headed for the kitchen. "Cook says lunch is in ten minutes."

Franco watched her disappear into the kitchen. Through the fluted columns flanking the dining room, he glimpsed Tino's young wife, Maria, setting the twelve-foot-long table. Lingering shadows still marred her pale skin from the last time Tino used her face as a punching bag. The fear in her eyes when Tino was around disgusted him. She'd scurry away like a frightened animal whenever her husband was near.

Traditional Italian families like his frowned upon divorce, but Franco had half a mind to help the poor woman disappear with a hefty sum of cash he would be more than happy to provide. Sadly, his son would only track her down and beat her to a pulp. That was, if he didn't kill her outright. At least this way, Franco could keep an eye on things.

Maria caught him staring and immediately came over, plastering a wan, though genuine, smile on her face. "Can I get you anything, Franco?" She tucked a strand of her long dark hair behind her ear, inadvertently giving him a close-up of the purple mark high on her cheekbone.

"No, thank you, honey." He returned her smile, but inside he seethed. How could he have spawned an animal such as Tino?

As Maria headed back to the dining room, he sighed heavily. The woman was once quite vibrant and lovely. Now she was pale, bruised, skinny, and lifeless.

Acid churned in his gut as he ran through the growing list of clusterfucks he had to deal with because of his son. Tino still hadn't nailed the thieves, and time was running out before the big meeting. Even Rocco had to abandon his apartment after it was hit three days ago. If a burglar could get in, so could the FBI to plant one of those listening devices. Though he hadn't found it, Rocco suspected they had, and he'd already found another place to stay.

Franco slammed his fist down on the armrest. All five Families operating in the northeast knew damned well someone was stealing from Falzone soldiers. That kind of news hit the rumor mill and kept right on running. He needed to strut into the Commission meeting with decisive news that these thieves had not only been caught but appropriately dealt with. He also needed that FBI agent off his ass pronto, but not the same way as the first one.

Snuffing an FBI agent was the stupidest thing his son had ever done. They could have dealt with that undercover rat some other way. A *quieter* way. All Tino accomplished was to piss off the entire FBI, particularly Jack Gates.

The man was a pit bull and smart, way smarter than any fed had a right to be. The guy's constant vigilance and persistence was another thorn in his ass. How could one agent put such a dent in his family's business?

"Dammit." If it came down to it, he might have to order a hit on Gates. Not ideal, but if the man continued to come between him and his one and only opportunity to secure a Commission seat, well... What was one more dead fed?

His cell rang with the theme from *The Godfather*.

"What do you have for me?" He craned his neck to check for prying ears.

"Nothing. All's quiet."

For once, Franco thought wryly. "Keep an eye on Tino and report to me directly. After this thing Saturday night, I'll be out of town, but not far away in case that other thing goes down." *This thing,* being the charity event. *That other thing,* being the Commission meeting.

All code used to protect against listening devices and turncoats. In the event the FBI flipped one of his soldiers or they missed a bug, all the government would get was worthless conversation about this thing, that thing, or this or that guy.

"Got it."

"Be extra careful when you guys meet at that place Sunday night." *That place* being Tino's shore house where Franco's soldiers met once a month for turn-ins—cash made from jobs pulled during the previous month.

"Yeah, I know."

Franco ended the call. He felt as if he'd aged ten years in the last month. He loved Tino. Sadly, he trusted the man he'd just spoken to more than his own son.

Chapter Twelve

It seemed to Gina that half the rich and famous of Manhattan had turned out at Clayton Manor for the fundraiser. Good thing, since there was no predicting when Jack's investigation would be over. Until then, this fundraiser was the only answer to their prayers.

She glanced at the slim gold watch on her wrist. Ten thirty. Having done the whole hobnobbing thing for the last three hours, she was exhausted, and from the way her stomach growled, starving as well. Plastering on a happy face for three solid hours and sweet-talking people into writing checks was hard work.

The orchestra at the far end of the ballroom played lively but traditional music, catering to both the city's old-world money and its newfound wealth. Enormous crystal chandeliers glistened overhead, reflecting off the multitude of haute couture sequined and beaded evening dresses twirling around the dance floor. Any of the chandeliers or even one of the outfits worn here tonight would be enough for a down payment on a small car.

Circular, white linen-draped tables with lush centerpieces surrounded the dance floor. Seated at the tables were several city counsel members and celebrities, including two rock stars, three actors, and one professional baseball player for the New York Yankees. Kinsey, clad in a slinky, strapless red gown, leaned down to whisper something to Mr. New York Yankee. As anticipated, he responded with a smile and moments later whisked Kinsey onto the dance floor.

Gina grinned. The man didn't know it yet, but before the night was out, he'd be writing a big fat check to the Center.

"You've outdone yourself tonight." Margo handed her a flute of champagne, the color of which matched Margo's silk dress. "And you look stunning. I'm fairly certain your dress has something to do with half the checks we acquired tonight."

"I had to hold my breath to squeeze into it." The shimmery copper folds of fabric hugged her body, except for the significant slash up the side of one thigh. Thin spaghetti straps were the only things keeping the heart-shaped bodice from slipping down and giving the guests a real show for their money. "I'll be happy when this is over and we can tally the receipts." She took a healthy swallow from the glass, allowing the cool, bubbly liquid to trickle down her throat.

"Anna says the checks are coming in, though most don't have quite as many zeros as we'd hoped for." Margo canted her head to where Anna stood at the buffet service table.

"I know." She sighed. "Money's tight for everyone these days, even the rich. Linda says overall donations are significantly down from last year." Leaning over to whisper into Margo's ear, she added, "The money we grabbed from Rocco's apartment, combined with the stack of cash I *unintentionally* stole from Psycho's, still leaves us short. And

Linda just informed me several more women and their families have been taken in at the Center."

Margo leaned in closer. "I'm surprised Jack didn't strangle you on the spot when that money fell out of your suit."

At the mention of his name, the far too vivid recollection of that soul-rocking kiss slammed into her, and she shivered.

"Cold?" Margo arched her brows and chuckled. "You miss him, don't you?"

"Miss who?"

"Jack." She uttered another laugh. "Don't try to deny it. You *do* miss him."

"Don't be ridiculous," she said, louder than intended. Embarrassed, she glanced around, but with all the chattering and music no one seemed to notice. "Why would I miss the company of someone who can still throw us in jail any time he chooses just by snapping his fingers?" And who'd rocked her world with one kiss, then walked out on her as if it was the biggest mistake of his life.

Kinsey sidled up to them. "Me thinks she doth protest too much."

"Putting aside for a moment the bizarre circumstances under which you two met," Margo continued, "have you ever wondered what would have happened if you and Jack had met somewhere else?"

"Nothing, that's what."

"Are you sure?" Kinsey expertly snagged a flute of champagne from a passing waiter.

"Yes, I'm sure. I could never have a relationship with an FBI agent." Thinking about Jack separately from the same agency that ruined her family wasn't possible.

"Why not?" Anna's bright green gown swished as she joined the group, carrying a plate heaped with pasta.

As the rich smell of Anna's dinner wafted to her nose, Gina's stomach growled even louder. She hadn't eaten a thing all evening, and the champagne was beginning to get to her. She'd much rather tackle a piece of the decadent chocolate mousse cake on the dessert table.

Kinsey slanted a knowing look at Anna's dinner. "I thought you said you were going to ease up on the carbs?"

"I tried, but I can't. I give up. I'm a carb slut." She shoved a bite into her mouth, chewed, then swallowed. "Now back to my question, Gina. For the sake of argument, can't you—for even one moment—forget Jack is an FBI agent?"

"No." She frowned, not wanting to explain the many hazards of *any* relationship with the FBI. Her friends had no idea of her past connections to the Mafia, and she'd just as soon keep it that way. "Besides, we *did* meet under these circumstances, and there's no way we could ever pursue a relationship." Didn't matter how much that line of demarcation had begun to blur.

Blunt, painful rejection aside, beneath that tough, muscular exterior was a man consumed with guilt over the death of his colleague. During their little drive to Psycho's she'd glimpsed yet another side of him, one with family ties that had obviously suffered as a result of his determination to avenge the other agent's murder.

Last, but by no means least, there was *the kiss*. Even she could accurately gauge a man's physical response, and she'd been undeniably sure he'd been equally floored. As if on cue, goose bumps crept up her spine and her face heated. She took another healthy swig of champagne, praying it would cool her off.

"Uh, Gina?" Kinsey smirked. "Your cheeks are flushed. What, pray tell, are you thinking about?"

"Nothing," she lied. For the last four nights since Jack had walked out of her kitchen, she'd gone to bed with the taste of him lingering on her tongue and the feel of his strong arms imprinted on her back.

Kinsey tipped her chin. "Who is Linda talking to?"

Grateful for the change of subject, Gina looked at the table where Linda sat next to a young man she didn't recognize. "I don't know who he is, but whatever they're discussing, Linda looks ready to scream."

Abruptly, Linda stood and made her way over. Her jaw was tight, anger flaring from her eyes. "I've just been informed by one of the mayor's top aides that the city has decided to audit all nonprofit organizations. Some kind of special initiative the mayor is implementing in response to all the financial schemes these days."

"Why is that bad news?" Gina asked. "The Center's books are clean."

"The audit is in three weeks. Until then, the city is putting a freeze on any new assets. Whether it's cash, checks, or endowments, any donations from tonight can't be touched until after the audit, and we're nearly tapped out."

Anna handed her plate of pasta to a passing waiter. "I'm suddenly not hungry."

Neither was Gina. Moments ago, she'd been ready to wolf down some of Anna's pasta with a chaser of chocolate mousse cake. Now, all the wonderful smells from the buffet table made her nauseous.

Linda held out her arms. "We could raise a million dollars tonight, but we won't be able to use it for quite some time."

Gina put an arm around Linda's shoulders. "We'll

figure something out. I promise." She worried that was a promise she couldn't keep.

"I'm sorry." Linda looked at all of them. "I don't mean to sound ungrateful. You've been wonderful. *Really* wonderful. I'm just so frustrated and worried. I think I need a drink." True to her words, she took off for the bar.

The gears began turning in Gina's head. There was only one way they could get cash now and quickly. The timing had to be perfect. Tomorrow night, to be precise.

"Gina?" Margo pursed her lips. "I hope you're not thinking what I think you're thinking."

"I am." She lowered her voice. "There's only one way to rectify this."

"No." Anna shook her head. "No, no, no. And if you didn't hear me, *no!* Jack will skin us alive. We gave him our word, and we can't go back on it."

"Look," Gina whispered, scanning the crowd. "I'm not exactly thrilled at the prospect, either, but Marilyn is recovering at another safe house, and it's only a matter of time before her husband's bloodhound private investigators find her. You heard what Linda said. We can't wait for the audit. Marilyn and so many other women need that money. All I'm talking about is one more rip, big enough to fund the Center for a long time. And," she added, giving Anna a pointed look, "for the record, there is no *us*. I'm doing this alone."

"The hell you are." Margo clamped a hand on Gina's shoulder. "This rip will be dangerous enough with all of us there. Doing it without backup and countersurveillance is just plain stupid, and you know it."

Kinsey cocked her head. "*What* rip? And where?"

Again Gina glanced around, searching for prying eyes and ears. "Tino Falzone's place. I don't think Jack planted a bug there. Tomorrow night, all Tino's soldiers are bringing their monthly payouts to his shore house. The place isn't impenetrable, but it's going to be more difficult than Rocco's or Psycho's. I'll make it work because there is no other option."

Again, Anna shook her head. "I'll never understand how you come by all this insider information."

"Informants," she answered, then bit her lower lip. "All I have to do is slip them some cash and they talk. It's that simple." She prayed her friends never discovered just how many informants she actually had, and that most were contacts she'd made while she was still Angelina Perotti, daughter to a mob bookie. They were all low echelon Falzone associates, but their intel was usually reliable.

"A rip that big is bound to make someone take notice." Margo pursed her lips. "You can bet Jack will hear about it."

Margo was probably right. Jack always seemed to know everything. "All the more reason for me to run this solo. That way, he'll only have one hide to skin. *Mine*."

"Not a chance." Kinsey leaned in, her eyes glittering with fierce determination. "Remember our pact? Where you go, we go."

"Even I have to agree." Anna pointed at Gina. "We are *not* letting you do this alone."

Slowly, Gina looked at each of her friends. The lump rising in her throat was the only thing cutting off the sob bubbling up. She should have known they would never let her do this without them.

"Okay." *Please, God. Don't make me regret this.* "We'll meet at my place tomorrow at noon. It's going to be a rush job, so we've got lots to figure out."

"Uh, oh." Kinsey nudged Gina. "Here comes Mr. Boring."

She turned to see her ex, Paul, heading their way. As he bore down on them, she groaned. Dealing with him tonight was the absolute last thing she needed.

"I told you to delete his name from your mailing list," Anna said. "And if I haven't mentioned it, he's been watching you all evening."

"Good evening, ladies." He ingratiated himself into their circle with the smoothness and ease of one accustomed to getting his way.

His suave demeanor and blond good looks had once charmed the pants off her until she realized his charm wasn't even skin deep. Beneath the surface was a positively dull human being. Not that he wasn't a decent enough guy. He just wasn't the right guy for her.

"Gina." He took her hand and held it to his lips. His unwavering intensity conveyed a less than subliminal message: he wanted back in her life.

"Hello, Paul." His lips were cool against her fingers and she felt...absolutely nothing. All it took was a glance from Jack to boil her blood and set her skin on fire. Not even Paul's kiss could stir the slightest physical response. She tugged her hand away. "How have you been?"

"Missing you."

Oh, boy. Even his choice of words was cliché. He might be every woman's blond dream, and there was no doubt he was exceptionally good looking. Too bad he held not one ounce of attraction for her.

Her lack of reaction did nothing to deter the man. "Dance with me," he said, rather than ask.

"Paul, I really don't think that would be a good—"

"Oh. My. God." Anna's eyes widened.

"What is it?" Kinsey's gaze followed Anna's, her eyes going equally wide. "More like *who*, I should say."

Gina's jaw dropped. Suddenly there was no oxygen in the room, and she couldn't breathe. The pounding in her heart drilled right up into her throat.

Standing at the entrance, surveying the room and looking hotter and sexier than ever in a black tuxedo, was Jack. When his gaze lit on her, every coherent thought in her head turned to pudding. *Chocolate* pudding. Something she could generally eat anytime, anyplace.

As if he hadn't looked yummy enough before in a rugged, Rambo-esque kind of way, all that strength and power harnessed in a perfectly fitting tuxedo was enough to draw the attention of every woman in the room, even some of the men.

"Who is that?" Paul asked.

The tightness in her throat worsened, and she swallowed. It didn't help. She still couldn't breathe.

"What's he doing here?" Margo whispered.

Conflicting emotions bubbled up inside her, although that could have been the three glasses of champagne she'd downed in the last hour.

"Whatever the reason is," Margo added, "it can't be good."

"I agree," Gina mumbled. So why was her body sparking with excitement?

"Do you think the FBI bugged the ballroom, and that he knows what we're planning?" Anna's worried expression mirrored what Gina had already considered and discarded as impossible.

"Shhh!" Kinsey nodded at Paul, who, luckily enough, had stepped away from them and seemed fixated on watching Jack as he maneuvered through the crowd.

Unexpectedly, Jack seemed to know several people, sharing a few words here and there. Those who didn't shake his hand, parted for him like the Red Sea. There must have been over a hundred people in the ballroom, but for her, there was only one person. Watching him eat up the distance between them with his long legs, she could practically feel his hands holding her again, cupping her bottom as he'd pulled her tightly against him. The memory of his lips on hers, his tongue sweeping her mouth, was so vivid, she had to lick her lips.

Paul moved closer, then leaned down and repeated, "Who *is* he? Did I hear Anna say something about the FBI?" As his lips brushed her ear, Jack's face hardened.

"Hello, Kinsey," he said as he joined them.

"Hi, Jack." Kinsey took his hand, bestowing him with her classic royal smile.

"Margo, Annabelle, how are you?" He shook their hands. "Gina." Without hesitation, he rested his hand at the small of her back and leaned down to kiss her cheek as if they'd known each other for years—not one week, eighteen hours, and approximately forty minutes. Not that she'd been counting. His lips were warm and firm, and there was that annoyingly sexy grin she was actually beginning to like.

His fingers made lazy circles on her bare back, rendering her speechless. Worse, making her bones and muscles liquefy. Whether it was voluntary or involuntary, she couldn't say. Somehow, she found her hip snugged against his upper thigh. Where her leg was soft yet toned, his was lean and rock hard.

The other night she was sure they'd never see each other again. Yet, here he was. Aside from the looks he'd sent toward her and her friends, the smiles he bestowed on everyone else were far from genuine. He was in total work mode. She already knew him well enough to pick up on those little nuances.

Common sense told her he wasn't here because of their newly formed plans to rip off Tino's shore house, but him showing up at that exact moment had her nerves screaming with panic. Especially given his uncanny ability to read her like an open book.

She didn't know if he really was just aces at his job, or whether there was some cosmic telepathic link between them. Either way, distance was key. Right now, there *was* no distance, and the heat between them was palpable, leaving her skin hot and sensitive to his touch.

Paul held out his hand to Jack. "Paul Bartholomew."

"Jack Gates." He accepted Paul's hand with his good one, keeping the other possessively at the small of her back.

Unable to miss the gesture, Paul's jaw tightened. A smile tipped Jack's lips at the obvious irritation he was causing her ex.

Jack's warm, lean fingers on her bare skin continued working their magic. She didn't understand it, but she felt tense and relaxed all at the same time. She leaned in closer to that comfy spot against his shoulder and chest.

This is not good. She had to get out before she did something stupid, like...like... She didn't want to find out, yet she couldn't leave. Not with a ballroom full of guests.

"What brings you to a charity fundraiser on a Saturday night?" she asked overly brightly.

"Supporting a worthy cause." He pulled two checks from his jacket pocket and handed them to her.

The first one had his name on it. *A thousand dollars.*

"Thank you." A lump formed in the back of her throat. The man was full of surprises. "This is unexpectedly generous."

He leaned down. "I'm not as cold and unsympathetic a bastard as you think."

"I never said that."

"Actually, you did."

She caught the brief glimmer of humor in his eyes—and was that a scooch of hurt? Couldn't be. Then she remembered. She *had* said that to him the night he'd broken into her apartment. She'd accused him of having absolutely no feelings whatsoever for the women and their families at the Center.

His display of emotion lasted only a second before it was gone. The realization she had the power to hurt this man—this tough federal agent—tugged at her heartstrings.

"Jack, I'm sorry." When she touched his arm, his biceps bunched. "I don't know what to say."

"Forget it."

He began making small talk with Margo, Kinsey, and Anna, pointedly ignoring Paul.

She looked at the other personal check Jack had given to her, also for a grand. This one had another man's name on it. Kyle Gates. *Kyle.* Jack's brother, the one he'd been talking to while they'd driven to Psycho's. She recalled him saying Kyle was also an FBI agent.

She tugged on Jack's sleeve, and he leaned in again. His clean, freshly showered scent enveloped her in a blanket of yummy manliness. "Please tell your brother we greatly appreciate his donation as well."

"I'll do that." He speared her with one of his sharp, penetrating looks.

When he returned his fingers to the small of her back, her belly fluttered, overriding the signal from her brain to flee. *Oh, dear lord.*

It was wrong to use Paul, but he was her only escape route. "Paul, do you still want that dance?" His grin made her grimace.

"Thought you'd never ask." He tugged her out of Jack's one-armed embrace and onto the dance floor. Within seconds, she was beginning to regret her invitation. The way Paul's hands slid all over her bare back was far too intimate, as if they were still lovers. Then again, the torture was self-inflicted, and she really did feel horrible about using him this way.

Jack remained talking with her friends, but his eyes followed her and Paul around the dance floor. His jaw set, and the furrow between his brows kept getting deeper every time she looked at him.

Hah! A sliver of repressed joy shot through her. He was jealous of Paul.

After the second song, she realized Paul had been rattling on about what he'd been doing since they split, and she hadn't absorbed a single word. What was Jack really doing here? Despite his and his brother's generous donations, she didn't doubt he was here on government business.

Paul's continued caressing of her bare skin pulled her back to reality. His touch wasn't exactly unpleasant, but it was nothing compared to those incredible zinging sensations every time Jack touched her.

Lord, but she might have to dance the entire evening with Paul just to maintain distance from Jack. Her friends would help keep him busy. It was nearly eleven, and by New York City nightlife standards, technically still early. Most of these shindigs lasted well past midnight. How would she ever manage to dance with Paul all night?

She could do it. She had to.

"Excuse me, may I cut in?" came a familiar, deep voice.

Gina's heart sank and her resolve went straight down the toilet.

Chapter Thirteen

Jack didn't give a damn what Paul's answer to his question was and didn't wait for it. Blondie opened his mouth to object, and Jack ignored him, whisking Gina halfway across the dance floor before the guy could utter a word. He cast a glance over his shoulder and smirked at the annoyed look on the pampered moron's face. *Too bad. Mine now.*

Gina's slim fingers were warm, as was the bare, silky skin of her back. When they'd been standing together, he'd stroked her back just to piss Blondie off. But the more he'd touched her, the more he liked it.

"You know that was quite rude." She shot him a look of indignation.

"It was, wasn't it?" He grinned. "Who is that guy?" Not that he cared. He was only curious. Maybe a little jealous, he had to admit.

"Paul and I dated for a couple of months."

"Then you should thank me." He tugged her closer, trying not to gouge her with the edge of his cast, while at the same time discreetly scanning the crowd for his targets: Franco and Tino Falzone. They hadn't shown yet, and that was a good thing. He'd have a tough time concentrating on the job with Gina's soft, curvy body molded to his and her scent penetrating his body like a .40 caliber bullet.

"*I* should thank *you*? Why?"

"Blondie's pathetic groping was making a scene." And he hadn't liked the way the guy's hands had slithered up and down her back. He'd wanted to rip the guy's nuts off. As an FBI agent, he could make Paul disappear and no one would ever find his body. He'd learned a thing or two from investigating the mob.

He intentionally twirled her back to where Paul stood scowling on the edge of the dance floor. He adjusted his hand, making a show of caressing her back. Paul's scowl deepened and yeah, it was juvenile, but he couldn't keep from smirking. *Amateur*.

"What's the difference between what *he* was doing and what *you're* doing right now?" Gina threw back at him.

"You tell *me*." He grinned again as he maneuvered them away from the orchestra so they could hear each other better.

Her mouth opened, then closed, as if she was about to answer his taunt but rethought the wisdom of it. To his amusement, the barest hint of red crept up the smooth line of her neck.

He chuckled. "Fine, don't answer. I already know."

"Know what?" When she angled her head to look up at him all he wanted to do was kiss her incredible lips again. "What are you talking about?"

"A person's body language says a lot about what they're thinking and feeling. Yours, for example."

Her eyes narrowed. "What *about* mine?"

"When I touch you, you relax. When that soggy-faced wimp lays hands on you, you get stiff and resistant."

She smiled, and a look of satisfaction bloomed on her face. "I hadn't realized you were watching us that closely."

Yeah, right. The slight twitch of her lips told him she knew full well he'd been watching them, and that he hadn't liked it one bit. Truth was, he didn't like the prospect of *any* guy laying hands on her, especially not after that kiss. Not even the best sex of his life had haunted his every waking and sleeping moment the way that one kiss had for the last three days and nights.

"Truce?" he asked, seriously needing to change the subject. Making out with an FBI cooperator had definitely not been the most stellar point in his career. Then again, she wasn't a cooperator. Not officially.

"Truce." When she returned his smile, his heart squeezed, a sensation he'd never felt before. Except right after running ten miles.

Shaking it off, he rescanned the room, dissecting it into quadrants. Ironic that Franco Falzone, a man who had undoubtedly ordered the deaths of over a hundred people during his criminal reign, was a staunch opponent of violence against women. Also ironic was that Gina and her friends were ripping off the Falzones and giving the money to a women's shelter.

In the recesses of his mind something bugged him about that, some piece of a puzzle that refused to slide into place.

According to Meat, Jack's informant, Franco and his entire family would be in attendance tonight. Franco liked a public show of family solidarity, anything to bolster his whole pillar-of-society image. Ridiculous, since it was no secret he was a mob boss. Sadly, the public ate that crap up.

If only he could keep his mind on the job. Being near Gina undermined his normally fully focused, one-track mind.

179

The orchestra transitioned into a sultry rendition of "Smoke Gets In My Eyes." When their thighs touched, he nearly groaned. He took what was supposed to be a steadying breath but wound up making him feel as if he were wading into quicksand and sinking like a lead brick.

He'd known running into her tonight was a distinct possibility. When he'd caught sight of her in that incredible dress with the slit up the side, his heart started pounding like a Gatling gun. Seeing her again had lit the fuse on his libido and made him realize he not only wanted her but missed her.

It *had* been regret he'd experienced when he'd left her apartment, but not for kissing her. His only regret was that he wanted more. If he hadn't stopped when he had, he wouldn't have stopped at all. They were better off not going there. He was the proverbial moth attracted to a flame, and that flame had a name: Gina Perot.

If only it were just physical attraction. *That* he could deal with. Once or twice in her bed and he'd have her out of his system. For him, that plan would never work, because there was so much more to Gina than physical allure.

She had everything a man could wish for—intelligence, guts, staunch loyalty to her friends. She was a successful businesswoman and philanthropist, donating her time and energy to a seriously worthy cause. He admired her for that. He'd even begun to enjoy the way she constantly wriggled under his skin. Her tongue was as sharp as a bullwhip, flaying him wide open one minute and making him laugh the next, something he'd forgotten how to do.

Doing his best to ignore the enticing way her hips undulated, he searched the room again. Part of him wanted the Falzones to be a no-show so he could spend the rest of the night with Gina in his arms.

"Are you going to tell me who you're looking for?" she asked.

"What makes you think I'm looking for someone?"

She gave him a *duh* look. "To anyone else, you probably seem like a really smooth dancer in an expensive tuxedo, but I know better. You're in work mode. Alert. Serious. Ready to kick ass any second. And while I hate to use such a tawdry cliché, 'Is that a gun on your belt or are you just happy to see me?'" Her chin dipped to the slight bulge beneath his jacket.

"I *am* happy to see you." He couldn't stop the smile tugging at his lips. "Maybe I'm just here checking up on you and your friends." He'd meant that crack to change the direction of their conversation away from his mission tonight. Instead, her eyes flashed with something he couldn't identify, and she went rigid in his arms. "The gears in your head are churning so loudly I could hear them over a barrage of gunfire. What's on your mind?"

"Nothing."

The hesitant look on her face told a different story. She was lying. He wanted to pursue it, but with every step they took to the music, her hips brushed against him, and he couldn't help noticing her long, slim leg provocatively exposed by the slit of that jaw-dropping dress.

"See something you like, sailor?" Her eyes twinkled.

He laughed. Tonight had started off all about work and would most likely end that way. Right now, he was thoroughly enjoying himself.

"No thigh-highs?" he asked innocently.

"Ahhh." When she smiled, it ignited something warm inside his stomach. "So you *did* look at my legs the other day."

"How could I not?" He grinned again like a damned school kid. He'd never grinned so much in his life.

She readjusted her fingers in his, calling attention to the fading mark on her hand where the rattlesnake had nearly bitten her. All humor fled. When she told him that seemingly absurd tale about the snakes in Psycho's freezer, he'd been about to cuff her and lock her up for breaking their deal. Then he'd glimpsed the mark on her skin, and the truth of her story became apparent. All he could think about then had been how close he'd come to losing her.

His heart lurched. *Losing her?* He never had her and never would.

"How's your bug?" she asked. "Getting anything juicy?"

"Let's just say the device is operational and we're getting useful information." Not enough and not fast enough. If that bug didn't get him some pretty hot intel and soon, he'd have nothing to show for their efforts. He was not a patient man, and that's why he was here tonight.

"Are you going to tell me why you're really here?" she asked.

To provoke the Falzones. "So I can enjoy dancing with a beautiful woman."

She pursed her lips. "Liar."

"Yeah." *That makes two of us, babe.* He knew what *he* was lying about. What was *she* holding out on?

Franco played things close to the breast, but Tino was a hotheaded prick, and Jack intended to push every one of his buttons until he said something stupid or did something reckless. Might not work, but it was worth a shot.

"How's the view from up there?" she asked a minute later.

He lowered his gaze first to the yellow gemstones twinkling on her earlobes, then to the matching pendant dangling just above her cleavage. "Outstanding." Did the woman live to torture him? He imagined dancing her out to the balcony and kissing her for a solid hour. Taking her home, stripping off that dress, and making love to her all night had serious merit.

"I'll bet it is."

"You really do look beautiful." Tight catsuit or slinky evening gown, the woman was stunning.

She smiled at him in a way that made him think no one ever said that to her, which was ridiculous since any man who couldn't see her beauty needed his head examined.

"Let's get a drink." He led her off the dance floor, snagging two flutes of champagne before heading them to a corner. Tipping his glass, he downed half the contents and nearly gagged. What he craved was whiskey, not bubbly grape juice. He took another swig of the offensive liquid just as Gina bit her lower lip, her *tell*. "Do you want to tell me what's on your mind?"

"Nothing's on my mind. It's just that—" She frowned.

"Just what?" He found himself wishing more than anything that he could erase the worry etched into her beautiful features.

"I'm concerned about funding for the Center."

"Won't they be flush after tonight?"

"Maybe, but not right away." Again she frowned, creasing her forehead more. "We just found out the city is auditing all nonprofits, and they can't use any money until after the audit. Everything we take in tonight is essentially frozen. If the Center violates the city's edict, they could lose their permit and their nonprofit status. They'd have to shut down."

"That doesn't sound good," he agreed.

"Yeah, well." She made a nondescript sound in the back

of her throat as she momentarily averted her gaze. "So tell me more about your brother Kyle. What's his interest in the Center?"

She was good at changing the subject. He'd let it go. For now.

"Kyle worked for the FBI in Chicago." Normally he was as tight-lipped about his family as he was about himself. On the other hand, if anyone could help him understand what Kyle was going through, it would be Gina. "When he came back to New York he was different."

"How so?"

"Something happened in Chicago. I don't know the details and Kyle refuses to talk about it. I do know it involved a woman." When his brother returned to New York, barely speaking, Jack made some discreet inquiries through his own contacts. "She was nearly beaten to death by her husband. Kyle risked his life *and* the undercover op he was working to save her."

"Did he? Save her, I mean?"

"Yes, but he hasn't seen or spoken to her since he left her in a Chicago hospital. That was ten years ago."

"He must have had deep feelings for her."

"I think he did."

"Why hasn't he spoken to her in all this time?"

"A shelter, just like yours, relocated her and got her a new identity. He doesn't know where she is."

She gave him a skeptical look. "It sounds as if he was in love with her, so why wouldn't he track her down? He's FBI. You guys can find anyone."

"It's more complicated than that."

"What's so complicated about love?"

He couldn't answer her question because he'd never been in love. At least, he didn't think so. "Sometimes," he

184

said after a moment, "even when there's a deep connection between two people, they're better off apart. Maybe Kyle thinks she's better off without him complicating her life."

Jack didn't know for sure if he was talking about his brother or himself. The more he wanted Gina, the more he knew he should stay away from her. Their lives could never mesh, and she could never be a one-time thing. After tonight, he'd go back to concentrating on what he'd come here for in the first place.

To nail the bastards who killed Jim Spencer.

Gina smiled, but she wasn't laughing at him. "You know, I think those are the most words I've heard come out of your mouth at one time."

In her eyes he was beginning to see things he shouldn't. Like a relationship with her. He deposited his empty glass on a passing waiter's tray. When he turned back, her jaw was tight. She'd balled her hands, and her body tensed. She looked ready to go ten rounds. "That *man* has the most unbelievable audacity showing up here."

He turned to see who'd lit Gina's fuse, then *he* tensed.

Targets in sight.

Standing just inside the entrance of the ballroom were the Falzones. Franco and his wife, Carmen. Tino and his wife, Maria. Jack understood the fury coursing through his bones at the sight of Jim Spencer's killer walking around free. What he didn't understand was the look of pure, unadulterated fury on Gina's face.

"Rat bastard," she growled and took off.

He had a hard time keeping up with her as she stormed through the crowd on her four-inch stilettos. "Gina, wait!" She ignored him and kept right on going like a torpedo shot from a submarine. He didn't know what was about to go down, but it clearly involved the Falzones.

"Get out!" she shouted at Franco. "You're not welcome here." Her body trembled, and her hands clenched and unclenched at her sides.

What the hell?

He slipped his arm around her waist and pulled her resistant body tightly against his just before she launched at one of the most powerful mob bosses in the country. Good thing, since the two goons in black undertaker suits standing behind Franco moved closer, primed to intervene. If that happened... He'd destroy anyone who touched her.

Franco raised his gray brows, a genuine look of curiosity on his face. The man had aged considerably since the last time they'd crossed paths. Franco was about sixty and, while still trim, his once brown hair was now as silvery as the satin handkerchief sticking out of his breast pocket.

"Franco." He gave a curt nod to the man who'd been his target for over a decade.

"Special Agent Gates." Franco nodded in return, an old-fashioned, gentlemanly display between longtime enemies.

If the evidence presented itself, he wouldn't hesitate to toss Franco in jail, yet there was an underlying air of respect between them. Each considered the other a worthy opponent, and both understood the first one to slip would go down. Hard.

"Who is this woman?" Carmen Falzone clutched her husband's arm.

In the years he'd been on the FBI's Strike Force Team, he'd never seen Carmen Falzone up close in the flesh, only in photos or from a distance. Wearing a full-length dark green dress, and with her hair piled on top of her head, she looked every bit the regal Mafia queen she was.

Gina struggled in his grip, trying to twist free. "Let me go," she spat.

"What are you doing?" he whispered harshly, doubting anything he said would get through to her. Her body was vibrating with enough fury to fuel a fighter jet.

"Good question, *Gates*." Tino sneered. Not even the expensive, double-breasted suit made that sonofabitch look or act any better than the lowlife piece of trash that he was. Franco was no saint, but at times Jack had a hard time believing Tino really was the fruit of his father's loins. "Control your bitch, or I'll call the police and have her charged with assault."

Jack fisted his good hand so tightly several bones popped. There was nothing he wanted more at that moment than to smash Tino face first into the wall, then repeat the process multiple times on the floor. If he gave in to the urge, *he'd* be the one in jail, or at least on suspension for thirty days. Meanwhile, his investigation would go down the crapper.

"Assault? That's a laugh." Gina turned her attention back to Franco. "After all the people *you've* murdered? You bastard."

"My dear," Franco said, "I assure you I've murdered no one."

Jack snorted. The list of murders Franco was suspected of having committed or ordered others to commit was longer than his arm. Was Gina's accusation specific or in general? Given the heated way she'd flung it at Franco, Jack's gut told him it was specific.

"This event is by invitation only," she continued, "and you are most definitely *not* on the guest list." A crowd had gathered around them. Miraculously, the orchestra played on. Margo, Kinsey, and Annabelle tucked themselves protectively at Gina's other side, all wearing the same dumbfounded expressions.

"We're all here for the same purpose, contributing to charity. I'd think that would more than make up for me crashing your party." Franco pulled a check from his suit pocket and held it out to her.

She grabbed the check and ripped it in half, letting the pieces fall to the floor. "Your money's no good here. You need to leave. *All* of you." She glared at every one of the Falzones, including Tino's wife. Not even the poor woman's makeup could hide the dark purple shiner just below her left eye.

Jack tightened his hold around Gina's waist. "Franco, I'd take the lady's suggestion and leave while you can." He still didn't get what was going down here, but this kind of hatred went beyond outrage at seeing a criminal pretending to be a pillar of society. This was personal. He recognized that kind of anger in himself.

"Franco, perhaps we should leave." Carmen tugged on her husband's arm.

He patted her hand, then his bushy gray brows bunched. "Young lady, have we met before?"

Gina didn't answer. Jack looked from Franco to Gina. There was sincerity in Franco's words and expression, as if he really thought they'd met previously. The same way *he'd* felt when he first met her. Again, something in the deep recesses of his memory tried breaking free, something critical his gut told him he needed to remember.

"Listen to your wife," Jack said evenly. "Leave now." So much for shadowing the Falzones tonight.

Behind them, the crowd murmured something about a mob boss.

"What's going on?" Margo shot Gina a look of concern. Kinsey and Annabelle's expressions mirrored Margo's.

"They're trespassing," she spat. "That's what's going on."

"Trespassing, my ass." Tino put his arm around Maria, who flinched. "The FBI trespasses all the time. Isn't that right, *Agent* Gates?" A smug smile spread across his face. "Although, I've heard they prefer solitary walks in cornfields."

"Tino!" Franco shot his son a look of warning.

"So young to die so soon." Tino smirked. "Whoever sent that boy in to do a man's job was an idiot."

Franco's eyes were murderous. "That's *enough.*"

Jack's blood boiled, and he gritted his teeth at the obvious reference to where they'd discovered Spencer's body. He wanted to rip Tino's head off. Then again, goading him into saying something stupid was precisely what he'd come here for. Everything Tino had said was public information the press had already reported. It wasn't anything he could use in court, but it was a good start.

"Agent Gates," Franco said, his tone gentling, "I'm truly sorry to hear what happened to your colleague. Such a tragedy should *never* have happened." He shot Tino a derisive look, confirming what Jack already suspected.

The old man was sending him a message. Franco hadn't sanctioned the hit. That had been all Tino's doing. Didn't matter. They were both going down for it.

His chest heaved at the effort it took not to plow his cast into Tino's face and smash his nose to a bloody pulp. *Get your shit under control.* "I appreciate the sentiment," he growled. "That doesn't bring Agent Spencer back, and it doesn't make things right."

"I'm sure it doesn't." Franco nodded briefly, then turned back to Gina. "I don't know who you are or why you're angry with me. All I wish to do is make a significant donation to a worthy charity. I would be happy to send you another check in the mail."

"Don't bother," she snapped. "I won't allow you to use this charity in some ridiculous attempt to make the public believe you're a fine, upstanding citizen, because you're not and you never will be. If you think you can waltz in here and throw your blood money around, you're sadly mistaken. You're nothing but a ruthless criminal who murders people."

Jack ground his teeth as Tino's hot gaze slithered down Gina's body. If he so much as touched her, Jack would kill him on the spot. Witnesses be damned.

"Forgive me. It's your party." Franco gave her a mock bow, then hooked his wife's arm over his and left the ballroom with Tino and the rest of the Falzone entourage in tow.

Gina took a deep breath before turning to the sea of people whispering around them. "Ladies and gentlemen, I apologize for the disturbance. Please go back to enjoying the evening." Her face paled. "Who am I kidding?" she whispered. "I just ruined everything."

Slowly, the crowd melted away, but not before darting furtive glances her way.

Jack admired her ability to regain her composure so quickly and execute triage damage control. Then he was just plain pissed. His assignment had been shot to hell and, once again, Gina was the cause. He could no sooner control her than he could a tornado.

"Way to go, girlfriend. Telling off a mob boss." Even

lighthearted Kinsey looked worried. "A sight to behold, but maybe not the wisest thing you've ever done."

"Begging the question, why?" Margo demanded in a less than pleased tone.

"How in the world do you know him?" Annabelle's eyes held accusation.

"All excellent questions I sure want answered." Jack sent Gina a meaningful look. He'd suspected for some time now that it was more than pure coincidence she'd been ripping off *only* the Falzones, courteously leaving the other five mob families in the Tri-state area alone. Tonight's event confirmed his theory.

She gulped in a deep breath. "I need to get out of here."

"We'll take you home." Kinsey draped an arm over Gina's shoulders.

"No!" She shook her head. "You need to stay here. All of you. You need to get more people to write more checks. I'm sorry, but I can't stay." Jack had to agree. She looked on the verge of either exploding again or having a total meltdown. "I'll be fine alone."

"No, you won't," he said. "I'll take you home."

She lifted her chin. "There's no need to put yourself out."

"Too late for that. I'm *already* put out." Whatever was up with her had screwed with his investigation and jumpstarted major protective urges inside him. Either way, letting her escape without an explanation... *Not happening.* "We need to talk."

He clasped her arm gently but firmly. "Good night, ladies. I'll make sure she gets home safely." At the skeptical look on Margo's face, he added, "I promise I won't cuff her and take her in for questioning."

"Maybe a little handcuffing would take the edge off." Kinsey winked, eliciting a grim smile from him.

That idea had occurred to him more than once while they'd been dancing. Now all he wanted were answers. And he wouldn't back down until he got them.

Chapter Fourteen

What have I done? She'd let her emotions get the best of her, and now she'd exposed not only herself but her friends.

Gina could practically feel the heat of Jack's suspicion as he closed her apartment door behind them. To say his professional curiosity was tweaked was a gross understatement. He wanted answers about her outburst, and she had no idea how she was going to give them.

The heels of her shoes clicked on the floor as she headed to the kitchen for a fix. After tossing her woolen coat onto the sofa, energy drained from her body like air from a tire. Even chocolate couldn't fix the disastrous mess she'd created.

There was no denying now that she had more than a passing interest in the Falzones, but admitting to it would make her charitable motives for ripping them off seem like outright revenge. Maybe that's all it had ever been. Maybe she'd been deluding herself all this time that her motives were solely to help others.

Memories of her father and how much she loved him threatened to crush her. She missed him so much her heart hurt. She hadn't laid eyes on Franco in over fifteen years. Even though he'd attended her father's funeral, he didn't remember her. She'd barely been out of high school at the time and hadn't known Franco was the one who'd ordered the hit. She knew it now, having heard the secondhand accounts from more than one low-level associate in the Falzone food chain. Nothing concrete and certainly nothing provable she could take to the police.

Seeing Franco again tonight lit every one of her smoldering fuses. Now she was absolutely drained and craved so many other things besides revenge.

Like a strong shoulder to lean on. Someone to hold her and tell her everything would be all right. More money for the Center. Mostly, that her friends wouldn't abandon her if they knew the truth. Would Jack throw her in jail if he knew? Would he see her differently?

Of course he would. He'd think she was no better than the scum they'd been stealing from. Her father always told her there was no getting out from under the heavy hand of the mob. Once associated, always associated. She couldn't risk her past tainting her friends in Jack's eyes.

Gina stared at the pantry doors but didn't open them. Tonight, not even chocolate would help.

"You want to tell me what that was all about?" Concern emanated from Jack's eyes.

She shook her head. "No." She turned to face him, knowing full well he wanted to grill her about the confrontation with Franco. Confessing the truth wasn't an option. Stalling for time was. "Can't this wait until morning, I—" His hands went to her waist, the warmth from his long fingers heating her body and making her shiver at the same time.

"How do you know the Falzones? It's obvious you and Franco go way back. Even if he doesn't know it."

Every ugly burden she'd been shouldering for more than a decade barreled into her. No matter what she did from this point forward, her father was gone. Nothing would bring him or her mother back.

A sob bubbled up her throat. Her past was about to become her present, and soon there'd be no hiding it from her friends. Or Jack. The thought was terrifying.

"Gina." His voice was soft yet insistent.

Tears leaked from her eyes and slid down her cheeks. Something deep inside her—yearning—uncoiled like a snake waking from a long nap. She slid her hands up Jack's chest, tracing every hard muscle. His body went rigid, and he pulled away. *No.* She wanted him. *Needed* him.

She stood on her toes and kissed him. He didn't part his lips, so she kissed him again with more pressure. Her heart raced, and just when she thought her efforts were a lost cause, she felt his heart jackhammering against her breasts. "Jack, please."

The blood in her veins grew hot and thick, leaving her trembling and desperate. If only the man standing before her wasn't as cold and unmoving as a two-ton block of ice. "I'm sorry," she began, pulling away. "I'm so embarrassed, I—"

His lips crashed down on hers, his tongue hot and demanding, sweeping the inside of her mouth. Strong hands gripped her waist, hauling her against his body. His hands roved across her back, sending ripples of pleasure to the very center of her that craved him so badly.

He broke the kiss, his chest heaving, nostrils flaring as he stared at her lips, her throat, her breasts. His hands skimmed her shoulders and down her arms, leaving a trail of goose bumps on her skin. When he cupped her breasts, she arched into his hands and moaned.

He hooked his fingers around the thin straps of her gown and slowly, teasingly, tugged the bodice to her waist, exposing her bare breasts to his dark, hooded gaze.

"*Please,* just...do something," she all but whimpered. If he didn't, she'd go up in flames on the spot.

He leaned down and took one of her tight, sensitive nipples into his mouth, plucking gently at her other nipple. She gasped and leaned into him. The rough edge of his cast rasped against her breast and she didn't care. A bolt of sensation shot straight from her nipples to her throbbing core. This was crazy-wrong on so many levels. So why did it feel so, so right?

He shifted his mouth to her other nipple, laving it with his hot, wet tongue as he pushed her gown lower, past her waist. The dress slithered down her legs, leaving her wearing nothing but beige panties, four-inch stilettos, and more goose bumps racing across her skin.

Again, he cupped her breasts, skimming her tight, sensitive nipples with his thumbs. His nostrils flared, and he drew in tight breaths. "Jesus, you're beautiful."

Her body ached and throbbed until she couldn't take it anymore. Like a crazed woman, she roughly shoved his tuxedo jacket off his shoulders, letting it fall to the floor. She tore his bow tie loose and threw it on the sofa. Somehow her trembling fingers made quick work of unbuttoning his shirt and tugging it from his waistband. He helped her by removing his gun and the rest of his clothes until he wore only a pair of briefs and... *Wow.* The bulge beneath the tight black fabric was totally in proportion to the rest of the man.

Gina bit her lip. Sexy didn't begin to describe the

sculpted body standing before her. Massively wide and heavily muscled shoulders made him appear even bigger than when he was fully dressed. Thick pectorals and a distinct six- or eight-pack rippled and bunched as he snagged his pants from the floor and withdrew a black leather wallet. Something shiny appeared in his hand. A condom.

Eager to speed up the get-inside-me-now process, she hooked her thumbs in the waistband of his briefs, tugging them to his ankles. He kicked them away, and when she looked up, his erection hung low and heavy.

"Now," she whispered on a ragged exhale, then stood and looped her arms around his neck. "Take me *now*." Before she self-combusted with lust.

With a groan, he slipped his hands beneath her panties, cupping her ass and lifting her as if she weighed no more than a butterfly. He laid her down on the sofa and tugged off her panties.

Wetness seeped from her core, slicking her thighs. He nudged her legs apart and pushed two long fingers inside her. She gasped and thrust her hips upward, impaling herself on his fingers. He thrust deeper, cupping her as he rubbed his palm against her sensitive nub.

Her body trembled with anticipation. Orgasmic tremors threatened to implode, and she forced herself to slow down, or it would all be over too fast. Wasn't that what she wanted —hard and fast, for one night only and with no strings?

He withdrew his fingers and tore open the condom wrapper, sheathing himself. He positioned himself at her entrance and thrust deep. The breath whooshed from her lungs. Her back arched off the sofa, and he pulled out, almost completely. His concerned, gray eyes met hers, assessing, as if he was making sure she was okay. In answer, she gripped his ass and pulled him back inside her until their hips met.

While she appreciated his concern, she didn't want slow, and she didn't want to give herself time to think about how sex with Special Agent Jack Gates was a huge mistake.

"If you do that," he groaned, squeezing his eyes shut and pressing his forehead to hers, "I won't last long."

"That's okay." She nudged her hips against his, urging him to keep going. "Me either."

He began thrusting, slowly at first, then increasing the pace until their bodies slapped together. The sofa shook beneath them. Then her entire world shimmied as the most fantastic orgasm blasted her from the inside out, and she screamed her release.

Jack groaned again as he thrust twice more, arching against her, his biceps and pecs bulging.

Their breaths came harsh and raspy. Slowly, he lowered his weight on top of her. Wordlessly, they lay that way for several minutes as their heart rates slowed.

Eventually, Jack eased out of her, then stood and disappeared. A light came on at the end of the hallway. Her bedroom light. Just like that, it was over. A feeling of heaviness settled over her. *What have I done?*

She'd wanted it hard and fast, and that's exactly what she'd gotten. That and the most amazing orgasm of her life. So why did she feel so alone at the prospect that he would, once again, walk out of her life?

"Hey."

She opened her eyes to find him standing beside her. He'd ditched the condom and was still gloriously semi-erect. She'd expected him to be dressed and beelining for the door. Instead, he slipped one arm behind her back, the other beneath her legs. He swung her into his arms and carried her to her bedroom.

The light was on, and he'd already pulled down the duvet on her bed. He laid her on the mattress, then came around the other side and slipped in, tugging the duvet over their bodies. Leaning on one elbow, he tucked a lock of hair behind her ear. The look on his face was so tender it stole her breath. When he skimmed the backs of his knuckles over her cheek, her heart did a little somersault.

"Let me stay the night," he whispered as he trailed sweet, gentle kisses along the curve of her neck.

No, her mind screamed. *This can never be*. Yet she wanted it to be. Whatever *it* was with Jack, she wanted to find out. "Yes."

What am I doing?

Jack kissed the hollow below Gina's ear. Even as he dropped more kisses on her smooth skin, warning flags snapped wildly in the back of his mind.

He'd gone soft. *Marshmallow* soft. For one naïve moment, he'd thought he could resist her. When she began kissing him, her sugary vanilla scent filled his lungs and every pore of his body until he'd lost all control. And every stitch of common sense. Then he'd gone and opened his big mouth. Spending the night? An even bigger mistake.

What he ought to do was bolt out the door. From the look on her face moments ago, that was exactly what she'd expected him to do, but he couldn't. More importantly, he didn't want to. Why, he didn't know. The only thing he was certain of was that he cared for Gina. A lot. There'd been something electric crackling between them since day one.

The timing sucked, and one thing he had no time for was complication. He had to finish his investigation before even thinking of getting involved with anyone. Then again, he was *already* involved. He could easily get *uninvolved* by getting dressed, walking out the door, and never seeing Gina again. The thought had his gut clenching with... Fear. Fear of missing out on something good in his life.

As he inhaled her scent deeper into his lungs, he held back a chuckle. If nothing else, he could justify sticking close so he could keep tabs on her. *Keep her safe.* Unlike what he'd done by sending her into Psycho's house. Making decisions that led to someone dying filled him with the kind of desperate fear he couldn't live through again.

He pulled away as a not so deeply embedded suspicion crept into his brain.

Big, soft, brown eyes peered up at him. "What?" she asked. He didn't answer right away—*couldn't*—because *damn*. His throat was clogged with six kinds of emotions he couldn't name. Didn't *want* to name. "Ah, I see." She nodded and rolled her lips inward. "You regret what we just did."

"*What?*" he blurted out. "I not only *don't* regret it, I'm thinking about us doing it again." Even as he said the words, his dick began springing back into full fighting form.

"Then why do you look like you want to vomit?"

He hadn't realized he had *any* look on his face. Except worry, maybe. "There's something personal going on with you and Franco. What is it?"

She tensed. "He's a mobster. A criminal posing as a pillar of society. Showing up at our fundraiser was an insult to all of us."

Her gaze was rock steady, and he already knew she wasn't a good liar. Every fiber of his being sensed there was more to it. Her reaction to Franco had been off the charts. "What else aren't you telling me?"

She took a deep breath and stared at the ceiling. "Nothing I want to talk about. Please, let it go."

It was the pleading tone in her voice that got to him. "Okay." *For now*. Eventually, he'd get to the bottom of why she'd gotten so stoking hot. "My investigation aside, I'm worried you and your friends will get hurt." *Or worse*. His stomach rolled at the idea of Gina or one of her friends lying dead in a cornfield.

When she refused to look at him, he had the answer to at least one of his questions. She'd never stop. "You know I can arrest you if you impede my investigation again."

"Jack," she said, a grim expression overtaking her features, "there are women and children out there who will suffer if we can't get more money."

"How much does each person need to get set up somewhere?" He honestly didn't know. Kyle probably did.

"A *lot*. Discretion and secrecy are expensive."

From the determined look in her eyes, he could see where this was going, and the direction wasn't good. He shook his head. "You can't keep doing this."

"I have to," she whispered. Tears glistened in her eyes. "I can't stop."

He clasped her chin. "If you and your friends get caught, there'll be no police, no charges filed, and no trial. Tino Falzone's nickname is 'the Beast.' If he catches any of you, he'll torture you just for fun. That's what that sadistic bastard does. He collects body parts from his victims—fingers and toes, souvenirs from everyone he's ever clipped. Did you know that?" She shook her head, and he released her chin. "He cut off my colleague's finger and blasted him full of holes. Taking out a federal agent meant nothing to him. Trust me, he won't hesitate to kill you or your friends. If you don't stop, eventually you *will* get caught. I don't want to lose you." Did he really just say that? Yeah, he did.

Her lips flattened. The tears he'd glimpsed were quickly replaced by something else. Exactly what that something else was he couldn't pin down. "What's really going on here?"

Again, her eyes glistened, but she blinked the tears back. "You wouldn't understand."

"Try me." Right then, he'd do anything to ease her pain.

"I can't lose them," she answered on a shuddering breath.

"Lose who? The families at the shelter?"

She shook her head. "No. My friends. We have a common goal that bonds us together. Once we stop doing this, I'll lose them." She covered her face with her hands, and her shoulders quaked with quiet sobs.

His mind fought to understand, but he was still missing something major here. "Why do you think you'll lose your friends if you stop stealing?" He tugged her hands from her face and stroked her cheek. "Help me understand."

Tears streamed freely from the corners of her eyes. "You have family. Your mother and your brothers. Without Margo, Kinsey, and Annabelle, I have no one. They're the only family I've got. Without them I'd have nothing. I'd *be* nothing."

Jesus, what in the world had Gina gone through that she actually believed she was nothing without her friends? He shoved his fingers through his hair, struggling for the right thing to say and coming up blank. With every passing second, he watched her pull away from him both physically and emotionally. The misery on her face gutted him.

"I'm sorry." She waved a hand. "I shouldn't have said anything. It's my problem. Not yours."

Somehow, it *was* his problem. He ran his fingertips down her cheek. "I don't think you're giving your friends or yourself enough credit. I've seen the way you are together. You're as tight as any blood sisters. Maybe tighter. As for you being nothing without them, that's baloney. You're smart, talented, a successful businesswoman. You're amazing, and people care about you. *I* care about you." He hadn't meant to say that last part.

"Why?" Her voice took on a bitter, challenging edge. "Why do you care?"

"Because—" It was killing him more than he could admit to see her in so much pain. "I just do." No, he more than cared, and he didn't know how or when that had happened.

Gently, he rolled her onto her back and kissed her until she sighed and parted her lips, allowing his tongue to tangle with hers. The second he settled between her thighs his dick hardened painfully. He could easily push inside her the way he'd done on the sofa. Now that they'd gotten all that pent-up passion and emotion out of the way, he wanted to make love to her properly. Slower and sweeter, and he wanted it to last.

"Jack." She sighed as he took her nipple into his mouth, sucking on the tight bud and rolling it around with his tongue.

Condom.

"Be right back." Seconds later, he had a fresh condom rolled on and was pushing inside her incredibly wet heat.

She gripped his ass, and he loved the way her fingernails dug into his muscles. When she wrapped her legs around his waist, he angled deeper, thrusting slowly, deliberately, gauging her responses by every intake of her breath and every tightening of her body around his.

"That's it," he murmured against her ear, knowing she was close. Knowing he was even closer to losing it and going straight over the edge.

Beneath his weight, her breasts mounded, her nipples rasping against his chest as he moved and making him impossibly harder inside her. He gritted his teeth, willing himself not to come before she did.

"Oh. Oh, Jack." She clamped her thighs around his waist and came hard, arching her neck and back.

Her tight walls squeezed him, sending bolts of pleasure shooting to his cock and up his spine. He groaned and let himself go.

Jack pressed his face to Gina's neck, breathing as heavily as she was. He should run from her. Run hard and run fast.

As he touched his lips to hers, he doubted he had the strength of will to take his own advice.

Chapter Fifteen

"Are you sure we should be doing this?" Annabelle asked.

"Park here." Gina indicated an empty spot on Ocean Avenue a hundred yards south of Tino's house and closer than where they'd been parked for the last two hours. "And no, I'm not sure." In fact, she'd been vacillating over the wisdom of going through with it. Especially the part about involving her friends.

There was still time to call it off. All she had to do was say the word. Coming back alone for next month's payouts would protect her friends, but many of the women at the Center—especially Marilyn—didn't *have* a month. Without the money this rip would net the Center, they wouldn't stand a chance. They'd be forced to return to the hellhole from which they'd fled. They needed to relocate *now*.

Gina took an unsteady breath, praying for the umpteenth time in the last hour that they would get through this unscathed.

Tino's newly renovated, one-story house perched high on stilts overlooking the river, a testament to new construction codes enacted in the aftermath of Hurricane Sandy.

They'd been surveilling the location all day, brainstorming on a last-minute plan to access the house, get into the safe quickly, and vamoose without being seen. Not an easy task.

The pricy shore home lay on a narrow spit of land surrounded by ocean on one side and the Navesink River on the other. One main road in, one main road out. If they needed to blast out of there in a hurry, there'd be no place to lose a tail. Less than ideal for emex.

To their left lay the sandy beaches of Sea Bright, New Jersey. Beyond that, nothing but distant ship lights twinkled in the inky blackness enshrouding the Atlantic.

"Okay, spill it." Margo laid her arm on the headrest and twisted in her seat. "What was up with you and Franco Falzone last night?"

Anna unzipped her jacket and adjusted the earpiece of her com unit. "And what did Jack say about it when he took you home last night? I thought he was about to punch Tino's lights out."

Her stomach twisted into knots. What to tell them? Not the truth, and certainly not when they were about to pull the biggest rip of their thieving careers. Afterward, yes, because Jack was right. It *was* too dangerous. If it weren't for the Center's dire financial straits, they wouldn't be here. This was their last job. Putting her friends in any more danger after tonight was selfish.

"Franco Falzone is a criminal," she said, feeling horrible for withholding the truth. "His presence at the fundraiser tainted the Center and all the good it does. That's all there was to it."

Margo arched a brow and twisted her lips. "That's lame, Gina. Really lame."

"Let it go. Please." In an effort to derail the conversation, she began stripping off her jacket, grimacing at the slight stinging sensation across her nipples—a reminder of Jack's voracious, then sweet, lovemaking.

She dropped the jacket on the seat between her and Anna, fully aware her friends weren't buying her bullcrap.

When she'd awoken that morning, Jack was gone. No note. Not even a hearty *thanks for the sex* on the way out the door. For a moment her heart had clenched with disappointment. Eventually logic and sound reasoning had won out, and she'd accepted it for what it was. Jack had used her for sex. Maybe she'd been using him too. Last night, her emotions had been the driving force and overridden every stitch of her common sense.

Breaking into Tino's house and stealing the cash could very well impact Jack's investigation, not to mention she was putting her friends' lives on the line, but she worried for the women and children at the Center more. There was no other choice. Saving lives was the priority.

She shimmied out of the black sweatpants and gasped at the achy soreness between her thighs.

"Are you okay?" Kinsey eyed her with concern.

"I'm fine." Other than worrying about Jack's reaction when he heard what they'd done.

"You don't look fine." Margo's eyes narrowed.

"It's nothing," she reassured them, practically laughing at the ridiculousness of the conversation. Her pain was a bittersweet reminder of the most amazing sex she'd ever had. Sex. That's all it was. So what had he meant when he'd said *I don't want to lose you?*

"*Gee-nuh.*" Kinsey sported a knowing smirk. "You still haven't told us what Jack said to you after he took you home last night. Or maybe the correct question is, what did he *do* to you last night. Were there handcuffs involved?"

"Really?" Anna gasped. "You guys *did* it?"

Margo groaned. "I hope you know what you're doing. Getting involved with him—an FBI agent—could land us in some serious trouble. Especially after tonight."

"We're *not* involved." She fell back against the seat. "It was just sex, and it won't go anywhere. It can't." Although one tiny part of her brain wanted it to.

It was just as well he hadn't stuck around this morning. Nothing good would come of it. Partly because after tonight, he'd probably arrest her.

"Why can't it go anywhere?" Anna pressed.

"Because he's an FBI agent, and the only thing between us is physical attraction and sexual chemistry." Okay, *amazing* sexual chemistry, but that's all there was to it.

"Why can't you get something going with an FBI agent?" Kinsey piped in. "Especially one as hot as Jack."

"Because—" Because if it weren't for Franco Falzone *and* the FBI, her father would still be alive. "It was only a one-time thing." Then why couldn't she stop thinking about the man?

Ironically, she feared being in a relationship because he'd only leave her. On the other hand, she feared being alone, unloved, and with no family of her own. Which was worse, she didn't know.

"So how was it?" Kinsey's face lit with such excitement Gina couldn't stop the grin forming on her lips. "Yeah," Kinsey nodded as her smile broadened. "That's what I thought. I want to hear all about it later while we're counting the cash."

Not. A. Chance. Reliving last night would only make her think about Jack even more.

"Tino." Annabelle pointed to the cream-colored Cadillac sedan as it backed from the driveway and sped north on Ocean Avenue. In the dim light, Gina could just make out his face. His was the last of six vehicles that had been parked outside the house.

According to her informant, Tino wasn't spending the night there. Which meant the safe was loaded with cash and the house would be empty.

"Radio check, ladies," she said, grateful for the diversion and eager to get this job behind them. No matter how she rationalized it, defying Jack's orders left a terrible ache in her heart.

He'd be so angry with her. Sex with him was a big mistake. It was messing with her normally logical decision-making process. Because whatever had happened between them last night was more than just sex. For her anyway. Now she cared about him and what he thought of her.

"Loud and clear," Margo answered. "One of us should go in there with you."

Gina pulled the hood over her head, tucking in her hair and adjusting her earpiece. "That's not necessary. This won't be different from any job we've done before." Then why was the anxiety in her belly worsening by the second? "Just wait nearby to help with the bags." There should be enough cash in Tino's safe to fill *two* duffel bags. *Can anyone say jackpot?*

She slung the empty duffels over her shoulder. "Everyone ready?"

"Ready," her friends replied as one.

"Then let's do this." She opened the door and closed it quietly behind her.

The air was cold with a stiff breeze blowing off the ocean. On nights like these, her suit provided little protection, and she shivered.

She began a steady jog to the driveway, her breath condensing as she ran. Seconds later, she stood at the foot of the stairs leading to the house. Her heart hammered, and she waited for it to slow. This was the final time they would do this. She prayed the women waiting in the car would still be her friends after she told them the truth. After everything they'd been through together, they deserved to know.

Gina tiptoed up the stairs, searching for cameras near the door. There were none, reinforcing the intel she'd received. At the top step, she lifted the edge of the doormat, checking for a pressure sensor. *Nope.* She reached into her pouch for the strip of supermagnetized metal to fool the door's sensors but stopped. The wood door had two glass panels, allowing her to see inside. The house was completely dark. Except for the steady green light on the control box just inside the door. Meaning the system was deactivated.

Her scalp prickled with unease. Leaving the alarm system off made no sense. Tino hadn't left with any cash. They'd have seen the bags.

She stuffed the thin piece of metal back into her pouch and cocked her head to listen. No sounds came from the house. She pressed her hand and cheek against one of the glass panes and closed her eyes, feeling for telltale vibrations. She couldn't detect any movement inside.

Using her tools, she easily picked the lock, then cracked the door open an inch. Sure enough, no beeps came from the wall box. The system really was deactivated. No time to worry about why.

Letting out a silent breath, she went in, being careful not to step on the mat in case a pressure sensor lurked beneath. She nudged the door closed and listened again. Still nothing.

With her tiny penlight as her guide, she padded softly down the south hallway to the small office where the safe was hidden. So far, everything was exactly the way her informant described.

She swung the beam to a large air conditioning intake grate low on the wall. *Bingo.* She put the end of the penlight in her mouth, holding it steady with her teeth while she plucked a screwdriver from her toolkit. Seconds later, she had the metal grating off and was staring at a one-foot by three-foot— *WTF!*

The rapid beat of her heart slowed. This was definitely *not* the Grandy safe she'd been expecting. She ran the red beam over the safe's make and model, confirming what she suspected. This was a Burnbridge 5000, the queen—no, make that the *king*—of all high-end safes. What in the world was Tino doing with this puppy? It cost as much as a Porsche.

Duh. She and her friends were to blame. He'd probably bought it because of all the rips they'd been doing.

The Burnbridge 5000 had 10-gauge steel-alloy armor plating on the door and all five sides, eliminating typical safe vulnerabilities and making it virtually torch and drill resistant. Not that she'd brought along a borescope and a drill with diamond or tungsten carbide bits, all of which she'd need to drill a hole through this type of reinforced metal to watch the tumblers align.

She sank to her knees. The duffel bags slipped off her shoulder and fell to the floor. All their plans had just gone down the crapper. She'd come prepared for the Grandy's digital keypad, one for which her robotic dialer could run all possible combinations.

Think. Think! Gina rubbed her forehead, wracking her brain for a solution.

This beast was old school, using a combination dialer. With massively thick alloy surrounding the locking mechanism, it would be nearly impossible to feel—let alone *hear*— the notches as they lined up on the multiple interlocking wheels inside. *I'm not good enough to crack it.* Dear god, she'd been arrogant. And stupid.

She fisted her hands. *I have to try.* Giving up wasn't in her genetic makeup.

Unzipping the largest pouch on her belt, she slipped out her stethoscope, one with astounding acoustic sensitivity and earpieces specially molded to fit her ears. She pulled off her gloves and stuffed them in her belt. Leaving prints behind was a risk, but she'd need every bit of touch for this job. Besides, it didn't matter. She'd never been fingerprinted in her life, so her prints weren't in any database, and Tino would never call the police. What would he say? Officer, someone ripped off all my illegal cash?

She yanked off her hood and plucked the com unit out, letting it dangle against her shoulder. Next, she positioned the pink rubber tubes in her ears, adjusting them until the world around her went dead silent. She pressed the chest-piece firmly on the door and closed her eyes. Slowly, she turned the dial.

At first she heard nothing except the beat of her own heart. She had to slow the darn thing down. *Just breathe. In. Out. In. Out.*

It wasn't working. The earpieces were so sensitive she'd have to hold her breath. She held her breath and tried again, turning the dial nearly a full revolution before she heard it. *Click.*

One number down.

After letting out the breath she'd been holding, she inhaled and turned the dial in the other direction. *Slow it down.* If she turned too quickly, she'd miss it. *Click.*

Holy cow, I'm really doing it. This was safecracking in its purest form.

Exhale. Inhale and hold. Again, she turned the dial in the opposite direction. Nothing. Nothing. Nothing. Her lungs screamed. *Whoosh.* She exhaled, keeping her fingers in place on the dial.

She took in another breath and held it, turning the dial painstakingly slowly. Nothing. Nothing. Noth— *Click.*

Gina snapped open her eyes but didn't move. With trembling fingers, she released the dial and grasped the silver handle. She cranked down and tugged. The door opened.

Did I really just crack a Burnbridge 5000? Yep. She smiled, wishing she could tell Sergio about it yet knew she'd be taking the secret of this triumph with her to the grave.

Inside the safe were three shelves and cash. *Lots* of cash. Again, her heart raced, only this time from sheer joy. She unzipped one of the duffels and shoveled cash into it from the top shelf. She zipped the bag closed, then began the same process with the second duffel, emptying the middle shelf and most of the bottom one. As she tugged the last of the bills out, her fingers contacted something hard. She stuffed the cash into the bag, then swept the flashlight beam into the back of the safe.

Eight small jelly jars stared back at her. Grabbing one, she turned it around, trying to identify the contents—a flap of something fleshy and dripping with black goo. *Blood.* Bile rose in her throat. It was an ear. Fairly fresh, judging by its condition. Jack was right. Tino really did collect souvenirs from his victims.

Unable to stop herself, she reached inside for another jar. The flashlight's beam glinted off something metallic—a gold ring with a green gemstone. Something dark and shriveled was stuck through the ring. More bile rose in her throat, nearly making her gag. *A man's finger.*

A whisper of sound. The stethoscope's chest piece hung between her breasts, and she hadn't removed the earpieces. She'd definitely heard something.

She wasn't alone.

The lights snapped on, blinding her. The jar fell to the floor. She squinted, but not before glimpsing the slim woman standing in the doorway. The other woman gasped and held a hand to her throat.

Gina jerked back and fell ass first on top of one of the duffels. She yanked the stethoscope off and stared. Her heart thundered faster than a thoroughbred galloping down the track.

The woman's face was puffy, but not from crying. From being beaten. Fresh bruises marred her cheekbones. Her eyes were bloodshot, and even from this distance the broken blood vessels were obvious.

"Wh-who are you?" the woman asked in a shaky voice.

Now it was Gina's turn to gasp. "You're Maria. Aren't you?" Tino's wife. While they hadn't been introduced, she'd been at Tino's side last night at the fundraiser.

So where was Tino? She could swear it had been him in the Caddy that had driven off.

"Y-yes. Do I know you?"

"Not exactly." With her heart still thudding, she pushed to her feet. This was bad. *Very* bad.

The woman looked at the open safe. "You just robbed my husband."

There'd be no getting out of this one. She nodded. "I did."

Hysterical laughter bubbled from Maria's throat. When

it stopped, she put a hand to her heart and wavered, looking a second away from passing out.

Gina rushed forward and helped her to a chair, crouching beside her. "Lean over. Take deep breaths in slowly, then let them out." At this point, she couldn't be certain whether Maria was ill or having a panic attack. She clasped the woman's cold, clammy hand.

After another minute, Maria's breathing evened out, and she sat up straighter. "Why are you doing this?" Her eyes clouded with confusion. Eyes filled with pain and suffering.

At this point, what could the truth matter? "Because that money is blood money, and there are families that need it more than Tino and Franco Falzone." It was impossible to conceal her bitterness.

Maria uttered a strangled laugh. "No. I meant, why are you helping me?"

She tried taking her hand back, but Maria held fast. "Because you're in pain. I know what you're going through."

Maria shook her head. "How could you possibly know? You don't—" Through puffy, beaten eyes, she stared harder at Gina. "Oh. *Oh.* You're the woman from the fundraiser. You work for the women's shelter." She released Gina's hand.

"In a way." She nodded. Maria might be a Falzone, but Gina's heart went out to her. "I help women like you. Women who can't get free." She waited to see what Maria would do. She'd expected her to scream or run for the phone and call Tino, but she didn't. By some bizarre stroke of luck, she was listening. *Really* listening.

What she ought to do was take the money and run, but no way could she leave this woman. "I know he's hurting you. Come with me. There are wonderful people who can help you make a life somewhere safe. Without Tino Falzone."

"No." Maria began shaking her head. Tears leaked from her eyes. "It isn't possible. He'll never let me go."

She nodded. "He probably won't. Which is why *you* have to leave *him*. It won't be easy, but I promise I'll help you if you come with me."

Maria stared at the floor. Eyes that had been bloodshot and dead were now lit with a flicker of something else. *Hope.*

"Gina," came Margo's distant voice. *The com unit.* She'd never put it back on.

She picked up the unit, holding it to her ear and the mic to her mouth. "I'm here."

"A light came on inside the house. Are you okay?"

"I'm fine. I'll explain later." To Maria, she said, "I have to go. Come with me."

When she lifted her face, the ray of hope Gina had glimpsed only moments ago was gone. For most victims of domestic abuse, escaping wasn't solely a matter of opportunity. It often took months to wrap their brain around leaving their spouse and to believe they could do it and survive. They had to want it bad, and they had to know there was help on the outside.

Gina spotted a pen and pad on a table. She scribbled down her cell phone number and was about to tear off the page.

"Gina!" Margo shouted. "A car is slowing down. Jesus, it's turning into the driveway. It's Tino! He's back!"

She tore off the sheet and handed it to Maria. "I have to go. Call me when you're ready. I'll help you. I swear it."

A car door slammed outside.

"Gina! Get out of there!"

"On my way." Her heart tripped. Tino would be coming in the front door, so that was out. She unlocked the nearest window, cranked it open and punched out the screen with her fist. Thankfully, this window didn't open over the driveway.

"Maria!" Tino bellowed.

Gina grabbed the duffels and heaved them out the window. They were so heavy they landed with a hearty *thunk* on the grass. "Maria," she whispered. "Please don't say anything."

"I won't." With surprising speed, Maria stood. "Go. Hurry. I'll try to buy you some time." She left the room, closing the door behind her.

The house was on stilts, making the drop to the ground at least twelve feet. Gina grabbed onto the sill and climbed out. To minimize the distance to the ground, she clung to the ledge, letting her legs dangle. This would hurt like a bitch.

"Maria!" Tino's angry voice bellowed from the other side of the door. The door flew open.

Gina let go of the ledge. A second later, her feet hit hard. Pain shot from her feet to her shoulders and she fell to her side, rolling several times. Her heart pounded, and she squeezed her eyes shut, willing the stabbing pain in her ankle to subside.

"Motherfucker!" Tino leaned out of the window, his expression furious, his eyes blazing. Then he disappeared.

"Kinsey, I need you! Emex, emex! End of the driveway, now!" She pushed to her feet and took a step toward the bags. Her ankle screamed in agony, but she kept going. Leaving the cash behind wasn't an option.

She grabbed the bags and fast-limped to the end of the driveway. The heavy weight of the cash made the stabbing pain in her ankle stab harder. Tires screeched as Kinsey braked the Charger. The rear door flew open, and she heaved the bags in first.

"Get in!" Anna screamed. Her eyes flew wide. "He's coming!"

Footsteps pounded behind her.

Pop. Pop. Pop.

As Gina dove onto the seat, something pinged against the open door.

Bullets.

"Go, go, go!" she screamed, and Kinsey hit the gas, flinging her and Anna against the seat.

Gina pressed Anna face-first into the seat cushion just before the rear window of the Charger shattered.

Anna and Margo screamed.

Gina risked a look through the rear window—the one that was no longer there. Behind them, the dim glow of headlights turned onto the main road. "Punch it, Kins!" They had a good head start, but like the Charger, that Caddy had a lot of horses under the hood.

"You got it." Kinsey's voice was strained and higher than usual, but she kept her cool and gunned the vehicle north on Ocean Avenue.

Gradually, the distance separating them from Tino's oncoming headlights grew until she could no longer see them.

Kinsey blasted onto the ramp for the Garden State Parkway. Cold air swirled into the car through the busted window. The vehicle swerved, and they nearly drove off the ramp.

"Kinsey, be careful." Margo shot her a worried look.

At first, Kinsey didn't answer. She gunned the Charger

onto the highway. "Is he following us?" she asked in an unsteady voice.

"Kins?" Gina leaned between the headrests. In the dashboard glow, Kinsey's mouth was pinched, her knuckles white where she gripped the wheel. "Pull over," she ordered. Something was wrong with her friend, and it wasn't just fear.

Kinsey slowed the Charger and braked to a stop on the shoulder. Gina punched on her penlight, twisting the top to switch over to white light. "What's wrong?" She aimed the flashlight beam at Kinsey's face, then her neck and chest, and—

Gina gasped. Blood poured from an open wound just below Kinsey's rib cage.

She's been shot.

Chapter Sixteen

Jack burst through the ER doors. All he could think was that Gina was lying somewhere in this hospital bleeding to death.

Given that it was Sunday and nearly midnight, the waiting area was quiet. A grand total of three people sat in the rows of plastic chairs. The only things Meat had told him was that a woman emptied out Tino's safe, and there'd been shots fired. He'd known instantly it had to be Gina and her friends, and his head had nearly exploded. She'd gone and done precisely what he'd warned her not to.

He'd driven to her apartment and waited for over two hours. While he'd sat in his SUV, he'd wavered between wanting to arrest her for obstruction of justice and paddling her bottom until she couldn't sit down for a week. By midnight, she still hadn't come home, and his anger had bled out, morphing into something else. Worry and stark cold fear.

He stormed to the reception desk and flashed his badge. "A woman was brought in with a GSW. Where is she?"

"Third floor. Surgical unit." The woman pointed. "Elevators are down the hall."

He strode to the elevator bank and punched the up arrow. He wished his instincts had been wrong, but they weren't. After Meat contacted him about what had gone down at Tino's shore house, he'd called the Sea Bright PD, inquiring if neighbors had called in shots fired near the house. There'd been no such reports made, but there *had* been a mandatory GSW report made to the PD and State Police.

When the elevator doors opened, he stepped in and hit the button for the third floor. It seemed to take forever to get there. When the doors opened again, he followed the signs to the surgical unit. Outside the unit sat three women in sweat suits, one on a hard chair with her arms wrapped tightly around her belly. *Gina.*

His throat tightened. He'd come to like all of Gina's friends, but the instantaneous relief that it wasn't her who'd been shot nearly sent him to his knees. Slowly, she raised her head, her red, watery eyes locking with his.

"Oh, Jack," she whispered. "It's all my fault."

Words still wouldn't come. What he ought to do was arrest her. What he *wanted* to do was take her in his arms and hold her so tightly he could feel her heart beating against his, verifying she was really alive.

Her body began to shake violently, and he didn't hesitate. He scooped her into his arms and sat on the same chair, holding her, rocking her while she sobbed openly. Every cry and every tear that slid down her pale cheeks was a slice to his heart. Despite everything, he'd come to care way too much for the thief in his arms.

Knowing there was nothing he could say to ease the soul-wrenching guilt she must be experiencing, he kept his mouth shut, absorbing her tremors as her body shook. He stroked her hair and kissed her forehead, not caring that her friends were watching. Over Gina's head, he glimpsed Margo and Annabelle holding hands, their expressions tight with worry. Silent tears trickled from their eyes.

"Are you going to arrest us?" Margo asked, releasing Annabelle's hand to drape her arm protectively over the other woman's shoulders.

"What I need are answers." Any minute now and Sea Bright officers, the New Jersey State Police—or both—would show up to investigate the GSW. In fact, he was surprised they weren't here already.

"Gina," he whispered, then glanced over his shoulder to see if anyone else was in earshot. "What happened?"

She took a shuddering breath. "I didn't listen to you. I *should* have. Kinsey got shot."

"I know." Using his thumb, he gently wiped away her tears, but it was no use. They just kept coming. "Tino was there, wasn't he?"

"Y-yes. How did you know?"

"I have eyes and ears on the street. Anything that involves the Falzones, I get a call."

"Oh. Right." She wiped her face. "Informants."

He nodded. "I waited outside your apartment, but you never came home. I was worried. Turns out the local PD received a report from the hospital of a gunshot wound." Since she hadn't come home, he really had thought it was Gina. He cleared his throat. "I need you to tell me every-thing that happened. Okay?"

"Okay." Sighing, she closed her eyes, then described what had gone down, including her run-in with Maria and the fact there was at least a hundred grand locked up in the trunk of their rental car.

After what Gina had orchestrated tonight, getting any probable cause to arrest Tino or Franco Falzone *before* the Commission met was about as likely as either of them strolling into FBI headquarters and confessing to murder. Gina's actions would most assuredly result in the Falzones and their soldiers clamming up entirely, relegating all the bugs he'd planted to expensive, worthless hardware from this point forward.

He should be furious. He should be railing into her. She'd been reckless with her life and the lives of her friends, but she already knew that. Guilt would haunt her over this for the rest of her life. He, better than anyone, understood what it was like to be responsible for someone's death. For her sake, he prayed Kinsey survived.

"I need to ask you a few more questions." First and foremost... "Did Tino see you?"

"No. I don't think so." She frowned.

"You don't *think* so?" He wasn't convinced. "I thought you said the lights were on."

"Yes." She nodded. "But I dropped to the ground just before he came into the room, and that side of the house was pretty dark."

"What makes you think Maria Falzone won't rat you out?" The woman was as much one of Tino's victims as anyone. That didn't mean she would keep Gina's secret.

"I guess I don't know for sure," she admitted. "But she wants to get away from him. I could see it in her eyes. I gave her my cell number." She grabbed his arm, her red-rimmed eyes lighting with hope. "I think she'll call me, Jack. When she does, I want to help her."

"We *all* want to help her," Margo said firmly.

Annabelle nodded.

"No." Gina shook her head. "After what happened

223

tonight, I won't involve either of you in any of this ever again. This is on *me*. If she calls, I'll handle it."

"Not happening." He pressed his lips together. It was bad enough that Gina had handed over her personal cell number to a Falzone capo's wife. No way would he let her handle this on her own. "If she calls, you'll tell me, and the *FBI* will handle it."

Her eyes flared hotly. "Promise me you'll help her."

"I promise." He seriously doubted the woman would ever call.

Booted feet echoed down the hall. Two uniforms came into view, one wearing a Sea Bright PD patch and the other that of the state police.

"Stay here while I talk to them." He stood, taking Gina with him before setting her back on the chair.

She grabbed his hand. "What will you tell them?"

I have no idea. "As little as possible." Even though Tino was the worst kind of criminal, the truth would land Gina and her friends in jail. What he was about to do was beyond stupid, but he owed these women.

As of four hours ago, the FBI now knew the Commission meeting was set for this Saturday. That intel came from the bug he'd planted in Psycho's house. The only missing piece was the exact location of the meeting. If it weren't for Gina and her friends, the FBI would still be completely in the dark.

Jack whipped out his creds and flashed his badge at the cops. "Special Agent Jack Gates, FBI."

The Sea Bright cop, Officer Schwartz, according to his name tag, frowned. The state trooper, Patrolman Hernandez, arched a brow. Most departments didn't like it when the great and powerful FBI swooped in on their territory, and neither of these guys was baby-faced and fresh out of the academy. No doubt they'd both had run-ins with feds before. Jack shook hands with Schwartz, then extended his hand to Hernandez.

The state trooper narrowed his eyes but shook Jack's hand anyway. "What's this got to do with the FBI?"

Jack tipped his head to the waiting area. "These women are my informants, and I'd sure like to keep this incident quiet. Blowing their cover would kill a major federal investigation. Any backup you can give me in making that happen would be greatly appreciated. I can't do this without you. The success of this case depends on your cooperation." Most of what he'd just said was true. Along with a little BS and a big serving of ego grease.

Officer Schwartz scratched his chin. "You gotta give us some idea of what happened. The hospital reported a GSW. We need to put something down in our incident logs."

He didn't really think he'd get off that easy. Time to pile on more BS. "They were working on something for me when they were shot at by an unknown assailant in a blue sedan on Main Street in Long Branch." Another town five miles south of Tino's house. "Wrong place, wrong time, and purely coincidental. You might want to notify Long Branch PD."

Hernandez, the older of the two men, pursed his lips but said nothing.

"Take my card." Jack pulled two business cards from his cred wallet, handing one to each officer. "If there's ever anything I can do to return the favor, don't hesitate to ask."

Both cops looked at his card, then at each other, and Jack knew precisely what each man was thinking. They were being handed a line of crap, and there was nothing they could do about it. The women would back up Jack's story, and they'd have nothing to prove the shooting didn't go down as Jack said.

"Good luck with your case." Hernandez tipped his head to Schwartz, and the two men turned to leave.

Jack watched them until they rounded the corner in the direction of the elevator banks. He didn't think they'd say anything. If they did, he was toast. As he'd once informed Gina, in the federal world, providing a false statement was a five-year felony. By lying to those cops, he'd strayed *way* outside acceptable boundaries.

He returned to the waiting area where a doctor in light blue scrubs was talking with the women. As he joined them, Gina winced, favoring her right foot. She'd been hurt and hadn't said a word.

"The bullet nicked her large intestine," the surgeon said. "We repaired the damage, and she'll be okay."

Margo put a hand to her chest. "Thank God."

Gina covered her mouth and squeezed her eyes shut. She'd get through this. Her friends would help her. *I'll help her.* He didn't know how, but he would. Despite the havoc she'd created in his life, he couldn't just walk away. She was a loving, caring woman, and she needed his help.

He wrapped his arm around her waist, enfolding her in his arms. Her body shook with renewed sobs as she clung to him, slipping her hands beneath his winter coat and digging her nails into his back.

Margo and Annabelle wrapped their arms around Gina as well, leaving them standing in the waiting area in a football-like huddle. Despite what Gina thought, these women would never leave her. She just didn't know it yet.

Two hours later, Gina, Margo, and Annabelle sat at Kinsey's bedside. A nurse had thoughtfully procured an ice pack for Gina's sprained ankle, which turned out not to be as bad as she'd originally thought.

Kinsey had been transferred to a private room and was awake but groggy. The paleness of her friend's normally cheerful face and the discomfort contorting her beautiful features tore at Gina's heart.

I might as well have pulled the trigger myself.

She didn't know what to say. Somehow, *I'm sorry I was so eaten up by revenge that I orchestrated this cockamamie scheme and you got shot* didn't cut it. So what *would* cut it?

The truth. It was time.

With her heart in her throat, she took Kinsey's cool hand in hers. "How are you doing, Kins?"

"Well," she said, reaching for the cup of ice Margo handed her, "considering I just got shot by a mobster and lived to tell about it, I'd say I'm doing all right."

Anna snorted. "The term is *plugged*. I saw it in a movie."

Despite the humor Anna was attempting to interject into the somber mood, Gina rolled her lips inward, desperately trying not to cry.

"Do you want us to call your parents?" Margo asked.

"God, no." Kinsey crunched on an ice shard. "They're floating somewhere off the French Riviera. Besides, how would I explain this?"

"Good point," Anna said.

How would *any* of them explain this? And what would Jack do to them?

"Gina." Kinsey gave her hand a light squeeze. "I'll be okay. Really. The doctor said so."

"I know but—" Seeing Kinsey this way was so much

harder than she expected. Guilt came roaring back, souring her stomach and leaving a giant lump in her throat. "It's my fault you were hurt. This shouldn't have happened in the first place. Jack warned me this was too dangerous to keep doing. I disobeyed his orders, and you paid the price." She shook her head, still not quite believing that one of them had actually been shot. "I'm so, so sorry, Kinsey. It should be me lying in that bed, not you."

"Don't say that." Her mouth curved up in an impish little grin. "Look at it this way. Now I'll have this cool scar to talk about at the beach when I wear my itty-bitty blue bikini."

Anna snickered, and Margo made an exasperated sound.

Kinsey's eyes widened. "Where's the money?"

"Locked in the trunk of the rental," Anna said as she tugged the thin hospital blanket higher on Kinsey's torso.

"Jack is letting us give it to the Center." While they'd waited for Kinsey to be moved to her own room, he'd informed her there was no giving the money back, so it might as well do some good.

"Jack?" Kinsey arched a brow. "How does he know already? Did one of you call him?"

Margo took the cup of ice Kinsey handed her. "He heard about the shooting and tracked us down."

"He's here?" This time, both Kinsey's brows hit her hairline. "At the hospital?"

Gina tipped her head to the door. "He's out in the hall on the phone." *Probably making arrangements for my jail cell.* That was a conversation they still needed to have, and one she dreaded.

Her friends stared at her, the unspoken question written plainly on their faces.

Anna said it first. "What do you think he'll do to us?"

"Nothing. He won't do anything to *you*. I pushed things too far. I'll take the full hit for this fiasco." Not only did one of her best friends get seriously injured but she'd obstructed Jack's case. Again. Only this time she'd done it knowingly and willfully.

Her friends shook their heads at the same time. Margo was the first to speak. "No, Gina. When we signed on for this, we knew there were risks. Those risks always included the possibility we'd be caught one day, either by the people we were stealing from or the law. We've had this conversation before. Whatever happens, it happens to all of us."

Kinsey reached for Gina's hand. Margo and Anna leaned in to rest theirs on top of Kinsey's. The gesture was so unbelievably supportive, so painfully poignant, her heart swelled.

"When we have our day in court," Margo continued, "we'll tell the absolute truth. We did this for the Center."

"Exactly," Anna added. "We'll tell the judge and jury everything and let the chips fall wherever chips fall."

"Our motives were pure," Kinsey said. "That has to count for something."

Their motives were pure. *Hers* weren't. At least not entirely.

Tell them.

A lump bigger than a baseball lodged solidly in her throat. Even if by some miracle she didn't wind up in jail for the next ten to twenty, after what she was about to confess, they would hate her. They'd never want to see her again, and she would be totally alone in the world. *That* would be the worst of her punishment.

"I have to tell you something," she choked out. "I haven't exactly been honest with you."

229

"About what?" Anna narrowed her eyes.

"About my motives for stealing money for the shelter. You already know my mother was a victim of domestic violence. But there's more."

Margo canted her head. "We all know someone close to us who was victimized. That's why we agreed to this in the first place. Isn't that enough of a reason?"

"For you, yes. For me, there was something else." She looked at her friends. *Here goes.* "There's a reason we've stolen only from the Falzones."

Anna's brows scrunched. "You told us you happened to know someone on the inside, an informant who fed you information on when and where we could grab some cash."

"That's true." She nodded. "But I didn't tell you everything. Like how and why I *had* that informant." She took another fortifying breath. "My father was a mob bookie. He ran numbers for Franco Falzone and—" A shot of renewed hatred punched her in the gut, and she clenched her hands. "Franco murdered my father."

Anna gasped. Margo pursed her lips. Only Kinsey's expression was neutral, probably due to residual effects of the anesthesia.

"When did this happen?" Kinsey asked.

"Fifteen years ago." Sometimes, it seemed like only yesterday. "He got caught up in an FBI sting. To avoid going to prison, he agreed to wear a wire to get incriminating statements from Franco. Franco found the wire and shot him in the head." She'd never seen her father's body, but that's what she overheard her mother repeating over the phone.

"My god." Margo's expression turned sympathetic, which only made Gina more determined to get it all out. "No wonder you've been keeping Jack at a distance."

Exactly. No matter how much the man insinuated himself into her thoughts, a real and lasting relationship with him wasn't possible. Maybe it was time to tell him everything too. Given his own quest for revenge, wouldn't he understand her motives?

Anna and Kinsey's expressions were similarly sympathetic. She didn't deserve their sympathy. Because there was more to tell.

"My name isn't really Gina Perot," she continued. "It's Angelina Perotti. I had my name legally changed after my mother died. The media did such a bang-up job of plastering my father's murder in the newspapers and on TV, I couldn't go anywhere without people talking about me behind my back. I went away to college and, before coming back to New York City, I changed my name, so I could start fresh."

"Wow," Anna said. "Virtually, a blank slate."

Not quite. No matter how much she wished it, changing her name could never change the past.

She clasped her hands tightly to keep them from shaking. "Do you remember when we all met at that fundraiser a couple of years ago?" They nodded. "We overheard Linda Hernandez saying they hadn't taken in as much money that night as she'd hoped for. One of you brought up that news story about oodles of cash the FBI had just seized from some mobsters after a big raid in Chicago."

"And," Margo interjected, "how that money would probably go to waste in some government bank account when it could be spent on something far more worthy."

"Like the shelter," Kinsey piped in, although her eyes were slowly closing.

"There's more." Gina uttered a bitter laugh. "Two nights after that fundraiser, we were drinking martinis at my place while watching *Robin Hood* when I jokingly said we should steal that money from the mob and give it away. Like Robin Hood stole from the rich and gave to the poor."

Gina swallowed the bitter tang in her mouth, sorely regretting the sequence of events her personal vendetta had set in motion. "I wasn't lying when I said I used to work for a locksmith, and that's where I picked up lock picking and safecracking skills. The man I worked for actually *was* a safecracker who did time in prison for breaking and entering."

"Oh," Anna said, her eyes widening.

"Yeah. Oh." Gina nodded. "Knowing I had those skills, I concocted this crazy plan to steal from the Falzones. I convinced myself I was doing it to help battered women, but it was also for revenge. And I nearly got Kinsey killed because of it. I should have told you sooner, but I was afraid."

"Afraid of what?" Kinsey asked in a sleepy voice.

"Afraid you'd think less of me." For her motives *and* for the Mafia blood running through her veins. She still hadn't told them all of it. The last bit would be the hardest.

"But it wasn't *all* for revenge." Margo touched her shoulder. "You were donating to the Center long before we started stealing. You sold thousands of dollars of your own personal belongings to help those women."

"Please, let me finish." She hung her head. "After my parents died, I had no family. When I met all of you and we became friends, *you* became my family. I was afraid this scheme we've been running was the glue that held us together, and that if we weren't doing it anymore..." *I'd lose you.* She couldn't say the words, but they hung there in the air just as surely as if she'd spoken them out loud.

"You could never lose us." Kinsey held out her arms to

Gina. "Come here. I love you, I forgive you, and I want to hug you. But if I get up, I'm afraid my intestines will fall out of the hole in my belly."

Gina's mouth fell open. Disbelief nearly took her to the floor. As she leaned in to gently hug Kinsey back her heart was so full of joy she thought it would burst. How could Kinsey—a woman she'd nearly gotten killed—possibly be magnanimous and forgiving enough to say *I love you*?

Margo and Anna joined in, hugging Gina from behind.

"We all love you," Anna whispered in a trembling voice.

"And you're right," Margo said. "We *are* your family, and you're *ours*."

They remained that way for another long minute, none of them speaking, just holding one another. Gina's throat constricted so tightly she couldn't speak the words she so desperately wanted to say. *Needed* to say. That she hadn't felt this loved since her parents died. "I'm so lucky to have you," she managed to whisper.

"Am I interrupting something?"

Gina straightened and turned to the door. *Jack.* Her heart was torn between beating faster because his nearness always did that to her and galloping away from sheer terror. This was it. He was here to arrest them.

In his good hand he held a decorative jar brimming with flowers. Handcuffs she expected. Not flowers. Stupidly, she stared at the pretty yellow daisies and carnations.

He set them on the rolling metal table next to the bed. "How are you feeling?" he asked Kinsey.

"Like I just got plugged." She winked at Anna, who giggled. "Thanks for the flowers. They should go great with our orange jumpsuits."

The mood in the room instantly went as somber as a funeral. *Theirs.*

"Are you going to arrest us?" Gina held her breath.

"No. I can't. Even if I wanted to, which I don't."

Gina's jaw dropped. "Wait, what?"

At first, he didn't answer, dragging out her misery. "If I arrest you, there'll be no keeping it quiet. Tino would put a price on your heads, and you wouldn't last a month. In *or* out of prison. You said he didn't see your face, so he doesn't know who any of you are. Let's keep it that way."

"What about your investigation?" Nailing Tino for killing his colleague was the most important aspect of Jack's case. "Did I just destroy it?"

He shoved a hand through his hair. "Probably. Maybe. Hell, I don't know. Locking you up won't help anything. What's done is done. For now, I covered for you."

Margo eyed him suspiciously. "What does that mean, exactly?"

"It means I lied. I told those cops you're all working for me, and that if tonight's events came out it, it would destroy a major federal investigation."

"Why did you do that for us?" Gina touched his arm. "You didn't have to."

His gray eyes softened as he clasped her hand, linking their fingers. "I don't want anyone else's death on my conscience. Especially not yours."

"Thanks again for the jar of flowers," Kinsey murmured as her eyes closed.

Gina jerked her head up. *The jars.* "Wait! I forgot to tell you something!" She squeezed Jack's hand. "I forgot to tell *all* of you something. In the back of Tino's safe were small jars filled with body parts."

"Eew." Anna grimaced.

Jack tensed. Eyes that only moments ago were soft, were now steely hard. "*What* body parts?"

"I didn't look at all of them. One had an ear in it, and it looked fresh. You know, still kind of pink and with gooey strands of...something." Just thinking about it made her nauseous.

Jack's brows drew together. "What else?"

"A finger. It was dry and dark, and there was a ring on it." He'd said Tino cut off that agent's finger before killing him.

His jaw tightened. "Can you describe the ring?"

"It was gold. A man's ring with a green gemstone. Maybe an emerald."

"Jesus." He turned away, parking his hands on his hips and tilting his head back to stare at the ceiling.

"Does that finger belong to the agent you told me about?"

"Yeah. Jim Spencer." When he faced them again, his eyes blazed with fury. "That was his wedding ring."

Chapter Seventeen

Jack set the duffel bags on the floor. It was 6:00 a.m. and he was beat.

As Gina walked to the sofa, favoring her twisted ankle only slightly, he was glad to see the injury wasn't serious. She sat and lowered her head to her hands. They'd both been awake for twenty-four hours. She'd insisted on one of them remaining with Kinsey at all times, at least until she was feeling better. Naturally, Gina had insisted on taking the first shift, and he'd stayed with her while Margo and Anna went home to get some shut-eye.

He sat beside her and tugged her to his side. Despite the lack of sleep, his mind still spun with the vital information he'd just obtained.

Jim Spencer's wedding ring—and *his finger—are in Tino's shore house.*

He should be jacked up and banging on a federal judge's door for a search *and* an arrest warrant. Locking up Tino for Jim's murder was why he'd been working his ass off for the last six months. Gina had just dropped the probable cause he needed right in his lap. And he couldn't use it.

She'd described details of the ring to a T. To establish a fair and reliable eyewitness identification, he'd followed protocol and shown her a photo array of six rings, including Jim's, and five fillers—rings similar in overall appearance to the one Spencer had been wearing. Gina positively identified Jim's ring. Problem was, if he used her ID as probable cause for the warrants, he'd have to explain where the information came from and the circumstances under which it had been obtained.

She sighed and rested her head on his shoulder. He'd been over and over it in his head. He had to keep her out of it. He hadn't been exaggerating. Even from a jail cell, Tino would send someone to kill her, and Jack couldn't protect her 24/7. He could try to persuade her to go into witness protection, but he wouldn't do that to her either. Besides, she'd never agree to it. Gina could never be confined to a life she didn't want to be in. She was too stubborn, too unpredictable and spontaneous, everything he wasn't. They were polar opposites in every way, but the laws of physics never changed. Polar opposites always attracted, and that was the way it was with them. No matter what she did to turn his world upside down, he wanted her like nobody's business.

A strand of thick, silky hair fell in front of her face, and he tucked it behind her ear. When had she gotten so far under his skin that he'd do anything for her? Including giving up the most important evidence of his career. There had to be another way. Whether it took another six months or six years... If it took the rest of his life, he'd find a way to nail Tino Falzone.

"C'mon," he said. "You need to get some rest. I'll send someone out later today to fix the window on the Charger."

Tired eyes pinned him. "You'd do that? Why?"

"So you don't have to answer questions about what

happened to it." He'd do everything possible to distance her from his investigation and the Falzones.

"What does that matter anymore?" She shook her head in confusion. "I'll have to give a statement about the ring I found and where I saw it."

"No. You won't. I can't use the information you gave me. Ever."

"I don't understand." Her brows furrowed. "Why not?"

He touched his fingers to her cheek, loving the softness of her skin. "I'd have to turn over your statement to defense counsel during discovery." Not for the first time, the image of her cold, lifeless body came to him with such vivid clarity his throat constricted.

"Oh." Understanding flared in her eyes. "I'm sorry."

"I'm not." The Falzones were responsible for so much death. He didn't want to add to the body count. Especially, not with her.

He stood and held out his hand. When she rose and wavered on her feet, he picked her up.

"You don't need to carry me," she protested.

He arched a brow. "You're still limping."

"Okay, fine." She uttered an exasperated breath as he carried her to her bedroom. "I don't think I can fall asleep. I can't stop thinking about everything."

He knew the feeling. "Try." He unzipped her sweat suit jacket and tossed it on the bed. Then he knelt and tugged off her black sneakers. When he peeled down the matching pants, his hands slid along the smooth, snug material of her catsuit. As tired as he was, his dick jerked. Sex wasn't what she needed, and he wasn't that much of a dickhead to take advantage of her after everything she'd been through. "I'm going to run you a bath, then I have to go take care of things."

Without waiting for a response, he went into the bathroom and turned on the taps in the giant soaker tub that was big enough for a small rhinoceros. He didn't dare go back into the bedroom just yet. One look at Gina's naked body and his stalwart determination to remain honorable would go south in a heartbeat.

While the pounding water filled the tub, he checked his phone for emails and missed text messages. No news regarding the break-in at Tino's or from the Sea Bright PD or the state police. A little of the tension that had been grinding away on his nerves for the last twenty-four hours eased.

A flash of green had him looking up to find Gina standing in the doorway. She'd artfully arranged her hair on top of her head, with thick, wavy strands framing her face. Though he willed it not to, his selfish dick jerked again.

The shiny, midthigh satin robe wasn't nearly as tight fitting as the catsuit, but the way it draped lovingly over her breasts, outlining their taut nipples, didn't help his honorable intentions. If only he didn't already know how good it felt to bury himself inside her while she clutched at his ass, pulling him in deeper until—

The zipper of his jeans tightened over his crotch, and he stuffed his phone into his jacket pocket. "Your bath is ready. Relax, then get some sleep. I'll call you later."

He started past her when she untied the robe and let it slip from her shoulders. Jack swallowed. *I'm toast.*

"Jack, don't."

"Don't what?" His voice sounded strangled.

"Leave." She stepped into the tub and held out her hand to him.

He swallowed hard, taking in the lushness of her creamy breasts with their dark, rosy nipples, her flat belly, and the sleekness of her thighs and dark curls—the doorway to heaven on earth.

With a groan, he shook his head. "Gina, no. What you need is a relaxing bath followed by sleep."

"I know. I just don't want to be alone. Please stay."

Oh, Christ. How could he get naked in that tub and not make love to her? It would be torture, but he'd do it. For her. Because she asked. *Because she needs me.*

While she settled in the tub to wait, he shrugged out of his jacket, then shucked every stitch of clothing while she checked him out.

"Tit for tat." She gave him a sexy smile, and two seconds later he went from half-mast to full mast and a half.

He stepped into the hot water, and when he would have seated himself facing her from the opposite side of the tub, she shifted position, indicating he should sit behind her. When she leaned back against his chest, her buttocks settled against his iron-stiff cock, sending a jolt of arousal to every cell in his body. He tensed and groaned audibly. Luckily, his cast was waterproof and wouldn't disintegrate into a lumpy mess. He wrapped his arms around her torso beneath her breasts, then buried his face against her neck, inhaling her sweet scent deep into his lungs.

"I'm sorry." She shifted, the movement snuggling her ass more firmly against his groin. "I should have listened to you. If I had, none of this would have happened."

"That's true." There was no sense denying it, and they both knew it. "But you can't beat yourself up over it for the rest of your life." Or she'd wind up a shell of a human being. Like him. Although, around her, emotions he'd thought dead had been slowly coming back to life.

Beneath the water, her hand skimmed down the side of his thigh, which didn't help his horny predicament. "You didn't pull the trigger," he said. He hadn't pulled the trigger that sent a dozen bullets boring into Jim's body, so why couldn't he take his own advice?

"No, but I put Kinsey in front of that speeding bullet."

"Only time can erase the guilt you're feeling right now. So give it some. Time, that is." As if it were the most natural thing to do, his hands splayed over her breasts, massaging them lightly and rubbing his fingers over her tight nipples.

"Mmm." She covered his hands with hers, urging him to continue. "That feels nice."

Sure does.

She hooked her legs over the tops of his thighs. "Did you know Jim Spencer well?"

His hands stilled on her breasts. "Yeah." He couldn't explain why...maybe it was the beautiful woman draped over his body... His mouth opened and he began spilling his guts. "Jim was my trainee. He died on my watch because I sent him in undercover. Somehow they found out who he was."

"And you feel responsible."

"Of course I do. It was my fault he was killed."

"Did you pull the trigger?" She twisted her neck to look at him. Even though he'd just thought the same thing, hearing his own words flung back at him was a slap in the face. It was on the tip of his tongue to regurgitate what he'd been torturing himself with for months. Jim was too inexpe rienced and Jack had been in too much of a hurry to get someone on the inside.

As he stared into Gina's eyes, counting the gold flecks in her irises, the truth punched him in the gut. Jim *wasn't* inexperienced. Maybe he didn't have as extensive a UC resume as some of the older agents, but he had an outstanding record of UC busts. Jack had selected him because he was the right man for the job. "Maybe it wasn't my fault," he muttered, the first time he'd ever said those words, let alone actually believed them. Sometimes things just happened and cases went bad.

She settled back against him. "I guess we both made decisions we have to live with."

He snorted. "Imagine that. A thief and an FBI agent having something in common."

When she giggled, the vibrations sent a shaft of lust shooting to his dick. He reached for the soap, intending to rub it over every inch of Gina's body.

"I told my friends the truth tonight," she said. "That I had ulterior motives for stealing from the Falzones because..." She blew out a long, heavy breath. "Because Franco murdered my father."

"*What?*" The soap slipped from his hand, splashing as it hit the water. He wasn't aware of anyone with the last name Perot having been killed by the Falzones, and he pretty much knew everyone Franco was rumored to have taken out. How could he have missed that?

"*Please*, Jack." She gripped his good wrist and turned in his arms. He couldn't miss the fear burning in her eyes. "Don't hold this against my friends. They thought we were stealing from the Falzones *only* to help the Center. They didn't know about my personal reasons."

Which explained a lot. Like her violent reaction to Franco at the fundraiser.

He let his head fall back against the bathtub rim. Gina's confession didn't change anything. No matter what they'd done, turning her and her friends in would serve no justice. When it came to the Falzones there might not ever *be* any justice.

"Who was your father to Franco?" he asked finally.

She sighed and settled back against his chest. "My father was... No one of importance, except to me and my mother."

Hmm. Jack wanted to pepper her with more questions. Now wasn't the time. She'd been through enough in the last twenty-four hours. Tomorrow he could dig into the FBI database and read the details for himself.

"How did your friends take it when you told them everything?" Well, he assumed. Before leaving the hospital, the four women had hugged, kissed, laughed, and cried like they'd be BFFs for all eternity.

"They told me they understood," she said in a choked voice. "That they loved me and we'd always be family." She shook her head as if she still didn't believe it, and his heart melted a little bit more.

He gave her a gentle shake. "I told you to give them and yourself more credit."

Like him, they'd both been through a lot. Unlike him, Gina had no parents left alive and no siblings. His isolation was of his own doing, but he always knew all he had to do was pick up the phone and talk to any one of his brothers or his mother and they'd be there for him in a heartbeat.

He snagged the bar of soap from the water, then slid it back and forth across her abdomen in slow, lazy circles. Spooning in a hot bath with her was hard enough; touching her this way could only go in one direction. With a groan, he shifted to ease his growing discomfort. Like that would help. But again, this wasn't about him. It was about what *she* needed.

Gina raised her arms over her head, linking them behind his neck. She arched her back, pushing her beautiful breasts into his waiting hands as he skimmed the soap over taut, wet nipples and down her belly. He set the soap on the ledge, then thoroughly massaged her torso, grinding his teeth as he hardened even more painfully.

She unlinked her arms from around his neck, taking his good hand and guiding it down her slick body, under the water, to the juncture of her thighs. If she needed release, he was happy to give it to her. Even if it killed him not to sink deep inside her.

Using two fingers, he pumped into her, rubbing her swollen nub in slow circles with the pad of his thumb. When she began undulating and meeting his thrusts, water sloshed against the sides of the tub. With the fingers of his casted hand, he pinched one of her nipples and was rewarded with a throaty groan that made his balls so hard they were probably turning blue.

"Faster," she moaned. "*Faster.*"

"You've got it, sweetheart." He picked up his pace, pumping harder *and* faster.

"Yes, that's it." She met his thrusts again and again. "Yes. Oh god, yes. I'm *sooo* close."

Water sloshed over the lip of the tub onto the floor. Jack was so turned on by her slick, undulating body writhing against him and the feel of her throbbing pussy beneath his fingers, he needed to... He bit down gently on her shoulder to keep himself grounded.

She slipped her hand behind her and grabbed his dick, rubbing up and down as she tightened around him and cried out. Her body arched and bucked, sending a small tidal wave shooting from the tub, and *damn*. Watching her in the throes of orgasm was the sexiest thing he'd ever seen.

Her chest rose and fell as she sucked in breaths. She released him and turned to straddle his thighs, again taking him in her hands and stroking him up and down.

As much as his body craved release, the sight of her

sleepy eyes was too much. "Gina, no. This is about you. Not me." His balls were on the verge of exploding, but he still wouldn't take advantage of her while she was so emotionally wrung out.

She gave him a weary smile. "How 'bout we make it about *both* of us?"

There was nothing he wanted more, but... "I don't have any more condoms."

Gina grinned. "I do." She stepped out of the tub, then pulled a condom from the vanity drawer and tore open the wrapper.

"Was that for that soggy-faced wimp, Paul?" A stab of jealousy hit him dead center in his chest.

"It was." The corners of her mouth quirked as she stepped back into the tub and straddled him. "The key word being *was*." She began rolling on the condom. "Are you jealous, Special Agent Gates?"

In response to her question, he grasped her waist, ignoring the stab of pain in his fractured wrist. "Jealous my ass." She giggled as he held her suspended half an inch above the tip of his cock. He lowered her just enough to rub himself against her swollen clit.

"You're killing me." Her hands settled on his shoulders. She tried scooting down on him, but he wouldn't let her, preferring to tease, rubbing the top of his cock back and forth against her slick folds until she gasped, writhing helplessly above him. "You always need to be in charge, don't you?"

"Like I said, it's an FBI thing." He leaned forward, just enough to capture one of her nipples in his mouth and roll it between his teeth and tongue.

"Jack, *please*."

"Please *what*?" he asked around her nipple, knowing

exactly what she wanted. For the first time in his life, he was not only totally aroused but thoroughly enjoying the fun of sex. *No, not sex.* He wanted to make love to her. To thoroughly and permanently banish any lingering memory she might have of making love with any other guy and replace them with new ones. Of him. *Only* him.

He released her nipple, lifted his hips, and thrust deep. Her eyes flew open and she uttered a cry of surprise. The groan that flew from his own lips was loud, feral, possessive, and he nearly came on the spot.

Sleek thighs clenched around his, and he slipped his hands beneath her ass, guiding her body up and down as he thrust harder. She rode him like a bronc rider, sending his pulse rocketing, but he held back, waiting for her to come and shatter around him.

With every merge of their bodies, she gasped, louder each time until her head fell back and her cry echoed against the tiled walls. He thrust deep one last time, coming right behind her and bellowing her name.

She collapsed against his chest, and he wrapped his arms around her, holding her tightly as the last spasms of his orgasm rocked his body from head to toe.

The only sound in the bathroom was their heavy breathing. He continued holding her, eventually realizing her back rose and fell evenly in a steady rhythm. She'd fallen asleep.

He needed to get them out of the tub before they shriveled into raisins, but he wasn't quite ready to move. Sated was the word that popped into his head. He couldn't remember the last time he'd been so content, so utterly at peace. *Try never.* Which shocked the heck out of him.

Still buried inside her warm body, he managed to rise and step from the tub onto the bath mat. Seemed like half the water in the tub was now on the tile floor. Jack eased out of her and lowered her to the mat. He grabbed a towel and gently rubbed her body dry. She wrapped her arms around his waist and mumbled something incoherent. The woman was asleep on her feet.

Working quickly, he dried himself off, ditched the condom, then carried her to the bed and lay down next to her. He pulled the covers over them and rose on one elbow, watching her pink lips part as she breathed softly. He could watch her like this for hours.

Gently, he unclipped her hair, sifting his fingers through the thick, silky strands. The tug on his heart was unfamiliar yet identifiable.

He was falling for her.

Nailing the Falzones was still a priority, but somehow it had ceased to be the one driving obsession in life. Now he had another priority.

The beautiful woman lying next to him.

Chapter Eighteen

Tino sneered at his trembling wife as she clutched the bed sheet to her body. She'd become skin and bones and barely worth fucking anymore. He preferred a woman with sexy curves and tits he could hold in his hands. Not Maria's sorry excuse for breasts. If she didn't have nipples, she wouldn't *have* breasts. And she just lay there, unmoving, while he'd pumped inside her and shot his wad.

He fisted his hand, barely resisting the urge to plow it into her face again. She deserved everything he'd just done to her.

The stupid bitch lied to me.

He grabbed his slacks from the floor. His own wife had stood by while that other bitch emptied out his safe. Then Maria tried to cover for the woman.

His lip curled with satisfaction. Neither his wife nor the bitch knew anything about the tiny, high-tech camera he'd embedded in the back wall of the safe. Anytime the safe door opened, the camera was triggered and he received notification—and video—on his cell phone.

He shoved his legs into his slacks. By the time he'd

hauled ass back to the house it was too late. He'd just missed the thief getting away with his money. There'd been close to a hundred grand in that safe. *Uncrackable, my ass.* He'd have to pay a visit to the lying, dead man walking who'd sold him that piece of shit. That guy's days were numbered, but he *would* get his money back. As of ten minutes ago, he knew who'd taken it.

Gina Perot.

He watched the recording three times before he recognized her from the fundraiser. The same woman with FBI Special Agent Jack Gates. *That motherfucker.* Confirming she wasn't an agent had been easy enough. He hadn't quite figured out what she was to Gates, but from the way he'd been holding her, he'd bet his ass the guy was fucking her.

I'd fuck her.

He sat on the bed and pulled up the video again on his phone. At first, the image was hazy green. Until Maria had flipped on the lights. Gina fell backward onto one of the bags of cash. The camera had caught her in profile, showcasing one hell of a hot body and a set of perfect tits beneath that skintight ninja suit.

His dick hardened to steel just thinking about her. He snorted. Unlike his wife, this chick would fight him, and that turned him on more. Soon, he'd know everything there was to know about Gina Perot. Thanks to Maria, he had her phone number.

The camera had a wide enough angle lens to record everything. Including the part where Gina wrote down her number and gave it to his wife. A few well-placed smacks and Maria had spilled everything.

His upper lip began twitching uncontrollably. The bitch actually thought she could convince Maria to leave him. That wasn't going to happen. *Ever.*

Glaring at his wife, he ground his teeth. "You'll never leave me." She'd rolled onto her side, facing away from him. He lunged for her shoulder, forcing her onto her back. "Do you hear me?"

"Yes," she cried, nodding as tears spilled from her swollen eye sockets and making her look so hideous he couldn't understand what he ever saw in her.

He raised his arm, and she cringed. His anger melted away as an idea came to him. He unfurled his fingers. Maybe Maria wasn't so worthless after all.

Grabbing his phone, he cued up Rocco's number. "Rocco," he said when the man answered. "Grab Meat and Psycho and get to my place. We've got plans to make." Before Franco returned from Florida for the big meeting this Saturday.

He stood in front of the mirror, buttoning his shirt, and he was actually grinning. By this time tomorrow, he'd have it all. He'd capture the thief who'd been ripping them off and get his money back, something that would elevate him in the eyes of the Commission. Then—and this was the icing on the cake—he'd have Gates's woman.

He'd fuck her until she begged for mercy, then leave her naked, bullet-riddled body in a cornfield. Maybe the same one he'd dumped that agent in. After all, he wasn't nick-named "the Beast" for nothing.

Chapter Nineteen

Gina leaned in to kiss Kinsey's cheek and breathed a sigh of relief. Less than ten hours ago, her friend's complexion had been pasty white, her eyes weary and pain-filled. Color had since returned to her face, and while she still occasionally grimaced, her eyes once again sparkled with life.

"How is Jack taking everything?" Margo asked as she adjusted Kinsey's pillow.

Gina sat in one of the chairs surrounding the bed. "Fine, I guess." Judging by the sated grin on his face after they'd made love again just before he'd left for his office. "He's making arrangements for the Charger's windshield to be replaced, no questions asked. He'll follow me later tonight when I bring it back to the rental company."

Anna yawned. "And?" She'd taken the last shift and was due to leave shortly.

Gina shrugged out of her coat, draping it on the back of a chair. "Then he's driving me to the Center to give Linda the cash."

Kinsey sipped water through a straw. "That's a lot of money to have sitting around."

"I know," she agreed. "They can't put it in the bank, or it will be subject to the audit. Linda said she has a safe place to stash it for now."

"What else?" Margo asked, and three sets of eyes turned to Gina.

Her skin heated at the memory of *what else*. Like the part where she and Jack had hot, wet sex in her bathtub. "Well..." She looked at her hands, praying her friends couldn't see right through her. "He can't use the information I gave him about Jim Spencer's ring." Or his finger.

"Why not?" Anna scrunched up her face. "After what he told us last night, that's what he's been after—rock solid evidence tying Tino to the murder."

That's what she'd thought too. "To use it, he'd have to divulge the source of the information—me—and the circumstances under which I discovered the ring. Eventually, Tino and his attorneys would hear about it." Silence filled the room. "Jack will find another way." Although she wasn't sure how.

Kinsey set her cup on the table. "He's giving up a lot for you, isn't he?" She let the question hang in the air as if there were a more meaningful implication.

Was there? Okay, so they'd made love. Technically, three times. That didn't mean he felt something deeper for her. Despite her adamant disdain for all things FBI, her feelings for him were growing every day. More than they should.

"Did you get any sleep?" Anna asked. "I crashed the second my head hit the pillow. I'm guessing you did too."

"Uh, yeah." Again, she stared at her hands. Not a total lie, but miles from the truth.

"Uh-huh." Kinsey snickered. "You and Jack did the horizontal mambo again, didn't you?"

Heat scorched her face. She really was a terrible liar. Cracking into a high-tech safe was child's play. Lying would never be a skill she acquired.

Margo sat in an empty chair and simply raised her brows. "Does this mean you've gotten over the fact that he's the scourge of the earth?"

"No." She shook her head, but the denial sounded hollow. "But things have changed between us. We're—" What *were* they? She honestly didn't know. They'd made love several times, but always following extreme duress. Was that making love or just sex in the heat of the moment?

"Wonderful together?" Margo's lips twitched.

"Maybe," she said, still not willing or able to admit to anything too deep. Then again...

They'd broken their deal with him, yet he'd shown immense kindness to her and her friends last night. He'd covered for them with the police, and that was huge. She didn't have to be an FBI agent to know how much hot water he could find himself in for doing that. And that barely scratched the surface.

After last night, his investigation might very well be in jeopardy once again. Despite that, he'd held her while she cried in the waiting room and again when she'd spilled her guts in the bathtub. He was always protecting them, always there when they—when *she*—needed him. Not everyone in a person's life did that. Most people in her life hadn't.

"Maybe you should give him a chance." Kinsey squeezed her hand. "At least think about it."

She already was thinking about it, along with his bold, sweet kisses and the way he made her feel when they made love—like she mattered. Like she was precious to him. Was that love? She'd never been in love before. She'd certainly never felt this way about Paul.

"You know," Margo said, resting a hand on her shoulder, "all he's ever done is help us. Help *you*. Stop thinking about that badge in his pocket."

Maybe it *was* time to finally put her father's memory to rest in a way that didn't tie her stomach in knots. If she wasn't willing to take that giant leap of faith, she'd never know if whatever was between her and Jack could turn into something real.

A heavy weight floated from her shoulders. Whatever the future held for them, she wanted to find out.

The evening air was chilly with a light breeze as Jack and Gina left the Center's administrative office in lower Manhattan. He held the door of the SUV while she slid onto the passenger seat.

Today had been a good day. A *quiet* day. Unlike every other since Gina Perot had blown into his life like an F5 tornado. She'd not only ripped the roof off his world but sent it spiraling totally out of control. Yet for some reason he couldn't understand, contentment still surrounded him like a warm blanket whenever they were together.

After getting into the SUV, he turned on the engine and adjusted the dials to blow warm air. Gina's scent filled the truck, reminding him of the way her bedsheets smelled. He hadn't woken in a woman's bed in so long he'd forgotten what it was like.

"Thank you for letting us keep the money." She gifted him with a smile that made his heart flip-flop like a speared fish.

"You're welcome."

Her smile widened, and damned if his heart didn't flip faster.

His cell phone rang and SAC Morrison's name lit the screen. Jack's gut tightened. There was no doubt he was about to get his ass chewed. He cued up the call. Before he could say a word, his boss lit into him.

"How in the world did you get that last bug planted?" Jack held the phone from his ear. "What part about me ordering you *not* to do any fieldwork until you're medically cleared did you *not* understand?"

"An opportunity presented itself, and I took it. Sir," he added, praying the added show of respect would get him some mileage.

"An opportunity?" Sarcasm dripped through the phone. "Do I even want to know?"

He glanced at Gina, who politely pretended not to hear. "Probably not." He'd never reveal the identities of Gina or her friends. Even if it meant withholding information from his boss.

From the heavy breathing on the other end of the phone, Morrison was gearing up for another salvo. *Time to head that off.*

"Did you read the transcript from yesterday?" He already knew Morrison had. The team monitoring the bug in Psycho's house had informed Jack that his SAC had pretty much danced a freaking jig when he'd read it.

"I did."

"Then you know it's gold." Pure gold. As in 24-karat. When he'd told Gina they'd been getting useful intel from the bug, he'd been downplaying it in a big, *big* way. Since then, they'd gotten even more critical information. Now they not only knew the Commission was set to meet five days from now—this Saturday—but they knew its location.

Cottekill, New York, about two hours north of the city. A criminal enterprise meeting of this magnitude hadn't taken place since 1957, and Morrison knew it.

"Yeah, I know, dammit!" his boss boomed, but his voice had lost some of its pissed-off edge.

Morrison would forgive him this transgression because he knew Jack got it done. Based on the transcripts, his boss also knew if they busted up the Commission meeting, they'd net some heavy Mafia players, including a few wanted for murder here in the US and in Italy. If that happened, Morrison would move to the short list for the next FBI directorship. All Jack had to do was let his boss vent.

"When this case is over, we *will* discuss this again!"

The call ended and Jack let out a heavy breath.

"Was that your boss?" Gina asked.

"Yeah." He guided the SUV from the curb, heading north on Broadway.

"Are you in the doghouse?"

He grunted. "When am I not?"

"Are you ever going to tell him what my friends and I did and what happened last night?"

"No," he answered without hesitation. If Morrison ever discovered what she'd seen in Tino's house, she'd never be safe. The FBI would move heaven and earth to get her testimony before a jury, even if it meant forcing her into witness protection. Before last week, he would have too. Now, he couldn't. She'd finally found a family—her friends. WITSEC would take that from her, and she'd have to start over somewhere far away. *Without me.* The selfish part of him couldn't stomach that either.

"Thank you," she said softly, momentarily resting her

hand on his shoulder. "By the way, I still haven't heard from Maria Falzone."

"I don't think you ever will." As much as he wanted Tino's wife to get free of the bastard, he didn't think the woman would call. Good thing because he didn't want Gina anywhere near that situation.

"I hope you're wrong," she said wistfully. "You should have seen her. He'd beaten her. Badly."

Jack didn't doubt that. Tino beating his wife was an extension of the sadistic monster lurking beneath those silk suits. "If she does reach out to you, call me right away. I don't want you meeting with her alone."

His cell phone rang again. *Kyle.* Jack wasn't exactly in the mood to talk to his family right now, not with everything else on his mind. Starting with putting together the biggest ops plan of his career.

"Are you going to answer that?" she asked when the phone had rung three times.

He really did need to stay in touch more with his brothers. With the cast on his hand, he fumbled with the phone, nearly dropping it. "Kyle, what's up?"

"You missed Sunday dinner," Kyle growled. "Again."

He grimaced. Anger from his SAC he could take, but from his brother...that sucked. "Yeah, well, a lot happened last night that I couldn't get out of."

"Did you take care of everything last night, then?" Kyle's tone was matter of fact, but Jack had a bad feeling.

"Yeah." He narrowed his eyes. "Why?"

"I read your draft ops plan," Kyle said. "Seems like it's almost done."

"Yeah," he repeated, narrowing his eyes even more. Instinct told him he wasn't going to like where this call was going.

"Well, good. We postponed dinner last night because Deke and I couldn't make it. It's tonight."

"Shit," Jack muttered.

"Dammit, Jack! Get your head out of your ass and get it to Ma's. Dinner's at six. For chrissake, be there." Kyle hung up.

He groaned as he set the phone in the console. Glancing at Gina, he caught her slightly amused expression. "Heard that, huh?"

"Hard not to. You really *are* in the doghouse tonight." There was both humor *and* sympathy in her tone.

When it rained, it poured buckets. It was pushing seven months since he'd sat down with his family. Maybe it was time. Only now his decision was more complicated. He'd never, *ever* taken a girlfriend to his family's dinner before.

Girlfriend? Was that what Gina was to him?

He turned to her. "Hungry?"

Chapter Twenty

They arrived at his mother's house a little after 6:00 p.m. The first things Gina noticed were the heavenly smells of garlic and herbs and the noise—voices raised in heated discussion, followed by raucous laughter.

"Word of warning. We can get a little loud." Jack hung their coats in a closet, then led her to the dining room.

"Jack! You actually showed up!" A deep voice chuckled.

"About friggin' time," another man said in a decidedly acerbic tone.

"Kyle, language!" a female voice admonished.

When Jack took Gina's hand, pulling her into the dining room and tucking her to his side, the room went so quiet she could have heard a tumbler falling into place. Three sets of eyes pinned her with undisguised shock.

The two men seated at the table exchanged quick glances and shot to their feet. Jack's mother's jaw dropped, but she recovered quickly, wiping her hands on her napkin, then pushing back her chair to rush over and give Jack a big, motherly hug.

Jack released her hand to wrap his mother in a warm embrace, and she instantly felt the loss of his protection. The other two men continued eyeing her—one with outright suspicion, the other with mild curiosity.

"Son, I'm so glad you're here." Jack's mother's voice trembled.

Gina was left with the distinct impression Jack hadn't been to a family dinner in quite a while.

"Ma," he said, releasing his mother and placing a hand at the small of Gina's back. "This is Gina. Gina, this is my mother, Elaina."

She extended her hand to Elaina, who made a dismissive gesture, then engulfed Gina in a hug. For a woman about thirty years Gina's senior and several inches shorter, Jack's mother gave one heck of a hearty embrace.

"Welcome, Gina." She pulled back and smiled. Like Jack, she had gray eyes, but where his were hard and flinty, hers were soft and twinkling with joy.

"Thank you for having me. These are for you." She handed Jack's mother the bouquet of pink calla lilies she'd insisted they stop for at a flower shop.

"How beautiful!" Her lined face brightened as she accepted the bouquet. "Jack, put these in some water for me."

"Yes, Ma." The look on his normally stern face was now adorably gentle as he dutifully accepted the flowers.

Well, whatdya know? As any good son should, Jack had a soft spot for his mother. Gina didn't know why she was so surprised. And he'd just confirmed something. He hadn't been grown in a clandestine laboratory test tube after all.

Jack headed down the hall, turning to give her a wink over his shoulder, one that made her belly flutter like a teenage girl with her first crush. Only it wasn't just a crush. Somehow it had turned into more. So much more. Deep in her heart she knew what was happening, and it was one of the scariest things she'd ever faced. She was falling in love.

"And bring another place setting," Elaina shouted after him.

Only then did she realize the table was set for four, as if Jack's mother had expected—or rather, hoped—he would show.

"Okay, Ma," came Jack's shout.

"Now," Elaina continued, linking arms with her, "these are my other two sons. Kyle and Deacon."

Like Jack, both men were well over six feet and strikingly handsome. The family resemblance was obvious in their muscular physiques, square jawlines, and overall bearing. That's where the resemblance ended.

"Call me Deke." The man's large hand engulfed hers as he shook it, his green eyes warm and smiling. A single dimple appeared out of nowhere on his right cheek. Thick, honey-brown hair gave him a California surfer-dude look. He was the kind of guy any red-blooded female with a pulse would fall head over heels for. "Welcome to our humble house of insanity."

"Thank you," she said. "I hope I'm not intruding."

Deke shook his head. "Not at all. Ma loves the company."

"And I want grandchildren." She guided Gina to where Kyle still stood by his chair, eyeing her like a hawk honing in on his prey right before pouncing. "Lots of them."

Gina nearly stumbled. *Whoa. Grandchildren?* That was jumping the gun just a tad. The woman had known her for less than five minutes.

"Don't worry, dear." She patted Gina's hand. "A mother knows things. And this," she continued without missing a beat, "is Kyle."

A tiny shiver ran up her spine. With hair verging on jet-black and the most amazing eyes—bright gold—he reminded her of an eagle.

"Gina?" Kyle said, and she looked down to see he'd extended his hand.

"Sorry." She'd never seen eyes like that on a human being.

His lips quirked, softening the harsh angles of his sculpted face. "It's all right. I get those kinds of looks a lot."

Heat crept to her cheeks, but she appreciated his understanding. *And, good golly, Miss Molly.* Jack's mother had spawned a brood of the handsomest men she'd ever met.

Elaina chuckled, a low but feminine sound. "We're not sure where Kyle got his eye color. I think they're beautiful." She reached up and pinched his cheek as if he were a ten-year-old.

Kyle gave his mother a gentle smile. "Thanks, Ma."

Deke snorted. "Didn't the milkman have gold eyes?"

"Deacon!" Elaina slapped Deke's shoulder, and he winced, even though Gina was sure he barely felt it.

Jack returned, carrying a plate, silverware, and a napkin that he set on the table opposite the setting clearly meant for him. He held out the chair, waiting for her to sit. As he pushed it in, his hands brushed her upper arms, sending warm tingles to her neck.

"Let's eat," Elaina said, taking her place at the head of the table while Jack sat across from Gina and next to Kyle.

A glass of red wine appeared in front of her, along with a plate piled high with roast pork, potatoes, and root vegetables, all smothered in dark gravy. The meat was beyond tender, the gravy so rich and delicious she had to hold back a sigh of pleasure.

"So how are things going with your ops plan?" she vaguely heard Deke ask.

The next forkfuls were the potatoes and vegetables, so herby and garlicky she couldn't keep from shutting her eyes and practically groaning out loud.

"Good," Jack said as she swallowed the vegetables. "I should have a final draft to send out by tomorrow afternoon."

The second bite of meat sent her taste buds into a tizzy, and this time she did sigh, smiling and closing her eyes as she savored the incredible food.

Conversation ceased. She opened her eyes to find Elaina smiling proudly at her. The men—including Jack—had smirks on their handsome faces. *Whoops.* She set down her fork to take a sip of wine, hoping to douse the heat that had been in her cheeks from creeping up her neck.

"Enjoying dinner, dear?" Elaina's smile broadened.

"Very much," she admitted. "I can't remember the last time I had a home-cooked meal." Probably when her mother was still alive. Despite the beautiful kitchen in her apartment, she rarely had time to cook. "Takeout dinners are my usual fare."

"Bro, you never did say how that happened." Deke tipped his chin to where Jack fumbled to cut a piece of pork. The plastic cast had barely been visible beneath his shirt, but he'd rolled up the sleeves.

"Fractured wrist." He speared the hunk of pork with his fork and shoved it into his mouth. "That's all you need to know."

Elaina gasped. "Is it bad? When did this happen? Will you be all right?"

"*How* did it happen?" Kyle asked.

Jack chewed slowly, then swallowed.

What in the world will he tell his family? Gina wondered. Certainly not the truth.

"Got hit by a car," he answered matter-of-factly.

"Seriously?" Deke snorted. "I hope you nailed the driver's ass."

"Deacon! Language."

Deke grinned sheepishly. "Sorry, Ma."

The corners of Jack's mouth lifted. "Yeah, I nailed them."

Kinsey had been driving, but Gina understood what Jack *wasn't* saying and why he was holding back a full-fledged grin. He *had* nailed them. More specifically, he'd nailed *her*.

Gina nearly choked on the gulp of wine she took next.

"I hope it's nothing serious." Jack's mother eyed his cast warily.

"Anyone know where Lance is?" He looked from Deke to Kyle.

"Nope," Kyle said, and Deke shook his head. "Wherever he is, he's gone dark."

"I worry about all of you boys." A wistful expression overcame Elaina's face. "Not knowing where Lancelot is makes me worry most about him."

Gina raised her brows. *Lancelot?*

As if answering her unspoken question, Jack said, "Ma was going through a Knights of the Round Table phase when little brother was born. The rest of the free world calls him Lance."

"Ah. I see." She grinned. Wherever the missing brother was, she was reasonably certain he was as strikingly handsome as the rest of the Gates boys. *Boys*. Gina stifled a giggle. No one could ever mistake these enormous men for boys.

"Where did you two meet?" Elaina looked from Gina to Jack.

She swallowed her wine, trying not to make an audible gulping sound. Where all couples met these days. In a mobster's closet. *With your son's hand on my breast.*

"At the fundraiser for that women's shelter," Jack supplied, then took a sip of his wine.

Kyle's dark brows drew together. "The one I gave you a check for?"

Something seemed to pass between the two brothers, but she couldn't determine what.

"Gina volunteers there," Jack said, which was true. Kind of. "She helps raise money for them."

Raise? Again, kind of.

Kyle pinned her with those golden eyes, the intensity of which made her heart thump faster.

"It must be expensive to run a shelter," Elaina said.

"It is." She set down her glass. "Most women—and the occasional man—who go to a shelter have nothing. Many have to leave their spouse or significant other with little or no cash and often with only the shirts on their backs. It costs a lot to establish a new life, and that's where we come in."

From across the table, Jack smiled at her. Was that pride in his eyes?

"What happens when the spouse or significant other goes to the shelter looking for them?" Elaina asked.

Gina was about to respond when Kyle interrupted. "Shelter locations are kept secret. No one is ever told where these people go when they get set up with a new life." He picked up his wineglass, staring at it without drinking.

"That's right." Gina nodded, sensing a dark undercurrent from Jack's brother. "The shelter may relay a message, but there's never any direct contact."

"Ever," Kyle added.

The woman in Chicago? Jack had said his brother saved her from a vicious beating, then she went into the system and disappeared. Judging from the faraway look in Kyle's eyes, she really had been important to him. Perhaps, she still was.

Thirty minutes later, Jack and Deke helped their mother clear the dishes and went into the kitchen, leaving Gina with Kyle to set out dessert plates and coffee cups.

"It's a good thing you're doing." Kyle pulled out fresh paper napkins from a sideboard. "People are clueless about the cash flow required to make the program work."

"You know someone who went into the system," she said softly. "Don't you?"

He stopped setting out the napkins and raised his head. This time, she didn't flinch under his unnerving golden stare. There was pain in his eyes, as surely as if it was stamped on his forehead. "She was...a friend." He resumed placing the napkins on the table.

She'd bet they were more than friends. "How long has it been since you've seen her?"

"Ten years."

She began setting out the plates. "Did you ever make a request to have a message relayed to her?"

"No."

"Why not?" She paused before putting down another plate.

He shook his head. "It's better this way."

"How so?" she prodded. "If she cares about you—"

"It's complicated. But thanks." As he set down the last

napkin, he gave her a fleeting smile, then went into the kitchen.

Her heart went out to him. She understood how difficult it was when someone you loved disappeared from your life. Whatever had happened between him and this woman was meaningful enough to last over a decade. That kind of emotion could only be one thing: love.

Was that really what she felt for Jack? The feeling of impending loss struck as surely as if she'd been run over by a truck. If he disappeared from her life, she had a horrible suspicion she'd be just as tormented as Kyle was. Acknowledging that sent a bolt of fear directly to her heart.

Drawn by laughter, she headed for the kitchen. The atmosphere inside the Gates family home was everything she was missing in her life. Everything she'd been robbed of when her parents were taken from her.

Pausing in the doorway, she watched Jack and his brothers huddled together like little boys, joking about something while their mother finished slathering white frosting on a giant layer cake.

Somehow, Jack being an FBI agent was beginning to matter less and less. The man beneath the badge was starting to matter more.

Catching sight of her in the doorway, the men lifted their heads. Kyle whispered something to Jack, and Deke grinned. Jack's expression went utterly blank as he continued staring at her. Then he smiled, his eyes sparking with something she'd never seen before. Whatever it was, it made her heart flutter wildly, and suddenly the idea of giving Elaina grandchildren wasn't so frightening.

"Am I ever going to see where *you* live?" Gina unlocked the door to her apartment. They hadn't discussed it, but his coming home with her seemed so natural.

Home. This was *her* home. It was too soon, but did she want it to be his, too, someday?

Jack didn't answer right away. He watched her, his expression once again inscrutable. "You really want to see it?"

"Yes." She flicked on the foyer light, tossing a flirty grin over her shoulder. "For all I know, you could be some kind of weirdo with a clown fetish or"—she hooked her fingers into quotation marks—"have a 'red room'." In truth, she just wanted to see his home. He kept that part of his life separate from hers, and she wanted to know all there was about him.

He stared unsmiling at her from across the foyer, but his eyes lit with banked humor. "Red rooms are for guys that can't get it up any other way. I don't need one to satisfy me *or* my woman."

"Really?" She took off her coat and hung it in the closet. She loved the witty banter that sprang so easily between them.

"Haven't I already proven myself?" He shrugged out of his jacket and reached over her shoulder to drape it on a hook on the closet door. As he did, he intentionally brushed his arm against her breast, making her shudder.

She closed the door. "How do I know that wasn't a one-shot deal?"

"One shot?" He gave a snort of disgust. "I believe I've made it clear that it wasn't."

"Maybe I need periodic reminders." She stepped back and pulled her sweater over her head, knowing he'd like what he saw.

His nostrils flared. Beneath the warm, bulky purple sweater, she wore a black, low-cut, lacy-edged bra that barely covered her nipples. His eyes darkened like a storm cloud ready to unleash everything it held inside.

He advanced on her slowly, and with each step he took forward, she took one back until they were in her bedroom. Foreplay she'd had before but never like this—teasing, tantalizing, and their bodies were still three feet apart. Electricity hummed and sparked between them. This was fun, exciting, and sexy. Like him.

The backs of her legs hit the edge of the bed. Without touching her anywhere else, Jack began kissing her neck.

"If you really want to see where I live," he said, his deep rumbly words like a warm, gossamer caress on her skin, "I'll take you there."

Her body trembled with need she could barely contain. "Okay." If he didn't put his hands on her soon, she'd scream.

"Not right this second." He backed away. "Take off your pants."

"Why don't *you* take them off?" she teased, really, *really* wanting his big hands all over her.

Slowly, he shook his head. "I'm calling the shots."

"Ooh, bossy tonight, aren't we, Special Agent Gates?"

He grinned wickedly. "I keep telling you. It's an FBI thing."

She could totally buy into this change of plans. *Game on, big guy.* She kicked off her shoes, then unzipped her jeans and slid them down her legs. Bent over as she was, Gina knew he was getting an eyeful of her breasts. She tugged off her jeans and socks, tossing them aside.

As he took in her tiny matching black panties, his mouth parted and he took a deep shuddering breath. "You are so incredibly beautiful."

His appreciative words went straight to her core, lighting up every feminine part of her body that wanted him deep inside her.

He swallowed, his nostrils flaring wider. "Touch your breasts."

She did as he ordered, cupping her breasts and pinching her nipples through the lacy fabric. A ripple of lust zinged from her head to her toes. Not from her hands on her body. From watching *him* while she did it.

The thick bulge behind the zipper of his pants told her how turned on he was. His eyes had gone smoky gray, backlit with so much lust and desire she could practically feel it on her skin, stroking and licking every square inch.

"Take off your bra." His voice was gravelly, commanding.

Reaching behind her, she unhooked her bra and let it fall to the rug. Cool air washed over her nipples, making them pucker and tighten.

He swallowed. "Now your panties."

A thrill ran through her, and she did as he ordered.

"I want to watch you pleasure yourself," he said. "Do it now."

Parting her legs a few inches, she ran her middle finger between her pussy lips, finding her plump, throbbing clit. She was wet and totally turned on.

"Push your finger inside." His eyes were glued to her hand. "Pinch your nipple."

Yes, sir. She pushed her middle finger deep inside her wet folds, undulating her hips and pinching one of her nipples. She let her head fall back, gasping as waves of pleasure converged in her core. He was absolutely right. No red room needed. No whips, chains, or handcuffs. She was on the verge of coming, and he hadn't even touched her.

She took shallow breaths, plunging her finger faster, rocking harder against her hand.

"Stop!" His voice was tight. "Get on the bed."

Yessiree. She sat on the bed and started scooting back when he clasped her ankles, kneeling on the floor as he tugged her hips to the edge of the mattress and draped her legs over his shoulders.

He fastened his mouth on her wet folds, sucking, biting, nibbling until she writhed and moaned, gripping the duvet in clenched hands. He drove her to the brink of a sexual precipice so intense she nearly screamed. When he pushed two fingers inside her and began pumping to the rhythm of his tongue sucking on her clit, she gasped at the powerful spasms rocketing to her core.

"Jack, I'm going to come!" She arched her back and cried out as the orgasm blasted through her. He fastened his mouth tighter, drawing out the near-painful ecstasy and making her body jerk from wave after wave of pleasure.

Her mind went completely blank. The pounding she heard and felt was her pulse roaring in her ears and her heart thumping wildly in her chest. She could barely draw in a breath. That uneven, raspy sound was her own pathetic effort at breathing.

They should write books about the orgasm Jack had just given her. Sexy, erotic, no-holds-barred, tell all books with diagrams and instructions, because that orgasm had been world class.

Slowly, she opened her eyes. Jack's lips tipped up in a smug, satisfied grin. The man definitely took pride in his work, and she wasn't just referring to his abilities as an agent. With the same appreciation he'd shown her while she'd stripped out of her clothes, she watched him do the same as he peeled off his shirt and jeans, taking in his powerful shoulders and thickly muscled chest and arms.

His cock hung low, thick and fully erect as he tore open a wrapper and rolled on a condom. She'd expected him to push into her and take her hard and fast, but he didn't.

Bracing his arms on either side of her face, he lowered gently on top of her, tucking wayward strands of hair from her face and kissing her softly on the lips. She looped her arms around his waist and dragged her nails up and down his back, loving the ripple and play of his body beneath her fingertips.

He deepened the kiss, slipping his tongue inside her mouth. His erection pressed against her hip, but still he made no effort to enter her. "You okay?"

"Mmm," she mumbled, loving his masculine scent and the minty taste of his kisses. "Never better." Never in a million years, would she have expected anything to happen between them. "I need to ask you something."

He continued dropping kisses on her neck. "What?"

"What were you and your brothers talking about in the kitchen when I walked in?" She'd meant to ask him that on the ride home but had chickened out. Whatever they'd been discussing, it had seemed like a private matter.

He lifted his head. For a long moment, he said nothing. Then he stroked his fingers down her cheek. "They told me that I shouldn't let you go."

As it had at his mother's house, her belly fluttered. "And what did you say to them?" she whispered.

"That maybe they were right." He lowered his head again, kissing her as he nudged her legs apart and entered her, filling her core and stretching her walls.

She sighed, rocking her hips to meet his rhythmic thrusts. The merging of their bodies was different this time, not fast and furious but equally amazing in its sweetness and tenderness.

He clasped the sides of her face, watching her as they both neared their release. In his warm gray eyes, she saw everything she'd ever wanted. Home. Family. The future. And just like that, she tumbled head over heels and fell in love. With an FBI agent.

Chapter Twenty-One

Jack woke to light streaming through the windows. Gina's head rested on his chest, her arm draped over his rib cage and thick waves of her chestnut hair tickling his abs.

As he sifted his fingers through the strands, that now-familiar sense of peace surrounded him. Along with a life-changing realization. His brothers were right. He shouldn't let her go. More importantly, he didn't *want* to let her go. Somehow amid the darkness, danger, and chaos that his life had become, he'd found something special. A perfect rose in a garden of thorns.

Gina stirred and lifted her head. Sleepy eyes met his. "Hi," she said, and when she smiled, his heart tumbled over and over. He was falling in love. With the most complicated woman he'd ever met.

"Hi, yourself." He dropped a kiss on her forehead. Waking up like this, with her naked body using his as a pillow... *Yeah, I can totally wrap my head around this.*

"Are you hungry?" She glanced at a small digital clock on the nightstand. "It's only seven. I can scramble some eggs."

He *was* hungry. Not for eggs. He rolled her onto her back, gazing down at her for a long moment without saying anything.

An impish grin lifted her lips. "Why are you looking at me like you want to dissect my brain?"

"Is that the way I look?" He'd always been careful to keep emotions from his face. He suspected he'd never be capable of hiding anything from her again—a dangerous position to be in.

"Yeah, it is." She snaked her hands to his back, then lower, squeezing his butt cheeks.

Blood surged to his cock and balls, and he shuddered. Her hands on his body first thing in the morning was better than coffee, scrambled eggs, a Denny's Grand Slam breakfast, or anything else he could think of.

He wondered if she felt the same way. No way could he have misread all the emotions pinging between them last night. It hadn't just been passion hot enough to singe the paint off the walls. They *had* something.

"Well?" She began massaging his ass and pulling his groin tighter against her hip. "Are you going to tell me?"

He kissed her, cupping one supple breast and rolling the taut nipple between his fingers. The urge to tell her that he loved her pounded inside his head. It was too soon, and the timing sucked. His workweek was about to go off-the-charts insane. With the Commission meeting this Saturday and an ops plan involving over a hundred law enforcement officers from three states, he'd be pulling all-nighters until then and dealing with the fallout for weeks afterward. Big cases, big headaches.

"Mmm," she moaned into his mouth, arching her breast into his hand. "That feels really, *really* nice."

"It sure does." It was about to feel even nicer. His dick

was as stiff as a telephone pole. He touched his fingers to her already-wet folds and positioned himself at her entrance.

Something vibrated. His phone. With everything going on, he couldn't risk ignoring a single call. Not even when he had a beautiful woman beneath him and he was about to explode.

He groaned and reached for his cell. The number on the screen wasn't familiar to him. *Robo-call?* Not *this* early in the morning. Using his thumb, he swiped to take the call. "Gates."

"Special *Agent* Gates?" an unfamiliar voice said.

"Who's asking?" The only people who had his number were FBI personnel and those he knew and trusted, which was a very small circle.

A pause. Sounds of motor vehicles and jet engines came through the phone. "My name is Danny Viggiani. I hear you're looking for me."

Jack's heart thumped faster. This was the witness he'd never expected to hear from—the one who might have witnessed Jim Spencer's murder. He'd given Meat permission to give Viggiani his phone number if the guy ever surfaced and was willing to talk. Neither of which he actually expected to happen.

He rolled off Gina and sat on the edge of the bed. She rose up on one elbow, watching him with concern.

Another roar through the phone told him the guy was at an airport. "Where are you?"

"JFK, but not for long. I can't afford to stay out in the open. As soon as Tino gets word I'm back in the US, he'll come looking for me."

That jibed with Jack's information. On Tino's orders, Viggiani had been directed to Sicily and to stay there until the heat over Jim's murder died down. Apparently, Tino didn't trust his own men not to dime him out. With good reason.

"What was Jim Spencer wearing when he died?" He had to be sure this guy wasn't lying. He wouldn't be the first Mafia witness to perjure himself in exchange for a pass on other crimes. Like aiding and abetting the cold-blooded murder of a federal agent by dumping the body in a field. Jack's information was that Viggiani and Psycho Fiori not only witnessed the murder but followed Tino's orders to make Jim's body disappear.

"Black pants and a blue polo shirt."

He gripped the phone tighter. Very few people knew what Jim had been wearing that day, and his clothes had never been returned to his wife. No photos were ever released, nor would they be. The file was still classified.

Adrenaline pumped harder through Jack's veins. His gut told him Viggiani was telling the truth, but he had to be sure. "What else can you tell me about the body?"

"Tino cut off the guy's finger, wedding ring and all. Had a green stone in the ring. The sick bastard keeps it in the safe at his shore house. I've seen it there myself."

Bingo. Viggiani just confirmed what Gina had seen. The guy was legitimate. His testimony and a search warrant at Tino's shore house would get him the PC he needed to arrest Tino for murdering a federal agent. He had to act fast before Tino emptied out the safe. He also had to grab this witness before he disappeared in the wind. Or Tino killed him.

Viggiani's return to the states without sanction would be a red flag that he was about to throw Tino under the bus. According to Meat, Tino trusted Psycho Fiori with his life but wasn't certain about Viggiani's loyalties.

"Stay at the airport," Jack ordered, reaching for his pants. "Go back inside the terminal, get to a restaurant, and stay put. I'll call you when I get there." He ended the call, shoving his legs into his pants and searching for his socks.

Gina sat up, clutching the sheet to her breasts. "Is everything all right?"

"Better than all right." Everything was kick-ass. By the end of the day, Tino Falzone would be behind bars.

He tugged his shirt over his head, then sat on the bed again to phone Smitty before calling SAC Morrison. In addition to the op on Saturday, he needed Smitty's help scooping up Viggiani and finding a safe place to stash the guy.

She touched his arm as he cued up Smitty's number. No sooner did he drop a quick kiss on her lips than his partner answered.

"You on your way in?" Smitty asked. "I've got bad news and some seriously interesting news. Which do you want first?"

Jack stiffened. "Give me the bad news first."

"Your clownfish—John Wayne—died yesterday."

Some of the adrenaline bled from his veins. Ten years was a long time for a clownfish to live in captivity, but he'd miss the little guy.

"Where is he?" Jack asked.

"I wrapped him up and put him in the freezer. In case you want to give him a proper burial. ASAC Standish wanted me to flush him down the toilet, but I convinced him not to."

"Thanks, man." If Standish so much as touched John Wayne, he'd ram *his* head down the toilet.

His chest felt tight. *For chrissake, it's just a fish.* He'd known it was coming, but now Annie Oakley was alone.

When things died down, he'd have to get her a new companion.

"What's the seriously interesting news?" He cradled the phone between his chin and shoulder, tugging on his socks.

"Remember that in-depth background check you ordered on Gina Perot because her records only went back twelve years?"

He'd been about to pull on his last sock but froze. He glanced at Gina, who still watched him silently. "Yeah?"

"If you aren't sitting down, you might want to."

Whatever Smitty was about to tell him, he doubted sitting would help. He stood and began pacing the bedroom. As if sensing his need for privacy, Gina rose and went into the bathroom.

"She still has no criminal record," Smitty continued. "The thing is, twelve years ago, Gina Perot had her name legally changed. Her real name is Angelina Perotti. Her father was..."

Jack stopped pacing and froze. "Tony Perotti," he whispered at the same time Smitty said the name. The bookie Franco Falzone murdered when he was caught wearing a wire—*Jack's* wire.

A sick feeling welled up from the pit of his stomach. *No. Oh, hell, no.* He sank onto a chair. This couldn't be happening.

On more than one occasion, he'd thought Gina looked familiar. That night at the fundraiser, even Franco Falzone had thought the same thing. Now he knew why.

I sent her father to his death.

That sick feeling began burning a hole in his gut. An image of a young girl, barely eighteen years old, came to him. Angelina Perotti, holding her mother's hand, tears streaming down their faces as her father's coffin was lowered into the ground. Her face had matured since then, her gangly teenage body filled out with graceful curves.

"You there?" came Smitty's voice.

"Yeah," he choked out, too stunned to say anything more. With the utterance of one name, his entire world was spinning completely out of control, and there wasn't a thing he could do to stop it. But he had responsibilities that couldn't wait. "We have to get to JFK. I'll pick you up outside 26 Fed in forty minutes."

He ended the call, his mind a jumbled mess. He would have told Smitty twenty minutes, but he couldn't just leave. Keeping a secret of this magnitude would only fester until it consumed him. What would Gina say when he told her he was the case agent who'd sent her father to his death? She'd hate him for all eternity.

As he lowered his head in his hands, it felt as if it weighed a hundred pounds. His heart was seconds from cracking in two.

He'd lose Gina. And he'd only just found her.

The bathroom door opened. Gina held a glass of water and wore the same green satiny robe that draped so lovingly over every one of her curves. He soaked in her beauty like a dying man. This might be the last time she'd ever look at him without hating his guts.

Her eyes widened as she set the glass on the bureau, then rushed over to kneel in front of him. "What's wrong?"

He swallowed as a giant lump lodged securely in his throat. The shroud of guilt that had plagued him for fifteen years tore open. He *had* done it right. She wouldn't see it that way.

"For god's sake, tell me what's wrong." She rested her hands on his knees and gasped. "Is it Kinsey? Did something happen to her?"

"No, it's not about Kinsey." Her question snapped him out of his stupor.

"Then what is it? I can tell something's happened. Please, Jack. *Tell me.*"

Without looking up, he clasped her hands, interlacing their fingers. There was no sense putting off the inevitable. "Angelina Perotti," he whispered.

The fear faded from her eyes, replaced by shock. She yanked her hands from his, and he let her go. Slowly, she rose to her feet. "How did you find out?"

"When I first met you, I ran a background check. It just took a while to come through."

Her shoulders slumped as she nodded. "That's part of what I didn't want to talk about. After my mother died, I changed my name because I couldn't get away from the stigma of being the daughter of a mob bookie. Despite what he did, I loved my father very much, and he didn't deserve to die the way he did."

"I know," he said quietly, letting his words sink in. He knew the very moment when they did.

Her brows lowered, her eyes lasering into him like a double-barrel shotgun coming on target. "*What* do you know?"

Part of him wanted to lie or say nothing. As much as it killed him, he had to tell her. "I knew your father."

Her nostrils flared. "How?" she asked tightly.

"He got caught up in a small sting operation. It was the first case I ran independently as an agent." He could barely choke out the words. "I was the arresting officer."

For a moment, her face went slack. "It was you," she whispered. "You forced him to wear a wire. You didn't give him a choice. It was either that or go to prison. And then *you* sent him to Franco Falzone."

The breath he took next was so painful it might as well have been poison gas. "Yes."

Her body trembled. She clenched her hands into tight fists. "*You* killed him."

"Dammit, Gina!" He bolted from the chair to grip her forearms. "I'm sorry. You have no *idea* how sorry I am."

She attempted to extricate herself from his grip, but he wouldn't let her.

Her eyes went wild and stormy, like the Atlantic in a hurricane. "How long have you known? How *long*?"

When she tried jerking away from him again, he let her go. "Two minutes."

"How could you do that to him?" Her trembling intensified, and her knuckles went white. "Why did you force him to wear that wire? *Why*, Jack? He wasn't a hardened criminal. He had a wife and a daughter he loved. *Me*." She jabbed a finger at her chest, then advanced on him. "Because of you, I have no father. If my father were still alive, my mother wouldn't have taken up with a man who beat her to death."

Jack knew her mother was dead but hadn't known how she'd died. Now he felt even worse. He dragged a hand down his face. "If I could change the past, I would. But I can't." The look of fury on her face ripped into his heart like nothing else could.

"No. You *can't*." She stood less than six inches from him, but it felt like a mile, and she was slipping further from his life with every passing second.

"Gina, please." He didn't know what to say or do to make her believe him, to help her understand that this was the world he lived and worked in, and it had been her father's world too.

She took a step back. "You and Franco took *everything* from me. Everyone I held dear and loved."

"*I* wasn't the one who pulled the trigger." The words sounded stupid, even to him. He had nothing else left in his arsenal.

"How can you say that?" Tears streamed down her pale cheeks, each one gutting him as surely as a knife strike. "*You* put him in front of the gun. *You* put him in front of that bullet. Just like I did to Kinsey. *That* will always be *my* fault."

Jack exhaled a short breath. He'd been hoping they'd gotten past that trail of guilt. It would suck hearing it, but she had to hear the truth. "Your father was working off criminal charges. He got caught up in the system, and—"

"The system?" Her eyes widened. "The *system?*" She lunged for him, pounding at his chest with her fists, and he let her. "You bastard," she cried, and kept pounding until her hits lessened in strength and she crumpled to the floor, covering her face with her hands while she cried.

Jack gritted his teeth. She was in pain, and he was the cause. There was nothing he wanted more than to pick her up off the floor, cradle her against him, and find a way to make her love him the way *he* loved her. That wasn't possible now. Or ever.

Just when he'd convinced himself otherwise, doubt crowded in. Maybe he *had* killed her father. As surely as Franco had pulled the trigger.

"Get out," she said quietly, then with more volume until she was shouting at the top of her lungs. "Get out, get out, *get out!*" she screamed.

He couldn't believe it had come to this. Numbly, he shoved his feet into his shoes, then collected the rest of his clothes and his weapon. Gina remained on the floor, staring glassy-eyed at her fists. This wasn't the right time to tell her, but he might not get another chance. "There's one more thing you should know." She lifted her red, watery gaze to his. "I love you. I love you so much..." *It hurts.* More than that. He loved her so much it was killing him.

Her eyes widened a fraction, flaring with acknowledgment. Little by little, the light in them died. "Get out," she said in a voice completely devoid of emotion.

His heart thudded dully in his chest. He resisted the urge to shake some sense into her, to convince her they could get past this. The vacant look in her eyes told him otherwise. He was a man of action, and he was utterly powerless to fix the mess he'd created. Fate really was a bitch.

He turned and walked out of the bedroom, rubbing the center of his chest with his palm. The grandfather clock ticked away in the foyer, reminding him of all the time he and Gina had shared and all the time they never would. He stepped outside the apartment and into the hallway, closing the door behind him and feeling as if he were leaving his entire world behind. Five minutes ago, he'd stupidly, naively imagined having a life with the woman he loved. Now, he had nothing.

Anger balled in his gut at how many lives the Falzones had destroyed over the decades. He punched the elevator button so hard the plastic cover cracked. When the elevator arrived, he walked in and leaned against the wall.

Without knowing it, the Falzones had extracted the ultimate vendetta against him. They'd taken away what he loved and cherished most.

Gina.

Chapter Twenty-Two

Gina's head pounded and her heart ached with so much grief she could barely draw a breath. The front door clicked shut as Jack walked out, taking what was left of that stupid, beating muscle in her chest with him.

I love you. Words that should have made her heart flutter madly with joy. Instead, they killed everything inside her.

Her stomach lurched violently, and she covered her mouth with her hand and raced into the bathroom. Falling to her knees, she flipped up the toilet seat lid and heaved the few sips of water she'd downed only minutes ago.

Jack had been the nameless, faceless man she'd hated all this time. She still couldn't believe it. Neither did her stomach, which racked with violent dry heaves. She crumpled to her side on the floor, wrapping her arms tightly around her body. Tears flowed like twin rivers from her eyes.

Why, of all people, did it have to be him? The man she'd fallen inescapably in love with.

To hear him say he loved her after what he'd confessed made a mockery of everything they'd shared.

How was this even possible? He had to have been so young when her father died, probably no more than twenty-three. How could she love *and* hate someone so much at the same time?

Absently, she rubbed her arms as the chill from the cold tile floor began seeping into her. Never in her worst nightmares could she have imagined Jack was behind the death of her father. He'd admitted it, and she had to accept it.

Her body shook with renewed sobs, and she pulled her knees to her chest, tucking into a tight ball and trying to muffle the wounded animal sounds emanating from her throat.

She lay there for several minutes until her sobs lessened and she could think somewhat clearly again. She'd get through this. After losing her parents, she'd reinvented herself and made a new life. She could do it again.

If only her heart didn't hurt so badly that she wanted to cut it from her chest with a knife. Life would go on, because it had to. Even while she was dying inside.

Pushing from the floor, she rose on unsteady legs and rested her palms on the vanity. The face staring back at her in the mirror was red and wet with tears. She licked her lips, imagining she could still taste his as he'd kissed her with a passion she never knew existed.

"No," she said, softly at first. "No, no, *no!*" She cranked on the tap, splashing water in her face, as if she could wash away his taste, his scent, everything about him. It didn't work. Every poignant memory was permanently burned into her mind and her very soul.

More tears stung the backs of her eyes. Crying over something she couldn't change was a waste of...well, everything.

She grabbed a towel from the ring on the wall. When

she pressed the fluffy terrycloth tightly to her face her heart gave another painful squeeze. He must have used this towel, because she could still smell him on it.

Low ringing filtered into the bathroom, dragging her out of her pity-fest. She went into the foyer and dug the phone from her shoulder bag. A number with the 718 area code lit the screen. Normally, she'd let unknown numbers go to voicemail. A niggling feeling she couldn't explain had her swiping to take the call.

"Hello?"

The barest intake of breath came through the phone. "This is Maria. Maria Falzone."

Gina tightened her grip. She hadn't wanted to admit it, but even she'd begun to think Maria would never reach out to her. "I'm glad you called. Are you all right?"

"Um, yes," she said in a hushed tone. "But I can't take it anymore. I want to leave my husband. If he ever finds out I called you, he'll kill me. *Please*, can you help me?"

Leaving Maria alone with that bastard husband of hers a moment longer wasn't an option. A lot of logistics had to be set in motion to make this happen.

"Are you really ready to leave him? Today?" Many people needed more convincing and time for the full implications of leaving their spouse to sink in before actually going through with it. Others simply made the decision and were ready to act on it immediately. She hadn't figured Maria Falzone to fall into the latter category.

"I'm not sure," Maria said, her voice hesitant. "I think so. Yes."

"Where are you?" She opened a drawer in the foyer table and pulled out a pen and pad. "I can pick you up at noon." She had to call Linda Hernandez and make arrangements so there'd be a spot for Maria at the Center and a plan in place to protect her.

"No! We're leaving for the airport at ten o'clock to go to Florida. I can't spend another minute with him. I have to get away from him *now*."

"All right. Stay calm." The quick timeframe wasn't ideal, but she'd make it work. "Do you have a car?"

"No."

"Where are you now?"

"Staten Island. At my father-in-law's house."

Gina's hand stilled. Maria was calling from Franco Falzone's mansion in Todt Hill on Staten Island.

"I can walk somewhere nearby and meet you," Maria said. "Willow Swamp Park, by the entrance to the bike trail. Do you know where the park is?"

"Yes." She glanced at the clock. It was seven thirty. "I can be there by nine. Will you be able to slip away?"

"I have to," she whimpered.

"I'll be there. I promise." She jotted down the location. "And Maria? My name is Gina."

"Thank you, Gina."

When the call ended, she stared at the phone. She couldn't fix her own life, but she'd do everything in her power to fix Maria's. Or at least hook her up with people who could.

She untied her robe and quickly dressed in slacks and a blouse. The more she thought about it, the more Maria's call surprised her. From their brief encounter, she'd have pegged the woman as needing significant coaxing before leaving her husband. *Kudos to you, Maria Falzone.*

After tugging on a pair of low-heeled boots, she called Margo. There was no way she'd reach out to Jack for help, nor would she ever risk putting her friends in danger again.

Still, wisdom dictated she inform someone what she was doing and where she was going.

"Morning," Margo answered.

"You won't believe who I'm on my way to pick up," she replied without preamble. "Maria Falzone."

"*What?*" Margo's shock echoed in Gina's ear.

"You heard me." She grabbed her coat from the closet. "I'm just as surprised as you are. She wants help leaving Tino."

"Is Jack with you?"

She flinched, mentally *and* physically. Hearing his name had the same effect as ripping a Band-Aid off a raw, bleeding wound. Her resolve nearly crumbled on the spot. "No. He's out of the picture and I'm going alone."

"What do you mean, he's out of the picture?"

"We..." *What, broke up?* They'd never even dated, so how in the world had he made her fall in love with him? Who was she kidding? He hadn't *made* her fall in love. She'd taken that leap all by herself. Naive fool that she was. "Whatever we had, it's over. I'll fill you in later."

"Okay, but you still can't meet her alone," Margo insisted. "It's too dangerous. Annabelle and I will go with you."

She opened her mouth to give Margo the location at the park where she was meeting Maria but stopped.

These women really were her family. They hadn't abandoned her after she'd told them everything, and they weren't abandoning her now. All the more reason why she couldn't accept their help. There was no way she'd put any of them in front of a speeding bullet again. This was a dangerous situation she'd created, and she alone would clean it up.

Gina shook her head. "No. This is something I have to do on my own."

"No. It's not!" A car door slammed. "I'm going to get Anna. Tell me where to meet you."

She swallowed the lump in her throat.

"I'll be fine." At least she hoped she would be. "I'll call you after I get Maria settled at the Center."

"Gina wait—"

She ended the call and took a deep breath. There was no point in dragging out the conversation. She was going alone, and that was that. Besides, there wasn't much time, and she still had to contact Linda. With finality, she slammed her apartment door behind her and hastily made her way to the elevator bank.

There'd been no opportunity to save her father or her mother, but she'd give everything she had to make sure Maria Falzone at least stood a fighting chance.

Chapter Twenty-Three

Jack parked at the end of the curb at JFK's Terminal 8. He tossed a placard on the dashboard, turning to see the other team of agents pulling up behind him and doing the same.

"You've been waiting a long time for this," Smitty said, undoing his seat belt.

Jack fisted his fingers around the plastic cast, expecting to feel pain but didn't. "Too long."

He and Smitty met the other agents—Turner and Pandya—on the sidewalk. Dozens of cabs and private livery cars discharged passengers and their luggage. The sliding doors to the terminal opened and closed nonstop.

Jack had already texted Smitty and the other agents Danny Viggiani's old arrest photo, taken when he'd been hauled in several years ago by the NYPD for selling cocaine —the charge Viggiani wanted to work off by cooperating. "The plan is simple. He's waiting for us at Jo-Jo's Café just outside the checkpoint. We go there, get him out to my vehicle ASAP, then take him straight to the US Attorney's Office to make a statement. Any questions?" Smitty and the others shook their heads. "Let's go."

He led the way inside the terminal, heading to the checkpoint. Adrenaline surged through his system but not with the excitement or gratification he expected, because the moment was bittersweet. He'd lost Gina. There'd be time for whining later. Focusing on getting his witness to the federal prosecutor's office—alive—was the priority.

With Smitty and the other agents directly behind him, he wove through the milling passengers, heading for the café dead ahead. Even as he tried pushing his last conversation with Gina from his head, he couldn't. The more he thought about what he'd lost, the heavier the unsettled feeling surrounding his heart became. Although in truth, he'd never really *had* Gina. Their relationship was a supernova that had shined brightly for one fleeting, glorious moment, only to go completely dark the next and disappear without a trace. As if it had never been there in the first place. He still couldn't believe how their lives had been intertwined all these years, and neither of them had a clue. Until today.

As they neared Jo-Jo's Café, he spotted Viggiani at the bar. The similarities between what he was about to set in motion with Viggiani and what he'd done to Gina's father bit deep into his conscience.

Like Tony Perotti, Viggiani was a criminal cooperating with the FBI to work off some serious charges. Perotti was snuffed out for wearing a wire. Viggiani was about to give a statement that would send Tino Falzone to jail for the next thirty years. So far, Viggiani refused to go into WITSEC. Either way, the guy would have a target on his back for the rest of his life. Somehow, he'd convince the man WITSEC was the only way to survive this.

The closer they got to the café, the more guilt ate at him, but this was business. He needed to shove his personal reservations into a deep, dark hole and keep them there. If there was any other way to nail Tino without someone else getting hurt, he'd do it in a heartbeat.

Twenty feet from the cafe, his cell phone vibrated, and he tugged it from his belt. Margo Kim's number showed on the screen. He kept walking and was about to send the call to voicemail when something stopped him. Throughout his dealings with Gina and her friends, Margo had always been the practical, no-nonsense one. If she was calling him, there had to be a good reason.

Ten feet from the café, he held up his hand to Smitty and the other men to wait while he took the call. "Margo, what is it?"

"Jack, Maria Falzone called Gina this morning. She wants to leave her husband. *Today*. Gina is on her way there now. *Alone*. She refused to tell me where she's going."

His chest tightened. How could she be so foolish and reckless? After what went down between them, he understood why she hadn't called *him*. Why hadn't she at least taken her own friends as backup?

The answer hit him like a sledgehammer. After what happened to Kinsey, she'd never put her friends in danger again. She was riddled with enough guilt to fill a boxcar.

"Jack, are you there?" The worry in Margo's voice cut through the loud sounds of the terminal. "I'm worried. *Really* worried."

"Yeah, I'm here." A knot began twisting in his gut. This was too easy, too quick, and coming directly on the heels of Gina nearly getting caught inside Tino's house. Gina had assured him Tino didn't see her face and that she'd never given Maria her name, but she *did* give the woman her number. He assumed Gina's cell number was private, but with all the invasive online search engines out there, it wouldn't take a forensic expert to easily discover the subscriber name.

"When is she meeting Maria?" He looked inside the café to where Viggiani sat sipping a drink.

"Nine o'clock."

He glanced at his watch. That was in ten minutes. There was still the possibility Maria really did want to leave Tino. Jack didn't believe that. Not so soon, anyway.

"Hold on," he said to Margo, then to Turner and Pandya, "Go keep an eye on him. Brown coat, jeans, second guy from the left at the bar." He jerked his head to the café, and the men took off, leaving Smitty staring at him in bewilderment.

"Tell me something, Margo. From everything Gina said, she couldn't have had more than a five-minute conversation with Maria Falzone. Is it typical for a domestic abuse victim to make such a snap decision?"

"It usually takes more time than this," she said. "Despite the beatings, the belief that a victim can not only leave their abusive partner but make a happy life for themselves takes time to sink in. It does happen once in a while, but no. It's not normal."

Deadly foreboding crept over him. Again, he glanced at the café. The timing couldn't possibly have been worse. Gina might have kicked him out of her life, but he still loved her with every beat of his heart and every breath he took.

"I'll find her, Margo. I'm leaving now." He clipped the phone back on his belt.

"You're *leaving*?" Smitty narrowed his eyes. "This is everything you've wanted. Everything you've been working for."

Not everything. Falling in love had altered his priorities.

"I have to go." He hadn't kept Tony Perotti safe, but he

intended to protect the man's daughter. "I've got a fifteen-year-old debt to repay." He clapped his hand on Smitty's shoulder. "You've got this. Get this guy to the US Attorney's Office, take his statement, and get started on the charging document. Keep Viggiani there, and I'll call you later." The last things he saw before bolting to the sliding doors were Smitty's eyes bulging and his brows hitting his hairline.

He raced from the terminal and hit the sidewalk at a dead run. He had absolute faith his partner and the other team would get the job done. Like Gina, he'd keep his friends out of the mess he'd created because he had no idea how all this would end. First, he had to find Gina.

Once inside his SUV, he called her cell, knowing it was unlikely she'd pick up. Sure enough, his call went directly to voicemail. "Gina, it's Jack. Don't do this. Do *not* meet Maria Falzone alone. It could be a setup. I know you hate my guts, but you need backup. Tell me where you're going, and I'll meet you there. Call me back, *dammit!*"

The Expedition's digital clock read 8:52. He was running out of time, and with each passing second, he was more convinced something was off about Maria calling Gina out of the blue.

He pulled up a photo on his phone that he'd taken of Gina's Porsche Cayenne in the garage. After jotting down the tag number on a piece of paper, he punched in the number for the NYPD's Real Time Crime Center.

"Detective Salazar," a gruff voice answered.

"This is FBI Special Agent Jack Gates. I have an emergency. I need LPRs on a tag starting today at 0730 through now." He gave the detective Gina's tag. The NYPD had license plate readers and CCTV cameras located all over the city and in every borough. She might not even be in the city anymore, but if he could track her last known location, it might tell him where she was headed.

"Stand by," Salazar said. "What's your email?"

Jack recited his government email address, then began tapping his fingers on the wheel, barely able to keep still. "Give it to me verbally. Start with the last known location."

"Stand by," Salazar repeated. "Pulling it up now."

C'mon, c'mon. Jack glanced repeatedly at the clock.

"At 0836 hours the vehicle was on the Gowanus Expressway heading over the Verrazzano into Staten Island."

Jack waited for another LPR location but was met with silence. "That's it?" That meant she could be anywhere in the island's sixty square miles. JFK was at least forty-five minutes from Staten Island with no traffic. Running hot, he might make it in twenty. He flipped on the strobes and siren to clear a path from the terminal. "Anything else?" He hit the ramp for the JFK Expressway and floored it. The last LPR data was nearly twenty minutes ago on the bridge.

"Negative," Salazar said. "Wait. This just popped up. At 0855 the vehicle went through the intersection of Todt Hill Road and Ocean Terrace, heading east on Ocean Terrace."

Jack's insides vibrated with more fear than he'd known in his entire life. He knew the Todt Hill section of Staten Island like he knew his last name. That intersection was less than a mile from Oceanview Lane. There was only one residence on that road.

The Falzone compound.

Gina could be rash, and she was running on instinct. Still, he couldn't believe she'd meet Maria at Franco's compound. That would be suicide. The meeting had to be somewhere nearby.

"Any more data?" He hit the air horn as he sped onto the Belt Parkway.

"Negative."

Dammit. He pounded on the air horn, scattering cars in front of him. "Detective, I need you to send patrol cars to search the area of that vehicle's last known location. The woman driving it is in danger."

"Copy that," Salazar said. "What can you tell me?"

Not much. All he had was a gut feeling something bad was about to go down. "Just tell patrol to find the driver and keep her safe until I get there. Have them call me when they locate the vehicle." He gave Salazar his cell number. "And ping me if you get any new LPRs."

He hung up and hastily made another call. Mobilizing the entire NYPD on nothing more than a hunch was a bad idea, but he couldn't stand by and do nothing. "Kyle," he said when his brother answered. "I need your help. Gina's in trouble."

Gina pulled over just inside Willow Swamp Park. The park was located in one of the most secluded and rural neighborhoods in New York City. No other cars were visible, and the nearest house was a good quarter mile behind her. She pressed the home button on her phone.

9:05 and still no Maria.

Her phone dinged for the second time in the last ten minutes. *Jack*. He'd left two messages, neither of which she'd listened to. A sensation of emptiness surrounded her. Whatever he wanted, she no longer cared. *Liar*. He was out of her life for good, and that was the way things had to be. If only she could forget him that easily.

She looked behind her at the empty road. When she turned back, a lone figure stood in the tree line not twenty feet away.

Maria Falzone.

Gina stepped out of the Cayenne. Despite the frantic phone call, part of her hadn't thought the woman would show. A gust of wind nearly tugged the car door from her hand before she could close it. She pulled the collar of her wool coat tighter around her neck. Todt Hill was the highest elevation on the Atlantic seaboard south of Maine, and the wind was brutal this time of year.

As she neared the other woman, Gina's blood boiled. Maria's right eye was nearly swollen shut. An ugly purple bruise took up half her face. The bastard must have beaten her for what happened at the shore house.

Maria tugged a phone from her pocket, tapping something into it before putting it back in her coat.

What is she doing?

Gina's scalp tingled. She twisted her neck to look behind her. The road was still empty. The only sound she heard was the wind roaring through the trees.

When she turned back, Maria had stepped a few feet closer. "I'm sorry," she said, her lips trembling.

"Sorry for what?" Had Maria shown up only to back out at the last minute?

Screeching tires cut through the howling wind. A car blew over the top of the rise, bearing down fast. Gina barely had time to jump out of the way as the car skidded to a stop.

"Please, forgive me," Maria cried.

She spun to face the car again. Her blood went as cold as ice.

The vehicle was a cream-colored Cadillac sedan. *Tino's* car.

"No," Gina whispered. *I've been set up.* Stupid didn't begin to describe how she felt.

The car doors opened. Instinctively, she backed up. Tino stood by the driver's door. A lecherous grin curled his upper lip. Two of the largest, bulkiest men she'd ever seen got out of the car. One of them was Rocco. The other man she didn't recognize.

She took off, running across the road to her car. One of the men lunged, snagging the edge of her coat and jerking her back against his chest. She twisted in his grip, but he was so huge it was like being restrained by King Kong.

"Got her, boss."

"Hang on tight, Psycho." Tino slammed his door shut and sauntered closer, as if he were in no hurry. "She's one slippery little bitch."

Psycho? As if Tino wasn't enough of a sadistic killer. This was the infamous Psycho Fiori.

"I had to tell him," Maria cried. "I *had* to." Tears streamed down the woman's face, and she shook harder than the nearby trees getting hammered by the wind.

"Shut up and get in the car," Tino bellowed, pointing to the Caddy.

Maria obeyed like a trained seal, running for the front passenger seat and all but flinging herself inside.

Gina gasped for air, struggling to take in a breath as Psycho tightened his apelike arms. She tried kicking back with her legs until he bit the tip of her ear, holding it between his teeth. "Knock that shit off," he said around her ear, "or I'll chew it off."

Pain shot from her ear to her scalp and she froze. After seeing the body parts in Tino's safe, she believed him. These two men were cut from the same bloody cloth.

Tino stood directly in front of her, so close she could

smell his cloyingly thick musk aftershave. He jerked his head to Rocco. "Check her pockets."

Rocco jammed his beefy hands into her coat pockets, coming up with her cell and handing it to Tino who threw it to the pavement and rammed his heel down on the cover. The phone cracked, its cover shattering into tiny pieces.

"Hold her arms," Tino ordered. "I need to check her for a wire."

Psycho adjusted his grip, pulling her arms behind her back with such force that she cried out.

Tino grabbed the lapels of Gina's coat and ripped it open. Buttons popped off and flew to the ground. His eyes met hers, a dark, fathomless brown and filled with hatred. Before she could blink, he tore open her blouse. Cold air washed over her skin.

"Nope." Tino leered at her breasts. "No wire. Just a great pair of tits." He grabbed her breasts, squeezing viciously and twisting her nipples through the lacy fabric of her bra. She gritted her teeth, squeezing her eyes shut and refusing to give him the satisfaction of letting him know how much it hurt.

"No wonder Gates kept you all to himself." He squeezed again. "You are one fine piece of ass."

Despite the freezing cold biting at her skin, heat flooded her veins, along with a rage she didn't know she had in her. She kicked out, missing her intended target—Tino's balls— and grazing the inside of his thigh.

He jumped back. "Bitch!" he shouted, then backhanded her across the face. Pain lanced through her skull, and stars danced before her eyes. "You'll pay for that." His gaze traveled down her breasts, then lower as he licked his lips. "Get her in the car."

Her belly clenched with absolute fear. There was no mistaking the fate he had in mind for her.

Psycho jerked her off her feet, carrying her to the Caddy and tossing her inside. She lunged for the opposite door's handle when the door was flung open and Rocco cut off her escape. With Psycho on her left and Rocco on her right, she was sandwiched between the two men. Panic bubbled inside her. She tried tugging the sides of her blouse together to cover herself, but it was no use. The shirt was in tatters.

Tino spun the Caddy in a one-eighty and gunned it back down the hill. His eyes met hers in the rearview mirror. She couldn't see his lips, but from the way the skin crinkled at the corners of his eyes, she'd bet he was grinning.

He's going to kill me. She'd been beyond stupid for not letting her friends know where she was going. *No, not stupid.* If Margo and Annabelle had come with her, they'd only wind up dead too.

As the enormity of her situation slammed home, she swallowed the rising bile in her throat. Tino *would* kill her and probably dump her body in a remote part of the city.

First, he'd torture and rape her.

Chapter Twenty-Four

Jack parked behind the patrol car on the outskirts of Willow Swamp Park. While en route, he'd gotten the call from patrol notifying him they'd spotted Gina's Porsche. Kyle and Deke were already there, searching the vehicle.

"Anything?" he asked as he ran over to join them.

"Sorry, bro." Kyle shook his head. "No sign of her."

"Except for this." Deke held up the remnants of a cell phone with its cover bashed to bits, the frame and casing broken in half. "The only other things are these buttons." He pointed to several black buttons scattered on the pavement.

Jack crouched and picked up one of the buttons, turning it over in his hand. It could have come from her coat, but he couldn't be sure. He clenched his hand around the button and stood, searching in all directions. Fear and panic drilled him with enough force he nearly fell to his knees. There was absolutely no proof, but he knew with unerring certainty what had happened.

Tino had Gina.

"You want to file a missing persons report?" one of the uniforms asked.

What he wanted was to tear the island apart until he found her. "Yeah. Gina Perot." He gave a quick description, then indicated to his brothers he needed to speak with them privately, out of earshot of the uniforms.

Kyle's dark brows lowered. "What's really going on, Jack?"

In the interest of time, he hadn't told his brothers much over the phone. Keeping them in the dark was no longer an option. "It's a long story. I found out Gina and her friends are the ones who've been ripping off the Falzones. In exchange for not arresting her, they helped me get one of those bugs planted. Their last break-in was at Tino Falzone's shore house. Gina got away with a hundred grand." Deke whistled. "Yeah, and Maria Falzone caught her in the act. She was beat up badly, so Gina gave Maria her number. Maria arranged to meet Gina here so she could leave the bastard. My guess is Maria never had any intention of leaving, and that it was a setup to get Gina here. Either that, or Tino *convinced* Maria to call Gina."

Kyle nodded in understanding. "Meaning he beat her and forced her to make the call."

"Yeah." Jack nodded. His brother had witnessed the horrors firsthand of what a domestic abuser would do to a woman. "He'll punish Gina for having the audacity to try to take his wife away *and* for stealing from him."

"Jesus." Deke shook his head. "She's got guts. I'll give her that."

Too much, and Jack was afraid it would get her killed.

"Where would he take her?" Kyle asked.

They were standing not half a mile from the Falzone

compound. Would Tino be so stupid as to take her there? Bringing business into Franco's home was a violation of the code. *Don't shit where you eat.* Franco would shit a brick if Tino pulled a stunt like that. But why else would the meet be arranged here?

"Bro?" Deke threw him a look of concern. "Talk to us. Whatever you want us to do, we're in. You know that."

"I do know that." He was more thankful for family than he'd ever been in his life. For what he was about to do, he could kiss his career good bye. He hadn't known how this would go down. Now that he did, he couldn't risk his brothers' careers along with his own. He shook his head.

Kyle held up his hand. "Don't. Don't say it."

"I can't ask you to do this."

"You don't have to." Deke rested a hand on Jack's shoulder. "Do you love her?"

"Yeah. I do."

Kyle rested his hand on Jack's other shoulder. "That's all we need to know. Just tell us the plan."

He gave his brothers a grateful nod. They'd always been there for him, good times and bad. Today was no exception, and today was exceptionally bad. Jack looked over his shoulder at the two cops standing by the patrol car, one of whom was on the radio. He had one shot at this. Calling in a marker of this magnitude might lose him one of the best informants he ever had because it would repay a debt owed to him. None of it mattered if he couldn't save Gina.

He called his informant, and it went right to voicemail. He left a brief message about Gina. "C'mon," he said in a low voice to his brothers. "I think I know where she is. First we need to lose these guys." He'd done more off the books in the last two weeks than in his entire career. What he was about to do now would trump it all. "Let's roll."

He and his brothers ran for the Expedition.

"Hey!" one of the cops shouted. "Where are you going?"

"False alarm." Jack got in and slammed the door shut in the cop's face. The guy pounded on the window, but Jack ignored him and gunned the SUV down the hill. Kyle sat to his right with Deke in the rear seat.

Jack redialed the last number he'd called. "Pick up, *pick up!*" Voicemail kicked on again. "Dammit!" He dropped his cell into the console and pounded the wheel with his bad hand. Pain shot up his arm, and he welcomed it.

"You headed where I think you're headed?" Kyle asked in a deceptively calm voice.

He glanced at Kyle, then caught Deke's face in the rearview mirror. "Yeah."

"Well, then," Deke muttered. "Looks like we're going to war."

Beside him, Kyle nodded.

The address he was heading to was one he knew by heart. Twelve Oceanview Lane—the Falzone compound. If he had to storm the place by force, he'd do it.

The side of Gina's face where Tino had backhanded her throbbed. A strip of duct tape covered her mouth, forcing her to breathe in the stench of oil and gas through her nose.

They were inside Franco Falzone's garage. Seated on a chair with her hands tied behind her back and her coat and blouse gaping wide open, she was so cold her teeth chattered. Not even the residual heat from the engine in Tino's Caddy did anything to warm up the place.

Tino and his men—correction, goons—stood by the

connecting door to the house, talking in hushed voices. Psycho and Rocco were there, along with another goon —Meat—she didn't recognize. Meat's phone rang, the second time in less than five minutes. He glanced at the screen, then shoved it back into his pocket. Maria still sat in the front passenger seat of Tino's car, her shoulders slumped and her head hung low.

Gina clenched her bound hands. *Bastard.* How a man could ever do that to a woman she'd never understand. Maria Falzone was not only physically battered but emotionally beaten to a pulp.

She had to get out of there, and she'd take Maria with her. Easier said than done. Not telling anyone where she'd been going was the right thing to do but had bitten her in the ass. She was alone but refused to give up. Certainly not to these assholes. Slowly, so as not to attract attention, she assessed her surroundings.

The only vehicle in the cavernous three-car garage was the Caddy. Two other vehicles were parked in the circular driveway in front of the house; she'd seen them as they'd driven through the large iron gates.

A wood workbench took up half of the rear wall of the garage, over which hung sheets of pegboard with various tools hanging on silver hooks. Tools she could never get to. Aside from the three closed garage doors, there was only one other way out. The connecting door to the house.

Meat's phone rang again. Again he ignored it. Next to where he and the others stood was a short set of stairs leading to the connecting door. Leaning against the side of the stairs was a large crowbar. Even if she could somehow manage to grab it, with her hands tied as they were, she wouldn't be capable of making any good use of it.

Not for the first time since Tino and his goons had grabbed her, a frisson of fear shot up her spine, only this time it was worse. *I might be totally screwed here.*

She could have told Margo where she was going. She *should* have told Jack. Then she wouldn't be in this no-win situation. Coulda, woulda, shoulda. Three completely useless, after-the-fact words.

"I gotta make a call." Meat headed up the stairs.

"What the fuck, Meat?" Tino's brows slammed together. "Now?"

"Yeah, now." Meat flung his arms wide. "My little girl got in a fight at school. That's a big deal these days. I gotta talk to the principal before she gets expelled." He pushed open the door and disappeared. The door banged shut behind him.

"Jesus Christ," Tino muttered. "Kids. Goddamn pains in the asses."

"Fun making them, though." Psycho chuckled. His eyes lowered, taking in her exposed breasts. "Right?"

Behind the duct tape, Gina gagged. Tino had surrounded himself with an army of disgusting, slimy clones.

"Right." Tino grinned. "Business before pleasure."

He came toward her, and with each step her heart raced faster. When he fisted one of his hands, she tensed, preparing to take a punch to the face, but it never came.

"You stole something from me. From *all* of my men." He canted his head to Rocco and Psycho, who'd come to stand on either side of him. "You didn't know about the camera in my safe, did you?"

Camera? Uh, nope. Maria hadn't necessarily dimed her out, after all. Judging by Maria's apologies, Tino must have forced her to make the call and pretend she wanted to leave him.

"I recognized you from that fundraiser. You were with Gates. Are you his girlfriend? Or is he just fucking you?"

She gritted her teeth, exhaling through her nose. Even if her mouth wasn't covered by duct tape, she wouldn't give him the satisfaction of answering his questions.

"Doesn't matter." He curled his lip. "Whoever you are to him, it will make it that much sweeter when I fuck the shit out of you and leave what's left for him to find. First, you're going to tell me what I want to know."

She couldn't suppress the shudder that ran through her body. The idea of him touching her was so repugnant, she nearly gagged.

With one painful yank, he tore off the duct tape, leaving the skin around her lips stinging.

"Where's my money?" He leaned down, resting his hands on the arms of the chair. Hot breath washed over her face. "Where is it?"

Pain exploded in her other cheek as he backhanded her again. She opened her eyes, trying to focus, but the room spun. All she saw were bright lights and a blurry shadow looming over her.

Maria's muffled sobs came from inside the Caddy.

"Rocco, take Maria inside. Lock her in Franco's study."

"Franco ain't gonna like this," Rocco muttered. "You bringing all this into his house while he's out of town... Doing the broad here? I'm tellin' you, this is *not* smart."

"I don't give a fuck," Tino shouted. "Just do it!"

Gina's vision came back on line in time to see Rocco half dragging Maria up the stairs and the murderous look in Tino's eyes as he watched them go. His chest heaved and his nostrils flared. The man was about to explode, and Gina was front and center in the fallout radius. Frantically, she looked around for a way out, still finding none.

"The Commission meeting is Saturday. After that, this will be *my* house." Tino took a deep breath before turning back to her with cold, dead eyes. An eerie calm seemed to surround him, and that frightened her more than any outburst.

"Untie her hands. Bring her over here."

Psycho untied her hands and began dragging her to the workbench. She twisted in his grip and lashed out, punching him in the gut. He didn't flinch.

Tino lunged for her wrist, jerking her closer to the workbench. "Hold her still."

"Nooo," she cried, still trying to twist away as Psycho shoved her to the vise grip attached to one side of the bench. Before she could stop him, Tino shoved her hand between the iron sides of the clamp and cranked it closed, leaving her fingers protruding from one end.

She screamed as he cranked the vise tighter. Tears trickled from the corners of her eyes as pain radiated from her hand up her arm. Psycho held her other arm tightly. Any movement she made only intensified the pain.

"Now, let's have some fun." Tino grinned as he reached for a tool on the pegboard—a large wire cutter.

Gina gulped. Her breath came in heavy rasps as she shook her head. "Don't do this," she whispered. "*Please*, don't do this." Visions of the jelly jar in Tino's safe swam before her eyes. The one containing that agent's finger.

He clamped the wire cutter around her thumb, squeezing until the blades cut into her skin enough to sting like a bitch and draw blood. "Where's. My. Money?" He grabbed her hair and yanked her head back.

Several hairs ripped from her scalp and she cried out.

Sweat broke out on her forehead as harsh reality settled over her like a death shroud. There was no way out.

Her heart hammered in her chest. Her fingers were about to become the newest addition to Tino's treasure chest. Worse... It was only the beginning of the horror to come.

Chapter Twenty-Five

The Expedition careened on two wheels as Jack took the sharp curve in the road. He glanced at his cell phone in the console, gripping the wheel tighter as the road straightened out. No word from Meat.

"Have you ever been inside the Falzone compound?" Kyle asked.

"No, but I know the blueprints by heart. It's gated on all sides. Eight bedrooms, seven baths, full basement, and a three-car garage." Gina could be anywhere inside. The last thing he wanted was to go in guns blazing and get her killed. He needed insider information. He needed Meat to give him Gina's location. He glanced at Kyle. "I don't have a warrant."

"We know." Deke squeezed Jack's shoulder. "That's why lawyers make up fancy phrases like 'exigent circumstances.'"

His cell shrilled and he grabbed it, but it wasn't Meat. "Smitty," he said. "Everything good?"

"Yeah, we're pulling into the US Attorney's Office now. I'll let you know as soon as we get a warrant."

Jack exhaled a long breath. They'd get Tino, but Viggiani would likely be dead by the end of the month. Somehow, the Falzones would get to his witness. They always did. Was this really worth someone else dying? For the first time since identifying Jim's body, he wasn't sure. "Hold off on giving anything to the AUSA until you hear from me."

"Why?" The confusion in Smitty's voice was understandable.

"I need more need time to convince Viggiani to go into WITSEC." If he refused, Jack didn't know if he could go through with this. "Just do it."

"Okay. Later." Smitty hung up.

"Problems?" Deke asked.

"No." *Yes.* Because of his conscience, he was about to throw his entire case against Tino down the toilet. "We're good."

Before he could set his phone down, it vibrated again— this time with the call he'd been waiting for.

"You better get your ass here fast," his informant said in a low voice. "Tino has the girl tied up in the garage. Hang on a sec. *I'll be right there,*" Meat shouted to someone else. "Give me a few minutes to get to the front door and unlock it."

Jack's phone went dead. He braked to a stop a hundred yards down the road from the compound.

A few minutes. That could mean the difference between life and death.

He gripped the wheel so tightly his hands squeaked on the covering. He stared at the front door to the house, willing Meat to show his face. Until he did, this would be the longest few minutes of Jack's life.

The wire cutter dug deeper into Gina's flesh. Blood oozed from the gash, dripping first onto the vise, then to the floor. She clenched her jaw, refusing to give Tino the satisfaction of crying out.

"Last chance, bitch." He yanked harder on her hair, dragging her head back until he was face to face with her, his nose inches from hers. "Where's the money?"

No matter what she told him, she was about to lose her finger. After that, she was going to die. The only satisfaction she'd have in what was most assuredly a short life span was to give this sick bastard the bad news. As for getting a dime of his money back, he was outta luck.

"The money's gone!" she screamed. "I'll never tell you what I did with it. *Never.*" She squeezed her eyes tightly shut and tensed so hard her entire body quivered.

"Fine." With her eyes shut, she couldn't see him, but Tino's hot breath washed over her face. "I love trinkets."

The wire cutters squeezed deeper, slowly though, as if he wanted to draw out the agony. Her finger was on fire, the pain red-hot, like someone had shoved a burning poker straight into her flesh.

"That's enough!" a voice boomed.

"Oh, shit," Psycho muttered. "I thought you said he was gone 'til Friday."

Tino unclamped the wire cutter and spun. The tool fell to the bench, and Gina nearly wept with relief. Only Pyscho's tight grip on her other arm kept her from sagging to the floor. Through the haze of pain, she blinked to clear her vision.

Franco Falzone stood on the top step with Rocco behind him. The other man, Meat, was nowhere in sight.

Rocco looked from Franco to Tino, then back again. She couldn't be sure whose side the man was really on.

The head of the Falzone crime family glared at his son as he slowly descended the stairs. He glanced briefly at Gina but made no move to free her.

"Please accept my apologies." When the bastard bowed, she was tempted to ram her boot into his gonads. "What you're doing for the shelter is commendable. Stealing from me, however, is not." He gave a subtle nod to Rocco. "Get rid of her."

"*What?*" Gina could hardly believe her ears.

"It's just business." He gave her an apologetic look. "You understand."

"Business?" Her blood heated and not in a good way. "Just like killing my father was 'just business'?"

Franco's gray brows knit. "Ah. I knew you looked familiar. Tony Perotti. I liked him. And, yes. That was also just business."

The pain in her hand dissipated until all she felt was the fury shooting out the top of her head. If it weren't for the fact she'd leave her hand behind in the vise, she would have attacked Franco right then and there and ripped his eyes out of his head. Blaming Jack all these years suddenly seemed ridiculous. Jack wasn't a murderer. Franco Falzone *was*.

"Your behavior disgusts me." Franco spat on Tino's shoes. "You're nothing more than an animal that should be locked in a cage."

Amen to that. Yet Franco did nothing to assist her, telling her one thing. He might not like what Tino intended, but it was too late. She'd seen too much, and no one would save her.

Tino didn't say a word. His back was to her, but she could see his fists repeatedly clenching and unclenching.

Franco was several inches shorter than his son, but the power and authority exuding from the man was worth an extra half foot. "How dare you betray me?" He pointed a finger in Tino's face. "You're nothing but an insolent child who doesn't know his place and refuses to obey orders."

"I am *not* a child, and *you're* nothing but an old man."

The slap Franco gave his son echoed through the garage loud enough that even Gina flinched. Tino staggered back, giving her a glimpse of the rage blazing in his eyes.

"Worse," Franco continued, "you've been orchestrating a coup behind my back to take over this family. Your coup failed. I'm stripping you of any authority. You are no longer my capo. You are no longer my son. You're nothing. You're *dead* to me."

Gina could have been imagining it but could swear Franco's voice trembled. The man—a murderer many times over—couldn't possibly have feelings. Could he?

A low growl emanated from Tino's throat, then he lunged for his father, clamping his hands around the older man's neck and squeezing so hard Franco's eyes bulged.

Rocco leaped off the top step, latching on to Tino's arm, attempting to pull him off. Psycho grabbed Rocco's arm, dragging him away.

Oh my God. A Mafia power play was unfolding, and she was caught right in the middle of it.

She was also free.

Psycho had to release her when he jumped into the fray. All four men grappled, cursing and falling to the floor in a heap of flailing limbs.

Gina fumbled with the lever on the vise grip, praying she wasn't cranking it tighter. She opened the two halves of the vise, releasing her hand. It was so bloody, blue, and numb she could barely feel it at all.

She bolted up the stairs, pausing to grab the crowbar, then pushing through the door into the house. For a split second, she wondered where Meat had gone. Maybe he'd known what was coming and hauled ass out of there. The only smart one in the bunch. She was tempted to follow his example but couldn't. Maria Falzone was locked up in Franco's study.

"Maria?" she shouted. "*Maria?*" No response. She ran through the ground floor of the house, finding one room with its door closed. She turned the knob. It was locked, and the keyhole was empty. She pounded on the door. "Maria, are you in there?"

A second later, "Yes. Leave me here," a frail voice whimpered. "Just go while you still can."

Not a chance. "Get away from the door." She jammed the flat edge of the crowbar in what little space there was between the door and the frame and pulled. Pain shot to her injured finger. She hissed in a breath but kept pulling. Muscles in her already-cramped shoulders, arms, and hand screamed. It was no use. The door didn't budge. By the looks of it, she guessed the house was built in the 1930s, which meant the door was well made and solid. It also meant the keys that opened one door in the house might be used to open another.

Still gripping the crowbar, she spun and raced through the main floor, searching every door for a key and finding none. Oddly, she didn't see Meat anywhere. She bolted up the stairs to the second floor, checking those doors too. *Nada.*

Shouting from the garage filtered upstairs. Sooner or

later, they'd realize she was gone. Calling 911 was an option but the police would never get there in time.

Plan B. Improvise.

She ran into one of the bedrooms and yanked open the closet door. All the hangers were made of shiny wood. Gina bit back a growl. Who didn't have at least one cheap wire hangar in their house?

Think, think!

She looked down at her exposed bra. Her *underwire* bra. She tossed the crowbar on the bed and began working quickly, fighting through the pain in her finger as she jimmied the bra back and forth over the end of one wire until a hole formed in the fabric and she could tug out the curved wire.

The yelling in the garage had quieted some, and that worried her. She retrieved the crowbar, then pounded down the stairs and flew into the kitchen. She yanked open drawer after drawer until she found what she needed in one of the silverware trays—a metal pick with a slightly curved tip, the kind used to extract crabmeat from the shell.

She raced back to the study. Quietly, she set the crowbar on the floor. With shaky fingers, she inserted her makeshift tension wrench and hook tool into the lock. Sweat trickled between her shoulder blades. Normally, she'd use her sense of touch to feel the guts of the lock and listen to what the internal mechanism was doing. Her heart beat so fast, hearing anything would have been impossible.

She could do this. She could break into anything. Anywhere, anyplace, anytime. Gina jiggled the tools until the deadbolt gave way. She turned the knob and opened the door to find Maria curled into a tight ball on the sofa.

"C'mon," she said with quiet force. "We have to get out

of here. Now." She held out her hand, and for a dismal few seconds thought the woman would refuse to come with her.

One of Maria's eyes—the only one that could open fully —seemed to clear. She sat up and gave an audible swallow. "Okay." With surprising conviction, she rose and took Gina's hand.

A door slammed. *The garage door*. Someone was coming for her. Gina dragged Maria to the open door, releasing her to grab the crowbar. As she straightened, Maria gasped.

Gina sucked in a breath. The black barrel of a gun was pointed at her face not two inches away. Tino's upper lip twitched uncontrollably.

Her heart jackhammered against her ribs. *It can't end this way. I won't let it.* Not at the hands of this sonofabitch.

Ducking away from the gun, she swung the crowbar with everything she had.

Tino bellowed as the edge of the tool glanced the side of his head. He pressed one hand to his scalp, staggering back as blood spewed from a deep gash.

Batter up, bucko. She swung again, but he grabbed the end of the crowbar before it made contact, wrenching it from her hands. He threw it to the floor where it clattered and skittered out of reach.

With a snarl, he advanced on her and jammed the barrel of the gun against her forehead. "You bitch."

"No, Tino." Maria grabbed his other arm. "I'll stay here with you. Just let her go. *Please*, let her go."

He shoved Maria away with such force that she fell to the floor. The barrel pressed harder against Gina's skull. She stared into the face of the last person she would ever see.

Jack's face flashed before her eyes. She squeezed her eyes shut, wishing for a do-over and knowing her wish would never be granted.

This was it. Game over.

Chapter Twenty-Six

Jack and Kyle scaled the fence surrounding the compound. Deke remained on the other side, his Glock drawn and pointed at the house. Once their feet hit the ground, Jack and his brother drew down while Deke climbed over and joined them.

As a unit, they charged to the house. Jack's heart pounded the entire way to the door. Meat had never steered him wrong, and he prayed the door was really unlocked.

With his hand on the knob, he paused. From inside the house, a man shouted. Jack couldn't identify the voice or make out the words. A woman—not Gina—pleaded and sobbed.

He turned, nodding once to his brothers as he twisted the knob and nudged the door open.

More sobbing, then, "Tino, *please* don't do this."

Shouting came from the other side of the house. Jack pointed, silently directing his brothers to check it out. Kyle and Deke disappeared around a corner. Jack headed in the opposite direction, following the sobbing. He stepped quickly but quietly, doing his best not to alert anyone to his presence.

"I don't know which I want more"—now that he was closer, he recognized Tino's voice—"my money back or watching your head explode."

Jack didn't think his heart rate could spike more, but it did. Tino could only be talking about Gina.

He edged around the next corner and froze. Tino had her shoved against the wall, the barrel of his gun jammed to her forehead. Tino leaned in until his face was inches from hers. Maria Falzone lay on the floor, sobbing at Tino's feet.

Jack gripped his Glock tighter. He was an expert shot, but with his support hand still in a cast, holding the gun steady and aiming with any degree of certainty was dicey. If he missed, Gina could die.

He took a breath, exhaling it slowly.

"Die, bitch," Tino hissed.

Jack squeezed the trigger.

The woman on the floor screamed. Red spray peppered Gina's face as she slid down the wall.

Sweet Jesus, no!

For one heart-stopping moment, he thought he'd missed. His entire world felt as if it were caving in on him like a black hole.

The gun fell from Tino's hand. Blood trickled from a hole in his temple as he fell sideways, slamming to the floor.

Breath whooshed from Jack's lungs. He ran to Gina's side and crouched. He holstered and took in the disarray of her clothes. Her blouse was torn open, every single button gone. Blood spattered her face, neck, and the exposed tops of her breasts. Her chest rose and fell with ragged, uneven breaths. Quickly, he inspected her for injuries. The only things he found were a fairly deep cut on her right thumb and the beginning of a significant bruise on her face.

He ran to the bathroom and grabbed a handful of paper guest towels. Back in the hallway, he knelt and wrapped Gina's finger securely to stop the bleeding.

Booted feet pounded closer, and he redrew his Glock, spinning on his heels and aiming in the direction of the approaching sound. His pulse tripped back into the stratosphere.

Kyle rounded the corner. "Whoa." His brother quickly holstered, holding up his hands. "It's just me, bro."

Jack jerked his finger off the trigger. He'd been a hair's breadth from blasting his brother to kingdom come. He sucked in a tight breath and reholstered.

Kyle's brows snapped together. "She okay?"

He tugged the edges of Gina's coat together. "Gina?" he said softly, willing her eyes to open. "Are you all right?" He already knew Tino had hurt her, but if he'd *touched* her... He could barely think the words, let alone say them... Half Tino's brains were on the floor or dripping from the wall, and Jack wanted to empty the rest of his magazine into the man's chest to kill him all over again.

"Gina?" He touched two fingers to her cold, clammy cheek. Every second that passed made him worry more. "Can you open your eyes for me?"

Her lids flickered and opened. "I'm okay," she whispered.

"Did he—" Jack swallowed, again taking in her torn clothes. "Did he hurt you?"

She shook her head. "No."

Relief poured through him.

"I've gotta get back to Deke," Kyle interrupted. "We've got three in custody in the garage plus Franco. He's alive but unconscious. Turns out your boy, there"—Kyle dipped his head to Tino's lifeless body—"tried to strangle daddy dearest and nearly succeeded."

Jack stared at Kyle for a moment. He shouldn't have been surprised Tino tried taking out his old man, but he was. "Call 911. Let them know what's going on and request two ambulances." Behind him, Maria Falzone lay huddled in a ball, whimpering softly. One of her eyes was swollen nearly shut, and most of her face was covered in bruises. "Better make that three." Although he suspected the woman's emotional scars were far worse than her physical ones.

"Copy that." Kyle turned, and a few seconds later the door to the garage opened, then slammed shut.

"Maria!" Gina crawled to the whimpering woman, then took her in her arms, rocking her gently. She stroked the woman's hair. "It's all right. Everything's going to be fine. I promise."

Jack stood. Every one of his bones and muscles ached. His entire body felt as if it had aged fifty years in the last five minutes. Maria Falzone *would* be fine. Now that her POS husband was dead.

More blood had pooled around Tino's head but was finally slowing. Things hadn't gone the way Jack had expected. He'd fully intended to let the criminal justice system run its course in court. In the end, things were better this way.

Jim Spencer's killer was dead, and Jack's witness would never have to testify or worry about a bullet taking him out. Tino Falzone's murderous reign was over, and he'd never become head of the Falzone Crime Family.

At the sound of approaching sirens, he went to the front door and punched a button on the wall to open the gates.

He turned to watch Gina, still sitting on the floor, rocking Maria and crooning to her as if she were a small child in need of comfort.

On a scale of one to ten, his admiration for Gina Perot aka Angelina Perotti was already beyond a ten. She'd been kidnapped, had probably come close to being raped and killed, yet she sat on the floor comforting the battered wife of a murdering mobster. His estimation of her jumped to a solid twenty. Not that it mattered.

She could never forgive him, and he couldn't blame her. The scars he'd unknowingly inflicted on her fifteen years ago were permanent. He had to let her go.

"Jack," she said over Maria's head. "Thank you."

Not being able to hold her or touch her again was killing him. All he could do was nod. As he walked out the front door to wait for the rest of the troops to arrive, he wondered if there would ever be a cure for the gaping hole in his chest where his heart used to be.

Chapter Twenty-Seven

No matter how long Gina stared at the portfolio spreadsheets on her desk, the numbers refused to come into focus. With everything that had happened over the last month, her work was beyond backed up. That wasn't the real problem.

The last time she'd seen Jack was four weeks ago, when he'd walked out the door of the Falzone mansion. She hadn't stopped thinking of him since.

Groaning, she gave up on work for the moment and flipped open today's newspaper to read the front-page article for the third time. *Franco Falzone Indicted for Murder*. Her father's murder. Miraculously, the FBI had found the evidence to charge Franco with her father's death, something that left her mystified.

Rocco and Psycho were old-school mobsters. They would never squeal on Franco. Given the pricy lawyers Franco employed, and with no witnesses to back her up, Gina had been told by the prosecutor that her word alone wasn't good enough. The statements Franco had made ordering her own death and that killing her father was "just business" might as well never have happened. Somehow, Jack had found a way around that.

She should be happy. She should be bouncing off the walls with joy. Instead, she was numb.

As she turned the page, the pink scar on her hand stood out like a beacon, an ugly reminder of what Tino had nearly done to her. Ironic that Franco's arrival had stopped him before he could do any permanent damage. The wire cutter hadn't gone deep enough to sever any ligaments or tendons. All she'd needed was a dozen stitches that had already been removed.

Since the day Jack and the FBI had raided the secret, infamous Mafia Commission meeting in upstate New York, every newspaper in the country continued headlining the latest in Mafia indictments and arrests.

Antonio "Psycho" Fiori and Richard "Rocco" Lambrusco were indicted for kidnapping her the day Jack shot Tino. With Tino dead, Maria Falzone hadn't hesitated to relate how her husband had orchestrated the whole thing. The mystery henchman, Meat, somehow managed to avoid charges altogether.

She folded over the front page to keep reading. A grainy photo of Jack escorting a handcuffed Franco Falzone graced the center of the page. He had to be up to his eyeballs in work. She'd lost count of how many times she'd picked up the phone to call him. Each time, she'd lost her nerve. Facing him again was the second scariest thing she could think of. Never seeing him again was even scarier.

Laughter and voices from the office Christmas party grew louder. It was Christmas Eve, but celebrating wasn't on her calendar this year. Maybe next year. If she was lucky enough to stop missing Jack. *Or stop loving him.*

She threw down the paper and walked to the picture

window overlooking the city. From forty stories up, people scurrying about on the sidewalks looked like tiny bugs. Jack was out there somewhere too.

He said he loved her, and she'd pushed him away. After the horrible things she'd said that day in her apartment, he would never come to her. Yet when she'd needed him most, he'd been there, and he'd saved her life.

Her vision blurred, and she blinked rapidly, preventing the tears from falling. What's done was done. There was no going back. So why couldn't she let go?

The intercom buzzed. Before she could get back to her desk, the door flew open. Her friends stood in the doorway, smiling. Between the three of them, they carried two bottles of champagne, four glasses, two poinsettias, and a box of chocolates.

"Merry Christmas!" they shouted, rushing in to hug her.

Charlotte closed the door to give them privacy. Her admin always did have a knack for knowing what she needed. The woman totally deserved the hefty gift card Gina had given her this year.

Kinsey tore the wrapper from one of the bottles, then twisted the cork out with a resounding *pop*. "I love that sound. It's the sound of par-tay." With the skill of someone who'd done so many times, she deftly poured champagne into the four flutes without a single spillover. Warm color brightened her face, and her energy level was back to normal and then some. Courtesy of almost dying *and* a hot doctor she'd met at the hospital.

Tears backed up behind Gina's eyes, and she quickly blinked them away. Kinsey really had come close to dying, yet her friends were all here. This time, she let the tears fall. Out of sheer joy, love, and thankfulness she could never repay.

"Oh, Gina." Anna swiped at her own tears. "Don't start that. You know it's contagious."

Margo and Kinsey began sniffling, and they all laughed.

"Sorry." She grabbed the tissue box from her desk and held it out for them to pluck away.

"Ladies," Margo said a moment later when they held up their flutes. "It's been a difficult year. One filled with triumphs, failures, and—"

"Adventure!" Kinsey interrupted.

Anna rolled her eyes.

"I was going to say," Margo continued, throwing Kinsey a mock glare, "wonderful achievements."

"Amen," Anna said as they went around the circle. "Here's to a wonderful holiday season and an even better new year. Preferably one filled with less *exuberant* adventures."

Now that it was Gina's turn to add something, her throat closed up. "Here's to the best friends a girl could ever have. I love you all. I mean that."

"Here, here." Margo nodded.

"Back atcha, girlfriend." Kinsey winked.

"We love you too." Anna stood on her tiptoes and kissed Gina's cheek. "Don't ever forget that."

As they clinked glasses and took a sip, Jack's words came back to her. *You're as tight as any blood sisters. Maybe tighter.* He was right. Then, she hadn't been giving her friends enough credit. Moving forward, she would never doubt their love or friendship again.

"Gina?" Margo asked. "Is everything all right?"

"Of course." To cover the fact that it wasn't, she took another sip of champagne. She actually did get some good news today. "I stopped by the Center this morning to see Maria Falzone. She's doing much better. Her injuries are healing and she's getting counseling. Since Tino is dead, she may not even need to relocate. After she married him, he put a wedge between her and her family. Now that she doesn't have to worry about him coming after her, she's thinking about reconciling with them."

"That *is* good news," Margo said.

"I'll drink to that." Kinsey raised her glass in the air.

"So why do you look so sad?" Anna watched her intently.

"Duh." Kinsey nudged Anna's shoulder.

"Sorry." Anna held up a hand. "I didn't mean to bring it up."

"That's okay." She squeezed Anna's shoulder. She'd already told her friends every ugly detail of her conversation with Jack.

"Have you heard from him?" Kinsey asked.

"No." She shook her head. "I don't think I ever will again. It's my fault. I pushed him away."

Margo rested a comforting hand on her arm. "You had your reasons."

"I know." She let out a heavy sigh, staring at the bubbles in her glass as they rose to the surface. "I guess I needed time to sort things out in my head. To separate the past from the present and to understand things clearly enough to come to grips with them."

"Did you?" Anna asked quietly.

She pursed her lips, nodding. "I loved my father, but as Jack said, he was, in fact, a criminal." His motives might have been pure—to provide more for his family than his legitimate job could—but that didn't change what he was. "What happened to my father wasn't Jack's fault, not really. He was just doing his job, and his job was to take out the big fish: Franco Falzone. Franco hurt and killed a lot of people.

It was Jack's job to stop him, and my father was a way to make that happen."

Margo's brows lowered in concern. "Can you really forgive him?"

Her heart squeezed because she already knew the answer. Now, when Jack's face came to her, it was no longer associated with the same rage and need for revenge she'd carried around for the last fifteen years. It was with the pain of regret, loss, and love that could never be. "I already have. But it's too late."

"I say you get him back." Kinsey's dark brows bobbed enthusiastically.

Anna grinned. "We'll all help."

Margo set her flute on the desk and rested her hands on Gina's shoulders. "You'll need a grand gesture."

Jack threw down the pen, flexing his fingers before filling out the service portion of another arrest warrant. The cast had been removed, but his hand was stiff during a time when he needed it most. For typing reports.

He glared at the stack of case files on his desk that he swore had grown ten inches overnight. Red tape. The FBI was infamous for it, more so than any other law enforcement agency on the planet.

Taking a break, he leaned back in his chair, tracking Annie Oakley as she roamed slowly around the fish tank. Alone.

True to his word, Smitty had safeguarded John Wayne's little body until Jack could give him a proper burial in his mother's rose garden. He wondered if Annie missed JW.

He uttered a bitter laugh. Transference. He'd equated

his own emotional state with that of a fish because...he missed Gina.

He'd just taken down an entire crime family, busted up the Mafia Commission meeting, making over twenty arrests of high-level mafioso for more outstanding charges than he could remember. Professionally, it was a monumental coup for him and the entire FBI. Personally, he no longer cared because he'd lost the most important battle of his life.

He dragged both hands down his face. The hole in his heart wasn't healing. It had widened faster than a sinkhole. Truth was, he'd nearly gone to Gina's apartment five times over the last month. It wasn't his place to make a move like that.

Laughter came to his ears, followed by Deke's painful rendition of "Jingle Bells." His little brother never met a party he didn't like.

"Hey, bro." Deke poked his head in the door, a strand of silver garland strung around his neck and holding a mug of something Jack assumed was spiked with holiday cheer. "Brought you a gift." He plunked the mug on the desk and sat on one corner. "Trust me. That'll grow more hair on your chest."

Jack peered at the mug, inspecting its contents. "Nancy's homemade Irish cream?" One of the other agents made it every year for Christmas Eve.

"Yep." Deke grinned. Clearly he'd already sucked some down.

SAC Morrison and Smitty joined them. Jack's eyebrows rose at the ear-to-ear grin on his boss's face. The success of Jack's case would solidify his boss's position on an even shorter list for FBI director.

"Hot off the press." Smitty held up a newspaper and pointed to the headline about Franco's indictment.

"Nice work, Jack." Morrison held out his hand for him to shake. "I have to admit, you got it done."

"Thanks, boss." He took the newspaper from Smitty. Front and center was a photo of Jack hauling Franco to jail in cuffs. He should be fist-pumping, reveling in the accolades, but the victory was a hollow one.

Last night he'd returned Jim Spencer's wedding ring to the man's widow. With Tino dead and Franco facing hard time, at least justice would finally be served. For Spencer and his family. *For Gina.*

Despite the media coverage surrounding the Falzones, the Commission meeting had taken place. Though he was still a free man, with all the charges pending against the Falzone organization, Franco had been denied a seat at the meeting. For a while there, it seemed Franco would escape without prosecution. The evidence Jack needed had come from an unexpected source.

Meat, Jack's informant, decided to testify against Franco in exchange for a brand-new life for him and his family in WITSEC. Meat hadn't been in the garage to overhear Franco's statements, but it turned out he *had* been there when Franco had shot Gina's father. All this time, and Jack hadn't known that. Ironically, Jack's best informant was also one of Franco's most trusted men. Given that Meat had nothing to gain and everything to lose—including his life—his eyewitness account had credibility. Combined with Gina's witness statement, the prosecutor hadn't hesitated to file charges against Franco. Given his age, Franco would never again see the light of day from outside of prison.

"Thanks to you, there's chaos brewing in the Mafia." Morrison made himself comfortable in a chair. "All the East Coast families are in total disarray."

"For now." He tossed the paper onto the desk. "Until the players change and new bosses are anointed."

"Organized crime never ends," Kyle said from where he now leaned against the doorjamb, arms crossed. "It just keeps reorganizing. Consider it job security."

Nancy poked her head in the office. "Kyle, that visitor you've been waiting for is here."

"Thanks." Kyle turned and left.

His brother must be pulling another all-nighter, something he noticed Kyle did a lot since transferring from Chicago.

The laughter and singing outside his office suddenly hushed.

Kyle reappeared with someone hovering off to the side, just outside the door. "Someone's here to see you."

Deke slid off the desk. "About time."

Jack eyed his brothers suspiciously. He wasn't expecting anyone. Judging by the barely perceptible grin on Kyle and Deke's faces, whatever was going on, both of them were in on it. Kyle stepped aside, extending an arm to whoever stood behind him.

Gina walked into his office. "Hi," she said shyly, a tentative smile curving her lips.

Jack shot to his feet. Beyond that, he could only stare. She was even more beautiful than he remembered.

"Um, am I interrupting anything?" She looked nervously around the room.

"Nope." Deke hauled Smitty from his chair. "C'mon, Smitty. We got that thing to take care of."

"What thing?" Smitty's features twisted in confusion.

"Hi, Gina," Deke said. "This is Smitty, by the way."

"Hi, Deke. Hi, Smitty." She gave his partner a polite smile before Deke dragged him out the door.

Jack noticed she held a white Styrofoam box tied with a thick red bow.

Morrison stood. "Jack, are you going to introduce me?"

"Uh, sure." He cleared his throat, coming around the desk. "Gina Perot, this is Special Agent in Charge Michael Morrison, my boss."

"Pleased to meet you." She held out her hand for Morrison to shake.

"Boss?" Kyle sent Morrison a meaningful look. "I need to update you on that case before you head out tonight."

Jack couldn't tear his eyes from Gina. Her coat open, revealing a snug black skirt, sexy as all get-out black hose and heels, and a green blouse the same color as her satin bathrobe. He still couldn't believe she was actually here. In his office. His palms began to sweat.

"Right," he vaguely heard Morrison say as the man headed for the door.

"I'll make sure you're not disturbed."

He glanced up in time to catch the spreading grin on his brother's face and the stealthy way he twisted the lock on the handle before closing the door behind him.

For several seconds that felt like minutes, he and Gina stared at each other. Jack didn't know what to say. The ball was in her court and he was merely a spectator.

Gina stepped farther into the room, looking around his office. Her knuckles were white where she clutched the Styrofoam box. "So, this is where you work."

"Sometimes." His throat had gone so dry he had to keep swallowing. "Mostly I'm in the field."

"I see you got your cast off." She glanced at his right hand. "That's good."

"Thanks." He flexed his stiff fingers. "Looks like your finger's doing okay too."

"Barely a scar. See?" She held up her hand, giving him a glimpse of the pale pink scar below the knuckle of her thumb.

Jack ground his teeth together, much as he'd done after learning Tino had been seconds from cutting off her thumb for his collection.

Gina went to the fish tank, trailing her fingers along the glass. Annie Oakley swam gracefully to the surface, waiting for her gourmet meal of freeze-dried shrimp and seaweed. "Is this Annie Oakley?"

"It is." When he stepped closer, he breathed in her sugary vanilla scent. She gripped the box tighter, looking up at him and biting her lower lip. For the first time since he'd met her, she seemed unsure of herself, not the kick-ass, shoot-from-the-hip woman he'd become accustomed to. He loved this softer side just as much.

"Hi, Annie." She bent over until her face was even with the fish. "I'm Angelina Perotti. But you can call me Gina."

To keep from taking her in his arms, Jack shoved his hands in his pockets. It didn't take a trained criminal investigator to figure out whatever the reason for her impromptu visit, she wasn't ready to clue him in. The waiting was killing him.

"I brought you something." She held out the box.

"Thank you." When he accepted the gift, their fingers touched and awareness sparked up his arm. He set the box on the credenza.

"You really should open it." She twisted her hands together, biting her lip again.

"Don't you want me to wait until Christmas?"

"No." She shook her head. "You'd better open it now."

"Okay." He tugged open the bow and shimmied off the cover.

"Do you like it?" she asked softly.

Jack's heart was so far up in his throat he could taste it. Nestled in the scooped-out center of the box was a plastic bag containing water. And a clownfish.

"It's a male. At least I think it is. That's what they told me at the store." When he still couldn't speak, she added quickly, "Do you like him?"

Like him? To his shock, the backs of his eyes burned. "How did you know?" He'd never actually told her JW had died.

"When I called Kyle and Deke, I told them everything. I said I needed a grand gesture. They told me about John Wayne. I'm sorry."

"Thanks." He lifted the lid off the tank and gently set the bag in the water to acclimate the fish before releasing it into its new environment. This was, without a shadow of a doubt, the most thoughtful gift anyone had ever given him.

When he turned around, tears shimmered in her eyes. Unable to wait a moment longer, he swallowed. Hard, so he could get the words out. "Why are you here, Gina?"

"For so many reasons." A single tear rolled down her cheek, and he resisted the urge to wipe it away with his thumb or kiss it away with his lips. "To apologize for all the cruel things I said to you." She twisted her hands together. "It was such a shock to find out..."

"The role I played in your father's death," he finished for her, knowing how hard it would be for her to say it. "If there'd been another way to tell you, trust me I would have."

"I know." She nodded. "At least, I know it now. I needed time to process everything. To understand why he did what he did, and why you did what you did."

"And do you understand now?" Even if they could only be friends from this point forward, her understanding

336

would mean more to him than she could possibly know. Not that he'd ever truly be able to forgive himself, but her understanding would be a close second.

"Yes." Again she nodded, more emphatically this time. "My father put himself in that position. You didn't pull the trigger. Franco did. And I want to thank you for arresting him."

"It was my pleasure." It truly had been. Now they'd both gotten justice. For Jim Spencer *and* Tony Perotti. "You didn't have to bring me a gift or tell me all that in person. You could have called."

"No." She shook her head in a tight, jerky motion and looked away. "There are certain other things that should only be said in person."

"What other things?" he said softly. As much as he wanted to be near her, it was torture to be so close yet so far. The things he wanted to hear cross her lips—the things he'd *dreamed* of hearing her say for the last four weeks—were just that. Nothing but a dream. One that would never come true.

She locked gazes with him and took a deep breath. "Things like, I love you."

"*What?*" Warm tentacles surrounded his broken heart, fluttering in the vicinity but not quite touching it. He must have misheard her.

"You heard me." She rested her hand on his cheek and looked up at him, the same way she had in his dream. "I love you. I hope you still love me. Did you mean it when you said it? Because if you didn't, I'll be really embarrassed. I'll—"

He reached for her arm and tugged her to his chest. Those warm tentacles flitting around his heart latched on and didn't let go. "You'll what?" When she opened her mouth to answer him, he kissed her, soundly, deeply, and with every ounce of love he could put into it. "I love you," he murmured against her lips. "I love you, I love you, I love you." As she clutched at his back, he deepened the kiss, tasting her very soul intertwining with his.

To say he loved this woman was an understatement. He was hers, body and soul. He'd never been more certain of anything in his life.

Grinning, he slipped the coat off her shoulders and tossed it on a chair. "You know, I've never made love on my desk before."

Her eyes flared wide. "In an FBI office? We can't."

"We can." Chuckling, he began popping open the buttons of her blouse.

"What if someone comes in?" There was no mistaking the panic in her voice.

For the next twenty seconds, he kissed her before coming up for air. "They won't."

"How do you know?" Her breath washed over his face, her eyes glazed with desire.

"Kyle locked the door," he said, popping the last button and tugging the silk blouse from her skirt. One day, he'd have to thank his brother for that.

A mischievous glint flashed in her eyes. "This has to be a violation of FBI policy."

"It is." Not that he cared. He backed her to his desk, then reached out and swept the stack of newspapers, files, and arrest warrants to the floor. "I always was a rule breaker."

The gleam in her eyes went softer than velvet. "I love you, Special Agent Jack Gates."

"I love you, Gina Perot...Angelina Perotti... Whatever your name is, I'll love you forever."

Epilogue

Six months later.

"Pigs anyone?" Annabelle held out the platter of pigs in a blanket.

"Absolutely!" Gina set her margarita on the picnic table and picked up one of the pastry-wrapped sausages, dunking it in mustard. She crunched into it, groaning at the delicious, meaty spiciness flooding her tastebuds. There could be two-pound lobsters on the table, but pigs in a blanket would always be a crowd pleaser.

"Me too." Kinsey grabbed one and shoved it into her mouth, somehow managing to smile, chew, and sigh at the same time.

"Me three." Margo did the same.

Jack's mother, Elaina, put a plate of deviled eggs and a heaping bowl of macaroni salad on the table. "Quite a crowd."

"Indeed it is." Gina nodded as she surveyed Elaina's large backyard.

Maybe the fact it was Saturday and the weather couldn't have been more perfect had contributed. Not a single one of their last-minute invitations had been turned down.

At a comfortable eighty degrees, with the sun shining from a lovely blue sky and a light breeze fluttering the wispy branches of the enormous weeping willow tree, the afternoon had begged for a big ol' backyard barbecue.

Annabelle was here with her husband. Margo had brought her twin eight-year-old boys and had somehow managed to drag her hubby away from playing golf with his buddies.

Gina waved to Smitty and his wife. They sat in the shade of the willow tree, watching their four kids and Margo's boys play Frisbee.

Even Jack's boss, SAC Mike Morrison, had shown up with his wife, Nancy. Kyle had come alone, as was usual for him. Deke, on the other hand, was never without a date. That man's calendar was a revolving door of beautiful women, including his latest—a pretty blonde with the biggest blue eyes Gina had ever seen.

At the other end of the yard, Nancy Morrison chatted with Linda Hernandez from the Center. Linda held up her glass in salute. Gina returned the gesture with her own glass, her heart filling with joy because the woman sitting across from Linda was now one of the Center's many success stories: Maria Tedesco, formerly Maria Falzone.

Not wanting anything more to do with the Falzone clan, Maria had reverted to her maiden name. With Linda's help, she'd found a new job, rented a small apartment, and was gradually reestablishing ties with her family. There was a rosy tint to her cheeks that hadn't been there before, and she'd put on a few much-needed pounds. Maria didn't smile much yet, but every so often Gina detected the barest hint of one on the woman's lips.

Wordlessly, Gina turned and met her friends' gazes, knowing they were all thinking the same thing. They'd done a good thing.

They'd hung up their catsuits for the last time, but they still helped Linda out at various fundraisers around the city. Between the fundraisers and the city finally releasing the assets they'd previously frozen, the Center's bank accounts would be nicely flush for quite some time.

Like the original pact they'd made to steal from the mob and donate the loot to the Center, they'd made a new one— to meet once a month for movie-and-martini night. They'd also discovered another outlet for their unique skill set.

Since getting to know Kyle over the last six months, which in reality meant she'd barely skimmed the surface, Gina and her friends had begun assisting him with a free self-defense class he taught once a week at a community center not far from 26 Federal Plaza. While he'd never admit it, she suspected his passion for teaching the class had something to do with "the friend" he'd lost touch with after she disappeared into a relocation program.

Elaina tucked an arm around Gina's waist. "I'm so pleased everyone could come on such short notice."

"I am too." Although the short notice part had been all Jack's fault.

She smiled, recalling the exact moment less than twelve hours ago when he'd decided to host a barbecue in his mother's backyard for all their friends and family. He'd woken in her bed, tugged off her silk nightie, then, after making voracious love to her, declared he wanted to have a party that very afternoon.

Jack and his brothers stood in a manly huddle of testosterone by the grill, listening raptly to something their boss, Mike Morrison, said. Jack lifted a bottle of Yuengling to his lips—lips that had done their share of kissing every square inch of her bare skin this morning.

Gina shivered, her body still tingling from all the delicious things he'd done to her.

"What are you grinning at?" Kinsey asked, her gaze following Gina's. "Oh. I see." She hip-bumped Elaina and laughed. "I must say, Mrs. G, you've sired the most handsome brood of men I've ever seen."

"Thank you, dear." Elaina patted Kinsey's shoulder. "I think so too. And please, call me Elaina."

"Sadly," Kinsey continued, shaking her head, "I don't think any of them are available. Jack is most definitely taken. Deke is never without a woman"—as if on cue, the little blonde he'd been dating for three weeks latched onto his arm like an octopus, as if she knew her time with him was fleeting—"and from the looks of things never will be. And Kyle just doesn't seem interested."

"It's not you, Kins. Trust me." Gina patted her friend's arm.

To say Kyle was a man of few words who didn't open up to anyone was an understatement. Yet there was a lot going on behind those intriguing golden eyes. Only last month, Jack had fed her a few more tidbits about his brother's past. The man was grieving. Anyone would after going through something like he had. But it wasn't her story to tell.

Laughter from the kids playing Frisbee mingled with the party music Jack had set up to play from a speaker perched on one of the tables.

As if he could feel her eyes on him, Jack turned his head, pinning Gina from across the yard. A slow smile, followed by a sexy wink, sent her mind wandering back to that morning. Carnal images involving his naked beautiful body and, what he could do with said body, danced in her thoughts. But, she admitted, winking back, there were so many other things she adored about him.

That unbelievably sexy smile. The easy way he made her laugh. All the snarky banter that had set her on edge during their first meetings was now one of many things she looked forward to. Most of all, she loved that he loved her and showed her just how much every day. It could be something small, like when he and his brothers had been watching a heated football game on TV, and he would send her a look that told her everything she needed to know: she was special to him.

How she could have fallen so far and so completely for the last man on earth she should have, and one with a chocolate allergy, no less, she'd never know. But if someone told her she had to give up chocolate or kissing Jack, she would give up chocolate. Because he loved her, he would never make her do that. Common sense, however, dictated he was never without an EpiPen in his pocket. Just in case.

A sigh escaped her lips, one full of more contentment than she'd thought possible. "You're right about Jack, Kins." She let her gaze linger on his handsome face, then lower down the blue T-shirt to his khaki shorts and muscular legs. "He's definitely taken." *And he's all mine. Today. Tomorrow. And, she hoped, every day after that.* Only time would tell.

"Hmm." Elaina tapped a finger on her chin and narrowed her eyes on Kinsey. "You should meet my youngest." She grabbed her phone from the table and began scrolling through the images, searching, Gina knew, for the photo of Lance he'd texted her only last week. A photo with the geocoding turned off, of course. None of them—not even Jack—had any clue what agency he worked for or where he was at any given moment. "The next time he's in town, I'll have you over for dinner."

When Elaina handed over her phone, Kinsey's eyes went as wide as the golf ball-size truffles Gina occasionally treated herself to from the Godiva shop in Rockefeller Center.

"Oh. My." Kinsey put a hand to her chest. "Feel my heart aflutter. Unfortunately, it looks as if I'll be leaving for Kenya soon."

"Really?" Gina couldn't keep the worry from her tone. Kinsey's family dynamics were strained at best, and the last time she'd gone home to Kenya she'd been gone nearly a year. "You didn't say anything about that."

"I just found out last night." Kinsey's expression darkened, something it rarely did. "My father is sick, and my mother doesn't know if she can run the cacao plantation alone."

"I'm sorry to hear that." She gave Kinsey's shoulder a squeeze, as did Margo and Annabelle.

"That's a shame, dear," Elaina said. "I sincerely hope he'll be okay."

"Thank you." Kinsey's eyes glittered with unshed tears. "Me too."

Gina's heart filled with so much love for her friend—and heaviness too. Losing a parent was never easy. At any age. "We're here for you. *All* of us."

Truer words were never spoken. The bond they shared was as strong as any blood bond.

"Excuse me. I need to freshen my drink." Gina headed for the pitcher of margaritas, blinking back the tears.

Life had thrown her a curveball yet again. Thankfully, this time, the ball had curved in the right direction. She'd lost one family but had eventually found a new one. Never again would she be alone. Despite the losses she'd suffered as a teenager, she now considered herself the luckiest woman on the planet.

Jack's deep voice drifted over the music, drawing her attention back to where he and his brothers were still in heated discussion with their boss. Even at this distance, he could make her heart flutter and her pulse race. There was no other man in the world for her.

Before topping off her drink, she tilted her head back and looked up at the sky. Two lone fluffy clouds drifted overhead in a slow-motion dance, and the truth of the moment inserted itself with brilliant clarity.

"Mom, Dad," she whispered, this time letting the tears fall. "I'm going to be okay." For the first time since losing her parents, she actually believed it.

Jack kept one ear on what his boss was saying about the Bratva—the Russian mafia—and one eye on the sweet curves of Gina's backside as she looked up at the sky. The red shorts and matching halter top she wore were sexier than if she'd been strutting around the yard buck naked.

Blood shot directly to his groin. No matter how many times they made love, he'd never tire of it. Maybe when they got home they should dig out Gina's skintight catsuit from the closet and play a little game of cops and robbers. With handcuffs.

"Jack, you getting this?" Deke elbowed him in the ribs.

"Um, yeah." He cleared his throat, doing his best to pay attention to what his SAC was saying.

No easy task whenever Gina was around. They'd officially been a couple since the day she'd walked into his office carrying a clownfish to replace poor little John Wayne.

A breeze brought with it the scent of his mother's rosebushes along the property line. Some of them were blooming early, particularly the one where he'd buried JW. Luckily, his new clownfish—Wyatt Earp—and Annie Oakley had instantly taken to each other. In fact, he'd discovered transparent fish eggs in the tank with tiny eyes showing. Soon he'd need a bigger tank, and the credenza in his office could only support so much weight. Moving the tank to his condo made sense. Then again, with Gina staying at his place half the time, what he really needed was a house.

Dealing with the mistakes they'd made and learning to live with them would take time. As would finding a way to balance her chocolate fetish with his need to constantly kiss her, something he couldn't live without. "Being careful" had taken on a whole new meaning for them. It was less about becoming unexpectedly pregnant before they were ready and more about not wanting to accidentally send him into anaphylactic shock.

Kyle tugged a phone from his shorts pocket, and his brow creased.

"Everything okay?" Jack asked.

"Yeah." He shoved the phone back into his pocket. "That was the US Attorney's Office in Chicago. Semyon Novikov is ill and petitioning for release."

Their boss made a sound of disgust. "He'll never get it."

"Probably not," Kyle agreed.

"Who's Semyon Novikov?" Heather, the pretty blonde clinging to Deke's arm, asked.

Deke looked down at Heather, who had to be a good

twelve inches shorter than his six-foot-two. "He's a Russian mob boss Kyle put in prison ten years ago."

When Kyle's frown deepened, Jack had a strong suspicion it had nothing to do with Novikov.

"Another beer, anyone?" Morrison asked, and when they all shook their heads, their SAC sauntered off to the giant cooler in the middle of the lawn.

"I think I need another margarita." Heather held up her empty glass just, then headed over to where Gina chatted with her friends and his mother.

"You ever gonna stop thinking about her?" Deke asked, now that the three of them were alone.

The only people in the world Kyle had confided in about the woman he'd saved in Chicago were him and Deke.

Rather than answer, Kyle shot Deke a look that said *probably not and back off.*

Whoever this woman was, it was clear she was still a sore spot not even a decade could heal. Jack hated seeing his brother in so much pain. Kyle had experienced more loss than any of them. If there was something Jack could do to help, he'd be all in. "I could probably pull strings, get some information on her."

Kyle seemed to consider the offer for a moment, then shook his head. "Way too complicated. Besides, safeguarding domestic violence victims' locations is sacred. I don't want either of us to break that code. But thanks for the offer."

"Anytime." Jack clapped his brother on the back.

In a show of support, Deke did the same.

Feminine laughter drew his attention to the tight circle of women, in the middle of which stood Gina. All he had to do was look at her, and a sense of lightness wrapped itself around him like a warm blanket on a freezing cold winter day. Sometimes he felt guilty for being so damned happy when one of his brothers was suffering.

Kyle and Deke chuckled and exchanged smirks.

Deke aimed his beer bottle at the women. "You gonna make an honest woman out of her?"

"*Honest?*" Jack laughed outright. "After all the laws she broke?" Then again, if she hadn't broken them, he would never have met her and found what was missing in his life. What he *needed* in his life. Love. And Gina.

"You know Mom wants grandkids, right?" Kyle flicked his gaze from Jack to Deke.

"Whoa." Deke held up his hands. "Don't look at me, bro. I'm not even close to that, and I may *never* get there."

"Don't look at me either." Kyle shook his head. "I've been practically celibate for a decade."

"Guess it's up to you, Jack." Deke squeezed Jack's shoulder.

Again, he turned to watch Gina. The woman had nearly driven him out of his mind, yet he loved her with every cell in his body.

"Okay, guys." He let out a breath, feigning resignation. "I'm the oldest. It's time I took one for the team."

"Huh?" Deke's brows scrunched together.

Kyle's brows rose. "We were kidding."

Jack grinned. "Yeah, I know." Though they might think it, they hadn't planted the idea in his head. In reality, it had been there for several weeks. Since the day he'd purchased the two-carat chocolate diamond engagement ring.

"Watch and learn boys." He handed Kyle his beer and went inside the house to the kitchen cabinet where he'd stashed the box.

Half a minute later, he strode past his brothers, carefully holding the gold tissue box-size container in both hands. Jack's heart leaped into his throat, pounding harder than a New York cabbie had ever pounded on a horn.

The only flaw in his plan, one he hadn't considered, was that she might not say yes. God help him if she didn't. He'd broken up an entire Mafia family, put dozens of dangerous criminals in prison, but he'd be lost without Gina.

"Hi." She smiled up at him, sending his heart rate into overdrive. "Pretty box. Whatcha got there?"

"A gift. For you." He handed her the box, careful to turn it so the clear cellophane window faced her. *And is that my hand shaking?*

"Ooh, pretty." Her smile broadened as she accepted the box containing the elaborately decorated chocolate Faberge-style egg. She gasped. "Is this chocolate? It's beautiful."

She held it up for everyone to get a better look at the royal blue egg with gold bows and flowers seated on a pedestal.

When he'd bought the egg, he'd been educated by the seller that it had been fashioned after one made by Victor Mayer, a German artist and jeweler who'd been commissioned to resume the manufacture of original Faberge objects.

This one, however, had a surprise inside.

"Thank you, Jack." She stood on her tiptoes and placed a quick kiss on his cheek.

"Open it." He indicated the box. "There's something special inside."

"Okay." Moments later, Gina had taken the egg from the box, balancing the pedestal in her hand.

As she gently flipped open the top half of the egg, Jack lowered to one knee.

His mother gasped and clapped her hands to her face.

Annabelle and Kinsey grabbed onto each other's arms, jumping up and down as they both let out squeals high-pitched enough to wake the dead.

Margo, ever the pragmatist, Jack had learned, simply nodded, as if she'd known all along what Jack had planned.

"Holy shit," Deke whispered over Jack's shoulder.

Kyle chuckled. "I'll second that."

"Gina." Jack looked up into the eyes of the woman he loved more than his own life. "I love you. I can't live without you. Will you marry me?"

Her eyes had gone wide, and her mouth had fallen open. His four-word question had rendered this woman—who never stopped talking—utterly speechless.

"Gina," Kinsey whispered in her ear, nudging Gina's shoulder. "Say something. You never have nothing to say. Don't leave the man hanging."

Yeah. Don't leave me hanging.

Still wide-eyed, her mouth moved, silently forming what he hoped and prayed with every fiber of his being was the word *yes*.

Jack gulped. "Is that a yes?" Or had he stupidly, mistakenly assumed they were on the same page when they weren't?

Slowly, she nodded, then the nodding became more emphatic. "Yes," she whispered, as tears fell from her eyes. "Yes!"

Thank God he was kneeling because his legs felt weak.

After purchasing the egg, he'd inserted a gold velvet cushion and stuck the ring in it. Now, with trembling fingers, he plucked out the ring, being careful to avoid touching the chocolate. He slid the sparkling diamond onto Gina's left ring finger and gently kissed her hand.

Gina flung herself into his arms. Everyone around them

clapped and cheered. He held her tightly, burying his face in her nape and inhaling her sweet scent.

Finally, as the clapping died down, she pulled away. "I love you, Special Agent Gates. I'll love you forever."

This time, when his throat tightened it wasn't from anaphylactic shock. It was from love. Knowing he'd finally found it and would never let it go.

**Keep reading for a sneak peek at Exacting Vengeance!
And please leave a review of Perfect Vengeance on your favorite retailer sites.**

AUTHOR'S NOTE

I've done my best to accurately reflect the world of law enforcement. Any mistakes contained within this book are entirely my own.

ACKNOWLEDGMENTS

This is my very first indie-pub novel, and so many people have contributed to this story finally making it to print.

Many thanks to Kayla Gray for the *beta* read, all the constructive and insightful feedback, and for being such a wonderful friend all these years. I've lost count of how many of my manuscripts you've reviewed! I must give credit to LJ Anderson at Mayhem Cover Creations. You've created so many stunning covers for me in the past. When it came time to create one for my first indie novel there was no question – it had to be you! Once again you did not disappoint.

A very warm and special thanks to my editor, Karen Grove. You are my first editor ever, and it's such a great pleasure to work with you again.

ABOUT THE AUTHOR

Tee O'Fallon is the award-winning, bestselling author of the K-9 Special Ops, Federal K-9, and NYPD Blue & Gold Series. Tee spent twenty-three years as a federal agent conducting complex investigations, including undercover operations, and four years conducting multi-state investigations as a police investigator. It felt only natural to combine her hands-on experience in the field with her love of romantic suspense. Tee has lived in New York State most of her life with a five-year stop in Colorado. When not writing, she enjoys cooking, gardening, chocolate, lychee martinis, and kicking back with her Belgian Sheepdogs, Loki and Kyrie.

See all Tee's books at teeofallon.com. Stay in touch with Tee via social media, and sign up here for Tee's newsletters: https://teeofallon.com/subscribe/.

Contact email: tee@teeofallon.com

EXACTING
VENGEANCE

Sneak Peek

Chapter One

"Chicago Russian Crime Boss Semyon Novikov Dies in Prison" was the headline that caught Kyle's eye as he walked past the *New York Times* dispenser outside the deli.

Since he'd been the agent responsible for Novikov's internment in Club Fed, the Bureau of Prisons had given him courtesy notification last night of the old mob boss's death. But seeing it in print for the first time was a kick to the gut, triggering unwanted emotions that ate at him like acid.

Anger. Loss. Regret. Not for Semyon Novikov. It was for *her*. Always, for her.

Vicki Solonik.

"Hell," he muttered as hot coffee dripped onto his hands from the two Styrofoam cups he'd half crushed.

He didn't know what had happened to Vicki after he'd left Chicago, yet somehow she managed to be just as distracting now to his sanity as she'd been ten years ago.

Has it really been that long? Yeah, it had. And he'd never stopped thinking about her.

Technically nothing had happened between them. At

least not in the sexual sense. But there was no denying it had been there, glowing but never igniting into the passionate fireball he knew it would have if circumstances had been different. Those thoughts haunted him like nothing else could. *She* still haunted him. One of many ghosts hovering in his past.

His polo shirt and cotton outer shirt quickly dampened with sweat from the hot, humid early autumn air funneling down Broadway, making him feel like a wet rat. And the day had only just begun.

He'd gotten no more than twenty feet from the deli when he froze, pinning his gaze on the beat-up sedan parked at the curb in front of a bank across the street. The driver kept looking over one shoulder, then the other. Considering it was hot enough to fry an egg on the sidewalk, the knit cap the guy wore was a tad excessive. From this distance he couldn't be sure, but the driver looked a lot like Ilya Sorofkin, a notorious wheelman for the local Russian Bratva.

Kyle cursed himself for nearly missing it. Now that his mind wasn't cluttered with useless emotions it was as obvious as a fifty-caliber machine gun staring him in the face.

The bank was being robbed. He knew it as surely as if the silent alarm was hardwired directly to his brain.

He hurled the two coffee cups into a nearby garbage can and charged to the blue Ford Expedition.

"Hey!" Jim growled from the open window of the SUV. "Why'd you dump the coffee?"

Kyle leaned inside the truck, never taking his eyes off the car across the street. "Grab your cell. See the brown sedan parked outside that bank?" He jutted his chin in the direction of the bank.

Jim turned to look. "What about it?"

"The engine's running and the driver's real fidgety."

"So?" Jim shrugged and held out his arms. "Maybe he's gotta take a leak."

"He doesn't." Kyle clenched his jaw. "I think it's Ilya Sorofkin, and he's waiting for his buddies inside."

"Shit." Jim yanked out his cell phone and punched in 911. "Boss, I don't know how you pick up on this so fast."

Kyle nodded calmly, but inside his guts were churning like an Iraqi sandstorm. "Warn them this may be the same crew that tried to rob the Manhattan Bank two months ago. We never nailed those bastards. Different car, but could be the same guys."

Jim held the phone to his ear, waiting to be connected. "Didn't they shoot one of the tellers?"

"Yeah." Kyle clenched his fist. "And left three children without a mother."

As Jim spoke with the dispatcher, Kyle kept his eyes pinned on the bank. History would not repeat itself. Not on his watch. "I'm going inside."

Jim grabbed his arm. "Not without backup."

Kyle gave him one of his infamous icy looks that said he wasn't about to be countermanded, making Jim immediately release his grip. "No time," he shot back. "This could all go down before the troops get here, and these guys have killed before."

"Yeah, and Morrison's gonna kill *you* if you don't wait for backup again. Then he'll have my ass in a sling for letting you do it."

Kyle compressed his lips. If he waited, the body count could double or triple in a heartbeat. With that overriding fear burning a hole in his insides, he pushed from the SUV.

"Kyle, wait—"

"Dammit," he snapped. "Don't argue with me." He pivoted and made for the back of the Expedition. Behind him, Jim got out and slammed the door shut.

Kyle lifted the tailgate and reached inside for his Kevlar vest. "Wait here for NYPD and fill them in. Call the rest of the team."

He peeled off his sweat-soaked outer shirt. Using the Expedition as cover, he strapped the Kevlar vest around his chest, then redonned his sweaty shirt and buttoned it to conceal the vest.

Jim ran a hand through his close-cropped hair. "Boss, don't do this."

"Call the team." Kyle put an edge to his voice. "Do it now—that's an order!"

Grumbling under his breath, Jim began placing the call.

As Kyle grabbed other gear from the truck, he recalled the TV footage of a young man consoling three small children who had just lost their mother. The raw pain on their faces etched deeply into Kyle's memory. It was the kind of pain that comes from losing the person you love most in the world.

It was a pain he knew all too well. One he would never forget.

With no small effort, he shoved the ugly images deep down into the emotional pit where he kept them stowed. "If everything goes to shit inside and you hear shots, take down the driver." He didn't wait for a reply, and stepped off the curb.

Charging into the bank hadn't been on the morning agenda. Kyle and the rest of his team had just come off a long night of surveillance in Little Odessa, the Brighton Beach section of Brooklyn, home to the largest population of Russian immigrants in the western hemisphere. But Ilya

Sorofkin was at the top of the FBI Strike Force Team's list of suspected bank robbers in New York City. The man was as violent as they came. Waiting around, sitting on his ass, was something Kyle could never do.

Trying to act casual, he maneuvered across three busy lanes of traffic, barely avoiding several aggressive yellow taxicabs hurtling south toward Lower Manhattan. A number of other cabs and limo drivers pounded on their horns. One flipped him off, yelling a string of obscenities out the window.

On the other side of the street, and without pausing, he touched the trunk of the suspect sedan, tagging the hot metal with his fingerprints. If things went south, at least there'd be evidence on the trunk.

With a sweep of his trained eye, he took in a multitude of details.

The nervous dirtbag at the wheel was indeed the Russian Bratva driver he'd suspected. Smoke spiraled from a cigarette held out of the car window. Kyle caught a whiff of smoke as he walked past. Both passenger doors facing the bank were cracked open, allowing for quick entry and an even quicker escape. It also meant there were at least two more perps in the bank.

Kyle pushed open the bank's heavy glass door, and a blast of frigid air-conditioned air hit him full in the face. Dark wood tables dotted the cavernous lobby. Half a dozen columns stretched from the marble tiled floor to the ceiling. The columns would provide good cover if they were solid. He couldn't count on that.

He walked to a table located in the center of the bank. Blank withdrawal and deposit slips were stacked neatly in individual wooden boxes. He wiped the cooling sweat from his forehead and pretended to fill out a withdrawal slip.

Glancing up now and then, he searched for Sorofkin's accomplices.

The robbery hadn't gone down yet. The only question, was why.

From his strategic position, he took everything—and everyone—in.

Three other people filled out slips at other tables. Half a dozen others waited on lines. Two bank tellers serviced customers from behind a tall, wood counter with barred windows. The only talking was the occasional brief, subdued conversation at the counter.

With another sweeping glance, Kyle noted the bank's security guard—an elderly man in a wrinkled uniform slouched on a stool near the main door. Kyle wanted to shake him. The guard could have been asleep, for all his attentiveness to what was happening around him.

He continued his scan of the lobby. Somewhere lurked at least two people who didn't belong there, and it was his job to find them before they hurt innocent people again.

Seconds later, he spotted the lookout standing at the table nearest to the security guard. That meant the old guard would be taken out first.

The lookout wore baggy khaki slacks and an oversized camouflage coat, easily big enough to hide a rifle or shotgun. Also a tad warm for this time of year, something that incompetent guard should have picked up on. The lookout glanced around the lobby, his chest rising and falling like an accordion. The guy was nervous. It didn't surprise him that during the previous robbery they'd gotten spooked and killed a teller.

He'd seen the bank's videotapes, assisted in their review, looking for a motive for the killing, but he'd found nothing.

Other than the teller's lack of speed emptying the cash drawer. She'd paid for that with her life.

Kyle's gut still clenched at the senseless killing. It shouldn't have gone down that way. All the perp had to do was wait for the teller to give him the cash, and she would have. That told him something else about this crew—they liked to kill. And after the first kill, it only got easier. He knew that from personal experience, but that had been for God and Country.

High heels echoed on the tile floor as a woman approached the table where he stood. A little girl dressed in a pink frilly ballerina dress clung tightly to her skirt. The woman filled out a slip, then headed for the counter with the girl trailing after her.

Kyle narrowed his eyes, methodically dividing the interior of the bank into quadrants, checking each one repeatedly, searching for the other perp. He wasn't wrong about this. His innate sense of all things bad was tingling at the base of his neck. The robbery *would* go down. It was only a matter of when.

A tall man in one of the teller lines tipped his head discreetly to the lookout, who nodded emphatically in return. Now Kyle knew who the brains of the bunch was. The tall guy was calling the shots.

Protocol dictated Kyle had to wait for a crime to be committed before acting on what could only be articulated as "a hunch." But this guy was a cold-blooded killer. Kyle had to get closer. No way would he let this asshole kill again.

He stepped from the table, his body tensed and spring-loaded. The perp approached the teller and shoved a gun through the bars. She gasped. Her eyes widened, and she jerked back. The heavy metal stool she'd been sitting on toppled and hit the floor with a clatter that rang throughout the bank.

Customers' heads turned. The all-but-sleeping security guard leapt from his chair. He fumbled for his gun and took several hesitant steps toward the counter.

Kyle yanked his Glock from his holster. He raced forward, taking cover behind one of the thick columns. He hoped to hell it really was solid, because he had a bad feeling someone was going to be shooting back at him real soon.

Movement to the left caught his eye. The lookout standing near the guard yanked a rifle from under his coat and raised the muzzle to the back of the guard's head.

Kyle left his position, then aimed and fired. The gunshot blast reverberated throughout the bank. The front of the lookout's shirt blossomed with a bright red stain just before the guy hit the floor hard.

Customers dropped to the floor, screaming. The old guard moved with surprising speed and scrambled for cover behind a table.

Kyle ducked back behind the column, focusing on the second perp. He aimed in and started squeezing the trigger, but stopped.

The man had grabbed a hostage—the little girl in the pink ballerina dress.

Kyle ground his teeth. *Fucking bastard!*

The perp pressed his gun to the girl's temple. Tears trickled down her cheeks as she squirmed in his grasp.

Releasing his finger from the trigger, Kyle gripped the butt of his Glock so hard he thought it would crack. He could barely hold back the growl rising in his throat.

Even if he took the perp out now, all it would take was a dead man's grip—the involuntary tightening of the man's finger muscles—and the trigger would pull back, ending that sweet little girl's life in less than a heartbeat.

A barrage of bullets slammed into the column. Kyle squeezed his eyes shut, half-expecting one of the bullets to drill straight through the column into his head or back. Moans and whimpers came from the customers kissing the floor. One guy started to get up.

"Stay down," he warned in a low voice, tugging aside his overshirt enough to expose the badge clipped to his belt. The man's eyes popped open, and he dropped back down.

Leading with his gun, Kyle peered around the column, searching the interior of the bank in increments. No one else was standing except him. The perp must have hunkered down to reload.

Kyle raced to another column and took cover. His heart hammered, every beat shooting adrenaline through his body. Yet his mind remained calm. This wasn't the first time he'd shot someone. Nor would it be the second. He'd lost track of all the bodies he'd left behind in his life.

Still clutching the girl, the perp popped up from behind one of the wood tables. Kyle jerked his gun to the left and came on target. The guy hadn't seen him yet and was still aiming at the other column. The perp turned, his eyes flaring as he honed in on Kyle's new position.

As if in slow motion, the guy raised his gun. In that second, images flashed before Kyle's eyes. Those of his dead wife. She was never coming back, and it was his fault. He could finish this right here and now. Let the bullet enter his body and finally end the torment. But he had to save the girl.

Another image flitted into his brain. *Vicki*.

He gave himself a mental slap and squeezed the trigger. The lobby echoed with the blast of a .45 caliber semi-automatic gunshot. The perp stared, still standing but not moving. His eyes were wide, vacant and unseeing.

The little girl slid from the man's now-limp grasp and ran to her mother.

For a few seconds longer, the guy remained where he was, then he slumped forward, and his forehead slammed onto the table. The body slid to the floor and disappeared from Kyle's view. He remained aimed-in, but it was over.

Customers began to stand, some whispering in hushed tones, others weeping.

"Stay down!" he shouted and moved forward, rounding the corner of the table and aiming at the body on the floor. Blood seeped from a hole beneath the man's nose, marking the path of the jacketed hollow point bullet that had just severed his brain stem.

He holstered, then grabbed the Smith & Wesson from the man's hand and stuffed it in the back of his waistband. Not that it was necessary, but he checked for a pulse.

More customers started getting to their feet. Outside, Jim and the rest of his team had Ilya Sorofkin cuffed and face down on the sidewalk. Police cars swarmed into the area, red-and-blue lights flashing, sirens wailing.

"Wait!" Anyone rushing out the door risked accidentally getting shot by the good guys. He tugged out his cell and cued up Jim's number. He watched through the window as Jim snagged the phone from his belt.

"You okay?" Jim asked.

"Yeah." He took in the dozen shocked faces waiting for his direction. "We're all fine. Two perps down. Let the uniforms know we're coming out."

"You got it."

He ended the call, noting a green SUV pulling up beside the NYPD patrol cars. Sure enough, the boss of the

FBI's New York City Strike Force teams—Special Agent in Charge Michael Morrison—joined his team on the sidewalk. Morrison's lips were pursed. Even from this distance, Kyle could see the flames shooting from his eyes. *Great.*

He tucked his overshirt behind his belt, revealing his badge so he wouldn't get drilled by any of the cops swarming into the area. "Everyone follow me. Keep your hands in the air. Don't run, and don't leave the area. The officers will want to ask you some questions." He opened the door and held his hands above his head. The second his SAC caught sight of him, the man's eyes narrowed to angry, don't-fuck-with-me slits, confirming what Kyle expected. He was in for an ass-reaming of epic proportions. Disobeying protocol and going into the bank alone was bad enough. That was only part of why Morrison was so pissed.

Kyle stepped onto the sidewalk and drew a long, resigned breath as he approached his boss. This wasn't the first time he'd risked his life. It hadn't been the second time either.

Morrison's lips pursed, but that didn't stop the man from growling loud enough for Kyle to hear from ten feet away. He'd be lucky if he didn't get chained to a desk for six months and forced to spill his guts to a shrink about his death wish tendencies.

Slowly, he lowered his hands. "Boss—"

"Don't." Morrison shook his head, flattening his lips more. "Just. Don't. I'll stay with your team. You can send in your statement to the NYPD later. I'll cover for you here. The only things I want you to do now are to turn in your firearm, get your ass back to 26 Fed, and stay there. Somehow I have to miraculously convene a shooting review board out of thin air and get them to clear you in less than a week."

At this point, virtual steam was shooting out of Morrison's ears. Jim and the rest of Kyle's team wisely backed away. Aside from his older brother, Jack, Kyle was about the only one in the New York Field Office that had been on the receiving end of one of Morrison's ballistic tongue lashings...and lived.

"Yes, sir." Kyle discreetly tugged his weapon from the holster and handed it to Morrison.

Morrison stuck the Glock in his waistband. "Now get out of here."

"Yes, sir," he repeated, then headed back to his Expedition, weaving through the fleet of emergency vehicles that had completely blocked off Broadway.

Sirens wailed in every direction as a seemingly endless stream of emergency vehicles continued pouring into the area.

Kyle understood Morrison's concerns. He'd just created a mile high pile of red tape for his boss to wade through, and they both knew it.

Mikhail Lazovsky and Boris Kolbayev's trial started next week. With two protected witnesses to squirrel safely in and out of the courthouse there was a boatload of tactical and logistical coordination to go over. After a shooting, he'd be on the rubber gun squad until the review board cleared him. For the trial, he had to be fully cleared for active duty. He'd been through a shooting review before but never at such a critical juncture.

He got into the SUV but didn't turn the key. It felt as if there was a fifty-pound weight pressing against his chest. He closed his eyes, trying to blot out the ghostly images from his past that refused to leave him be. Vicki, for one.

Ironically, she'd saved his life today. He'd saved her life once, too, but it had cost him. It had cost them *both*.

He turned the key and put his hands on the wheel. They should have been shaking—normal physiological responses to shooting two men and coming a hair's breadth from being killed himself. His hands were rock-steady. That wasn't normal, even for a seasoned FBI agent who'd been to war for his country.

He was going numb. There was always the remote possibility all the normal PTSD signs would come later. Kyle didn't think so. Risking his life, at times not caring if it ended, then going on with his job and life as if everything were normal...

Was becoming routine.

He didn't know which would be worse, dealing with Morrison and the shooting review board or his brothers after they heard what he'd done. Again.

Kyle spun the SUV in a U-turn, intending to head south toward 26 Federal Plaza but slowing to watch paramedics in front of the bank examine the little girl in the ballerina dress. Her mother stood next to the gurney, holding the girl's hand.

Watching them triggered a soul-wrenching ache deep inside him that he'd thought was long buried.

Because of his actions today, *this* mother and child had been saved. But he'd never forgive himself for what he'd done.

When his actions had resulted in the death of his own family.

Exacting Vengeance is available here for preorder!